MW01200444

Sentinel Island
A Novel

World Writing in French
A Winthrop-King Institute Series

Series Editors
Charles Forsdick (University of Liverpool)
and
Martin Munro (Florida State University)

Advisory Board Members
Jennifer Boum Make (Georgetown University)
Michelle Bumatay (Florida State University)
William Cloonan (Florida State University)
Michaël Ferrier (Chuo University)
Michaela Hulstyn (Stanford Univesity)
Khalid Lyamlahy (University of Chicago)
Helen Vassallo (University of Exeter)

There is a growing interest among Anglophone readers in literature in translation, including contemporary writing in French in its richness and diversity. The aim of this new series is to publish cutting-edge contemporary French-language fiction, travel writing, essays and other prose works translated for an English-speaking audience. Works selected will reflect the diversity, dynamism, originality, and relevance of new and recent writing in French from across the archipelagoes – literal and figurative – of the French-speaking world. The series will function as a vital reference point in the area of contemporary French-language prose in English translation. It will draw on the expertise of its editors and advisory board to seek out and make available for English-language readers a broad range of exciting new work originally published in French. This series is published in partnership with the Winthrop-King Institute, Florida State University.

Benjamin Hoffmann

Sentinel Island
A Novel

Translated by Alan J. Singerman

Liverpool University Press

First published in English translation by Liverpool University Press 2024
Liverpool University Press
4 Cambridge Street
Liverpool
L69 7ZU

Sentinel Island was first published in French as *L'ile de la Sentinelle*
(© Editions Gallimard, 2022)

Copyright © Benjamin Hoffmann, 2022
English translation copyright © Alan Singerman, 2024

The right of Benjamin Hoffmann to be identified as the author of this work and Alan Singerman to be identified as translator of this work has been asserted by them in accordance with the Copyright, Designs and Patents Act 1988.

All rights reserved. No part of this book may be reproduced, stored in a retrieval system, or transmitted, in any form or by any means, electronic, mechanical, photocopying, recording, or otherwise, without the prior written permission of the publisher.

British Library Cataloguing-in-Publication data
A British Library CIP record is available

ISBN 978-1-83764-261-8 hardback
ISBN 978-1-83764-262-5 paperback

Typeset by Carnegie Book Production, Lancaster
Printed and bound by CPI Group (UK) Ltd, Croydon CR0 4YY

Contents

Some facts precede their emergence in your life.

They've always been *there*. On the horizon. You know that the time to meet them will be long in coming, but nothing can be done, ever, to circumvent them or get them to wander from their path. You just have to go through this, through them. They are like floating objects that you set on the surface of a liquid. Look how their intrusion provokes a violent rise of the water that swells then flees. The swollen wave doesn't move in a single direction. It grows in concentric circles that expand *infinitely*. On all sides. When you think the water has calmed down, you are mistaken. Become still again, it is traversed by invisible waves. These waves are the echoes of what is yet to come.

You become conscious of them at long intervals. It happens when you are at peace, in the darkness, just before you drift off to sleep. Or in plain daylight when you're driving, or when you're scurrying down the street. A surprising and reversible impression—the familiar universe becomes strange, unless the strangeness comes to seem familiar—suddenly possesses you. This impression comes from far away, you are sure of that, but from *what direction* you cannot say. It is called *déjà-vu*, but it would be just as proper to call it a "reminder." It is a gentle warning but nonetheless firm. "You are coming near," it tells you. "You are precisely where you should be. Just a little further, and you will be with me." It's only a matter of time, but time is an illusion. You cast about, make choices you regret; all that is a dream. Through our meanderings, we move straight ahead. Where are we going? Toward the shipwreck that awaits us.

Imagine a boat. A sailboat or motorboat, with one hull or several, as you wish. But a boat that would be alone, completely alone, in the middle of the ocean. The weather is magnificent. The water is calm, and there is a mild breeze. The sun is high in the sky, the azure, crystal clear. Not a cloud. The whole panorama offers no threat of any kind. And suddenly, here it is. At the horizon it is only, for the moment, a minuscule spot, scarcely more than a speck on your glasses. It grows, however, makes itself at home, something substantial; it spreads out, takes shape, becomes clearer. It is an island. No other coast can be seen; the nearest continent is far away—days, nay, entire weeks of sailing. You approach, and as the island fills the space, the weather grows foul. Behind the skiff, the cliffs close and march straight ahead toward you. The rain falls, first a light shower, then a muted pounding. You continue to approach and can now distinguish the forests, black, a dark canopy. Against the reefs around the island, the waves break thicker and thicker, more and more violent. You stay rooted in place, fascinated by the inevitable. And when the shock comes, when the hull is finally shredded on the shoals, you understand, with a strange smile, a paradoxical tranquility. You understand that your whole life was tending toward this moment.

Somewhere an island is waiting for us, and we are all traveling toward it. I've found mine. It is Sentinel Island.

FIRST PART

And a word carries far—very far—
deals destruction through time
as the bullets go flying through space.

Conrad, Lord Jim

1

The Double

I'm three, and I'm one of the thieves. I spin around, once and then again and again. I spin around with my thirty-nine comrades, and all the parents watch us from the playground of our school in Mumbai. That's what I remember: spinning in a light blue *jellaba* with a turban around my head. But take note: I do not remember the scene as I lived it; I remember it as I saw it on the television in our home. My father had filmed it with a camcorder that weighed around ten pounds. You opened it on the side to insert a rectangular videocassette. The magnetic tapes turn slowly around little plastic cogwheels, and I'm turning too, on the screen. But little by little, from rotation to rotation, something happens: the turban comes undone. I was only one thief among others, but now all eyes are on me: this little kid with a pathetic flap floating behind him. And most absurd of all, I am completely unaware of it and continue, conscientiously, to spin around the schoolyard. My older sister Kamala begins to laugh, and my parents too. I'm ridiculous, absolutely ridiculous, oblivious of this train that is growing behind me: Is it an animal? A tail? I protest in tears. And rather than admitting that I'm the one on the screen, I claim that I'm this other kid, there, in the swarm, this other kid who is walking with dignity, moving gracefully in full view of everyone, his head held high, in a light blue *jellaba* too, but whose turban remains perfectly in place. I tell them I am he, and not the one who is twirling around with his turban undone. My parents and Kamala know that I'm lying and laugh even harder. And I continue to stare at this other kid, convinced that I am he. All my life it seemed to me that this double truly existed somewhere, like a more perfect version of myself of whom I would only ever be a caricature. This *Doppelgänger*, I immediately understood that I had found it in Markus.

2

Physical Description of the Island

Sentinel Island is a phantom ship. At long intervals it emerges in the Western consciousness, observed by a bold traveler who draws its outline. Then it disappears for several decades or several centuries, unknown, forgotten, until the day of its return. It is the story of these intermittent relations that I'm going to tell, by tracing those isolated moments in which Sentinel has become visible in the gaze of others, by quoting those—they are rare—who have returned from the forbidden island. There is a good reason for moving from its history to my own. Sentinel always ends up reminding the West of its existence, and it has never strayed very far from the core of my life.

Let's begin like the ancient travelers, with geographical considerations. "North Sentinel Island" (hereafter simply "Sentinel Island," for it will never be about its little sister to the south, inhabited solely by coconut crabs) measures around twenty-three square miles, which, to give you a point of comparison, is the size of Manhattan Island. A million and a half people live on the latter; according to the most generous estimates, there are fewer than two hundred on Sentinel. A tourist arriving for the first time in New York already knows the city. The straight avenues, the bright yellow taxis, the ladders climbing up the walls: he's seen them a thousand times on the screen. Sentinel Island, on the other hand, is the realm of the *never seen*; it's the last place in the whole wide world that hasn't yet been explored. Even the omniscient Google Maps is incapable of delivering its secrets to you. Its little yellow man, the brave parachutist, is always ready to leave on expeditions to the four corners of the globe to lend you his eyes, but he stubbornly refuses to land on this square of jungle hemmed in by a turquoise lagoon and navy-blue abysses.

As isolated as they are, the Sentinelese are featured regularly on the front page of newspapers. All that is needed is for a foolhardy fisherman or a Westerner more or less well-intentioned to wash up on their coast and lose their life. The media then trot out the same old clichés showing black men on the shore, majestic and solemn like the *moai* of Easter Island; or this other image, blurred, taken from a helicopter that a warrior, brave and pathetic, tries to hit with an arrow. Then the experts debate the same questions of international law and of individual responsibility before concluding that it is better just to leave the body of the foolish fellow there, under the sand where the Sentinelese have buried it to prevent it from infecting them with diseases that could wipe them out.

Imagine the map of the world. No, not as it is today but rather five centuries ago when immense empty zones existed, and the form of the continents was a caricature of the one you know. And in marshalling the sum of your knowledge, imagine, as if a film were playing in fast motion before your eyes, the general progression of geographic knowledge in the West as the lines of the continents gradually become clear, North America's western border is revealed, Japan emerges from the water followed by Australia, Indonesia rises up, and Africa's depths take shape. The words *terra incognita* disappear. They disappear beneath bloody invasions, beneath railroads built with rows of victims, beneath the foam of slave-trader ships, beneath the mass of native corpses struck down by pandemics. Now we're in the 19th century. The travelers begin to complain that there is nothing left to discover, and it is true that now they have to hurry toward other truly inhospitable regions, the Northwest Passage and the Bolivian jungle, to fill in the persistent blanks in the maps, give one's name to a final mountain, another bay. In the end, with the constant surveillance of satellites, there is nothing left unseen or unexamined, nothing that is not observable in real time on the Internet, nothing, or almost nothing, except this island, Sentinel Island, a paradoxical name since it is a rearguard battle being fought by its tribe, who are keeping their distance from the modern world. Just one unfortunate event—a rise in the sea level, an influenza outbreak, a tsunami—is all it would take to find ourselves alone, without our guilty conscience, the reminder of all those peoples we've caricatured, exterminated, and forgotten.

The isolation of the Sentinelese is owed to their resistance but also to the characteristics of their territory. To begin with, it has little to arouse interest. Its size is mediocre, and there are hundreds of islands like this, with virgin forests, mangroves, and curving beaches, across the Bay of Bengal. To make matters worse, Sentinel is located six hundred miles from the Indian peninsula and hours by boat from Port Blair, the capital of the region. Technically, it belongs to the archipelago of the Andaman and Nicobar Islands, one of the eight territories of the Republic of India; the Sentinelese are virtually unaware of this and only wish to be left alone, which they make clear by threatening visitors when they arrive and by firing their arrows at those who don't get the message. Their coasts are surrounded by reefs that form an impenetrable defense; three openings alone in the ring around it permit access to the interior lagoon where they sometimes venture on narrow dugout canoes. Moreover, these access points are impassable from April to November when the rainy season is raging, and the waves are so high that any boats in the area are shattered on the reefs.

Between December and March, however, the weather in the Andamans is splendid. The air is warm, the skies clear. The waves open upon turquoise depths where the clownfish and the giant turtles maneuver gracefully around each other. It's the time of year when European and American tourists come to wallow in postcard clichés: coconut trees bowing down toward the sand, hammocks swaying in the breezes from Sumatra. They seek in these faraway places an ultimate exotic dream, cheap artificial paradises, the persistent memory of the glory of empires. It is also the time of year when Sentinel is most exposed to foreign incursions. The Indian government is aware of it, maintaining its vigilance since 1996, when it forbade anyone to come within five nautical miles of the island. This prohibition is not always respected. In 2006, two fishermen who had fallen asleep in their boat moored not far from the island had the misfortune of foundering on its shore. The Sentinelese killed them, and, after keeping their corpses buried in the sand for a week, tied them to stakes facing the sea—like scarecrows designed to frighten off any intruders. As crystal clear as this warning was, it was not enough to discourage visitors. Malaysian pillagers, Thai shark fishermen, explorers excited by this last remnant of the Age of Discovery, and, ah yes, missionaries determined to bring the gospel truth to this "bastion of Satan": all of them dream of finding a way to get onto this island.

Granted: the ships of the Indian navy patrol this zone constantly. But what about those who avoid them by taking to the sea in the middle of the night? There are frequent storms in this area. But what about those who manage to survive them? There are all the reefs that surround the island. But what about those who find the entrance to the lagoon? There are, of course, the Sentinelese's arrows. But if someone succeeds in getting onto the island, what will they find in the center, deep beneath the interlaced vines and branches, under the forest canopy? What secrets are hidden in the heart of the island where no one outside the tribe has ever ventured? It is the last mystery, the final frontier on the face of the planet, the completion of five centuries of conquests and iniquities. Whoever solves it will have snuffed out the last spark of magic in the world; and how many of us are heeding the ancestral call that drives us to destroy the very thing we cannot live without?

3

Markus

He arranged to meet me in a spot on campus where I had never set foot. First, go up Wall Street then continue on to Hillhouse Avenue, turn right in front of the residence of the president of the university, and continue on toward Orange Street. It's nearly four o'clock according to the watch I received from my parents: I have to hurry. Markus is waiting for me in this secret enclave. In the center, the branches of a cherry tree stretch over a stone bench and a bed of yellow and violet flowers. Subsequently, it always seemed to me that Markus held the key to these unique, hidden places whose existence only he could reveal.

"Krish?" he asked, getting up to shake my hand. I told him he could call me "Chris," like everyone else. The Americans tend to massacre my name, so six years ago I adopted another one: it's simpler. "So you have two identities," he replied mischievously. "You're lucky," he quickly added.

He's younger than me. On that day I'm twenty-five (it's September, and my birthday is the following month) and he barely twenty-one. In a certain sense, I resemble him. We're the same height, his hair just as black as mine, and our general bearing about the same. The principal difference is our skin: his is as pale as mine is brown. He's also more thickset; his body, beneath his clothes, must be more muscular than mine. I have to wince, lower my eyes, buckle slightly, as if his beauty had hit me in the stomach; I find him more handsome than I'd ever found myself, and all the self-confidence I lack is there, emanating from him. Flawless Markus—at least that is what I long believed. He had everything and the others, beginning with me, had nothing, or almost nothing, in comparison ... I've often wondered how it is that certain beings are born with so many advantages lavished on them: exceptional intelligence and a harmonious countenance, and then a complete education acquired in books and wide travel, the whole set of privileges that come with a multi-millionaire family. Markus's father is the beating heart of his life, a presence that reappears constantly in his speech, like a cold draft in a house. His father is an immense figure, an object of love and veneration, but also a shadow that is growing and growing and slowly crushing him. Markus knows that one day he'll have to come out from under this shadow.

Today is my second interview. One of three I have to pass to qualify—perhaps—for the rest of the trials. I met Joseph ten days ago, a Brooklyn type with a ponytail and turquoise eyes. He speaks Turkish fluently; he's already spent a year in Istanbul and intends to return there the following semester, a prospect that irks his Palestinian girlfriend, who would like him to stay in New Haven. When he isn't studying the history of the Ottoman Empire, this slight little guy, always dressed in black, is the drummer for a punk group that plays the local bars and the string of cities— Bridgeport, Stamford—that stand between us and New York. Moving up through the stacks, narrow like the passageway of a submarine, I found him on the top floor of the Sterling Library, seated at a bottle-green metal table, under a window that looked like a porthole. Joseph was observing me intensely, as if he were striving to uncover what I was hiding behind each word.

With Markus, it's different. The discussion is more cordial: I'm chatting with a friend, not sitting in front of a lie detector. He begins as usual, asking where I come from. I tell him that I grew up in Mumbai, and that my parents and older sister are deceased. It's odd that I share this information; normally, I keep that to myself. Delicately, he asks if I would like to tell him more.

I hesitate for a moment, but since I've already said too much, I explain that my parents and Kamala were at the Chhatrapati Shivaji railroad station on November 26, 2008. For me, it's as if I were telling him that they were in the World Trade Center on September 11, 2001. But Markus doesn't remember the attack or has never heard of it, and I have to explain to him that two men armed with assault rifles killed fifty-eight people that day, and that my parents and sister were among the victims.

Beginning to choke up, I changed the subject and announced that two years ago, near the end of my bachelor's degree at Columbia, I decided to stay in the United States—nothing and no one was waiting for me at home—and to apply to several doctoral programs. Ultimately, I moved here with my wife Eleanor to prepare a doctoral thesis in the Anthropology Department. Markus had taken some courses in this area and immediately brought up *The Gift*, no doubt happy to steer the conversation toward less painful subjects—unless he just wanted to prove to me that he was familiar with this discipline—as with virtually everything else it seemed. His knowledge of Mauss and Durkheim is precise and of considerable depth. I'm already learning that nothing is foreign to Markus. He has one of those rare minds that can embrace absolutely everything. He is currently enrolled in seminars on astronomy and mathematics and is also interested in law and English literature. Markus could become a diplomat, professor, scientist, senator, historian, or lawyer; every path is open to him, and this dizzying potential is, in fact, a handicap. It's a curse to be able to do too much.

Markus asks me the subject of my dissertation. I tell him about this tribe that is living far away off the coast of India in the Bay of Bengal on an island called Little Andaman. These are the Onge—pronounced "onjay." They are one of the most fragile peoples on earth; there are around a hundred of them, and almost half of the couples are sterile. In 2008, when eight Onge died of accidental poisoning, the whole tribe nearly died out. I could talk about all that for hours, but I tell him only what interests me particularly about them: their religious convictions. The Onge believe in the existence of spirits, in the real presence of invisible creatures. They belong to the last three native peoples living on the Andamans: there are also the Jarawas and the Sentinelese; the latter live alone on their island, and hardly anything is known about them. Markus seems intrigued. He wants to know more and is amazed that in the 21st century there still exist people who have no contact with the outside world. He listens to me for a moment then declares, enthusiastically, that the Sentinelese would surely have fascinated his favorite author, Joseph Conrad. I wonder if his curiosity is always so keen when he learns something new, or if this tribe really arouses a genuine interest in him.

Before we take leave of one another, he asks me a final question. I told him, a little while ago, that I had applied to several doctoral programs: Why had I chosen Yale? This query surprises me. Is he hoping for a flood of praise for our university that will confirm our feeling of belonging to the elite? Or is he in fact setting a trap for me, to see if I'm going to wallow in self-satisfaction? Unless he is hoping for a more personal response that will reveal something about my values and my decision-making process? I have no idea; this apparently banal question seems to me fraught with consequences. But it is certainly simpler to just tell the truth. I pause a moment before beginning; I haven't spoken of this to anyone, not even to Eleanor.

I tell him about my first visit to New Haven. It was the year before, in February. It was cold, and heaps of dirty snow clogged up the streets. Cars had to slow down to a crawl, and pedestrians had to watch where they walked. I took refuge in the Hall of Graduate Studies at the very end of Wall Street, a vast Gothic-style building with a huge tower on top, like a keep. I walked under the arch that leads to the main door, a carved wooden door decorated with ironwork. With the rain beating down, the inner quadrangle looked like the courtyard of a medieval cloister. At that precise moment, I had the distinct impression of having already come to this place, of having already seen this place—not in images on the Internet but for real, in person. Which was impossible, because I had never set foot in this city, not even in the State of Connecticut. But I felt absolutely sure I was rejoining something I had left here one day, I didn't know when, no doubt a long time ago. I had to make a decision very quickly: What program was I going to choose? What offer should I accept? In which town were Eleanor and I going to spend the next five or six years? I thought of the job openings for her, the amount of the stipend, the reputation of the Anthropology Department, of all the practical criteria that I could reasonably take into account ... But to be honest, I have to admit that what tipped the scales was the impression of *déjà-vu* I felt that day in the Hall of Graduate Studies. I had the feeling that in coming here, I was coming home.

Markus is silent. Without knowing it, I've just touched on the question he is obsessed with, the one that is going to stamp our friendship and, one day, lead to his disappearance.

4

Mysteries

The concept of the number three does not exist for the Sentinelese. Their mathematics has two signs and their music two notes: everything that exceeds "two" falls into the category of "a lot." This being the case, try to explain the Holy Trinity to them: this people is immunized against the Good Word.

If it is true that we are superior to them in the art of mathematics, does that mean we're more advanced? Beyond a certain stage, we drown in the abstraction of numbers. Take this one, for example: fifty thousand. Most of us have only a vague idea of what has happened during the last three millennia. The history of the 20th century, sure, but what about the Kamakura era, the Abbasid empire, or the golden age of the Gandhara? Add forty-seven millennia to those three, and you will find yourself at the origin of the Sentinelese. They've been isolated for fifty thousand years on their island; some colleagues go so far as to add twenty millennia more of seclusion, an easy jump. To compare, we note that Europe was populated forty thousand years ago by our ancestors, which means that the Sentinelese are one hundred centuries older than the West, which should count for something.

But instead of the respect that we normally reserve for our elders, the Sentinelese's distant origins have only earned them the nickname "Stone Age tribe." It makes no sense, but it's hardly the only thing explained by racism. If we are to believe the yellow press of Europe and America, meeting the Sentinelese would be tantamount to abolishing time: jumping onto their beach and going back to the Pre-Neolithic period. I condemn this phantasm that freezes them in time. Granted, the Sentinelese don't know how to make a fire, so they have no knowledge of metallurgy, any more than of agriculture. But they have learned to nurture the flames created by lightning and to attach to their arrows pieces of metal torn from ships that run aground on their reefs. And if they no longer leave their island, they nonetheless—before the British colonization disrupted their relations—did business with the other Andamanese tribes and formed alliances with them. There are thus changes, evolutions, and adaptations in their world as in ours: the fact that they steer clear of our modernity does not mean that the Sentinelese are outside History.

Among all the mysteries that surround them, their arrival on this island is one of the most troubling. While they've been living for thousands of years in the Bay of Bengal, they still do not seem to be at home there. Look at them for a moment through the eyes of a researcher from Stanford, Dr. Underhill, and you'll understand what I mean: "Their physical features—short stature, dark skin, peppercorn hair, and large buttocks—are characteristic of African Pygmies. They look like they belong in Africa, but here they are sitting on this island chain in the middle of the Indian Ocean." What are Pygmies doing five thousand miles from their home? There is no lack of theories to solve this puzzle. The most widely accepted one views the Sentinelese as the descendants of an exodus from Africa fifty thousand years ago, their ancestors walking on coasts that the oceans have since swallowed up. Are the Sentinelese scouts of sorts? The last isolated people on Earth is perhaps the first to have reached the borders of the Western world.

Their language is an additional mystery. The linguists distinguish two groups in the region: Great Andamanese and Ongan. These are agglutinative languages that are built on a combination of prefixes and suffixes. Like the language of the Onge, that of the Sentinelese belongs to the latter family. Alas, the attempts at communication between these two tribes have produced nothing conclusive; their languages have evolved separately for such a long time that they've become mutually incomprehensible. In short, all we know for sure about the language of the Sentinelese is that nothing, or nearly nothing, is known about it. In addition to finding a way to explain to them the number three, the individual aspiring to convert the Sentinelese to Christ would also have to teach them his language or find a way to learn theirs. It's enough to discourage any evangelical enterprise; at least, one would hope so.

5

Saint Andrew

It is impossible for me to speak to you in detail of Saint Andrew. In fact, I'm certain that discussing it in general terms is already far too much. I gave my word, you see. I promised not to say anything about what goes on in there, what is exposed behind these walls. My brothers and sisters will be furious if I break my word; even if threats remain veiled in our world, their consequences are no less real.

But now that I've decided to write this book, it is just as impossible to pass over the role played by this secret society in my relations with Markus. Our friendship grew in the course of scholarly discussions in comfortable, out-of-the way lounges cluttered with antiques, as we confided in each other in the security of the pact we shared and the feeling, rather exhilarating I admit, of belonging to a small community of *happy few*. But he was an undergraduate whereas I was working on my doctorate, and we had nothing in common, neither age nor national origin nor social milieu, other than Saint Andrew, without which we would have never met—and my whole life would have been changed.

Unsatisfactory, like all compromises, the one I found that permits me to speak of the secret society without going back on my word consists of distinguishing between the public and private rituals. It's wrong to believe that all the activities related to Saint Andrew are reserved for its members. Some of them take place in front of everyone, like our solemn entry on ceremonial days, when one of our superiors chants the ritual words, and we give the prescribed responses before mounting the stairs that lead to the top of the tower. The society itself—I mean the building that I'll call henceforth the *hall*—is in addition divided into two spaces, the first of which sometimes includes guests, while the other is jealously guarded, its very existence unsuspected by the uninitiated. In speaking of the ground floor of the hall, I'll only describe the lounges and libraries whose doors are regularly open to everyone and always dazzle the guests at our annual ball. Likewise, in sharing general information that, with a little perseverance, is available to anyone on the Internet, I hope to remain within the precise bounds of what is acceptable to reveal. And even if I were to go beyond them, I have to admit that at this stage in my life I have little to fear from the members of Saint Andrew—or from anyone as a matter of fact.

There is an additional reason why I cannot let myself simply dismiss the secret society. My membership in Saint Andrew revealed the first crack in my relationship with Eleanor. Not the very first, it is true—there were others before—but one of those that was impossible to shrug off by claiming it was a trivial bit of friction that all couples experience. Sometimes we would be walking on campus, and I would explain to her as we passed by someone who had waved to me discreetly, "He's a member." The same scene occurred several times and soon irritated her: "Yes, I get it," she would snap, "it's a member." Eleanor often put me down that way. She saw me begin to rise above her and couldn't tolerate it. Rather than competing with me with her own accomplishments, which she was never able to bring off, she devoted herself to petty actions, trying to bring me down a peg, infantilize me, convince me that I was unable to perform some minor task or other. "Here, let me do it," she would say, impatiently. My selection by Saint Andrew increased the distance between us: I was admitted into yet another space where she would never be permitted to join me.

It is true that I could have refused to join Saint Andrew, since it had a bad effect on my marriage, but you need to understand my social origins. When you are given everything at birth, an opportunity that opens up to you is of little consequence: there will be so many others. On the other hand, if, like a burglar, you suddenly break into a world that you weren't socially destined to inhabit, every chance offered to you is like a duty, an absolute order to succeed. I was an Indian immigrant in the second richest university in the entire world; it wasn't as if I had the luxury of letting this opportunity pass me by.

It's my friend Edmond who made me aware of the existence of Saint Andrew. He was taking courses at the law school and collecting signs of belonging to the social elite in order to exhibit them shamelessly, modesty never having belonged to his vocabulary.

Modesty, he maintained, as a faithful follower of Nietzsche, was "the typical excuse of the weak." Even the Yale students, accustomed to signs of smugness among their classmates, were shocked by the ease with which he confused the privileges of his social milieu with the rewards of his personal merit, by his tendency to reply, "I owe everything to my intelligence" when someone drew his attention to the fact that his success was not entirely unrelated to his uncle who worked in the Admissions Office at Princeton, where he had done his undergraduate work, nor to the advantages—which he considered overrated—of having a mother who was an engineer, a father who was chair of a neurology department, and a grandfather who was a Republican Congressman from Virginia.

His arrogance irritated me, and I would have avoided him if I hadn't found him appealing for other reasons, notably for the enthusiasm with which he discovered late in life the pleasures that his severe education had deprived him of up until then—the pleasures of parties that last until dawn and women you seek in the illusions of the nightclubs. I liked this party buddy who spoke loudly and returned from drunken nights with fantastic stories, one of his exploits consisting of surviving a kidnapping. To punish him for courting a girl too assiduously in a shady bar he had dared to enter alone, a band of bikers had loaded him onto the back of a truck and bounced him around like a box during a wild race through the sleepy streets of New Haven. Edmond came through it worn out and delighted: with such an adventure to his credit, this daddy's boy became a man, a real man.

Like most people, Edmond loved to speak about himself, but the enormity of his self-satisfaction made him oddly likeable, all the more so since his reasons for being enamored with himself were not entirely illegitimate; he was authentically brilliant and possessed an erudition that was at times dazzling. It was this swaggering, colorful side of him that attracted me despite everything, and when he renounced it to fall in line, he became completely what he had always been in some respect: a conservative, joyless spirit, bitter and reactionary, who detested independence in women and the very claim to exist voiced by minorities, concealed less and less the contempt he felt for the color of my skin, and reduced the immense complexity of social phenomena to a simplistic opposition between *them* and *us*. I learned from him to be wary of people who claimed that things are simple. A few years after leaving New Haven, the election of Trump to the presidency of the United States lit a fire under him. He claimed to be among those who wished to make America great again, without ever saying what period—before the civil rights movement? before the abolition of slavery?—he was referring to, becoming in time the incarnation of yet another paradox in this country: a highly educated Trump supporter.

To arouse my curiosity, Edmond had hinted about *his* society, putting on secretive airs and leading me to imagine Gothic ceremonies behind windowless stone walls, orgies of intelligence, and brotherhoods sealed in blood. After the first interviews and various other tests best left unmentioned, I waited several days with no news. Naturally pessimistic, I assumed I had been rejected and was licking my wounds when I found a letter that someone had slipped under the door of our apartment. Sealed with a bit of blue wax, it bore the seal of Saint Andrew, the "X"-shaped cross on which the apostle had been tortured. The society was summoning me: behind the law school, in front of the Grove Street cemetery, at thirteen minutes after midnight. I told Eleanor that I would be back very late that night, perhaps even the following morning. She did not respond and went into the living room to read. *"Above all, be obedient,"* the letter warned in closing.

"The Dead Shall Be Raised" proclaims the lintel above the gate to the cemetery. The ice on the roof of the mausoleums shines gently in the moonlight. I wait. It is the end of November and extremely cold. No more flakes are falling, but along the sidewalks mounds of snow gleam in the darkness. The salt strewn on the asphalt forms glittering milky ways. New Haven is splendid on winter nights; it looks like Prague, with its steeples and towers, as if the frost gave it an Old World patina. Bundled up in a heavy coat, wearing a scarf, gloves, and a knit cap, not an inch of my skin is exposed; nonetheless, I feel the grip of a glacial hand that moves up my legs and seizes my lungs in its frozen fingers. I'd like to walk around to warm up, but I'm afraid to leave the rendezvous spot. Suddenly a pair of hands grabs my shoulders, and another pair puts a blindfold over my eyes. I tense but do not resist: *"Above all, be obedient."* I'm shoved into a car that takes off immediately. The initiation begins.

The car rolls along. I'm in the back and, through the blindfold, I manage to perceive shapes and lights, as if I'm looking through a telescope at an object located several galaxies away. Someone is seated beside me; I can feel his shoulder rub against mine when we hit a bump. Who is it? No one speaks in the car. We travel long enough to be outside the city.

I'm standing in darkness; the blindfold is removed. Through signs that are impossible to reveal here a complete hierarchy is disclosed, with its attributes and functions. The procession begins. In the darkness a light is glowing in the window of a vast dwelling like the ones owned by old families in New England.

The blindfold is back on, and I'm mounting a winding staircase. My guide is holding me by the forearms. In front of me, behind me, I feel other people present. The ascent goes on and on; at the top awaits a challenge.

Later. We're all standing under a vault. The door is closed and will not open until we have survived yet another trial. A very old rule designates me as the one who has to go first. I hesitate before those who are watching.

Once again blindfolded, we are led into a room whose vastness is betrayed by the echo of our steps. We are seated and ordered not to move. Then something happens that I can say absolutely nothing about: I'm paralyzed by a moment of pure terror. We're finally allowed to take off our blindfolds; a stupefying, magnificent spectacle is revealed to us: from this day on, we will be brothers and sisters.

6

Cannibals

From the moment the Western world became aware of them, the Sentinelese acquired a bad reputation, through no fault of their own. Take the Alexandrian geographer Ptolemy. One hundred and fifty years after the birth of Christ, he warns us about the "island of cannibals" off the coast of India. Which part of the Andaman archipelago is he referring to? No one knows, so to be safe the sailors suspect all the peoples in the region of practicing anthropophagy—a generalization all the more unfortunate since, in truth, none of them do.

The first travelers nonetheless confirm this malicious gossip. In 953, in his work titled *Kitāb ʿAjāʾib al-Hind* or *The Book of the Marvels of India*, the Persian navigator Buzurg ibn Shahriyār al-Rām-Hurmuzi says that tribes of cannibals live off the coast of Burma and baptizes one of their islands Andaman al-Kabir or Great Andaman. Three centuries later, Marco Polo sails by the archipelago without setting foot on it, which does not prevent him from describing it with full confidence: "*Angamanan* is a very large island. Its inhabitants live like animals, governed by no king. They are idolatrous. All the men on this island have vicious dogs' heads, with the eyes and teeth of dogs as well. They are ferocious men who devour everyone who does not belong to their tribe." And if you go to the National Library of France, in the Manuscript Department, in a 15th-century copy of *The Travels of Marco Polo*, you will discover a rather troubling illumination. The Andamanese are portrayed as a dog-headed people: in a prairie festooned with flowers, beneath the mighty ramparts of a flourishing city, dressed in long, colorful tunics, creatures in boots conduct business, debate, and look human in every respect—with the exception of their mastiff faces.

In depicting them as animals, Marco Polo joins a tradition that may be traced back to Pliny the Elder. In Book VII of his *Natural*

History, Pliny places in the mountains of India a race of men with pointed snouts, barking instead of speaking, armed with claws, and devouring the spoils of their hunt. Marco Polo moved these creatures from continental India to the Andaman archipelago, with no concern about the harm he would thus do to the Sentinelese. This suspicion of cannibalism became so firmly associated with their tribe that it reappeared in the 21st century. In 2006, when the Sentinelese killed the two fishermen I mentioned above, the coast guardsmen were surprised they did not devour them.

But really, why does this rumor persist? Where there's smoke, there's fire—bad joke aside. In my opinion, it comes from an Onge ritual. When an outsider dies, the members of the tribe cut his body into pieces and throw them into the fire. Their goal is to destroy the bones, otherwise, so they believe, the spirit of the victim will return to torment them. What is actually a prophylactic rite for this people has long been interpreted as a cannibal feast—and I recognize that, seeing them around a fire where human body parts were being grilled, appearances were against the Onges.

7

Brothers and Sisters

Regarding the origins of Saint Andrew, there are different versions. Some claim that the society was born at the beginning of Western monasticism before seeking refuge in America at the time of the French Revolution, when the patriots were attacking the statues of monarchs and saints *en masse*. Others maintain that its founding was the result of the splitting of a Scottish branch of the Masonic order whose members emigrated throughout the world. Symbols were said to be found on rocks in grottos far off in the Orient, in Kyrgyzstan, and even in the mountains in Afghanistan. A competing tradition attributes the creation of this inherently rational order to Benjamin Franklin. Less venerable in terms of age, it is still held in high regard for the identity of its illustrious founder. In the course of time, lodges spread throughout the English colonies and, if we are to believe a minority school of historians of the Order, they played a little known but highly important role in the Revolutionary War by providing the insurgents with a network of support and spies. By virtue of an obvious tropism, based on the attraction of knowledge and abstract speculation, these lodges progressively implanted themselves in universities, on the east coast first, then in the South and ultimately all the way to California.

The members of Saint Andrew travel regularly between the lodges. Hospitality is one of our duties, and a brother from Pennsylvania knows that he will always have, in Indiana as in Georgia, a bed, food, and company. These visits, however, have a normative function of which the founders of the Order—whoever they may have been—were keenly aware in prescribing them in our statutes. Above and beyond the bonds of friendship and gratitude that they establish, they serve to monitor the rigorous application of the laws that govern us. A host is also an observer, always ready to inform our superiors of any deviation from our prescribed rites. We wish, in effect, our liturgy in New Hampshire to be exactly as it is in Louisiana and to remain today what it was yesterday. This faithfulness to our usages is scarcely a gratuitous constraint. Each time it is accomplished according to the rules, the ritual transports us outside History. Its vocation consists in effecting a momentary abolition of time.

I would like to reveal to you, as it was to me, the force of our underground sociability, these understandings that weave powerful bonds between individuals who apparently have nothing in common, and who nonetheless work together to initiate large-scale changes. It is in fact true that organizations like Saint Andrew play an unrecognized but decisive role in the advent of global phenomena. These fraternities now transcend national borders, because foreign students, enrolling in American universities in ever greater numbers, are broadly represented at Saint Andrew as in rival associations. The web of their invisible network extends throughout the world, and an Italian manufacturer has a close relationship with a Pakistani engineer and a Texan lawyer because, twenty years before, they shared nights they can only evoke with each other.

This solidarity between members, as is the case for the majority of human groups, results in large part from their antagonism toward rival and nonetheless similar tribes. I've often observed in fact that *similarity*, as much and perhaps more than *difference*, is a powerful factor in enmity. Why do we hate someone who resembles us? Because we recognize in the other what we detest in ourselves? Because we wish to be unique and cannot tolerate someone who is like us? Or is it because our attention to subtle dissimilarities leads us to exaggerate the superiority they seem to reveal in the other? All of the above, I imagine. In any case, these organizations, separated by scarcely a few minutes on the campus, are divided by grudges that last long after their cause has been forgotten. Before my induction into Saint Andrew, I hadn't the slightest idea of what was being plotted late at night in the streets of New Haven; no idea of those battles, of those perilous transgressions in tomb-like buildings, of those thefts of documents nor of the reprisals they provoked. It's a world with its own codes, shifting alliances, hereditary enemies, and heroes whose legend, exploits, grand gestures, brave acts, and dark betrayals are recorded in chronicles that a scribe maintains scrupulously in each organization, and that are exhumed by archivists to be read in public or to find within them the solution to a point of contention. Alas, even to hint at these things is too risky.

Likewise, I can only describe my brothers and sisters in general terms. It is not forbidden to reveal one's membership in the fraternity, but that is a personal decision, and I have no right to make it for others. All I will say is that I found in this community, more than in any other place before and afterwards, the effervescence that accompanies the rise of something new. Imagine yourself working on a revolutionary invention, alone against fierce competitors who possess financial means far greater than yours: the first to succeed will make a fortune while the others will be left to weep. That is how I saw the members of our society: they were all striving, under pressure, to change the paradigm.

Hadji—not his real name—was writing a program that three well-known corporations were eyeing with interest. He became a multimillionaire at the age of 19. Hanna was preparing a doctoral thesis on digital humanities at a time when no one was seriously interested in it. After becoming a member of the highly prestigious Society of Fellows of Harvard, she is now teaching at Stanford. Ayush's grandfather introduced him to the stars while sharing with him the legend of Einstein and Niels Bohr. Ayush began by following in their footsteps but, intuiting the potential of quantum computers, he was among the first to join this area of research. Victor became a partner in a big law firm in New York after having been the youngest editor-in-chief in the history of the *Columbia Law Review*; Daniel is the mayor of a city with a population of a million people in Mexico; and Lucy published an essay, translated into fifteen languages, on the Sinicization of Tibet. Each one of them accomplished something remarkable in their area of expertise, and that does not surprise me, since in our youth they were already seething inside, driven by something serious and somber that propelled them forward, kept them sharp, and prevented them from being satisfied with what they were. They were impatient like people who covet greatness and know that they haven't earned it yet. It is among them, at Saint Andrew, that I learned this fundamental lesson: I understood that anything, absolutely anything, is possible. In this world there is only willpower and renunciation; if the first prevails, there is no limit to what we can accomplish.

Several decades have passed, and it is time to take stock: have we proved unworthy of Saint Andrew, of this chance that was offered to us one autumn day in the form of a letter with a blue seal? This is a fear shared by members of exclusive clubs: each one dreads not having measured up to the hopes invested in them. At the reunions every ten years, no one wants to be the black sheep of the community, the one who must dodge and weave when asked what they've been up to. For a long time, I dreaded that I was the one, the imposter of the group. That is my flaw, my complex, that of the *thief with the turban come undone*. But if I were to question the others, ask them who didn't go as far as they could have, I know all too well what they would answer. No one had so much promise and ultimately accomplished so little than my brother and friend, who is also the man I most detested in the world: Markus.

8

The Diligent

A new chapter began on January 16, 1771: the birth certificate of Sentinel Island in the consciousness of the West.

The discoverer of the island is Captain John Ritchie. He's a maritime expert who spent nineteen years in the service of England, drawing maps, marking the shoals, carving a path in a labyrinth of forests and rivers, relentlessly exploring the Bay of Bengal. In 1787, he complained to his superiors of the arduousness of his work and petitioned them successfully to let him return home and retire with, as he put it, a richly deserved pension. He left the Andamans honored by a string of islands named after him but with one regret: he was unable to convince his government to establish a permanent colony there. The Crown eventually acquiesced but several decades later, after the Sepoy Rebellion of 1857, when it sent the heroes of Indian independence to rot in the Port Blair jails.

Ritchie left laconic notes in a work with a resounding title, in the 18th-century style: *An Hydrographical Journal of a Cursory Survey of the Coasts and Islands in the Bay of Bengal.* We learn that on January 16, 1771, he is on board the *Diligent,* a ship of the British East India Company whose mission is to take hydrographic readings. Ritchie writes that after sundown he observed on the shore of a neighboring island "a multitude of lights." "However," he notes, during the day there wasn't the slightest sign of houses or inhabitants. The entire island is covered by impenetrable forests that extend to the edge of the water." *The Diligent* continues on its way, leaving behind the lights shining on the shore—the shore of Sentinel Island.

It would be unfortunate to omit what follows in the journal. Ritchie recounts that shortly afterwards, around midnight, lightning pierces the darkness over to the southeast. An hour later a storm breaks out, a storm of driving rain and punishing hail that rages over the surface of the furious waters. "Reverberating between the hills, the thunder seemed atrociously sublime," Ritchie observes. A few years earlier, the philosopher Edmund Burke had declared, "Whatever is fitted in any sort to excite the ideas of pain, and danger, that is to say, whatever is in any sort terrible, or is conversant about terrible objects, or operates in a manner analogous to terror, *is a source of the sublime.*" The birth of Sentinel Island is a sublime spectacle: it occurs in an aura of surprise, horror, and danger.

9

Victor

For a long time, Markus remained inaccessible. I observed him from afar during the *soirées* at Saint Andrew, smiling, amiable, more charming than anyone else, and despite the invariable cordiality with which he treated me when we found ourselves face to face, it always seemed that there was an invisible obstacle between us. It was no doubt his perfect courtesy that produced an insurmountable distance between him and the others. Being rigorously polite permitted him to remind his counterparts of his social origins, to oblige them to join him at heights where they quickly faltered, while discouraging them from adopting a familiarity that would have threatened to lower *him* to their level. Markus spoke to you and then disappeared immediately, as soon as prolonged contact could have signified the birth of a type of intimacy between you.

During the first weeks that followed my induction into Saint Andrew, he was therefore not the first person I became close to but rather Victor, a Californian who had given me my last interview in the admission process. Never have I met anyone so clearly split between two personalities. Victor alternated between them as easily as a light bulb goes from day to night. At your first meeting, when he didn't know you well, Victor was the coldest, the most conventional, the most distant, conservative, and ceremonious fellow you can imagine. He was nonetheless far from belonging to the privileged classes with which his interlocutors instinctively identified him. His father was a Chinese immigrant, his mother American, and himself strikingly handsome, as is often the case of children of mixed heritage. He had grown up in Sacramento where his parents ran a grocery store, the kind that stays open at night, in which convex mirrors eliminate the blind spots, and where the liquor is out of reach behind the counter. Seeing him so constantly discreet and dressed with such studied elegance, hearing his melodious voice uttering just the right words, you would still have sworn that his childhood was in a British boarding school where gentlemen in blazers had introduced him to the classics and social graces. So perfectly did he master this pose as an elegant, fragile young man that most of his professors likely never suspected that there existed someone else behind this smooth façade.

But if he sensed in you something subversive and blithe, something that violated these conventions that he seemed to embody so impeccably, he would send you a signal that you would do well to respond to as expected or risk seeing him take refuge behind his well-mannered little prince role. It could be a smutty joke, an allusion to popular culture, an insolent reflection, or simply something vulgar; it varied according to the individual and he measured very precisely the intensity of his remark so that it would explode without being too destructive. It's what he called "making an opening": if you answered spontaneously, he continued to reveal his real self, to the point that it became impossible for you to recall his double, the well-behaved, serious individual, for he became obscene, uncontrollable, and excessive in his humor and impropriety. And if, on the contrary, you took offense, the complete opposite occurred: he instantly returned to his former self—and this time for good.

It didn't take Victor long to figure me out: he quickly understood that we were both interlopers at Yale, the type of people who have no business being in such a place, and who constantly wonder if there wasn't some error involved in their admission. One day when I was reading in the great lounge of the hall, he tried out his usual technique on me. Standing at the door, he called out to me: "So, how's the imposter doing?" Upon seeing my downcast expression, he stopped me immediately: "Relax, we're all imposters, beginning with me: I still haven't told my parents I'm gay." I said nothing; I just listened to his story. He told me that his father, having emigrated from Yunnan Province to join his cousins in California, had converted to evangelical Christianity, and his mother belonged to the same church. For them it was inconceivable for their son to be homosexual. To avoid raising their suspicions, he had himself photographed with a female friend at Saint Andrew, pretending she was his girlfriend; thus, his folks didn't have him exorcised when he came home on vacation. He seemed to be joking, but the need to hide the truth from them was clearly a serious source of discomfort for him. "And what about you? Tell me a little about yourself; something tells me that you have interesting things to share." I began by telling him that I had gotten married a little over a year ago.

"Didn't waste any time, did you? And is she Indian too?"

"No, she's American. Her name is Eleanor."

"Where does she come from?"

"Texas."

"From Texas? Let me guess: her family didn't appreciate an immigrant getting his hooks into their daughter, right?"

Victor had gotten it right: the conservative stereotype fit this case perfectly. When I had met them in Arlington, Eleanor's parents and four brothers—Cody, Cory, Connor, and Cooper—hadn't spared me their sarcastic remarks on my origins, including clumsy allusions to Bollywood, the Taj Mahal, spicy food, and slums. They were recycling the few clichés they had heard about a country in which, of course, they had never set foot. Having tried to talk her out of marrying me, they had led Eleanor to understand that she was always welcome in their home, but that there was no need for me to accompany her. The fact that she hadn't defended me was the source of our first real argument: Eleanor made every imaginable excuse for them while judging me too sensitive, or ridiculous, when I told her that their rejection had hurt me deeply. I related all that to Victor, who, to cheer me up after these painful revelations, invited me to the hall's bar, where we talked for hours.

A few days later, Markus invited me to a party he was having at his place. Since the beginning of the year, he no longer lived on campus, renting instead a luxurious duplex in the center of the city. And for the first time, without my understanding the reasons for this new attitude, he relaxed the wariness he had always reserved for me. I have to admit it: I was amazed by the honor he was doing me; Markus was showing me favor. That evening Victor did not show up, unless he had not been invited: he had no affection for Markus, and the two of them avoided each other as much as they could. Against my wishes I was forced to choose between them, and while maintaining excellent relations with Victor, I bonded more and more with Markus. It was he that I began to see every week outside of Saint Andrew, making him my closest friend during this period, and making my choice of him over Victor one of those decisions that, by a strange premonition, you understand commits you more deeply than you can say, a decision whose consequences you sense, somewhere deep within you, without being able to identify them, like those forgotten tunes whose melody remains on the tip of your tongue.

10

The Ninive

Here is the testimony left by the captain of the *Ninive*, a ship that was traveling from Madras to Rangoon in the summer of 1867:

"This dishonor, Gentlemen, I'll bear the stain of it until my final day. I beg you to excuse my brevity: it is made necessary by the painful impression that remains from these deplorable events. That night my second-in-command was in charge, and I was resting in my quarters. We were sailing towards the southeast and were supposed to leave Port Blair on the port beam before noon. Providence decided otherwise. At one thirty in the morning, while we were to the west of Sentinel Island, the ship ran into a reef. Fatally injured, the *Ninive* was lying in the shallows, torrents of water gushing into the hull through the open wound. Jolted awake, I went to survey the damage. Considering it irreparable, I ordered everyone to abandon ship immediately. On board there were eighty-six passengers and twenty crew members. They all reached dry land in our lifeboats, without the loss of a single person.

"For two days we remained on the shore, looking out to the sea. We were hoping for the friendly sail that would save us from our mishap. Unfortunately, these waters are rarely visited, and the length of our wait was uncertain. Not wishing to assume anything in this respect, I took the necessary measures. I began by leading multiple trips to the wreck of the *Ninive* to save the merchandise and food that we had been forced to abandon during the shipwreck. Alas, the gunpowder was lost, but we were able to bring large quantities of foodstuffs to the shore. I then gave the order to ration them and stand guard over them day and night. These precautions seemed all the more indispensable since without powder we were unable to hunt in the nearby forest. In addition, I forbade anyone from entering it. It was not difficult to get everyone to obey, since some of our crew had already shared alarming rumors concerning the island's inhabitants, ferocious cannibals and formidable warriors. I hoped that by establishing our camp on the shore, without ever venturing into the interior of their territory, the Sentinelese would leave us alone until our deliverance.

"In the morning of the third day, as we improvised a meal, a volley of arrows showered down upon us. It was the Sentinelese shooting at us as they ran towards us. These savages were entirely naked. They had short hair and noses painted red. As they approached, they cried out over and over: *pan on ough, pan on ough, pan on ough*, this horrible noise that I still hear sometimes in my nightmares. Seeing us at a severe disadvantage, I fled to my dishonor. Accompanied by three officers and my second-in-command, I reached one of the lifeboats of the *Ninive*, abandoning our shipmates to their fate. I would be lying, Gentlemen, if I said I was going for help: I was only trying to save my own skin.

"I can see in my memory, as I see you today, the survivors armed with sticks and stones facing the army of cannibals. As we were rowing with all our strength towards the open sea, a hideous struggle was playing out on the beach. The savages were attacking our people, who were standing up to them with a courage I was already reproaching myself for not demonstrating. But it was too late to come to their assistance: the battle grew faint as we bent over our oars, and I would have liked to believe it was only a bad dream.

"The rest can be told in few words. After days of suffering at sea—that didn't succeed in punishing a fault that was inexpiable by nature—we crossed the path of a Maltese ship headed for Burma. It took us to Port Blair, from where we set off immediately to rescue our shipwrecked companions on Sentinel Island. To our relief and shame, they informed us that the savages had fled without leaving victims and hadn't been seen since. Severely tested by their ordeal, they thanked me for returning for them, but their gratitude made all the more painful my feeling of having been derelict in my duty in abandoning them in the moment of danger. Shortly afterwards, I resigned my master's certificate and never again saw the coast of England. You'll understand if I say no more about this."

In saving the survivors of the *Ninive*, the British Navy took advantage of the situation to absorb Sentinel Island into their Empire. Symbolic in nature, this decision changed nothing for the existence of its people—at least not before 1880. That is when an officer of the Royal Navy arrives on the scene, a minor aristocrat, self-proclaimed anthropologist, historian, photographer, administrator, and pseudoscientist whose calamitous influence has never waned.

11

Block Island

Markus enjoyed the spontaneous majesty with which power is conquered and dynasties founded. This surprising charisma is in no way mysterious: it is explained by an overabundance of talent. As I mentioned earlier, he was extremely handsome. Later, when he became famous for dramatic reasons, and then for others less flattering, the hoi polloi of the Internet mocked his naturally aristocratic manner. I remember a remark on Twitter that described him as "the embodiment of a trust fund"—a wry dig that cut deeply. It is true that Markus's physical appearance was his first privilege: he had an athletic build, a distinguished bearing, and a charming smile that made you feel just as intelligent as he was.

Shortly before his birth, his parents had moved into a four-story home that a fashionable architect had renovated in the very chic Upper East Side. Markus had a sister two years younger than he, a brunette just as strikingly beautiful as he was; I'll have more occasions than I like to speak of Alexandra. Their mother handled fortunes in a Midtown law firm. She had begun her studies at Harvard, then enrolled in the law school at Yale after a year at Oxford as a Rhodes Scholar. Samantha had an impeccable pedigree and a fierceness in battle that could be perceived behind the predatory smile of these white, ambitious, brilliant, and highly educated American women. It's their perfect fangs and the glacial glow of their gaze when they pose for their professional portraits that give them a merciless expression even when they're trying to look warm and friendly. During a charity gala at the Metropolitan Museum of Art, she had met Joakim, a Swede who had come to New York a decade earlier. Their marriage had been announced in the *New York Times*, and the combined fortunes of the guests added up to billions of dollars.

It was thought at the time that their couple was a bad match. Samantha belonged to an old money family: a South Carolina clan whose wealth was already lavish before the Civil War. From the sixties on, her people's interests aligned perfectly with those of the Republican Party. Her family included a senator from the Grand Old Party and several CEOs of businesses specialized in aeronautics, steel, and arms that donated generously to the electoral campaigns of Nixon and his successors. Joakim not only came from another country; he came from another world.

After the death of his parents, he had been raised by his grandmother in the small city of Vallentuna, twenty miles north of Stockholm. He was older than Samantha, had no prestigious schools on his resumé—only a diploma in performing arts, earned at a time when he dreamed of becoming a theater director before abandoning the stage in favor of artists' studios—and, after a long apprenticeship with a gallery owner at the top of the New York food chain, had just opened, with a partner, his first spot in So Ho. Samantha's family would have preferred that she not choose an immigrant, even a Swedish one, but rather one of the suitors whose advantages they played up during parties organized in the posh districts of Manhattan. It didn't help Joakim's case that he created his gallery at the beginning of the nineties, during an economic recession when a gallery was created every month while four others closed their doors: sheer professional suicide, said the experts. But he had an unerring instinct for artists who would become successful, and Samantha's instinct reassured her over and over that she hadn't made a mistake in marrying him. This man would not prove to be unworthy of her. To succeed, he needed time and capital that she was in a position to find for him. Armed with this financial support and everything he had learned in Stockholm, Berlin, and then New York, Joakim had gone off in search of new talent and had spared no effort to keep them once he found them.

From the outside, singular success stories always seem to be in some way inevitable. A rising star in the art market, as if by predestination Joakim had become an essential actor. From his point of view, however, success was simply the result of many years of perseverance. Joakim knew just how much cunning, audacity, intuition, and relentlessness it had taken to reach the top; he could say what he had learned from each error he had committed along the way so as never to repeat it. Believing that others had a privileged relationship to fate, he said, was just a way of ignoring the sacrifices they had had to make. The dominant position he enjoyed had been built upon patiently negotiated steps. The space rented in SoHo with another gallery owner was eventually in his name alone. Then he had moved to an abandoned garage in Chelsea, transformed into a huge exhibition space whose industrial style was completely in tune with the times. He had progressively established himself in the secondary art market, acquiring works from their first buyers and reselling them to private collectors or to prestigious museums like the Guggenheim, the Pompidou Center, and the Tate Modern. The reputation of his artists grew steadily in his hands, and with rare exceptions they stuck with him once he began handling their work. Joakim had an affinity for the avant-garde postwar movements, and in particular for Arte Povera and conceptualism and minimalism in the style of Yves Klein. Sometimes disparaged by his competitors, who criticized his authoritarian style and the impatience with which he conducted his negotiations, he was nonetheless respected for the unconditional support he gave his artists and commended for the philanthropic activities he pursued with the same single-mindedness as his business ventures. At the time of our meeting, his success was already resounding. Owner of three galleries in Manhattan, he was contemplating opening a fourth in one of the great European capitals. Insiders were beginning to see in him a serious pretender for the throne of Larry Gagosian, the emperor of modern art.

I knew nothing of that world, and as Markus was discreet when it came to his family and very infrequently spoke of his father—and always with a somber air that discouraged questions—I was completely unaware of the milieu I was preparing to enter when I accepted his invitation to Block Island. Eleanor was going to visit her parents in Texas. I had no desire to go with her and, in all honesty, no one had asked me to. In learning that I would be alone in New Haven, Markus immediately invited me to join him at his family's home, where I would meet his father and sister—his mother, on the other hand, would be too busy to join us. Edmond said over and over, "You don't get it. Markus's father is *Joakim Holmberg*! He's one of the biggest art dealers in the world!" No, I didn't get it, but I was beginning to wonder how I would be treated by people with so much money.

My fears were groundless: Joakim was always extremely kind to me. He came to get us, Markus and me, at the helm of his sailboat, and we embarked on a luxurious vacation that I related to Eleanor, attaching photos to my emails so that she could admire the enormous house and its private beach, the wooded park, the infinity swimming pool, the Swedish sauna, and the recreation room where father and son battled on the billiard table while tolerating my pitiful efforts. Joakim was remarkably frugal. He could have transformed his home into a Gatsby palace and lined up on deckchairs a bunch of destructively temperamental artists, novelists acclaimed by the *New Yorker*, influential journalists, and rising Broadway stars, with a few political personalities thrown in for good measure. He gladly left this social whirl, that he often experienced in Manhattan, to the residents of Nantucket and Martha's Vineyard, more prestigious destinations than Block Island, which he had chosen precisely because it held no interest for the great and the good of the world. He had a need for authenticity that affected his taste in decoration, books, and friends. The house displayed no ostentatious luxury, and the furniture, charming and comfortable, mixed white with various shades of gray.

What Joakim preferred, during this all too short summer break, was simply to read. Reading had become a luxury for him, an activity increasingly threatened by the emails that required his immediate attention, or by the negotiations with the artists and the exhibits he was organizing in one of his New York galleries. During his rare weeks of repose, he liked to roll his pant legs up to his calves, slip his legs into the swimming pool, and read as far away as possible from any electronic device that could distract him, a frayed cap on his head and a pitcher of water within reach. And then he would get up suddenly, saying, "Come on, boys! Let's go for a walk on the beach." The three of us would leave for a stroll among the dunes and return, intoxicated with the sun and wind, in time for the dinner that we found served on the veranda. The personnel was so discreet that it became virtually invisible, as if everything we enjoyed—the cleanliness of the house and the coolness of the sheets, the plentiful supplies and exquisite meals—were the work of a magical domestic staff.

In every respect, knowing Joakim and Markus was an invaluable stroke of good fortune for me, and I just couldn't believe that I had received the father's friendship along with the son's. Both of them could be useful to me, help me enter a world otherwise inaccessible. However, I never tried to take advantage of my relationship with Joakim or, more broadly, to benefit from him or his son in any way or form. It was their friendship that interested me, and I sensed that the moment I tried to get something from them, they would give it to me and at the same time remove me from their life. Friendship demands equality, and in a case like this, where there was a prodigious gap between our respective social positions, I had no choice but to exhibit complete selflessness to avoid being transformed in an instant, in their eyes and my own, from a guest to a parasite. At the university, Markus was already constantly solicited by more or less distant acquaintances who all assumed, because his parents were wealthy, that he had inexhaustible reserves of time, energy, and generosity to spread around. Even more than his father, who had, after all, made his fortune out of nothing and could claim it fully as his own, Markus aspired to be appreciated for himself. My clear interest in him, independent of the advantages his family brought him, did much to solidify our friendship—at least during our time together in college.

During our walks, Joakim spoke affectionately of the novelists he often saw in New York. This art dealer had a literary side, most likely because artists were associated with his work whereas the company of writers gave him some relief from his professional activities. When he told us stories about Colson Whitehead, Atticus Lish, Joyce Carol Oates, or Zadie Smith, I was mesmerized. There is a well-known theory according to which it only takes six relations to put you in contact with the whole planet. I looked at Joakim, and only one degree separated me from the contemporary authors I admired the most. Among all his anecdotes, none fascinated me as much as those that concerned the brilliant Japanese writer Haruki Murakami, who, it turned out, was one of his close friends. They had met when Murakami was a visiting artist in residence at Harvard, and since he returned to the United States every year to run the New York marathon, Joakim took the opportunity to invite him over. Apparently, they wrote each other every Sunday to compare, with an affectionate rivalry that sometimes turned fierce, the number of miles they had run during the previous week. When Markus spoke to me of this novelist, the most brilliant of our time, in a manner he would have adopted to refer to an old family friend, I was terribly jealous—much more, in fact, than of all his father's millions.

When he wasn't leading us across the sand dunes, Joakim liked to bring out his sailboat and take us on a cruise around the island and sometimes even farther afield, toward Cape Cod or Nantucket. We boarded the *Samantha III*, where Alexandra, who wanted to learn from her father how to steer, would join us. The rest of her time she spent doing laps in the pool or with friends that I never saw, because she went to meet them at other spots on Block Island, at the wheel of a flashy red vintage convertible.

I imagine there are no longer any reasons to deny it. The protagonists of this story have been dead for a long time, or the relations that existed between them have changed entirely ... I was both violently attracted to Alexandra and viscerally repulsed by her. I didn't quite know if the most uncontrollable fantasy she inspired in me was of bedding her in her room or punching her in the face. Let's get beyond the obvious: she was magnificent, with her long-limbed body, narrow hips, and legs beating rhythmically in the pool. I avoided looking at her when, seated on the edge, she twisted her long hair, pulled forward in a plait on her shoulder, to press the water out. The heat of these summer weeks, and the abstinence I was condemned to by Eleanor's absence, transformed the attraction I felt for her into a growing obsession. Stretched out on my bed, I imagined each movement I would have to make to slip into her room, so close, just at the end of the hallway ... I have no idea what would have happened if she had given me any form of encouragement; it is difficult to even imagine, since everything in her attitude told me clearly that I was not to her taste.

There was at best a glacial indifference between us, at worst out and out contempt. Some women have a special gift that consists in making you feel less of a man. In their eyes, you're a stone, an object, an insect, sometimes vermin or just something transparent; and while they excite in you all the palpitations of the heart and groin, the boiling of your blood and the stirring of your flesh, they let you know by their words as by their silence, the gazes they direct at or simply through you, just how much your presence, far from arousing in them an erotic emotion comparable to the one they provoke in you, inspires in them, on the contrary, unremitting boredom, flashes of irritation, and, finally, complete indifference. It's not that they wish you were dead; they would just profoundly prefer that you had never been born. And because I couldn't prevent myself from coveting her heavy breast, her maiden's flat stomach, and those nervous thighs where I dreamed of plunging my head, I detested myself for feeling such an unrequited attraction. I've never fully understood why she disliked me so much. A polite lack of interest, a controlled antipathy, I could have accepted that; but why this almost physical repulsion?

While Joakim and Markus, sincerely, never seemed to be concerned with my origins, she saw me as a young male escort, a brown-skinned immigrant who helped to relieve their solitude on Block Island, or as a little David Copperfield they had taken in to salve their conscience. My anthropology studies—at NYU she was majoring in economics and international business—only inspired condescending remarks from her. She clearly wondered why, as poor as I was, I was devoting myself to such non-lucrative questions as the origin of the Onges' language and the kinship structures of the Jarawas. Alexandra would have respected me more if my main goal in life had been to earn money. It is also possible that something in my body, my odor, my manner of being, or my accent deeply displeased her. To speak plainly, racism was doubtless the principal cause of her hostility … Unless, sensing the attraction she held for me, she had used it as a means of asserting herself at my expense and compensating for the abyss of doubts she concealed as best she could—in her way, Alexandra too suffered from the crushing success of her parents. As time went by, I eventually responded to her aggressiveness with indifference, and as I had to feign it less and less—the businesswoman she became, with all the boyfriends she dismissed one after the other, not finding anyone good enough for her, with her manicures, her lacquered hair, and her large rings, frankly no longer appealed to me—she held that against me too, since it was also an offense to no longer be bound to my desire for her. There are certain beings with whom, whatever we do, however much we or they change, our relations can only ever lead to suffering. The simplest solution is to avoid them, and I would have continued to do so if, years later, Alexandra hadn't turned up unexpectedly in my office in Columbus.

Despite our tense relations, we shared that summer an experience that created a special bond between us. I've never forgotten it. Joakim had read until the middle of the afternoon, and, at a later hour than usual, he suggested we go out on the boat. Markus and I accepted immediately, followed soon by his sister. With the time it took to get to the boat and cast off, evening had already descended upon us. There was a cool breeze, and we were skimming along to the northwest. Alexandra was at the helm, supervised by Joakim, while Markus and I were chatting at the bow. I remember this particular intoxication, that included both the excitement of an unexpected adventure—Joakim was keeping our destination secret—and, more prosaically, the alcohol we were imbibing and that was slowly going to our heads. Made tipsy by the sun and the cool wine, we were sailing along, carefree and happy; Alexandra had forgotten her policy of ignoring me, and I think she even smiled at me that day.

An island rose up on the horizon: a beach and walls of boulders, with no house in sight. A few hundred yards from there, perhaps a little more, Joakim dropped anchor, dissuaded by reefs from getting any closer. Markus, who excelled at swimming as he excelled at everything, suggested we swim to the shore. Alexandra dared him to try it, reminding him of the great white shark whose presence along the coast had been noted in the local papers for at least a week. The shark hadn't taken any victims, but the papers stressed its impressive size and its dangerous proximity to the bathing areas. Without answering her, Markus took off his cap and shirt and dove over the boat's rail. I wasn't sure that this was a good idea; we had drunk too much, and this business about the shark was worrisome. But when Alexandra took off her jean shorts and the plaid shirt that covered her bathing suit and her golden body, I immediately understood that I wouldn't have the courage not to follow her example. I dove in as well, and something strange happened whose complete meaning was only revealed to me many years later.

I was swimming toward the shore, slowly. Markus was far ahead, and Alexandra had almost caught up to him. "Always last," I quickly thought, despite myself. I knew I was not able to join them (I had learned to swim in my late teens), so I preferred to pay attention to my breathing and not try to go too fast, to be sure to make it all the way. It was the first time that I had reached land from the water, and the first time I had swum so long in the open sea. If I had had any difficulties, no one could have helped me. The distance between me and Markus and his sister became ever greater, and before Joakim would have had time to come to my aid, I would have disappeared beneath the water. Nonetheless,

I thought I could do it: my body was reacting astonishingly well to my efforts, and the coolness of the water had caused the effect of the alcohol to wear off. The sun was dipping below the horizon when I set foot on the shore.

Everything was dark and orange around me. There was no sign of Markus and Alexandra; the beach was narrow and came up against black boulders that formed a wall around six feet tall. I climbed over them, discovering on the other side the edge of the forest, whose approach was marked by sparse, scrawny bushes. In the distance, Alexandra and Markus were standing still and looking behind the curtain of trees. I called them, and they walked back to me. The three of us began to look for seashells in the hollows of the rocks. We had become children again, roaming around happily in the twilight. There was no longer either desire or contempt between Alexandra and me, just the shared goal of finding pretty shells. And Markus was no longer this young man whose talents impressed me so much at the same time as they crushed me: he was just a playmate. All three of us returned fleetingly to an age of innocence, prior to any of the differences that we invent between ourselves and others.

It was getting dark, and Alexandra was shivering. With her loose, wet hair she no longer resembled a provocative mermaid but a little girl who needed to be taken home. In the distance, the silhouette of Joakim was gesturing emphatically. Soon night would have completely fallen. We went down to the beach before slipping back into the water, all three of us at the same time. Compared to the rapidly cooling air, it seemed almost warm. Each at our own rhythm, we headed back toward the boat, Markus far ahead, Alexandra following him closely, with me again bringing up the rear. And then I remembered the shark. At first it was just a game, an idea I was entertaining to frighten myself, like kids do with scary tales around a campfire in the dark. But little by little I began to feel its presence, and something strange, something uncontrollable gripped me.

I take a deep breath and dive straight down, as far as I can toward the bottom, where the water is inky black, where it's impossible to see a yard in front of you; at each stroke, the temperature drops several degrees. Above, there is only night, a tomblike ceiling that nothing can pierce; around me, more darkness. When the pressure begins to get to my ears, I stop my descent and just spin slowly around until I begin to run out of breath. I search the darkness, trying to make out the phantom I imagine so intensely that I think I can see its pallid sides, powerful tail, dead eyes, and fearsome jaws. My spine is shaken by such violent shivering that I curl up in the water, and when I'm very nearly out of breath, I finally go back up to the surface. When my face breaks the water, the stars are out. I dive again, several times, until the terror, the idea of this beast that I'm seeking in its watery lair, has run its course. Then I resume swimming toward the boat, with no comprehension of the urge that has just gripped me. I've since thought back on this urge, often in fact, when it drove me to take risks that were infinitely more serious. During this period, I was struggling with serious doubts about my masculinity that stemmed from Eleanor's domination of me. Putting myself in danger was a way to reclaim what she had taken from me and was holding hostage. To surmount my fears, I needed to confront them; fleeing them was not an option, for that would have given substance to the image Eleanor had of me. All of that contributed greatly, I believe, to the decisions I made after Markus's disappearance.

Long after him and his sister, I climbed back on board the boat. Joakim handed me a towel, and I dried myself vigorously while he set the sails. In spite of myself, I stared at the water, still trying to make out the pale shape I imagined swimming around the hull. I had the peculiar feeling that something important but for the moment incomprehensible had just taken place, that this excursion foreshadowed an event that I was, for the moment, unable to identify. That reminded me of the disturbing feeling you get as a child when an adult says something in your presence that they shouldn't have, because you are too young to understand it: you remember it without knowing what it means until the day when life finally unlocks its secret.

The boat was making slow headway, much slower than we would've liked. The wind had died down, and our return was growing increasingly late as we inched toward our port. Alexandra, Markus, and I had each taken our turn in the cabin to strip off our dripping, freezing swimsuits and dress more warmly. Joakim was standing next to his daughter, who had taken the helm again while Markus and I returned to the bow with another bottle of white wine. We remained silent for a good while, during which my memory was jumping around, reviving various moments separated by time. Most of them brought my parents and Kamala back to life for a brief moment, fragments of my childhood in Mumbai. How many times, I wondered, does one die in the course of one's life? As often as we lose those we love. The void they leave upon departing is the space where we have to reinvent ourselves; there is no other way to console oneself.

Markus kept his silence and drank, more than me, more than he should have, and it was the first time I had seen him abuse alcohol—or do anything that was contrary to the perfection I had seen in him since our first meeting. The boat was gliding gently through the night, noiselessly, as if it were weightless. Suddenly a curtain of clouds was drawn back, revealing on the other side an enormous moon, scarlet and pagan. It looked like it was floating on the horizon like a bobber left to drift away by a titanic fisherman. Markus stared at it with an unusual intensity, his brow furrowed, his forehead wrinkled by the effort; he was completely engrossed by this blood-red moon.

"Markus—Is everything alright?"

It was then that he pronounced this sentence that heralded all our misfortunes:

"This moon … I've already seen it."

12

Portman (1/3)

Every story has its detestable villain, and the villain of Sentinel Island is named Maurice Vidal Portman. Let's listen to him address the very prestigious Royal Geographical Society of London, near the end of his life, to sum up a career that posterity has judged quite differently than did his contemporaries:

"Mister President, Ladies, Gentlemen. I stand before you to speak of Man as we may observe him in the far recesses of the Empire. For twenty-two years I lived among those dark-skinned peoples who have occupied the distant Andaman archipelago since the beginning of time. I devoted to them my care, my work, my sleepless nights: in short, the very best of myself. With all the patience of which I was capable, I employed the tools and methods of modern science to document the details of their anatomical conformation. But it is first of all their soul that interested me: the extent of their intelligence, their capacity to receive the teachings of our civilization and the grace of our faith. I will soon share with you my conclusions on this matter.

"I arrived at Port Blair, the capital of our possessions in the Andaman archipelago, at the age of nineteen. It was in 1879, and the colony was only two years older than me. I assumed my duties as Officer in Charge of the Andamanese and strived, as young as I was, to be worthy of the consideration that this important title brought by following the impulses of the lively curiosity that these savages provoked in me. It is the natives of Sentinel Island that captivated my imagination, and it is to them that I devoted the majority of my reflections rather than to their neighbors on Great Andaman, better known because they live closer to our anchorage points in the archipelago.

"I had been at Port Blair scarcely a few months when I decided to pay a visit to the Sentinelese. It was the first time in human history that such an expedition had been prepared. It is true that my predecessor, Mister Jeremiah Homfray, approached the island in 1867, but he was frightened off when he saw some ten natives standing on the shore and quickly turned his ship around and headed back to port. As for me, I was resolved to explore Sentinel Island and to put my name on this important discovery.

"The crossing from Port Blair was short and uneventful, other than the necessity of mooring our ship away from the reefs that surround the island and then proceeding the rest of the way in our rowboats. Accompanied by my second-in-command, Colonel Cadell, I discovered in the jungle a veritable network of paths leading to villages—which their inhabitants deserted at our approach, leaving behind them only empty huts. I was greatly irritated by this and soon understood that our method had little chance of succeeding. There were too few of us to search the island methodically and seize a sample of its natives. I headed back to Port Blair with plans to return to Sentinel Island with a greater number of troops. I accomplished this in the last days of January 1880 on board an excellent schooner named the *Constance*. Upon setting foot on the shore of Sentinel Island for a second time, I swore not to leave it before seeing its inhabitants for myself. In this undertaking I was able to count on the aid of Captain Allen and lieutenants Hooper and Dobbie, irreproachable officers and true gentlemen as England alone is able to produce.

"During the first day of our expedition, we discovered a village of Sentinelese where three children remained. Without harming them in any way, we brought them to the *Constance*, where they stayed until our exploration was finished. The following night was the most perilous I've ever lived through. Lieutenant Hooper and I set up camp on an islet off the northwest coast of Sentinel Island. When night fell, we lit a fire to serve as a landmark for the *Constance*, which was cruising in the area. But the flames attracted so many sea snakes that they entirely covered the ground around us. And since their bite meant certain death, you can imagine how little sleep we found that night.

"A few days later, on a path in the middle of the forest, while we were crossing the island from the southeast towards the western coast, being careful not to make any noise, Lieutenant Hooper and I came face to face with an old native, followed by his companion and their child. The man immediately seized his bow and took aim at Lieutenant Hooper, who escaped with his life only owing to the action of my convict orderly, a Pashtun named Amirullah, who had got behind the Jarawa, jumped on his back, and spoilt his aim. Without doing them any more harm than we did to the children captured a few days before, we left with them on board the *Constance*. I hosted the six savages in my house in Port Blair in order to study them closely. Alas, their health declined rapidly, and the old man and his wife drew their last breaths after just a few days. It is possible that their premature deaths were the paradoxical consequence of the good care we gave them; I suspect, indeed, that the abundance of excellent food we served them proved to be fatal to them. After this unfortunate incident, I ordered the children to be returned to the island with quantities of presents.

"This expedition was not a success for, misled by Mr. Homfray's statements regarding the numbers and ferocity of the aborigines, they were met in a less conciliatory manner than was desirable, and we cannot be said to have done anything more than increase their general terror of, and hostility to, all comers. It would have been better to have left the Islanders alone, until the Onges of the Little Andaman were tamed, and then to have approached them with the assistance of the latter. The facts which justify this view were not, however, known at that time."

13

4 Wall Street

A few days after our excursion off the coast of Block Island, I returned to New Haven. Eleanor was back from Texas, and I was impatient to spend the month of August with her. New Haven is surprisingly pleasant in the summer. During the cold season, which, in Connecticut, lasts most often from October to April, the accumulation of snow is really a prison. The town green is completely white. At night it looks like the end of the world, under the pale light from the streetlamps; in the paths that cut through it diagonally, only gusts of wind dare to go. People are discouraged from leaving their homes and even more so from leaving the city, with the piles of snow at the corners of the sidewalks forming low walls of white that soon turn to dirty gray.

But when the slopes of East Rock shed their coats of snow over there at the end of Orange Street and display the ochre and orange of their steep rocks, the city opens up. People are out walking their babies in strollers along the rows of trees in blossom; neighbors greet each other from their porches where they're enjoying the cool of the evening. The stone façade of the Yale art gallery evokes the Old World; students sitting on little metal chairs sip soft drinks while they read or chat. They're also out on the old campus, where Frisbee matches spring up. But what is most striking in this general renaissance is the return of a very simple idea that had disappeared during winter: suddenly, people remember that New Haven is near the sea.

Like most of its neighbors in New England, New Haven is cut off from its coast. To reach a shore that is both charming and spoiled, one has to cross a whole network of freeways and railroad tracks. Just try to do it on a bike by riding under the bridges and along the industrial wastelands: enormous trucks will brush past you while you're pedaling near the warehouses of the harbor area. It'll take you an hour of toil to reach the edge of the parks along the water and the lighthouse that adorns the narrow beach. What is stretching out before you, however, is still not yet the ocean but just the Long Island Strait: the Atlantic is farther off, way over there, on the other side of this narrow strip of land, at the horizon. Despite the distance that separates them, the ocean, during the summer, is never far from the minds of the people of New Haven. The rapid passage of the clouds driven by the wind, a certain salty fragrance in the air, and the latter's bracing humidity combine to maintain the presence of the Atlantic at the edge of their consciousness. All of these impressions mixed together reinforced the maritime association of ideas attached to our strange abode.

Our apartment was located at the very end of Wall Street. Far from being the beating heart of world capitalism like its New York homonym, our street began in a desolate stretch where our residence was caught between a parking lot, the austere offices of the FBI, a four-lane highway, and railroad tracks. This building was a hideous anomaly whose triangular shape, gaudy yellow walls, and bright blue molding had the passersby shaking their heads. Fascinated by its ugliness and odd design, determined by obscure cadastral logics that must have gone back at least to the interwar period, my friends begged me for permission to visit the most ill-conceived four hundred square feet of the whole east coast of the United States. For others, this yellow wart was "the piece of cheese" or "that weird thing on Wall Street," but for Eleanor and me, it was our first home and our lighthouse at the end of the world.

The ceiling was unusually low, the floor so out of kilter that a ball released on one side of the room would quickly roll to the opposite side; the living room tilted like a listing ship. The downstairs neighbor had to bail the water out every time we took a bath, because beyond a certain level in the bathtub, the water poured down into his kitchen. As for the windows, they were set at hip level, and their meager size evoked the portholes of a transatlantic liner. There were three of them in the one bedroom: two of them opened onto a street that the police recommended we avoid at night, the third onto a ditch filled with rocks and weeds where some poor fellow often stepped over the barrier separating it from the street and spent the night there, leaving behind a sodden sleeping bag in the morning.

In the summer, squadrons of seagulls landed on our roof. Their heavy steps resounded above our heads, and we could see their white bellies when they launched themselves into the void from our blue molding. Constantly walking off balance on a floor slanted like the deck of a sailboat, hearing the cries of the seagulls as they brushed past our portholes, staring at the stretches of flat concrete that, after five o'clock in the evening, sparkled like the sea when the wind has died down, in a building where we put a deckchair in the emergency exit, we had the fleeting impression of living in the middle of the Atlantic Ocean.

After the disappearance of Markus and my divorce from Eleanor, I returned to New Haven. It was the first time since graduation twenty years earlier. I embraced Julia and our daughter, who had accompanied me to the airport, closed the car door, and took my flight to JFK. Always the same excitement in arriving here: New York! The city of cities. The taxi carries me off on the congested freeway: nearly two hours to reach New Haven. I don't open the book that I had taken out of my bag; I think of everything I've lost, and gained, in the preceding years; I think of Eleanor, with whom I've lost contact. Strange: a person is everything to you, your wife and best friend, your sister and travel companion; and suddenly this void—there will be no more discoveries or plans together; the house is empty in the evening when you come home. The families that you invent for yourself are the most difficult to preserve.

The taxi drops me off north of the city, near the campus. It's the end of the afternoon, but night is still far off; the days are long in May. I leave my suitcase at the hotel and go out immediately to "stretch my legs"—that is what I tell myself, but I know that I'm lying, that I am filled with impatience, with anguish too. In a few minutes I've reached the Hall of Graduate Studies, and suddenly I've returned to my body from before. I'm in my twenties again, writing my dissertation; I don't know if I'll ever get a job as a college professor, or if I'll have to do something else with my life. But I continue to work as hard as I can, for me, for Eleanor, for the family we're going to found; my day is finished, and I return home where I know she is waiting for me. At first I walk slowly, but as I get closer I begin to speed up, almost running.

At the end of Wall Street, I contemplate the triangular building: the yellow of the walls has turned pale, and the bricks are visible here and there under the chipped paint. One detail strikes me:

they've changed the curtains. It's stupid, but it seems scandalous to me. I remember the pretty curtains that my Eleanor had sewn, sitting calmly on the living room couch in the evening, so that they would fit the narrow windows, during our first year in New Haven. At that time, she still had plump cheeks that made her look childlike. It was so long ago, before meeting Julia and the vanishing of Markus, before Eleanor's accident and the move to Columbus, before Eva and the birth of our daughter. All of these periods are mixed up in my mind; I no longer know in what order they took place, and it seems to me that they're all still going on, parallel to each other in time. Other *me's* are developing over time, sending each other adumbrations of all the events that they still have to live, events that, they too, will be repeated—forever. I stare at the curtains and am traversed by a violent anger, full of distress, at the strangers who have replaced us. Alone in the declining day, I am overcome by a heartbreaking impression of nostalgia and regrets, for I'm standing in the street looking at the house where my love and I, in another life, were happy.

14

Portman (2/3)

Portman pauses. He clears his throat, swallows a mouthful of water, and mops his forehead with a handkerchief embroidered with his initials. In the amphitheater of the Royal Geographical Society of London, the gentlemen with muttonchops and spectacles become impatient: they would like him to pursue immediately his fascinating presentation. Finally, Portman continues in these terms:

"Now I would like to speak of the geography of Sentinel Island and of the mores of its curious inhabitants. The surface of the island is covered with blocks of coral whose sharp ridges make it difficult to walk there. The soil there is admirably favorable to the growth of coconut palms, the surface drainage being excellent. This is an advantage that could be extremely profitable for England, provided of course that it be guided in its development by men who have acquired, by dint of their devotion and perseverance, an intimate familiarity with these distant lands. At numerous spots across the island, the jungle opens up and is reminiscent of our delightful parks of London. The traveler finds himself before stands of beautiful evergreen trees whose sturdy wood lends itself to shipbuilding, an additional asset that our navy could take advantage of.

"Sometimes the Sentinelese camp among the buttressed roots of trees. They are few in number and excessively fearful. Their food, like that of other Andamanese, consists essentially of roots, fruit, fish, and turtles. As for their cooking methods, they resemble those of the Onges. In dry weather, the Sentinelese dig small wells and build huts that resemble those of the Jarawas. On the other hand, they have no knowledge of those large huts shaped like hives that are seen as permanent villages in the southern part of the Andaman Islands.

"Like other tribes in the archipelago, the Sentinelese regularly cover themselves with yellowish clay, and I found on their island, as on Little Andaman, natives with their lower jaws adorned with a fringe of twisted fibers that they wear around their neck. As a general rule, the Sentinelese resemble the Jarawas of Rutland Island, and we discover in the members of both tribes the same idiocy in their appearance, facial expression, and behavior. We frequently compare our English schoolchildren to savages. After twenty-two years of frequenting the Andamanese, I'm able to confirm that the Sentinelese are quite similar to the average schoolchild such as we see them in rural schools populated by the lower classes.

"If the Crown, in a plan conceived at the highest levels, thought one day, as it would be in its interest to do, to create a coconut plantation on Sentinel Island, I would strongly advise it to send a large contingent of soldiers whose mission would consist in capturing the male natives and conveying them to a camp that we will have built in the south of the island. There we'll teach the savages to live with us and will show our good intentions by feeding them turtles and yams. We could also teach them to smoke, creating in this way a need that they will only be able to satisfy by keeping company with us."

15

Brooklyn

I only saw Markus again once before the end of the summer. After his stay on Block Island, he planned to take a flight to Fiji with Alexandra and his parents. Samantha's birthday was in August, and every year the Holmbergs took a trip to some far-off place to celebrate it. When we had spoken of it, Markus seemed impatient to make this trip. As I understood it, his family was rarely together. In the summer his mother could only winnow out a dozen days from her lawyerly obligations and hardly ever visited their property on Block Island. The rest of the year was dominated by the pursuit of their respective careers, such that outside of summer vacation, Thanksgiving and Christmas were the only times all four of them spent together. Markus seemed to cherish these moments with his family, which appeared to be much more important to him than the exotic destinations where they took place. I was thus quite surprised when, around August 15, he invited me to spend the weekend at home with him: he had preferred to stay alone in New York.

I say goodbye to Eleanor and walk down State Street. The weather is glorious, and I'm only twenty minutes from the station. I walk briskly and, as always, remember the murder that took place here, between the barber shop and the consignment store. They had remodeled since then, but I could forget neither the impact of the bullets nor the marks on the ground. That too is America: streets where you walk on the memory of the dead. Today there are only splashes of sun on the walls. Even during the day I'm on my guard in this neighborhood, especially when I pass by a highway system that separates the railroad station from downtown, a sinister intermediate zone where pedestrians rarely venture. I pass huge desolate parking lots and, inside Central Station, quickly buy my ticket. The train arrives a few minutes later: in an hour forty-five I'll be in New York.

I take a seat beside a window facing forward, the train lurches, we're off. The locomotive holds its speed down between the stops while an impersonal male voice announces each stage, first with joyful anticipation (*Stamford!*), then with sudden regret when the traveler departs (*Stamford* ...). After a slew of little towns where you'd have to be paid to get off, followed by coves where dozens of sailboats are moored, a certain tremor among the passengers informs you that the apartment buildings on both sides of the tracks are forerunners of the approaching megalopolis. It is tiny at first, with all these houses that you look down upon from your seat in the train; then it expands like a huge wave on either side of the tracks—you feel like Moses cleaving through the Red Sea with these buildings that grow ever higher as you move forward. Soon you're in Harlem and, if you're paying attention, on the right you'll see a Gothic tower, absolutely incongruous, rise up at the end of a perpendicular street, dominating the campus of Columbia. You continue to move forward faster and faster, or so it seems, and like in amusement parks where the carriages plunge into the darkness, you suddenly enter a tunnel. End of the line. Everyone steps down onto the platform: you're in New York.

Markus arranged to meet me in the Grand Central Terminal, beneath the clock. I pass through flurries of hurrying passengers before I find him. I know him well enough to understand at a glance that he's in a bad mood. Markus is incapable of controlling himself. If he's happy, you can sense it immediately by the sweetness that radiates from him, by the tenderness of his gaze: you're snug in his vibrant countenance as you would be in a very chic lounge where you are served tea in porcelain cups while you recline on the most tasteful fluffy sofa. But when he is annoyed, he resembles a Romantic painter coming to life in front of you: his hair wild, dark rings under his eyes, a severe frown digging wrinkles in his forehead. Today I'm greeted by his tormented double. He shakes my hand and asks, "Is that all you're bringing?" I only brought a backpack for the weekend, with a t-shirt and a change of underwear: "I like to travel light." He shrugs and continues: "Can I offer you lunch? There's a restaurant in Brooklyn that I really like." I accept, and we hop onto the subway.

Markus is silent. So silent and distant that for the other travelers in the car we surely do not seem to know each other. We emerge from the subway, and I follow him as we stroll in the streets of

Brooklyn. We pass organic shops, bars that serve home-made soft drinks, e-cigarette stores, and others that sell imported Himalayan products. Markus pushes a door open, and we enter a Mexican restaurant where he promptly orders two glasses of tequila. I don't like to drink during the day, but I make an exception: something tells me that he needs to loosen his tongue.

We only really begin to talk later, after leaving the restaurant, after having walked for a very long time, our legs growing shaky, through Brooklyn. On the way there was a kind of open-air market where guys stripped to the waist gave virtuoso performances with machetes, cutting up a coconut for us in the back of a pick-up truck in under ten seconds while a dozen moist-eyed girls waited their turn. That reminds me of Hawaii, where Eleanor and I went for our honeymoon: some locals had prepared a tasty, soft coconut for us the same way, two minutes from a beach whose translucent waters were trapped in a setting of black rocks. I share this memory with Markus, which provides me with a perfect transition to ask him the question I've been harboring since the beginning of the afternoon: "By the way, why didn't you go to Fiji?" He doesn't answer and just goes on walking for a long while, until we reach a park on the banks of the East River, with the skyline of Manhattan on the other side. It's odd, because we're admiring this magnificent view from a ruined bench that leans to one side, our feet in a puddle, surrounded by a lawn that has known better days, near a playground where empty swings are moving back and forth, creaking, as if they were rocking a child's phantom. This park is a little like a balcony offered to the poor, overlooking the fabulous wealth of New York: just one more way to remind you of what you can never have. The city is there, within your reach, but there is much more than a river separating you from it. Markus finally answers me, as if my question, asked a good quarter hour before, had just registered. "I had an argument with my father."

That doesn't seem like much, but for him it is of extreme importance. I had seen it clearly on Block Island: Joakim is the keystone of Markus's psyche. His opinion is the only one that matters to him and is all the more important, in fact, since he has scarcely any interest in what the rest of the world thinks of him. Markus feels certain that it is not fair to others to compare them to himself: he is quietly convinced of his superiority. Paradoxically, this insolent hubris makes him a rather nice fellow, in any case pleasant to be around. With most people, tensions grow out of their desire to get you to admit that they are better than you because, in fact, they aren't so sure of it. Markus has no doubts: he knows that he is boxing in another category. It would be inelegant—worse, a kind of cheating—if he were to compare himself to you: what interest does a heavyweight have in fighting against a featherweight? The result is known in advance. Markus never fails, but now and then certain results aren't as good as he'd hoped—which doesn't lead him to falter, since he knows that occasional variations don't affect the general trajectory. His always goes upwards, and the mystery of his life does not consist in determining "What am I worth?" but rather "How far will I go?" As for me, I'm in some sense another himself, to the extent that I spontaneously recognized him as an extraordinary individual. He is grateful to me for this and holds me in unusual esteem for that reason: "Here's a guy who understood more quickly than the others" is what I suspect he thinks. There is nonetheless an exception, only one in the vast world, one person who can dislodge him from his throne. It's not his sister, whose efforts to measure up to him just amuse him, like the attempts of a child to knock down an adult by attacking his legs. Nor is it his mother, although a brilliant lawyer, whose profession moves him to offensive remarks since he considers it, quote, "more plodding work than intellectual." The one exception is his father. A single word from him can have a devastating effect on Markus. It's as if the price to pay for this absolute confidence in himself was this one weakness: Joakim's opinion of him.

Markus explains to me: he's beginning his third year and next semester has to choose a major. He discussed it with his father after my departure from Block Island, and Joakim recommended that he choose English literature, German, or philosophy, three subjects in which he excels. In fact, Markus agrees with him and was already thinking of one of these three disciplines. The problem is what motivates Joakim's advice: he would like Markus to work for him. Four years ago he created a publishing house that specializes in biographies of the most accomplished artists among those he exhibits, along with essays on modern painting and new translations of classic works on the philosophy of art. Brilliant and multilingual, his son would be an ideal director for this business. Markus already has personal relations with numerous artists and would have carte blanche in the choice of projects to pursue. Joakim has thought of everything: in the event his son would like to take a sabbatical to recover from four years of toil at the university, the business would wait for his return, whether he's spent time in Rome and Florence or Hong Kong and Singapore, whichever he prefers. Joakim hardly has to explain the ultimate goal of all that: it goes without saying that one day he would like Markus to assume the direction of the galleries. Not immediately—Joakim is still young and has many ventures to undertake—but, when the time is right, after showing him the way, it will be incumbent on his son to take up the torch. Everything is ready, weighed, organized, easy; and since Joakim is hardly a domestic tyrant, he is prepared to make all the concessions that will help Markus to blossom, like involving him directly in the organization of the next exhibits if that interests him more than publishing. Well, Markus does not want this future.

Or, more precisely, he isn't sure he wants it or doesn't want it; not at all sure, in fact, of what he wants. And that is exactly what he would like to determine, alone: what he is going to do with his life, with the enormous potential he feels in himself, without everything being decided in advance by someone else. Joakim, at his age, had just moved to Berlin after leaving Stockholm; then he fought to make his mark in America and, today, his name is among those at the top of the world ranking in *ArtReview*. Markus would like something similar for himself: success that he owes only to himself. Unfortunately, he's not sure he knows what he is seeking, that he knows why he disdains the position his father is offering him, this position that, if he had earned it through his own efforts, would seem desirable to him if only he didn't know that in accepting it, it would make him *the son of* forever. Markus predicts to me the articles that will describe him as "the heir to the empire." He doesn't want to inherit: he wishes to get out from under his father's shadow. "It's not so difficult to understand!" he suddenly rages to an invisible opponent. It's his refusal that provoked their quarrel. If he had declined his offer in order to devote himself to a clear plan, Joakim would've accepted it and, indeed, would've supported his decision—but Markus is foregoing an opportunity with no other plan in mind, and that's what Joakim doesn't understand. Joakim doesn't enjoy not understanding; nothing is beyond his capacity to understand, in any case nothing that is comprehensible. If he doesn't understand something, it's because it's not logical. A spirit that is fundamentally rational is an advantage as well as a weakness, for it tends to become indignant at the incoherence of all these beings that are impelled by obscure forces, by drives whose origin is a mystery even to themselves. Markus demands his right to be irrational, his right to make mistakes; he wishes, he says, to work in solitude, with no material support, on a project of which he can be proud.

At these words I understand that he hasn't told me everything, and that he has an idea of what he wishes to undertake that is more precise than he is willing to admit. That is the answer I give him, and he lowers his head with a smile that confirms my intuition. He pauses for a moment, then begins a long speech explaining that he is perfectly aware that it's ridiculous, a real cliché, but nonetheless it's true, he has a goal he didn't want to discuss with Joakim—what he would like, *really* like to do (he emphasizes it to dispel any suspicion of frivolity), is to get a room somewhere, anywhere but New York where there are too many distractions, and finish the novel he began the previous semester. If he gets involved with his father's gallery, he knows that it will be over, that there will be too many demands, too many social obligations, and he can say goodbye to the concentration required to write a book. And when I ask him why he didn't tell Joakim the truth, his reasons aren't very clear. If I have to reconstruct them, I would say that he fears his father's judgment of a text that he will surely ask to read, and he also fears ridicule as the nth literature student who aspires to become a novelist; he doesn't want to "conform to a stereotype," he repeats several times, it is apparently such a salient reason for him. When I point out to him that, with a father like his, his personal merit will be questioned come what may, since he will be accused of having taken advantage of Joakim's relationships to find a publisher, he replies that he is aware of this and intends to use a pseudonym. For a moment I don't know what to say; I finally ask him if he's made a decision.

He then speaks to me of this old professor whose courses he's taken. Thomas Young is such a luminary that he's already considered to be a classic. He's published books that are references for the whole profession; his doctoral students have taught several generations of students in their turn. He is so old and so necessary that one would be tempted to think that he's been teaching at Yale since its creation. The day he passes will feel like an aberration: how can he no longer be there? He will leave behind some fifty works, published in forty languages. Of course, Markus is one of his favorite students, and when he heard of his novel, Young offered to read his manuscript. If the professor is happy with his first chapters, Markus will show them to his father; otherwise, he'll consider doing something else, perhaps a doctorate in philosophy at Oxford or Cambridge, for he'd also like to study outside the United States. I reply that this is certainly a good idea, even if I can't help thinking that a writer, someone who thinks that they *must* write, will not depend on someone else's opinion, even that of an authority. He couldn't do anything else but continue to work, whatever he is told. That is perhaps Markus's weakness: having so many possibilities open to him that he finds it hard to choose among them, in order to convert one of his overabundant talents into something more. We both fall silent, contemplating the city on the other side of the river.

Since I've known him, I've managed to avoid being jealous; at this moment, however, I feel a crisis coming on. The differences between us are too vast. I'm no longer sure of liking him so much, this guy who's drowning in rich people's problems, whose major difficulty in life consists in deciding if he'll deign to accept a fascinating profession, who refuses to go to Fiji because his father offered him a six-figure salary, and who speaks to you of having his first novel read by Thomas Young—*Thomas Young* himself—as if it were his due. Does he realize the extent of his privileges? If I were to draw his attention to them, what would he say? That they have nothing to do with his talents? Or would he admit that the talents in question, as real as they may be, have only prospered owing to the advantages he enjoyed without deserving them, owing to his birth into what, in our era, corresponds most closely to what in times past was the aristocracy? I come from another country and don't have the right skin color; I'll always be a foreigner in the United States, even if I spend the rest of my life here, but the little I have, I earned it myself, all alone. In this instant, I have an urge to just ditch him there, with no explanation, for how can I tell him without losing his respect and managing to get him to understand me of the problems that they're causing *me*, all of *his* problems?

It is a sociological aberration, our presence together on this bench, our shared affiliation to Saint Andrew, certain of whose members, it is true, come from the underprivileged neighborhoods of Atlanta and Chicago and have had a childhood much more difficult than mine, but many others of whom are exactly like Markus, born with a silver spoon in their mouth. I do not belong to his world, in any sense of the word. If I hadn't been awarded a scholarship to study in America, my parents would never have had the means to send me here. This opportunity offered me the same path as individuals whose experiences, ideas, finances, and obstacles are so radically distinct from mine that it becomes insulting for me to listen to the qualms of this rich kid who summoned me to New York to display them before me. How many of these privileged individuals have the indecency to complain? They go to the trouble of being born, and for that all the joys of the world are owed to them. Nonetheless, I say nothing. I look at Manhattan, far off in the distance; I imagine the house where he goes back to his family whenever he feels the need; I think of the family I lost one day in November 2008; and at that moment, the gulf that separates us has never appeared so great.

16

Portman (3/3)

There is something ambiguous about Portman's interest in the men of the Andamans. That's the opinion, in any case, expressed by a certain "Respectable Lawyer," a Twitter user whose messages on the question have been shared by thousands of people. On November 23, 2018, he begins a vengeful thread in which he comments on images found in "Savage Bodies, Civilized Pleasures," an article published in 2009 by Dr. Satadru Sen. Taken by Portman between 1879 and 1900, these photographs show him dressed in white towering over a group of nude black men, the narrow strip of a belt the only dark mark on his immaculate uniform. We also see him sitting like a pope on his throne, surrounded by Jarawas, certain of whom are wearing chasubles adorned with a large cross, while others are seated and naked, a subdued expression on their faces. And since Portman is in uniform, he combines the authority of the Army with that of the Church to dominate these natives. Indeed, he looks like a white idol of the Old World whom this black people is forced to adore.

Even more troubling are the two photographs that follow in the thread. The first highlights the bodies of three Andamanese, buff naked with the exception of ornaments in their hair, finely worked necklaces, thin bright bracelets, and, for one of them, a belt with geometric motifs. Their male organs, at rest, are disposed on the same line at the center of the image. And to emphasize the eroticism of the composition, each body is attached to the next by a point of contact, the man on the right placing his hand just above the buttocks of the man in the center, whose arm is placed on that of his neighbor while their feet, legs, and upper thighs brush against each other. Their shoulders drawn back, their chests swelled out, their abdomens well defined, the three Andamanese are as handsome as Greek gods. As for the last photograph, a real nightmare, it shows a very small girl with swollen belly, standing sidewise with, behind her, a caliper's square attached to her skull and her spine by metal rods that are taking incomprehensible, absurd measurements.

The measurements, as it happens, were of great interest to Portman. In addition to these photos, he catalogued the physical characteristics of hundreds of individuals throughout the archipelago. In his eyes, the "primitive body" changes meaning: no longer a cannibal, the Andamanese becomes a sex object, an ethnographic phantasm. The hand of the White Man takes its measure as it cops a feel. Single until the end of his life, Portman exhibits his attraction to the masculine physique throughout his work. He enthusiastically notes each detail: the color of the skin, which he places on a scale from deep dark to pinkish white; the form of the nose, the mouth, and the lips. He examines likewise the size of the shoulders and the hips, the circumference of the torso and the calves. The goal of his work? "The identification of what he called 'the Andamanese average' and the utilization of that average to locate the Andamanese in a wider world of races and savages," answers Dr. Sen. His unavowed goal? To take pleasure in the male body under the guise of scientific objectivity.

For Portman lingers passionately on the length and size of indigenous penises, on the atrophy or vigor of native testicles that he gauges lovingly in completing the notes on his observations of the sexual temperament of his subjects, all of them more primitive, he thinks, as they are more drawn to lechery. Both scientific and sexual (or rather: sexual under the disguise of scientific interest), the action of the colonist is also political, legitimizing the White Man's claim to power over the natives of whom the foreigner has proclaimed himself master and protector. These three elements work together, the erotic emotion encouraging the scientific study, and the latter justifying the political control over the nude individual whose body is reduced to a series of data that contribute to the creation of an abstract average. Dr. Sen concludes his demonstration: "Portman integrated his erotic fascination into the practice of governance and into a decadent modality of being a colonizer among desirable savages." In popularizing his work, Respectable Lawyer reaches a similar, if less sophisticated, conclusion: "Finally, it seems that Portman in some small way acknowledged his transgressions against these people. Though I don't feel bad for calling him a foot-faced English pervert." It's difficult to judge either of them wrong.

Beginning with the first decade of the new century, his name often crops up in the press. Every time an intruder loses their life on Sentinel Island, it's Portman that the journalists accuse of being at the origin of the natives' hostility toward strangers. If the Sentinelese protect their territory so jealously, they claim, it's because they haven't forgotten the abductions the Englishman was guilty of in 1880, nor the deaths they caused; it's because the memory of the treachery of the White Man, who seizes whatever he desires, basing his right to do so on a self-proclaimed superiority, has been handed down through the generations, keeping alive a tradition of suspicion toward strangers who come from the other side of the sea. The history of peoples, like that of individuals, nonetheless discourages definitive judgments, for the value of a fact is often altered by subsequent events that force us to revise its meaning, sometimes even to reverse it. In the course of the 20th century, the population of the Jarawas has been divided by two, that of the Onges by seven; their culture was radically modified under the influence of the colonists whose numbers went from twenty thousand to three hundred thousand during the same period. If Portman is the cause of the Sentinelese's stubborn rejection of intruders, one is *almost* inclined to thank him for the harm he did them. From a certain point of view, those who hurt us deserve our gratitude, for they also force us to change.

17

Eva

A few weeks after this weekend in New York with Markus, at the beginning of the fall semester, I met someone—although I was absolutely not trying to meet anyone. Eleanor and I had been married for two years. I was deeply attached to her, so deeply that I couldn't imagine that it was possible to live without her. This unwavering bond was paradoxical. Ever since its beginning in Manhattan, just after the brutal death of my parents and sister, our couple was shaken by recurrent crises whose cause, at first imperceptible, became clearer over time: neither of us was what the other wanted them to be. Eleanor detested how hard I was: hard at work, hard with others and myself. I was traversing—as I impatiently repeated to give myself excuses—one of these decisive periods that young people must confront if they wish to make something of their life. And as I was determined to be successful, I treated myself with the intransigence of a drill sergeant in the Marines. I inflicted on myself a discipline whose excessiveness was self-destructive; I was tormented by ambition and the passion to conquer. It wasn't easy for Eleanor to live beside this anxious creature.

A vague rancor that swelled up in me with the regularity of a geological phenomenon, almost invisible and nonetheless inescapable, was moreover driving me away from Eleanor without my even being conscious of it—at least at the beginning. I saw her sink into whole days of laziness, phases of depression, spells of hypochondria that, eventually, occurred more and more frequently. And while I was adopting the inflexible rigor of a mechanism, slogging through hours of study and consumed by the pursuit of my goals, I heard her complain about each obstacle that arose in her path: one of her clients had been rude; one of her colleagues abused his authority; there was always another cause adding to her unwavering sadness. Often her recriminations culminated in elegies on Texas, a blessed land she had given up for me, she said, although she had been just as unhappy there as she was now in New Haven.

Eleanor did not like her current job in a luxury hotel, where she had managed to get hired as the person responsible for international clients—which represented an excellent opportunity for someone as young as she was, and even a promotion compared to her previous position in New York. She didn't like that former job either, nor any of those that, to tell the truth, she ever mentioned to me. Eleanor indulged in vague daydreams about what she would've liked to be, without ever really having done what was necessary to make it happen. For a long time, theater had been her passion; she had been sufficiently enamored of it to leave Arlington and try her luck in New York City. But instead of persevering on this path and considering the failed auditions as opportunities to improve herself before the next, she had thrown in the towel after a few months, and her day job had become her profession. She could have accepted the fact that the theater, Broadway, tours around the country—but also the rivalry between actresses, the directors' whims, the general precariousness of the profession—were not for her. Instead, she continued to cultivate the regret that this unfulfilled ambition had caused her, and although she had already given it up when we met—she was working full-time as a receptionist at a Midtown hotel when some friends we had in common introduced us—by dint of a subtle shift following a memory falsification, of the sort that bad faith and wounded pride conspire to contrive, she had convinced herself that I had turned her away from her destiny on the stage, that she had given it up to bury herself in a little town in Connecticut: I had become the gravedigger of a career she had never begun.

Occasional stabs at painting were her most recent attempts to rise above her current life: she wanted to sprinkle a little beauty on an existence she found too prosaic and continue to think of herself as an artist by other means. But between the world and her image of herself there remained an unbearable gap. Nothing in reality reflected what she thought she was; and to explain this persistent disconnect, which was destined to continue (for she denied herself the possibility to learn from her failures by never admitting the slightest responsibility for them, while her willpower, called upon in fits and starts, ran out of steam immediately in the effort), she needed a scapegoat to exonerate herself to explain why, with these treasurers of exquisite sensitivity she felt within herself and these rivers of hidden talent that flowed in her veins, she occupied the social situation that was objectively hers. I was the ideal culprit, and in the course of a slow but continual process that multiplied the tensions between us, as I was tasting the first successes in my university career, she was convincing herself that, without her, I would have been a good-for-nothing, that, in fact, my achievements were her doing and were obtained at the expense of those she would've enjoyed if only I hadn't been her husband.

She never said it outright, but the following conviction underlay her remarks, left unspoken because it was shameful and nonetheless crystal clear for anyone who bothered to complete her thoughts: she had done me a favor in marrying me, an immigrant. The independence she had sought to demonstrate in marrying me against her family's wishes was the public face of an attempt to free herself from their influence and assert a certain image she had of her person: a liberal bohemian individual, adventurous and devoid of prejudice, capable of leaving for New York on a whim and letting a brown-skinned foreigner put a ring on her finger. Her prejudice, however, came flooding back when it appeared to her that I was standing in the way of what she could have accomplished. I had at first brought her a kind of moral standing; now I was only a weight, the living reminder of an error. She looked at me and thought of her more desirable former boyfriends whom she occasionally mentioned in my presence and could have easily married. It took me a good while to understand that I was in fact only one way among others for her to think well of herself, and that in revealing myself incapable of filling the narcissistic abyss in her and thus being useless to her, I was only deserving of her hatred.

It is in this context, that of a couple whose problems were so deeply entrenched that they seemed to belong to the natural order of things, that I met Eva. From the beginning, and paradoxically, she provoked in me a kind of hostility. I immediately understood that she threatened my marriage with Eleanor—that is, the foundation of the life I had reconstructed after the murder of my parents and Kamala. I resented Eva for being so charming, for trying to spend time with me, and while I had only one wish— to abandon myself to the desire she inspired in me—I was cold, almost reproachful toward her. I kept her at a distance and toyed with my wedding band as if to say, "Can't you see I'm married? I have no right to be attracted to you." When she spoke to me of a boyfriend who lived in the Netherlands, I had felt jealous but also relieved in a way. The fact that she was involved with someone else gave me a pretext to avoid confronting my fears: the fear of her not being attracted to me and of having misunderstood the signs of interest she seemed to be showing; the fear, too, of destroying my marriage with Eleanor if I wasn't mistaken. Eva had given me to understand that her romantic involvement was not very serious. She had met her "boyfriend" a few months before, and she wasn't sure she was going to see him at Christmas. So it felt cowardly to stifle feelings that I had no good reason to hide—in any case, no other reason than this certainty: to be unfaithful to Eleanor would change our relationship irreparably and, eventually, put an end to our couple.

Still today, all these years later, it is difficult for me to think of this period, to think of Eva. I close my eyes; she remains in my memory as she was then. Eva is twenty-five and has long black hair. She is there ahead of time, and in the seminar room where the tables are arranged in a circle, she takes a seat across from me. I often lose my train of thought when I feel her gaze on me; I avoid looking at her, then take a quick peek and immediately look away. I can't do it, you understand: if I really looked at her, I would not be able to take my eyes off her narrow torso, her diaphanous skin, and her hazel eyes. It's more prudent to force my gaze to glide over her, telling myself that she is like those flowers whose petals capture you: a trap. It's the end of the class, and she walks toward me smiling; I would be sad if she were to leave without speaking to me, but it puts me terribly ill at ease to make the right gestures and not those I'd like to make, to say the prescribed words and not those that are burning on my lips. There is a protocol to be followed, a script from which one must not stray; to stray from it would be dangerous, too dangerous—where would that lead us? That would lead us where I have no right to go; I'm ridiculously polite; she says, "See you tomorrow." Eva wears colored t-shirts and white shorts, very short. She is slight, slender, so delicate that if I took her in my arms, I'd be afraid to break her into pieces, like those ballerinas that spin slowly in music boxes, suspended in the perfection of a single movement. Time goes by, I've not yet said any of the things I'd like to tell her, and I've already refused a first invitation. I can't, I said, while pulling at my wedding ring, and still, I really want to make a move, but to what purpose? Winter is coming. Eva is wearing one of those charming fur hats called *chapka*s and a chocolate-colored coat that clings to her slender body; she takes off the gloves that are protecting her exquisite hands, and in her hair scattered snow crystals shine like stars, far off, so far off, that fade little by little. Sometimes she speaks to me of Russia. Eva is from Moscow and will return there in the spring: our time together is short. We had a year, that could have become a life together; a life that I ruined.

I'll leave aside a few months that went every bit as bad as the preceding ones, which brings us to the end of the second semester. As she does every year, Eleanor has gone back to Texas; it's the middle of the month of May. I walk up Wall Street at twilight to meet some friends at GPSCY, a bar reserved for graduate students. At the entrance I show my student card, walk down the stairs, order a drink, and go out into the courtyard. The place is crowded this evening; the graduation ceremony has just taken place, and we're about to begin vacation. Among my classmates many are going home to their families while others will stay in New Haven to make as much progress as possible on their dissertation. I like this bar where beer is dirt cheap, and twelve-year-old whisky only costs five dollars a glass; the university subsidizes GPSCY generously, and the barmen serve you lavishly because the establishment doesn't have to make a profit. By and large, the customers are well behaved; of course, there are those who drink too much, and whose performance at karaoke on Tuesday nights is frankly pathetic. But the great majority of these young people never lose control of themselves, acting like the person they'd like the others to remember later, when it is time for recruitments and appointments. Polishing their public image preemptively, they are careful not to leave any skeletons in their closet. A legend says that it is here, at GPSCY, that Bill Clinton and Hillary Rodham met, and many people wouldn't mind being in their place, finding the relentless partner who will accompany them on their march upwards. I talk with Amitabh and Nathalie, Colin and Annie, Elizabeth and Marc; my glass is empty, and I'm going to get a refill when, at the top of the stairs leading to the bar, I bump into Eva.

Since we're no longer in the same seminar, we hardly ever see each other. The campus is not so big, but everyone had soon gotten into the habit of going to the same places but at different times. I often think of her, but as if she had returned to Russia, as if our relationship, which could still be saved, already belonged to the past. This evening she's there in the half-light, leaning on the wrought iron fence that overhangs the steps. It's a lovely night. I'm standing in front of her, and it's like I'm holding her prisoner. She explains to me that she came to Yale with a scholarship, and that the other day, in the thank-you letter she sent to the donor, she mentioned a certain man—me—with whom she took a course. She is leaving tomorrow, she says, and continues to stare at me, adding nothing, with a smile I don't recognize. I don't say a word.

I imagine what could happen in the following minutes; I see the scene that is ours to live: we leave the bar and walk down Wall Street together, staying separated until I grab her hand. Then we walk faster, enter the building, go up the stairs, embrace once, twice, and more, then clinging to each other enter my apartment, I don't quite know how, my apartment that is so close, scarcely ten minutes away, and where, this evening, my wife has left the bedroom empty. And it's during this second when this possible future is unfolding in a flash that she makes this gesture, a gesture I've never forgotten. As if despite herself, her hand touches my forearm; I feel that this movement was involuntary, like words that emerge from the depths of the subconscious. For a second, I don't move. Then I back off, stammer goodbye, I hope we'll see each other again and move away from her as fast as possible, leave the bar and walk up the street, alone, far from Eva.

My whole life is suspended on this gesture toward me. Not being unfaithful to Eleanor, does that make me a good person? Or does the unexpected violence of my desire for Eva prove that I shouldn't have controlled it but rather submitted to it, accepting the consequences? I don't know; I only know that it is a nodal point in my life, an event so full of forces, tensions, and meaning that it will never cease to exist. Somewhere in time, we have never left New Haven. This spring evening has not stopped, Eva's hand is still on my arm, the thrill it provokes continues to spread, infinitely. Yes, somewhere in time, we are still standing before each other, bound together by this touch that continues to promise us what we will never be for each other.

18

Phileas Fogg

1872: the Andamans enter French literature. A discreet entry since Jules Verne only mentions them in passing, while the *Rangoon*, the ship used by Phileas Fogg during the eighty days of his famous voyage, cruises a stone's throw from the principal island:

"This whole portion of the enormous bay that the sailors call 'the fathoms of Bengal' was a pleasure to navigate. The *Rangoon* had soon visited Great Andaman, the principal island of the group, whose picturesque Saddle Peak Mountain, two thousand four hundred feet high, identifies to us from afar. We sailed along close to the coast. There was no sign of the Papua savages that inhabit the island. These are beings at the bottom of the human scale, but who are not, contrary to popular belief, cannibals."

It's very kind of Jules Verne to rectify the accusation of cannibalism; it would've been even better if he had denounced the concept of racial hierarchy. In 1890, Sir Arthur Conan Doyle will propose an even more demeaning portrait of the Andaman people.

19

Deviations

Markus asked for my help at the end of summer. He wanted to discuss Sentinel Island with me, because the focus of his novel, the one he spoke to me about in Brooklyn, and that he intended to show to Thomas Young sometime during the fall semester, was the forbidden island and its inhabitants. I was surprised. The choice of this subject showed that I had had an influence on him that I would not have thought possible. Before that day in September a year earlier, when I had my second interview with him for admission into Saint Andrew, Markus knew nothing of the Sentinelese and didn't even know the Andamans existed. In choosing to devote his first book to them, he revealed despite himself that I had had a much greater impact than I had ever suspected on his imagination and the course of his life. Flattered, I agreed to answer his questions.

I've never forgotten the hours we spent together in the lounges of the secret society, sprawled in those huge, comfortable leather sofas, our feet on a hundred-year-old cherrywood table, talking about Sentinel Island and its people, surrounded by antiquated luxury: oil paintings representing whale hunts off Nantucket Island, stuffed stag heads, lamps with green shades, dark woodwork, emblazoned fireplaces and bronze andirons, thick rugs that were common at the end of the 19th century in grand homes on the East Coast where England was still considered to be a model of elegance to imitate; luxury from a bygone era preserved, intact, by the studious generations that had succeeded one another at Saint Andrew, whose exotism was mind-boggling to me, since I had never seen anything comparable in India. We spoke of Sentinel Island with an adolescent enthusiasm, as if we were really preparing for an expedition there, as if we were going to take advantage of his father's fortune to travel one day, both of us, to the Andamans, sail on the Bay of Bengal, and walk on the shore of the forbidden island. It was a game that we took seriously, his questions arousing detailed responses from me, his theories provoking my objections, his castles in the air my trenchant reminders of reality. All we had left to do was prepare maps and lists, lists of material to bring with us and glass beads to give to the *natives*, to truly be—like this obsolete decor gave us the fleeting impression, while we sipped potent liquors—adventurers of a defunct era when the discovery of the Earth was still exalting, because there were still forests from which people did not return, tribes whose names were unknown, and because we still found therein an opportunity, through action and risk, through the acceptance of suffering and the embracing of danger, to become men—without this inmost need becoming an object of ridicule, deconstruction, or criticism.

For me, these discussions were rather relaxing. They allowed me to make playful use of the anthropological knowledge I was acquiring quite seriously at the same time. But for him, they represented something else, a kind of groundwork composed of sessions of reflection on the plot of his novel. Markus got out of me everything I could teach him, and when he understood that I had given him the sum total of my insights about Sentinelese culture, that I had yielded all the knowledge I possessed and all the suppositions that this knowledge allowed me to construct, he put an immediate halt to these evenings in order to seek elsewhere, alone, in the works of the anthropologists who had studied this people—Man, Radcliffe-Brown, Chattopadhyay, Pandit, and Pandya, to name only the most important—what he could use to enrich the narrative on which he was working much more seriously than on his studies.

Markus never told me precisely what this story was about— Sentinel Island, obviously, but nothing about what was going on there, who his characters were, what they were doing. The only allusion that offered some kind of clue concerned the works of Joseph Conrad, to which he had decided at the same time to devote his senior thesis. Markus had finally decided to do a double major in English literature and philosophy. One day he described to me the mental fatigue he felt each time he reread *Heart of Darkness*. The silence of the forest, the river with its constantly identical bends, the river followed for such a long time that the travelers wondered if they had advanced at all; and then something immense and monstrous awaiting them in the shadows at their arrival. Reading all that, one really felt they were with Marlow on his infernal ship, blinded by the appalling greenness of the jungle, feeling the implacable sweltering heat on one's skin, the whistling in one's ears when the shrill cry of the steam sounded, frightening off the tribe gathered on the bank. "It's that *physical* effect I'd like to achieve"—and Markus smiled at these words, as if to suggest that he doubted he would ever be able to rise to such heights, the only doubt about his abilities I've ever seen him confess. It took a model of Conrad's stature for Markus to show a little modesty.

By this remark, I had deduced that his book was an adventure novel that would describe the interior of this island it was nonetheless forbidden to enter. I wondered if Markus had made the preparation necessary for such an undertaking, and if he was conscious of the problems he was, inevitably, going to have to confront. He had never gone to the Andamans, nor even to India, and then—I would never have dared to tell him this—I feared he lacked something more: quite simply, experience and maturity. His Conrad had spent twenty years in the merchant marine before publishing a single line. Markus persevered in his project until the end of the semester, assisted by Grace, his girlfriend at that time (at the university she was, to the best of my knowledge, the only one he ever had), who commented on and annotated the first hundred pages of his story.

Like Markus and myself, Grace belonged to Saint Andrew, but of all the members she was perhaps the one I knew the least, probably because she devoted most of her free time to Markus, whom she simply adulated. For her, Markus could say nothing that wasn't admirable. A petite brunette, Grace followed him everywhere, as if she were getting ready to become his biographer and finish, after fifty years of living together and the death of the great man, the work that would become a reference for future specialists of his life work. Given how she looked at him, it was clear that she desired nothing more than Markus's success, Markus's love, and Markus's children, whom she wished to bear to strengthen the bonds between them, each day more tightly. But the fact that he always said "I" and hardly ever "we," that he showed no impatience at their periods of separation—at Block Island he only spoke of her to me once or twice—made it clear to me that he only considered her his college girlfriend, his companion for a certain period of his life, a companion he would leave when it came time for him to move on to the next stage. I felt sorry for Grace in advance, for she didn't seem to suspect the fate that indeed befell her: Markus left her two months after graduation.

At the end of the semester, Markus didn't tell me right away that Thomas Young had hated his book. In fact, the august professor was careful not to use such a strong term, but what Markus eventually shared with me represented a polite way of expressing the same opinion: "You shouldn't begin your career with this text" was, word for word, the verdict Markus had received. This erudite man had immediately detected the influence of Conrad— legend had it that he had read everything of importance in world literature. The mark of *Lord Jim* seemed too obvious for him not to condemn the work of his pupil out of hand. Young had advised him to develop a universe that was more personal, to assimilate his references instead of imitating them so explicitly and, simply, to move on to a new project rather than persevering with this one. "It's of no use to continue on a bad path just because you've spent so much time on it," he had declared. "And ultimately nothing is lost, everything will be recovered in another form: even failures are good for something," he concluded.

Markus seemed to have recognized the soundness of this opinion and accepted it graciously. He spoke calmly of putting aside his text and returning to it later, perhaps in a few years. I found that reasonable but couldn't stop myself from seeing in this episode the first questioning of his infallibility. For me, Markus was the *perfect child of the forty thieves*. His life couldn't be anything other than a series of successes, each one leading him, invariably, to a more elevated plane. I was disappointed for him, but, in fact, disappointed *by him* as well. It seemed to me, it's true, that life had given him too many advantages, and I would have liked to see him, at the very least, recognize it, for his privileges were also a weight for those around him. At the same time, however, I felt no petty satisfaction at observing his failure; I would have liked him to achieve his goals, for his sake. That is perhaps the principal ambiguity of male friendship: it is a form of love that always includes a measure of competition, and one never really knows exactly which feeling is dominant.

Despite the laid-back manner he had adopted in relating Thomas Young's opinion, it was clear to me in the following weeks that something in his psyche had been perturbed. It was as if the questioning of his writer's vocation had deprived him of some internal support. He was no longer the same Markus who radiated such self-confidence and spirit, whose culture, phenomenal for his age, always made you feel that you knew nothing, or that you only possessed at best a superficial understanding of what you thought you knew. A muted anxiety was growing in him, revealed by the silences in which he fell, as by the new habit of biting his nails that he developed at that time and was never able to rid himself of afterwards. His raw cuticles offered an obscene denial of the appearance of self-control he affected; this superior man bore on his flesh the acknowledgment of his weakness. For my part, I thought—and didn't hesitate to tell him over and over at the time—that if he wanted to write, Young's opinion shouldn't prevent him from doing so: a failed novel, every author has one in their drawer. He just needed to move on to the next one—which is exactly what Young himself had recommended he do. But the negative opinion of the professor had severely discouraged him from facing the only judgment that mattered to him, that of his father. How could he justify his refusal of the enviable position Joakim had prepared for him if all he had to show was the beginning of a work he was incapable of finishing? He never lost the will to write—later events demonstrated that fact without the slightest doubt—but he felt deeply that he had to gain more maturity to become a writer.

For a very long time, I followed Markus's evolution solicitously. Thomas Young's negative judgment was the first true disappointment he had ever experienced, and I saw clearly that the only way he knew to respond to this new feeling was by plunging headlong into other work. All of his energy was now concentrated on his thesis on Conrad; he wanted absolutely to leave Yale with the highest honors possible, academic success being summoned to compensate for his literary failure. Then that fatal November day arrived, the day that marked a rupture in our life, Eleanor's and mine, and all our attention was absorbed by the interminable convalescence of my wife, such that Markus's problems became very secondary in my eyes. I was too occupied with my couple: each day we were on the verge of shipwreck, and I had to keep us afloat.

Night has fallen, and I'm reading in our apartment on Wall Street. Eleanor comes in the door in tears; I ask her what has happened. At the pool where she was taking a course, a swimmer veered out of his lane and struck her violently on the head. She nearly lost consciousness, sunk beneath the water, but managed to get back to the surface and make it to the side of the pool. She weeps gently in my arms like a very small girl. The next day and until the end of the week, she tries to lead a normal life but cannot do so: headaches and dizziness prevent it, sending her to bed as soon as she gets home in the evening. We hurry to the doctor: he diagnoses a concussion and prescribes anti-inflammatory drugs and rest, promising she would be over it in a week or two. A month goes by. A month she spends in the dark since the light hurts. She no longer leaves her room, neither to go out for some fresh air nor to take a shower; the slightest effort worsens her headaches, and she can no longer stand to read. To help her combat boredom, I find audiobooks for her: she listens to all of Dickens then moves on to Proust, and *In Search of Lost Time*, volume after volume, passes through her bedroom. The headaches become permanent; her doctor doesn't know what to tell us.

Sure, she received a blow to the head, but the resistance of the water certainly reduced the violence of the shock: it's not normal for the pain to persist. He prescribes other tests, leading us to entertain the possibility of other appalling illnesses lodged in her head. We await the results in the grip of anguish. No cancer. The doctor sends us to a psychologist; this lingering pain may be psychosomatic. Eleanor becomes indignant, detests her doctor, loathes her specialist, and lays claim to her illness as others do to their liberty. She loses her job. We lose thousands of dollars in treatments and visits to doctors that bring no relief; the second semester begins; I teach my classes, continue to work on my dissertation, think of Eva whom I no longer see, and go home. Eleanor is waiting. She's dirty, doesn't wash for days on end; a pungent odor permeates the darkness of her room. It's your fault, she moans, all your fault. At the pool where she was swimming, at the very second at which she was hit, she was thinking of me: I have to become as strong as he is, she was saying to herself. Tears stream down her face, her features drawn by insomnia and distress. She is unattractive; I give her a kiss. Progress is slow, very slow to come; it seems to us sometimes that with time, like daylight pierces little by little the night, a slow but real improvement is secretly making its way. We watch impatiently for signs, and when we think we see a favorable development, the smallest thing still sets it back: a film she saw, an effort a little too violent, and the pain escalates, bringing weeks of additional convalescence without any indication of a permanent healing.

I become the seismograph of her pain, sensitive to its slightest variations. I'm the barometer of her suffering, noting each change in her humor, in high spirits when she is, enduring all of her storms when they return, which is often. I continue to work. It is necessary; I have a dissertation to finish and a job to find, barring which we'll have no income or health insurance. She resents the time I spend outside her room; she would like my life to stop too, for me to spend it holding her hand at her bedside, reading to her, as long as she needs it, whether it be weeks, months, or years. More and more, something seems suspect to me in this illness that persists without anyone understanding the cause. It's the neurologist who makes me suspicious when he appears to be at his wit's end, eight months after the accident, repeating once again the advice she has never taken: consult a psychologist, a specialist who will help her understand why her pain persists despite the fact that all the tests and scanners find nothing worrisome. Eleanor bridles at the suggestion of hypochondria: "My headaches are real, my dizziness too. How dare he?" I say nothing; additional months go by in depression and darkness. I continue to work, shouldering the burden of preserving our couple while in the room where she is dozing, *Madame Bovary*, *Anna Karenina*, then all of Dostoevsky pass by.

We go out at night. Never very far: my twenty-eight-year-old wife is like a little old lady, disabled, walking slowly. "It's your fault," she repeats, darkly, bitterly, her eyes wild. "I followed you to New Haven; nothing would have happened if I had returned to Texas." She names all the friends she left, reminds me for the thousandth time of the theater career she quit on my account, speaks to me of the man, the heir to an oil fortune in Odessa, she could have married instead of me. She blames me for the end of a relationship that was over several years before we met. I protest, don't put up with it, argue with her—and I think of Eva, Eva with her brown *chapka*, Eva so slender in her coat, Eva with her black hair, the graceful Eva who still lives in New Haven. My stomach is twisted with desire, and my own rancor grows. My rancor against this little woman with shining eyes and imaginary ills. I believe less and less in this brain disease in which the neurologist himself has long ago stopped believing. Without yet admitting it, I sense the monstrous plan that these supposed pains are concealing: her attempt to enslave me, to chain me to her bedside, to reproach me for her abandonment of the theater, this vocation she never had the courage to pursue because she never had the courage to persevere in any undertaking. And I also suspect another plan; I understand that Eleanor is conspiring to achieve my own failure without even realizing it. She would like me to drown in her illness just as she is doing, to miss the opportunities that could widen even more the gap between us. I revolt, continue to work, no one will stop me—it seems to me that it is my duty, in the name of my parents who once, long ago, were proud of me. Eleanor changes her strategy; other difficulties arise that drag us down still more.

Gas. There is a gas leak in the apartment. I smell nothing, I say; yes, there is, she repeats impatiently, yes, gas, there's a leak, I'm sure of it. We call the company, and the technician finds nothing amiss. She isn't convinced, I tell you there's a leak, she won't let it go. Eleanor begins to speak of moving out, we have to leave, gas is filling the room, we're going to get sick, die; I resist, and she complains with tears and wild eyes, I'm the guilty party and the enemy, it's all my fault, why don't I want to leave? She calls the company again, and they send us specialists with a brand-new machine; the two men inspect the apartment from top to bottom and discover nothing other than a candle we'd forgotten behind a row of books. They bring it to Eleanor and ask, is that what you smell? She turns pale: the odor is the same. The men leave, and she falls silent for several days. Then the headaches return and capture our attention by intensifying: she is a prisoner in her mind, and it's all my fault; all her failures, all her disappointments come from me. I alone am responsible for everything she cannot become.

This autumn is a period of deviation: the one I refused to take in suppressing my desire for Eva; the one regarding the literary vocation of Markus, who abandoned writing for years; and Eleanor's, who was never the same after her accident. But perhaps the term *deviation* is poorly chosen, since it implies a variance in relation to what should've happened. It's just as possible that what occurred was precisely what had to occur. In thinking back on this period, from the other side of the considerable space created by the intervening years, I'm struck by the extent to which these few months, between the summer on Block Island and the beginning of the new year, marked a turning point in all three of our lives. As if temporal plates had collided, provoking a deep tremor whose waves have never stopped spreading throughout time.

20

The Sign of Four

A few years after Jules Verne, it was Sir Arthur Conan Doyle's turn to evince interest in the Andamans. And like him, he surely would've done better to just go on his way: that would have helped him avoid spreading racist ideas. It is true that this eminent novelist went generously to the aid of a lawyer of Indian origins found guilty of a crime he had not committed. In George Edalji, accused of massacring livestock in the English countryside, and whose only wrong was to be the son of a vicar of Parsi descent, he found his Captain Dreyfus. Doyle was nonetheless capable of denigrating an entire people in one scathing paragraph. Let's read this excerpt from *The Sign of Four*, the second adventure of his famous Sherlock Holmes:

"'The Aborigines of the Andaman Islands may perhaps claim the distinction of being the smallest race upon this earth, though some anthropologists prefer the Bushmen of Africa, the Digger Indians of America, and Terra del Fuegians. The average height is rather below four feet, although many full-grown adults may be found who are very much smaller than this. They are a fierce, morose, and intractable people, though capable of forming most devoted friendships when their confidence has once been gained.' Mark that, Watson. Now, then, listen to this. 'They are naturally hideous, having large, misshapen heads, small, fierce eyes, and distorted features. Their feet and hands, however, are remarkably small. So intractable and fierce are they that all the efforts of the British officials have failed to win them over in any degree. They have always been a terror to shipwrecked crews, braining the survivors with their stone-headed clubs, or shooting them with their poisoned arrows. These massacres are invariably concluded by a cannibal feast.' Nice, amiable people, Watson!"

Through his detective, Conan Doyle deliberately makes a series of fallacious declarations. He wrongly accuses the Andamanese of practicing cannibalism; he attributes to them poisoned arrows they have never used but which liken them to a fantasized primitive tribe; he exaggerates their small size to emphasize their monstrosity; the ugliness and gloominess he ascribes to them are belied by the evidence he has at his disposal. And even more serious, by drawing on physiognomy and phrenology, convenient justifications for numerous prejudices, his description conveys a racial hierarchy where the Andamanese occupy the bottom rung, bordering on bestial. As for the "efforts of the British officials to win them over," what might he be referring to: the English intrusion in Sentinel Island? The kidnapping of members of their tribe? The pseudoscientific work of Maurice Vidal Portman? He doesn't say, and the rest of the novel doesn't help. Without revealing the intricacies of the plot, I can tell you that we meet a native named Tonga (the name of a Polynesian monarchy is transposed to the Bay of Bengal: one "savage" is the same as any other), who is skilled with a stone club (which relates him to the age of the same name), a lover of raw meat (does the reference to cannibalism need to be emphasized?), and faithful like a bulldog (the black man is reduced to the level of a pet). For Sir Arthur Conan Doyle, the Sentinelese are exotic creatures; he speaks of them without knowing them, with the calm superiority of a British colonist.

All the same, I'm moved to contemplate a strange coincidence that brings together in the capital of the Empire the inhabitants of Sentinel Island and the dashing Dorian Gray. Allow me to explain. On August 30, 1889, Conan Doyle meets an American publisher at the Langham Hotel in London, Joseph Stoddart, in the company of the famous Oscar Wilde. This evening has been preserved in the annals of English literature, because Stoddart persuades the two novelists to publish a piece each in his review. A few months later, Wilde sends him *The Portrait of Dorian Gray* and Conan Doyle *The Sign of Four*. From this anecdote, I draw the conclusion that everything is so connected in world history, in the relationships that people weave among themselves, that the most distant cultures are always in contact, if not directly, at least by some secret bond. Sentinel Island: a little-known place, isolated in a faraway sea, to which we are nonetheless brought by Ptolemy, Pliny the Elder, Marco Polo, Jules Verne, and Conan Doyle; an island apart from the world but, still, bound to it on all sides.

21

Déjà-vu

Like the year before, Eleanor went back home to her family when summer arrived. And like the year before, Markus invited me to spend the beginning of the vacation on Block Island. I left Wall Street with a suitcase full of books whose weight surprised Joakim when he grabbed it on the New London platform.

"It's for the doctorate!" I explained.

As a mild breeze pushed the *Samantha III* toward the island, Joakim, at the helm, questioned me about my plans. I had two semesters left on my fellowship, I explained to him, after which I either had to find a teaching position at a university or try again the following year, with no financial support and no guarantee of success at the end of it all. My priority this summer was to finish my dissertation, for I foresaw that, beginning in September, my time would be monopolized by the job search.

"Are you going to apply at Yale?"

I couldn't help smiling: I would've been happy if things were so simple.

"Unfortunately, unsolicited candidacies do not work in this profession. In the first place, a department has to obtain the funds necessary to create a position. Then, you have to send in an application, wait to be selected for a preliminary interview, have the interview, wait for the result, be invited to the campus to give a lecture, wait again, and finally learn whether or not you've been chosen.

"How much time does that take?"

"In all? Around nine months."

"And how many positions are available each year?"

"Three or four in my discipline. Each position attracts around a hundred and fifty candidates, around twenty of whom are invited to preliminary interviews. Only three are then invited for a campus visit, and, at the end of the process, one is offered the position. That's why the overwhelming majority of candidates go from one short-term contract to the next: there are far too many people with doctorates for the number of positions available."

"You're lucky."

I didn't say anything: it was the first time my description of university recruitment in the United States had prompted such a response. I usually received condolences or pained looks that meant, "Why in the world would you want to put yourself in such a position?"

"Why so?"

"Because you must have a very clear idea what you want to do with your life if you're willing to face such unfavorable odds."

Part of me was proud of Joakim's approval, but the implicit disappointment in those words as regards Markus hardly escaped me. I was relieved that, standing at the bow of the sailboat, my friend had not overheard our conversation.

We spent a studious summer, all three of us—that year Alexandra did not join us on Block Island. She was doing an internship in Dubai, and I cannot really say how I felt about her absence: more disappointment or more relief? Every morning I worked on my dissertation. I had brought the books that were indispensable, and access to scholarly articles on the Internet helped me move my last chapter forward, a piece focused on the perception of outsiders by the Onge tribe and, more precisely, on the place they occupy in their cosmology. Named *ineney* or "spirits come from the sea," what roles do they play in the Andamanese conception of a world in perpetual metamorphosis? It seemed to me that a colossal amount of energy had been spent wondering what the White Man had thought throughout the centuries of the non-Western peoples, while the opposite proposition—how is *he* perceived, the White Man, by those who see him as the Other?—had scarcely been studied in comparison. While I was exploring this question, Markus continued his writing of a thesis on "The Idea of Loyalty in Conrad's Work." As for his father, he spent long periods shut up in his office. It was a key moment in his professional life, for he was investing an enormous amount of capital in the opening of an art gallery in Paris, a stone's throw from the Place de la Concorde and from the Élysée Palace, a project he had been contemplating since the year before. Having acquired this prestigious address, he also had to reconfigure the exhibition space. Hours were spent in discussions with his architect. In addition, Joakim was pondering which canvases would be presented to the public at the inauguration. Huge sums were in play, several tens of millions of euros as I had understood, and Joakim, without losing any of his kindness, often appeared tense when we took our meals together. This European gallery was intended to consolidate his position among the leaders of the world art market and preceded, if everything went as planned, the creation of another space in Hong Kong intended to cater to a wealthy Asian clientele.

Behind the balance that we all found on Block Island, where our vacation resembled an intensive writing retreat, the tension between Markus and Joakim surged up regularly, and I sometimes wondered if my presence on the island didn't serve above all to keep them at peace. They were far too well bred to sink to quarrelling in front of a man who, after all, was only an outsider. It's enough for a subject to be sensitive, and that there be a tacit agreement to avoid it, for it to loom behind all the others. What Markus would do in a year, his plans after Yale, was what we had agreed to say nothing about, and of course our exchanges inevitably brought us back to it. If by chance we brought up the following summer or the time Joakim would spend in Paris to oversee the work on the gallery, a heavy silence quickly descended upon us: it was better to stop there to avoid discussing whether Markus would be able to accompany him.

People like Joakim and his son are rarely worried about the present. Free of any material concerns, they have little fear of unforeseen mishaps: their fortune protects them from chance occurrences since, when you think about it, it is rare for hardships to resist the power of money. Their imagination, on the other hand, tends toward the future, much further out than the rest of us, and when their success has been secured, they find a way to look still further beyond: having nothing more to desire from life, they become concerned with posterity. Joakim was in his fifties, and ever since his first steps in the art world, at the end of the seventies, he was in the habit of planning each of his initiatives several moves in advance. What would happen to his galleries after his passing was hardly an urgent problem, but he would've liked at least to know *now* if he could count on his son. In the event that Markus had refused, I'm convinced that he would've resigned himself to it after a brief period of disappointment, and that he would've soon begun a search for another successor. Still, his son's foot-dragging irritated him: Joakim wasn't the type of man who was comfortable waiting for others to make up their mind.

Markus was aware of his father's growing frustration, but before giving him the response he was hoping for, he wanted to take full advantage of the period of reflection they had agreed to, which extended to his graduation from college. His plans, however, had been stalled since the year before. He no longer spoke of his novel. That didn't mean he was no longer thinking of it, as indicated by the questions he still asked me from time to time about Sentinel Island, but only that he was waiting to complete his studies before returning to it. "I've got enough work to do with my thesis for the moment," he said. I politely acknowledged what I nonetheless viewed as an excuse. In addition, he was still contemplating graduate studies in the UK and, when his father wasn't listening, questioned me on the academic world. At this time, I was too preoccupied with my own meager chances of success not to paint a pretty dismal picture for him. I told him, "You know, there are hardly any jobs anymore that lead to tenure: the huge majority of those holding doctorates, including those from the most renowned universities, go from one short-term contract to the next before giving up and looking for work in another field." Markus brushed off these warnings as if it were inconceivable that they could concern him: "Still, there are people who succeed," he insisted, and he had no doubt that he would be one of the happy few if he went to the trouble of trying.

I listened to him imagining aloud a career that would lead him from a dissertation at Oxford to a teaching position at an Ivy League school. But even while he already saw himself among the stars of the academic world, in an office on the campus of Harvard or Princeton from which he would sally forth to teach five hours a week, his enthusiasm for this profession remained lukewarm. He shared his reservations with a tactlessness that often upset me. After all, the future that he found unworthy of him for reasons he spelled out for me in detail was precisely the one for which I was preparing myself. With a kind of anti-intellectualism I often noted in people who had nevertheless come from the best schools, he scoffed at the futility of academic publications that are only read by a handful of specialists and never, so he said, had the slightest impact in the real world (and what did he know, in fact, of the "real world"?). This was followed by complaints about the declining level of students—which was pretty rich coming from a young man who hadn't yet earned his bachelor's degree—and, to top it all off, mockery of the insignificance of the professors, all of whom thirsted for intangible honors to compensate for earning hardly more than two hundred thousand dollars a year (a sum he deemed derisory, while it would've appeared princely to the immense majority of the individuals in question). I let him go on, because I didn't wish to begin an argument by answering with what I was burning to say, namely that before showing contempt for everyone around him, he still had to prove that he could be anything at all without his father's money.

Such a response would've doomed our friendship, and that's why I kept it to myself; but I'm convinced that deep within him the fear of being above all—and perhaps only—Joakim's son never really left his mind. When he put off the decision his father awaited by exclaiming, "We'll see after graduation!", the nonchalance he displayed rang false. He was playing the role of a carefree male lead without much conviction, a lie betrayed by the deplorable state of his nails. Their disgusting condition indicated the troubles that were increasingly brewing in him and whose violence I had never suspected before that summer on Block Island. In New Haven they were essentially invisible, because the moments we spent together were spread out over time: between each meeting he was able to put on a front, prepare a flattering image of himself. But in this context, a prolonged familiarity during which we shared the same routine, I couldn't miss certain surprising details.

His bathroom was adjacent to my room, and I noticed that he took three showers a day. One day when I was kidding him about his obsessiveness cleanliness, he blushed deeply before replying that he hated the feel of salt on his skin after swimming in the sea. I had, however, noted that when bad weather prevented us from our customary swim, he still, invariably, hit the shower three times. His hands too were in an awful state; not only his nails but his palms as well, which seemed to be eaten away from the inside, victim of an illness, like leprosy. Markus washed them much more than he should and never went out without a bottle of disinfectant that he used constantly, mechanically, so that the antibacterial agents, having become corrosive from overuse, attacked the skin, turning it reddish and white and swollen. Conscious of their unsightliness, he kept his hands closed or flat on the table, particularly when he found himself in his father's presence. But the most striking symptom, whose recurrence worried me most, consisted in pauses he would make in the middle of a sentence, as if he were in a freeze-frame, suspended in the contemplation of an object in his mind of which, in the end, he regretfully took leave, his eyes misty, like a man waking up. For the longest time, Markus refused to tell me what was happening to him. Then, on an evening when his father had left us to dine alone in order to make an important phone call to Asia, he suggested we go out onto the beach together.

It was the beginning of June. We had an hour of daylight left, and the shore, deserted, stretched out before us. Only a few strollers, silhouettes clinging to each other, could be made out on the horizon: lovers perhaps? I thought of Eleanor, who had sent me a message from Texas; I couldn't say I missed her, probably because I was completed engrossed in my dissertation. It did me good, however, to take a break walking on the sand after dinner while the heat, which was in advance of its normal season, persisted as night approached. On the other side of the dunes, the windows of houses similar to Joakim's, but smaller, looked out on the ocean. The water was calm, ruffled by astonishingly light blue ripples, almost exotic, evoking in their wake an impression of far-off unexplored seas. We set off spontaneously on the path we had often taken the year before with Joakim, and to which we hadn't returned with him a single time, since he was working morning to night.

Joakim had a power of concentration all his own—he could stay bent over his task, without losing his focus, for seven, eight hours in a row. Now that I was seeing him on a daily basis, I discovered something I never would have suspected about him too if I were only meeting him now and then, in those moments that we reserve for others to create an image for them. His will to work had something unhealthy about it, monstrous even: he had to exercise considerable violence over himself to achieve self-control to that point, to stifle the little voice that must have protested within him, encouraging him to take a break, allow himself some feeling of weakness, whether it be weariness, laziness, or discouragement. Joakim exhibited terrifying willpower and revealed now and then an unfathomable scorn for those who didn't possess his strength of character—that is, the rest of the planet, with a few exceptions, no doubt. I better understood how crushed Markus felt in the presence of this man. It was impossible not to prove oneself unworthy of him.

We remained silent for a long moment. After a half-hour of walking, we sat down on the sand. It was comfortably warm. There was, between us, a little fragile plant that had managed to survive despite the wind. Markus finally asked me this question: "You remember what you told me about your visit to Yale, the first time?"

"When I told you about the Hall of Graduate Studies?"

"Yes. You told me that you had a strange feeling of ...."

He didn't finish his sentence, as if those two words were painful for him to pronounce.

"Déjà-vu?"

"Yes. Has that happened to you often?"

"A few times, I don't really know ... Why are you asking me that?"

Markus paused and, very softly, so softly that everything threatened to drown it out—the noise of the wind on the dunes, that of the waves that stubbornly dug into the beach at high tide—he finally answered: "Because that happens to me all the time."

"What do you mean, all the time?"

He explained to me that he suffered from spells of déjà-vu. Not just once in a while, like most people, but constantly and without warning. This impression of abnormal familiarity with a unique event was happening to him more and more frequently of late, for example during common events of daily life. Breakfast, brushing his teeth afterwards, everything he did on a regular basis each day gave him the feeling that it had occurred previously in a *rigorously identical* way. It was the same gesture and the same light in the room, the same arrangement of plates and glasses; they weren't only comparable to previous occurrences, they had *already* occurred. He admitted that this phenomenon didn't appear to be remarkable in any way. After all, life is made of repetitions; we're always doing again what we have done before, like the phantom of the person we were yesterday. But this impression also came over him when he was visiting a place for the first time. During spring break this year, an astronomy course led him to northern Chile, to the Atacama Desert, where he had never been. Under the stars, a troubling feeling of familiarity had gripped him one night when he was observing the sky wrapped up warmly in a coat. The cries of his classmates, he had already heard them; the explanations of the professor, he already knew them; this moment, he had already lived it. He couldn't figure out what was happening to him, but the sensation itself was unmistakable: each new event he experienced appeared to be the memory of another that he had experienced previously.

It was worrisome, intolerable at times, because the beings and things around him seemed to lack coherence, to be illusory in nature. Had he dreamed what he was living, or was what he was living the dream, with reality relegated to his sleeping state? His explanations became more difficult to understand; he got up, clearly impatient with his lack of clarity, and began to walk with great strides, crushing without seeing them the little plants that had valiantly survived in the sand, like a giant indifferent to the tiny cities that collapsed beneath his feet. I had trouble keeping up with him, and as his face disappeared little by little in the growing darkness, it appeared to me that he was speaking to himself more and more excitedly, as if he could no longer control the theories he had hatched to explain his malaise and was exhibiting them openly in the night without taking into account how bizarre, indeed absurd, they were. Markus knew perfectly well the cognitive interpretations of déjà-vu, like the one that relates it to epilepsy, for example, and concluded that they did not apply to him—he brushed them off irritably, as if he were a world specialist on the question annoyed by the objections of a neophyte. This abnormal phenomenon was the beginning of a new concept of the mind, he declared, suddenly becoming bombastic, just as it is the explanation of the anomalies in physical phenomena that lead to scientific revolutions.

With a nervous laugh that he used in order not to appear to adhere entirely to conjectures that, nonetheless, had clearly preoccupied him seriously, he began to roll out a complete theory of knowledge. "Let's suppose," he said, as if he were announcing a hypothesis at the basis of a philosophical argument, "that before being born, knowledge of what our life will be is shown to us in a dazzling revelation. Chance will play a role in the details, of course, but the major events, the turning points in this future life are revealed to us because they've already been determined.

"Determined by whom?"

"By karma: a relentless law that makes our misfortunes proportionate to our misdoings, our good fortune commensurate with our virtues."

"So, you believe in karma and in reincarnation?"

"I don't believe; for the moment I'm just hypothesizing. Let's begin again: before we are born, the principal breaking points are set in advance. Then life begins, we have to grow up, change, we're in the grip of time, so to speak. But now and then we have premonitions, an intuition of these major experiences that await us. Déjà-vu is the same, it belongs to the same category. It's the sign that we've literally *already seen* what eventually happens; it's the proof that there remains in our memory a trace of the future before it occurs. And not only the future: a trace of everything we understood before. Learning something is recognizing a discovery made in a previous life. Think of innate talents, early vocations, beings we are immediately attracted to, those who trigger warning signs at the first meeting, the key differences between siblings who are nevertheless endowed with the same genetic heritage and grow old in an identical environment. If my theory is valid, it explains all these various phenomena.

"Markus, are you serious?"

"Not entirely. I'm rambling, formulating. But I also believe that no one has ever proposed a definitive theory of the mind. Of its nature, its origin, its functioning. And since I'm constantly experiencing it, it occurs to me that déjà-vu may perhaps be the way to reach a solution to these problems. It's frightening, you know ... I have the impression that I'm imprisoned in time, that I'm constantly reliving the same day, seeing the same things, the same people over and over again. Even this conversation, it seems to me that we've already had it ... This has been going on for years, but it's been getting worse recently."

"You should go to Sentinel Island, I joked, hoping to lighten the mood a bit. *There's* something you've surely never seen!"

Markus smiled, gave no answer, and we started back.

22

Epidemics

The Andamanese believe in spirits and are afraid to travel in the dark. Sometimes they put an ornament around their neck; it's a necklace made of bones. To dispose of bodies, they go deep into the forest. They lay the bodies of their parents between the roots of the kapok trees and return when they are completely decomposed: then they take the bones and use them to make their talismans. Between 1868 and 1892, a series of epidemics descended upon them: pneumonia, syphilis, ophthalmia, measles, mumps, influenza, and gonorrhea struck them one after the other. The native population of the archipelago had been five thousand people in 1858. At the census of 1931, there were only four hundred and sixty left.

Isolated on their island, the Sentinelese are protected from illnesses. But their immune system is fragile, and the germs of outsiders represent a deadly risk for them. Fortunately, the frequency of contact has decreased since the time when Portman dreamed of *taming* them. There was, however, a final meeting of our two worlds before the end of the 19th century. It was brief and without regrettable consequences—at least for the Sentinelese. Portman says that the convicts of the Andamans sometimes managed to flee. Three Hindu prisoners succeeded in doing so on March 18, 1896. In Constance Bay, to the west of Port Blair, they build a raft and put out to sea on it. But the current pulls them onto the reefs of Sentinel Island, their craft is smashed to bits, two passengers drown, and the third reaches the shore only to be riddled with arrows. His remains are found by the English on March 30, to the south of the island.

After this date, Sentinel Island disappeared from our history for seventy years, taking with it the secret of an unpredictable navigation, as if it had begun to drift across the Bay of Bengal, or as if a fabulous mirror had risen up around its coast, reflecting the image of the ever-changing sea to the sailors in the area.

23

Sterling

After our discussion on the beach of Block Island, my friendship with Markus grew deeper. His troubles endeared him to me more; I understood that behind this façade of invincibility that had impressed me so much at the beginning, there was a young man who was suffering like the rest of us, and who deserved my compassion. His weakness brought him closer to me; knowing him to be less perfect made me like him more. And then, I was beginning to worry about him. Having become aware of the emergence of a phenomenon whose existence I hadn't suspected previously, I now saw how regularly his déjà-vu episodes distressed him. Markus would suddenly fall silent, an absent look coming over him; it took him a long moment to come back to us. It happened often, and it hurt to see the effort it cost him to hide his anguish from his father, pretending to suffer simply from random headaches. Joakim took him at his word and returned to his office.

We said goodbye at the Block Island port. The following month he accompanied his parents and sister on a trip to the Maldives. On the platform where the ferry had just docked, we shook hands more warmly than usual, suspecting that this vacation would be the last we would ever spend together; in a year, our lives would have taken a new direction. I waved to him from the ship's rail, thinking about everything we had shared during the summer: long walks on the beach, kayaking on the open sea, swimming at twilight when we played at seeing who would stop first as we headed out into the open sea, and then a few memorable visits to the island's bars from which we returned much too late, trying not to knock anything over in the house. All that belonged to the past already, but we could think back on those shared memories, saying to ourselves: that summer, I had a close friend.

It was mainly my fault—or rather, it was mainly owing to obstacles I had to confront at that time—that we began to drift apart in September. My dissertation barely finished, I had begun to prepare for my job applications, around thirty in all since, out of fear of not finding work, I was applying to all the open positions and postdocs I could find, even those for which I was only remotely qualified. I still saw Markus, of course, during the weekly meetings at Saint Andrew. But though I had committed to attending them all, I occasionally stayed at home on certain Thursday evenings to take care of Eleanor, whose condition was still of some concern. If she hadn't returned from her stay in Texas completely cured, at least her symptoms were far less serious. Then suddenly, incomprehensibly, her headaches became more debilitating than ever, and she was again spending whole days shut up in her room. A year after her accident, we had returned to the darkest hours of her illness.

To take her mind off her misery, I had convinced her to go with me to one of the events organized by Saint Andrew. In addition to its annual ball, the society opens its doors now and then for special evenings to which members are permitted to invite guests. Eleanor had gotten ready, grumbling, to attend this classical music concert; arm in arm we walked through the cold night like a little old couple. "Night is my element; I become a vampire," she said, although I wasn't amused by her attempt at humor. She set one foot before the other with extreme caution, as if the vibrations of her steps risked increasing her pain. It was the very image of our couple, this walk in the night: she staggering and I holding her up, our bodies frozen in the shadows.

Everything was dark on Wall Street, and the street was empty. At the windows of the houses, the halos from the lights were dimmed by heavy curtains, as if the occupants were contriving to stifle any trace of life inside. New Haven at night has often reminded me of a city after the end of the world, a city deserted by its inhabitants, whose cellars contained horrors. Eleanor and I passed through this dystopian décor until we could make out, far off on our left, a bright glow from the windows of Saint Andrew. From the street below, we could see well-dressed young people looking serious and polite, conversing next to huge bookshelves and cheery fireplaces. I opened the door for Eleanor, and in the vestibule where authentic medieval armor greeted the visitors, we happened upon Grace and Markus. I think Eleanor had met them before that evening, but only in a rush, just long enough to say hello and exchange a couple of platitudes. I have no idea why we had never spent an evening together, the four of us. Probably because Eleanor's illness had prevented it? Nonetheless, they chatted while I went to greet other members of the society in the grand lounge with its woodwork and Saint Andrew's crosses engraved in the stone walls. Victor, our leader, was not happy with me: I had missed several gatherings. When he had finished his reprimands, he kept me company while the musicians were getting ready.

I've forgotten what works were played that evening, but all were performed by members of the society. One of those members has become an orchestra conductor in Canada. Alone in front of the crowd, Markus played a sonata for violin—music was yet another talent among all those he possessed. It was an incredibly difficult piece, a tour de force written to showcase the virtuosity of the performer. Markus did a beautiful rendition, then came to sit in the audience to listen to the rest of the concert. As he turned his gaze to the other musicians, Grace devoured him with her eyes, which were glowing with admiration. On the way home, Eleanor made fun of him: "Did you see how red he was when he was playing his piece? I thought he was going to have a heart attack!" Without knowing quite why, I felt obliged to defend him.

Twenty-four hours after the concert at Saint Andrew, I was invited to a preliminary interview for a tenure-track position. Other invitations soon followed, as if they had been encouraged by this good news. It is normal in my profession for hiring committees to meet candidates at the annual meeting of the American Anthropological Association. That winter it took place in Vancouver: I endured a nine-hour flight to have, on the other side of the American continent, four thirty-minute conversations on which my career depended. One of the oddities of these job interviews is that they take place in the hotel rooms where the committee members are staying. They question you on your research projects a few feet from an unmade bed you can see through a crack in a door left ajar. Three days later, I was back in New Haven; I had traveled five thousand miles, and it was only the first stage in the process. After a week of waiting, several anthropology departments wanted to meet me.

Armed with photos of the Onges and a lecture taken from the last chapter of my dissertation, I began my round of universities. My departure for New Haven airport marked the beginning of a series of more or less grotesque adventures. Having arrived in Ohio, I noticed that I had forgotten to bring my dress shoes; all I had to wear with my suit were thick hiking boots. I found myself running through the deserted streets of Columbus in minus-thirteen-degree weather looking for a shoe store that was open. Five days later, at a tiny college in Pennsylvania I had almost never reached because of a snowstorm that, after canceling my flight, had blocked my train without heat for four hours, a curt, arrogant woman who wanted to show off the advantages of her town found nothing better to boast about than the local oncologist. Having soon left for California, I fell violently ill there; I had to hide my fits of vomiting between the interviews. Then I took off for Florida, where the tipsy dean who had me to his home almost came to blows with a colleague over a sabbatical leave he had refused him a decade before. In short, I returned to New Haven having logged over fifteen thousand miles and, at the end of this academic odyssey, accepted a position in Ohio.

A few weeks later, at the graduation ceremony in May, Markus's path and mine crossed again. He had his whole family around him; Joakim shook my hand warmly while an indifferent hello slipped from the lips of his mother and sister, who kept to the side waiting for it all to be over, wearing outrageously expensive and, to tell the truth, rather vulgar dresses that flattered their bodies sculpted by the daily sessions in the gym. Markus was imposing in his navy-blue gown and wore the graduates' square cap with as much elegance as a Panama hat. He knew that Eleanor and I were leaving two days later for Ohio. "And what about you," I asked, "what are you doing next year?" He answered immediately, as if it had never been in doubt, that he would become the head of his father's publishing house beginning in September. During the summer, he would travel in Europe to interview the close friends and relatives of an artist discovered by Joakim, and whose biography he planned to write.

In short, everything was back to normal, the pre-established order of things. We shook hands in front of the Sterling Library, a few minutes' walk from the hidden spot where he and I had met three years earlier. We of course promised to stay in contact, but neither of us had any concrete plans for our next meeting; they were just words you say to mask the truth when it is too sad. All I had been for him was an acquaintance among others, playing a predetermined role in his years at the university: that of a good companion to enjoy vacations with. All in all, I'd only been the equivalent, in the area of friendship, of what Grace had been for him in that of amorous relations, and my time was up, that's all there was to it. I understood that at the time of this short exchange in front of Sterling and accepted it. I reconciled myself to the death of our friendship; after all, I had attained my professional goal, my wife and I were leaving for another state, another life in which other relationships surely awaited us. Markus and his family said goodbye and headed for the old campus to attend the speech that a guest of honor, the Vice President of the United States, would soon deliver to the graduates. Eleanor and I were expected at another ceremony, organized in the Hall of Graduate Studies. Markus and I each went our separate ways, and I would've bet that day that we would never cross paths ever again.

SECOND PART

The mind of man is capable of anything—because everything is in it, all the past as well as all the future.

Conrad, *Heart of Darkness*

1

Columbus, Ohio

The city of Columbus, Ohio, suffers from a reputation it doesn't deserve. The malicious call it *Cowlumbus*, a provincial town where you "chew" your boredom as if it were cud. Perhaps they were right once, when its rivals Cleveland and Cincinnati attracted the industries and arts, leaving to Columbus the governance of the state of which it is the capital. But they were already treating it unfairly when Eleanor and I moved there, for Columbus had already begun its metamorphosis.

Toward the end of the Obama years, the city was in a frenzy of development. Cranes rose up at crossroads, freeways were expanded, ethnic restaurants were opening up on every street corner, inner-city neighborhoods attracted new inhabitants who, sniffing out good investments, were spending fortunes building lofts, patios, skylights, and gardens on rooftops. National corporations were moving their headquarters to the financial district whose windows looked out upon the placid flow of the Scioto River. Well-heeled thirty-somethings drove the economy and in the evenings turned out in the Short North bars to flaunt their dates in short dresses. On summer evenings, pedal-driven vehicles rolled up North High Street to the joyous clamor of their passengers. Job openings were quickly filled, as were the attractive glass-and-steel apartment buildings that arose in every available space. Now diversified, the economy was booming. People came to Columbus to work in a bank or an insurance company, in medical research or in fashion, in arms companies or for The Ohio State University, one of the largest academic institutions in the country, with its sixty thousand students, its seven thousand professors, its four-square-mile campus, and its six billion dollar endowment. People came from very far away, from other states as from abroad, but especially from the smaller cities in Ohio—Dayton, Springfield, Youngstown, and Toledo—that were inexorably losing their youngest inhabitants as they converged on the capital. The rest of the country had not yet become aware that Columbus was already one of the most thriving metropolises in America. For the city, as for Eleanor and me, a new chapter was beginning.

We wanted a big yard, and there are hardly any in Columbus, so we settled in a tiny town, almost a village, about 15 miles away. The center of our new town sits on one main street, with three bars, two restaurants, a barber shop, an ice cream store, two churches, and a gun shop. Other than the disappearance of the Amerindians, nothing much has changed here since the conquest of the West. People's lives are organized around the same poles: they lead a peaceful existence installed in well-kept, imposing homes. Without admitting it, all the neighbors are in competition to some extent: whose house is the most elegant, whose garden the best groomed. So on Sundays in the spring, a symphony of lawnmowers can be heard in the neighborhood: the locals go at it upon returning from church. When autumn comes, leaves are gathered up as soon as they fall on the lawn, and in winter, complex displays—inflatable snowmen, floodlights trained on the houses where reindeer and sleighs leap about joyfully—come out of the basements where they will return, after the holidays, until the following year. Halloween is the other major holiday in the neighborhood. Normally the streets are empty, but that night, the families are outside, five-year-old Darth Vaders skipping about holding a plastic pumpkin, past lawns filled with a Gothic collection of bric-a-brac, plastic skeletons, and giant spiders. The rest of the year, life is dominated by invariable rituals. At seven in the morning, the garages open a few minutes apart, the neighbors go off to their offices and return around five o'clock; throughout the night, electric lamps burn on each side of the front door. That is life in the Midwest: orderly and tranquil. All of that is banal for Americans, but for me who grew up in the sweltering heat of Mumbai, it was wildly exotic, touchingly odd: I sometimes dreamed of an anthropological study that would portray the residents of American suburbs.

On our street, we were the only couple that didn't have any children. The house was ready, and I was too. Eleanor was still hesitant, and I was waiting for her to make up her mind. For this baby that wasn't yet born, I had made a gesture of love in advance. I had hung from the ceiling of the room planned for him or her a little white boat with blue sails. One day, I thought, this boat would watch over our baby's dreams as it sailed in the night.

2

Pandit

Seventy years of solitude. Seventy years pass by between the death of the Hindu fugitive beneath the arrows of the Sentinelese and the return of outsiders to the island. Seventy years of autarchy during which the Sentinelese have no knowledge of the two world wars that rage on out of their sight, nor of India's independence. Seventy years that see them slip into oblivion, for in the streets of Port Blair, scarcely anyone speaks of their tribe anymore. If there is a people everyone's talking about, it's the Jarawas, in the north, who attack intruders and then vanish into the jungle. But among those who haven't forgotten the Sentinelese, the tales are conflicting. Some describe them as little black smooth-skinned beings with kinky hair, while others assert that they are tall, light-skinned, and have long beards: they assuredly descend from prisoners who escaped from the penitentiary colony during the last century. In 1966, thirty miles from Port Blair, the Sentinelese are as little known as in the time of Marco Polo.

That's the year Triloknath Pandit comes into their history. He comes from another part of India, almost from another world: from Kashmir, where he studied hill tribes for his doctoral dissertation. Currently, he's a member of the Anthropological Survey of India, a leading government organization involved in anthropological research. Before his appointment to the Great Andaman group, he had never heard of the Sentinelese. And suddenly he finds himself on the way to their island. "It wasn't my idea to go there!" he protests.

I met Dr. Pandit twice. The first time during my studies and the second before receiving tenure, when I returned to the Andamans to finish my book there. He had retired in New Delhi, and I took advantage of a stop-over to visit him.

With his customary courtesy, Dr. Pandit invites me to wait in the living room while he makes tea. Sitting in the half-light, I almost fall asleep: the fatigue from a twenty-six-hour trip catches up to me and hits me hard. To stay awake, I force myself to look at the photos on the furniture and the walls. One of them shows Dr. Pandit standing in a lagoon up to his waist, offering a coconut to a black man as small as a child, a member of the Sentinel tribe. I know this image. It's a souvenir of his legendary expedition of 1992, the culmination of twenty-five years of perseverance. The tray trembles in his hands when he comes back, slightly stooped in his sky-blue *kurta*. That day, Dr. Pandit is over eighty. He's delighted that I've found a job since our last meeting, and that the study of the Andamanese people is continuing in America. And since he sees no problem with my recording him, I can listen to him, taking only occasional notes, while he relates to me his first visit to Sentinel Island a half-century earlier.

One day in 1967, not even a year after Pandit took up his post, the governor of the Andaman and Nicobar Islands called him to his office. He had decided to send an expedition to Sentinel Island, and Pandit would be in charge. "My mission consisted in establishing friendly relations with the tribe, which would have been seen as a victory for the government," Pandit explained as he held out a tray of *kaju barfi*. He pauses, and the tape-recorder continues to record the purring of the air-conditioning in the room as well as all the noises from outside, the horns of the auto-rickshaws, the shouts of the tea sellers in the street. Then he gives me a gentle, sad look before describing his arrival off the coast of the island.

An instant before, a group of Sentinelese was standing there, on the shore. But upon seeing the rubber dinghies approach, they vanished into the jungle. The policemen disembarked first, soon followed by the scientists they were there to protect. Pandit led them into the heart of the island. The forest all around them was full of life and noises, but none of it, apparently, came from the tribe. In which depths, beneath what shelters, on which heights had they taken refuge? Unless they were there, watching from behind the tangle of branches, silently following the intruders who had come into their territory, theirs by virtue of the countless generations that had succeeded one another there, who had found their subsistence there, then the ground in which to rest their bones.

Pandit and his team traveled over a mile before coming upon a deserted village. The huts in the clearing were made of branches and leaves, and a fire was burning in front of each one. "What I'll never forget is the light, the special manner in which the rays fell on the roofs of the houses when we came out of the darkness of the forest into their world." It was one of those moments for which anthropologists live: the revelation of a spectacle not yet spoiled, contaminated, and cursed; the entrance into a space exhibiting the enchantment of a culture still intact. Pandit asked his men to leave gifts in the houses—plastic buckets, sweets, pieces of cloth—and despite his protests, some policemen took objects belonging to the Sentinelese: bows, arrows, baskets, the skull of a wild boar decorated with paint. "There was a festive atmosphere that day. I no longer knew if we were participating in a scientific expedition or a school outing."

And for twenty-five years, Pandit made trip after trip to Sentinel Island.

3

The Vekner Foundation

At first Markus and I stayed in contact. Lengthy at the beginning, then more and more brief, his emails gave the impression that he was thriving in his editorial functions, and that he was always between two trips, two exhibitions. For my part, I told him about my research, the classes I was teaching, and my plans for a stay on the Jarawas territory, for which I had begun to gather the required authorizations. One day, I sent him a message to which he didn't respond. I was hurt without being too surprised; we were living in different cities, leading completely separate lives—it was foreseeable that our relationship would eventually wear thin. I could, of course, have tried to contact him again after several weeks, but my wounded pride stopped me; there was too great a social distance between us; I didn't wish to lower myself to solicit his attention if he didn't grant it of his own accord.

Despite the silence that continued between us, I never thought that he had completely disappeared from my life, especially since over time he began to occupy a different place in it through new intermediaries. I regularly searched the Internet for the latest news about him. My reasons for doing so weren't entirely clear—to me, I mean. There was probably still some emulation going on between us (at least on my part), and after so rapidly assuming I was his inferior, I wanted to see if he had deserved my surrendering so quickly, fulfilling the hopes we all had for him, those of us who cared about him.

In coming to live in Ohio, our mutual friend Edmond had also created a new bond between Markus and me. Markus's absence separated us a little more each day, of course, but this friend helped me to follow his evolution from a distance. Edmond worked in the legal services of a large insurance group that had opened offices in Columbus. Since he went to New York regularly for meetings at their headquarters, he was able to meet up with Markus, "his Saint Andrew brother." Much more than I, they had preserved an emotional bond with the secret society, to which they returned together from time to time. From their dinners in the chic restaurants of the West Village, Edmond brought me the latest news of the Holmberg clan. Since the triumph of the first exhibition in Paris, Joakim was working on the opening of a new gallery, in Singapore instead of Hong Kong, the city he had considered for a while before changing his mind, foreseeing before everyone else that its inhabitants would eventually revolt against the Chinese government. For her part, Samantha continued to pursue her career as a lawyer after a change of firms that she had cleverly orchestrated, pocketing a bonus sufficiently large to impress the members of a profession accustomed to indecent sums. And the beautiful Alexandra had created a brand of sportswear whose obscenely expensive bathing suits were promoted on Instagram by the slender bodies of pouting nymphets.

As for Markus, he was perhaps not as fulfilled as he had given me to believe when we were still writing to each other. When Edmond returned to Columbus, where I saw him in a cocktail bar downtown, a pretentious and trendy place he always insisted we meet at, he described Markus's chewed-up fingernails and the sudden pauses he made during their discussions before emerging from his silence with a haggard look. I knew these symptoms well, having often witnessed them myself. Markus had published two works in the house he directed, a translation of essays on aesthetics by the Swedish philosopher Hans Larsson, in collaboration with a professor at New York University, and a series of interviews with a South Korean woman specializing in video art. Markus was also working on a novel of which Edmond knew nothing, because he stubbornly refused to talk about it until he had finished it, and I wondered if it was still his work on Sentinel Island. According to Edmond, the relations between Markus and his father had deteriorated as soon as they began working together. As could be foreseen, Marcus wanted to establish his independence in his editorial activities, but his initiatives were regularly blocked by his father who, in the end, remained his boss. Markus repeated to Edmond that he was seriously considering resigning, but those words were never followed by any action—he gave me more and more the impression of being a prisoner of the advantages of his family: the rich too must have their reasons to be unhappy.

After a few months, I nonetheless lost the indirect contact with Markus that I had thanks to Edmond, because the latter took a hard turn to the right that put me off. It was the period when Trump was announcing his run for president by calling Mexican immigrants murderers and rapists. That anyone could support this vulgar individual, whose crass ignorance and absolute lack of empathy eventually degenerated before the whole world into paranoid lunacy and narcissistic outbursts, seemed to me a passion reserved for the lowest ranks of society, that could at least be excused by their minimal education and a diet of information dramatically reduced to Facebook and Fox News. But that my friend, a graduate of Yale and Princeton, could see a serious and even desirable candidate in this individual, who was fundamentally incapable of producing a coherent discourse, whose speeches were filled with retrograde ideas that he expressed in an appallingly impoverished vocabulary, struck me, in my moments of discouragement, as an irrevocable condemnation of the Western system of education, if not of the very concept of human perfectibility.

Edmond belonged to the class of people who thought themselves cleverer than everyone else in predicting, with an insider mien, that Trump would be a great president who, once the campaign was over, would put an end to his clowning around—which was unfortunate, of course, but necessary to win political power in our spectacle-driven society—and would soon endow the White House with his rigorous pragmatism and unequaled business sense: a sort of postmodern politician of hidden genius, capable of playing several chess games simultaneously, endowed with an intelligence commensurate with the excesses that masked it. I already wondered then what gave them confidence in the accomplishments of a reality TV star whose businesses had failed one after the other, and whose principal quality in life consisted in being his father's son.

But after the election, when Edmond continued to support Trump despite everything—despite the children he locked up at the border, in revolting conditions, the abandonment of the Puerto Ricans after the hurricane of 2017, a tax reform that only served to further enrich the most wealthy, his complicitous silence on the devastation wrought by firearms, the encouragement he gave to White nationalism, his guilty denial of climate change, his overt sympathy for dictators throughout the world, the racism in his repeated attacks against Latinos and Blacks, Haiti and the African continent in general—I preferred to reduce our meetings to a minimum, because in the end the hypocrisy of his responses, which were always reduced to asking if the Democrats hadn't done worse when Trump was accused of doing something wrong, drove me to distraction.

It was the last straw when he ranted before me against the immigrants who were going to drown the White population in their mass—the moron forgetting that he had a dark-skinned foreigner in front of him. There we have it, I said to myself: I understood that he was revealing to me the cause of his unwavering support, that I was finally seeing a sincere explanation. All of these Trump partisans usually refuse to admit this nightmare of theirs that goes back to 1619 and the sale of the first African slaves in America, but the fear of it happening goes a long way to explaining the dishonest moral compromises, the voluntary blindness, the hypocritical indignation they exhibit, all the while claiming to be good Christians. I left without saying a word to him; he would've ruined me with a lawsuit if I'd punched him out, as I was sorely tempted to do for a moment. Personal reasons I'll explain at another time were later added to the political motives that led me to detest someone who had been my friend, so that we acknowledged each other's existence less and less when our paths happened to cross.

My relationship with Edmond now broken, I only had the Internet to follow Markus's career path. I could've been distraught about it or reconsidered my decision not to write him anymore, but the deterioration of my relations with Eleanor during this same period distracted me from it. I had enough problems at home; I'd deal with this one when I'd gotten beyond my conjugal difficulties. Our move to Columbus that had begun a new life for us had quickly aggravated the tensions that already existed between us. I had become a professor; I put on a suit and went off to lead my seminars and came back home in the evening to find Eleanor in her pajamas, her hair a mess, sour-faced, with nothing to say about her day, and no interest in mine. The days I spent at home, writing in the morning and preparing my classes in the afternoon, she stretched out languidly like a cat on the living room couch or lazed around for hours looking at God knows what on her computer, her head full of vague daydreams, brooding over memories, disappointments, and regrets, over all the reasons she had to be dissatisfied with her existence without finding the strength to change it. Her creeping depressions, constantly renewed, her intrinsic weakness, her latent fear of life, her pathological incapacity to recognize her responsibility for anything at all: everything was eroding a little more each day, including, though I was not willing to admit it, the love that I had had for her.

Nothing I could say had any effect on her: enjoining her to see her situation in a better light was telling her how to think; inviting her to take steps to change what she disliked was picking on her; giving her leads to look for a job was dictating her conduct; doing something in her place was rubbing her nose in her inadequacies; leaving her free to decide what she wanted to do was abandoning her to her fate; my meeting any kind of success was turning the knife in the wound. With her, I could only be wrong. I tried everything. I tried affection and understanding, sympathizing with her about the headaches that were still tormenting her, about the difficulty of finding a job in our times. Meanwhile, I encouraged her to engage in other activities, painting and drawing, yoga and horse riding classes, but that wasn't enough either, nothing was enough to shake off this native sadness, entrenched in her since the depths of her childhood, this despondency that was the essential truth of her disposition, her natural and constant state, the instinctive determinant of her mood. And while she became an eccentric clown as soon as we got together with acquaintances—making others laugh at her expense to extort their sympathy, demeaning herself before strangers to flatter them into granting her a condescending friendship—she took off this mask as soon as we were in the car, exhausted like an actress who had given too much of herself on the stage. One evening, a colleague who was meeting her for the first time asked her what she did in life. Eleanor answered, "Nothing, because I'm nothing," bursting into tears. I didn't know any longer if I felt ashamed of her or pitied her. Sometimes it seemed to me that what she really wanted was for me to join her in her boundless depression, to agree with her once and for all that life is ugly and ambition ridiculous, that effort is useless, and that there was no reason, as she often repeated, her face creased by tears, to bring into the world a child who would share our suffering.

A Tibetan proverb says that a thousand paths lead to Buddha, and Eleanor's was her chronic depression. I'm no longer sure what drew her to a temple for the first time, but she nonetheless found there a kind of echo to her pessimism, to this manner she had of always assuming the worst, of viewing illnesses diagnosed too late and accidents that cut down families as much more likely than happiness and prosperity. For Buddhism—at least what I've understood of this religion, which is like space, ever more vast as one gets into it—begins by observing the omnipresence of suffering. To deliver people from it is the goal of its joyous teaching, full of hope, for pain, as protean as it is, is still surmountable provided you follow the path set out by its founder. I wasn't especially attracted to a religion that, born in northern India, within the current boundaries of Nepal, had eventually lost its importance in my country. In that regard, I was certainly influenced by my place of origin, in which I had heard from my childhood onward that Buddha hadn't invented much, since, all things considered, transmigration and karma were beliefs accepted by Hinduism well before him. So, I'm not the one who nudged her toward this Eastern religion, far from it, although I was sympathetic to her interest in it.

Eleanor began by going to the Sunday morning meditation sessions, then to those on Tuesday and Friday evenings, quickly building relationships with the members of this community, composed essentially of sweet, pious old ladies constantly between two meditative retreats and two fundraising events for the most destitute. She let herself be adopted, with disconcerting ease, by these enterprising ladies who saw in her, I imagine, a girl or friend that helped them feel a bit younger. And as Eleanor wasn't working any more than they were—widows in many cases and already long retired—she had all her time to devote to the events of the community.

One of her friends, Suzanne, had lost her husband a few years earlier. She had an only son, Julian Vekner, who had become wealthy in real estate in New York. Now retired, he devoted his time to the charitable organization that bore his name. The principle under which the Vekner Foundation operated was the application of the rational approach of the business world to that of philanthropy. In his offices, the personnel discussed the quantification of needs, risk assessment, and the forecast of results. Mr. Vekner financed projects in the areas of environmental protection, education, and healthcare, primarily in the northeastern United States. But he was trying to increase his activities in the Midwest as well and, particularly, in Columbus, his hometown, where the opioid crisis was the focus of much concern. Suzanne observed Eleanor for a while without revealing her intentions. Then she gave her a strong recommendation to her son. After bringing her to New York for an interview, Mr. Vekner gave her a position as an analyst in his newly opened offices in Columbus where, at the beginning, she had only two colleagues along with Suzanne, who, despite being over seventy, still found ways to be useful.

This opportunity was greatly beneficial to our couple. We both had a job, we enjoyed what we were doing, and I'd never been so proud of her as she put her energy to work helping others. After a brief outbreak, no doubt caused by the anxiety of taking on new responsibilities, her headaches suddenly disappeared. Diplomatically, I preferred not to point out to her this coincidence that confirmed for me what I had long believed, namely that her pain was largely psychosomatic in nature since it worsened in periods of stress and vanished every time her mind was on something else. I had also decided to speak to her no more about having a baby, at least for the moment. She wanted to prove herself in her new job before getting pregnant; I understood her reasons but hoped that we would eventually begin a family, perhaps the following year. She had had her job for around two months and I mine a little more than a year when I received news that provoked a sudden resurgence of a whole world of long-repressed feelings: Eva was moving to Columbus.

4

Man in Search of Man

1974. The IRA sets off bombs in London and Birmingham, Nixon resigns after the Watergate scandal, and Pompidou dies while president of France. 1974 is the year the skeleton of Lucy is discovered in Ethiopia, Stephen King publishes his first novel, and Aleksandr Solzhenitsyn loses his Soviet citizenship. In 1974, you can hear ABBA, the Beach Boys, Eric Clapton, and Freddie Mercury on the radio. *The Godfather II* and *The Exorcist* are in the theaters, and the West German soccer team wins the World Cup. It's also the year when another event, more modest in appearance but still historical, is being prepared very far from the West: the first filmed expedition to Sentinel Island.

It's spring, and a film crew sets out to sea. They are accompanied by policemen, a photographer from *National Geographic*, and Dr. Pandit. The dinghy approaches the island while a group of Sentinelese emerge from the forest. The pilot yells and changes course, just in time to avoid a volley of arrows. Wearing body armor and protected by shields, the policemen disembark a healthy distance from any projectiles. They set on the sand a collection of gifts as heterogenous as the verses of a surrealist poem: a pig attached to a rope, some red cloth, coconuts and bananas, a doll and knives, a little plastic car and kitchen utensils. Then everyone hurries back to the dinghy to observe from afar the reaction of the Sentinelese—which consists in firing more arrows, one of which hits the director in the thigh. On the shore, a huge laugh rings out. The triumphant archer returns to the edge of the jungle and sits down in the shade of a honey tree to savor his victory. Other Sentinelese stab the pig and the doll and bury them in the sand before vanishing with the utensils and coconuts into the forest, a forest from which five scrawny trees jut out against a stormy sky, like monstrous idols forbidding outsiders from entering the island.

In its very title, *Man in Search of Man* asserts the equality of visitor and visited, contrary to the British colonization, which is torn to shreds in the first few minutes of the film: "In spite of the progress of Western humanistic values," intones the voice-over narrator, "there were representatives of the British Raj who even in the 19th century behaved barbarously and tried to drive away the local tribesmen." The director is careful not to make any suggestion that his people is superior to the Andamanese: India also knew colonization, was part of the so-called White Man's burden. His work is rather an attempt to start over again, to rewrite the primeval scene of the age of discovery, peacefully this time; to begin History anew, from scratch.

On board the ship, the crew members look like proud explorers. At each stop, they are confronted with an ever-increasing strangeness. The expedition goes first to the home of the Onges, a contemplative people whose couples share interminable embraces, suspended in time. They are almost solemn in the expression of their affection, yet joyous and gentle in their rhythmic dancing. Then the crew discover the Jarawas, enveloped since the dawn of time in a false legend that depicts them as a warlike people, always ready to greet outsiders with poisoned arrows. Yet, as soon as they arrive on the island, the visitors are received by a smiling welcome committee who, intrigued, reach out to touch their beards, listen delightedly to music emanating from a tape-recorder, and draw them into a spontaneous dance.

The crew finally sets back out to sea. The soundtrack turns sinister, with drumming and whistling, as the sailors approach Sentinel Island. Brief shots reveal their worried expressions as they scrutinize the shore. The Onges and Jarawas were happy to be filmed close up, content to show off the beauty of their bodies; the Sentinelese are only silhouettes seen from afar, phantoms gesticulating wildly in the hope of driving away the intruders. It will take many more years, many more attempts, to progress from these human ideograms signifying "I'm hostile!" to the fullness of faces open to the arrival of outsiders.

5

Leaving

For two and a half years, I had had no news of Eva, who had finished her dissertation in Moscow before seeking a teaching position in the United States. Particularly dynamic, my university was creating positions in fields as varied as comparative linguistics, microbiology, Victorian literature, and environmental anthropology. Eva applied for a position in my department, although I only learned of it by chance. Since I was only an assistant professor, not even sure I would be given tenure, I hadn't been involved in the workings of the search committee where my more experienced colleagues were in charge. I pursued my professional activities without paying much attention to this process, knowing nothing about the candidates, neither those who had been eliminated nor those who were still in the running. One morning as I was walking toward my office, I discovered the flyers announcing the campus visits of the finalists. Eva was looking out at me from one of them. She was wearing a navy-blue blouse and a pearl necklace that could have made her look older if she hadn't had that sweet, luminous face, that porcelain doll's face delicately made up and radiating a frank, gentle smile. My heart began to beat as it hadn't, no doubt, since that night in New Haven that I regularly remembered with a mixture of regret, sadness, and resignation.

When she came to Columbus, I was required to interview her. The second I saw her I was transported back in time, into that body trembling with desire and hesitation before her majestic, serene features and poise. For a brief moment, I was flustered, as if our roles were reversed, as if she were leading a discussion on which my career depended. I managed to pull myself together, and everything proceeded in a professional manner, following a script written ahead of time; one could very nearly have thought we had never met before. "Barely," I'd answered the department chair when he asked if we knew each other, since we had been to the same university. Eva left my office after shaking my hand coolly—as if this hand, one spring evening in New Haven, an eternity ago, hadn't offered me her affection. When I had to meet with my colleagues to decide between the finalists, I didn't know if I was more moved at the idea of her coming to Columbus or more frightened at the idea of seeing her every day. Voting for or against her posed an ethical problem for me, for I would have been incapable of identifying the real reasons for my decision with any certainty. Would I succeed in making up my mind based on her professional qualifications alone, as I was supposed to do, or would it rather be this mass of unresolved sentiments within me that would tip the balance? I waited until a consensus had been reached without intervening before adding my vote to the majority that had already chosen her. A few days later, I learned that she had accepted our offer and would join us the next fall. The whole following summer, I neither sent nor received any news regarding Eva, and not a single day passed without me thinking of her.

In September, who knows which one of us determined the nature of our relationship? It's possible that I was the one, by behaving with a chilliness that concealed the violent feelings I had for her—now so close, a colleague and neighbor when I had thought I'd never see her again— who gave her to understand that I wished to maintain this distance between us. And how could she have thought otherwise when my wife, in a green-and-white summer dress, was chatting idly in the garden where we were dining with our colleagues? I had no idea what she thought of what I didn't dare call our "relationship" in New Haven, and as there was nothing, or almost nothing, that could be said on this subject, it was much simpler to pretend—which was barely a lie—that nothing at all had happened. Eva was an outsider in this country, and she too had to find her place, she too had goals, dreams, and ambitions to realize. Why compromise them by reviving, with a married man who was also her colleague, repressed, unformulated feelings that had no doubt been fragile and had surely died out by now? Some beings will always live on other emotional time zones than yours, and nothing will ever be able to correlate them.

I was already suffering from seeing her and having to keep to myself the words I would have liked to say to her, and this suffering became overwhelming when I learned that she had begun a relationship. It happened at the end of the first semester, when she came with a guest to the Christmas Eve party organized by our department. Of course, I would have detested any man I saw at her side (with consummate dishonesty, since I was jealous while still being married), but that she had chosen this individual was particularly painful for me. I would've liked to think she was only Edmond's friend, but when I saw them holding hands, I felt my legs grow weak. They knew each other casually when we were at Yale and had met again during an evening organized by the alumni association in Columbus.

I understood too late that Eva had been available, and had I shared my feelings with her, she would perhaps be living with me now—and not with this pontificating guy, so full of himself, whom I began to hate with an unreasonable violence, and whose relationship with Eva, even more than our political differences, made it unbearable to be around him. They chatted affectionately in a corner of the living room while Eleanor was gossiping at the other side of the room; I could hear her inane banter bringing giggles from the small circle around her, which left me no choice but to drink much more than I should have, much more than I had in years. "You hit the bottle pretty hard, huh?" Eleanor said as she took the wheel to drive us home. I didn't reply. I watched the city and its lights through the window of the car as it took us back to our suburb, our big empty house where a child's laughter would never ring out. It's at that very moment that I decided to return to the Andamans; once again, I was choosing to flee.

6

"The Finest Day of His Life"

Leopold III, exiled king of Belgium,
visited the world's most dangerous island.
Maurice Matthysen tells the story.

"Leopold III was a tireless defender of unspoiled nature. In 1951, after yielding the throne to his son Baudouin I, he devoted himself entirely to his two passions: anthropology and zoology. They led him to Venezuela and Brazil, Zaïre and Colombia. The former king gave his name to two specimens: the *Gehyra leopoldi*, a gecko from Indonesia, and the *Polemon leopoldi*, an African snake. The high point of this life spent traveling the world was the creation of the Leopold III Fund, in support of unharmed nature and disinherited ethnic groups.

"The monarch contributed widely to our knowledge of the animal kingdom, as witnessed by his archives at the Royal Institute of Natural Sciences of Belgium. He also devoted himself to the protection of peoples threatened with extinction. In the village of Isleta in New Mexico, he met with the Pueblo Indians. A few years later, during an expedition into the Amerindian reservations of Mato Grosso in Brazil, he spoke with Raoni Metuktire, the grand chief of the Kayapós and protector of the Amazonian forest. But who remembers this event in the biography of the deposed king? Who knows that he went, at over seventy years of age, to the domain of the most dangerous tribe on earth?

"This tribe lives on Sentinel Island, an Indian possession in the Bay of Bengal. For centuries the Sentinelese have been repelling outsiders. They make no exceptions, as Leopold III learned for himself in 1974. Accompanied by Dr. Triloknath Pandit, an Indian anthropologist, the king got into a lifeboat to leave gifts on the shore of Sentinel Island. The visit took place at twilight, and the lagoon was so perfectly calm that everyone forgot the danger they were in. They were reminded by the sudden passage of a ten-foot arrow a couple of inches from Leopold III's face. The boat turned back immediately, carrying the former monarch to safety, in the comfort of his ship, and to the nine years he had left to live. Dr. Pandit relates that the king was enchanted by the adventure: 'He was thrilled and repeated that it was the finest day of his life!'"

7

Port Blair

A paradoxical lucidity sometimes comes over you on long-haul flights. Completely worn out, when your watch shows six o'clock in the morning and, back home, it's the afternoon of the previous day (or the day after?), when the plane, after a trip that seemed to take forever, is in the last half-hour of the flight, and the darkness is banished by the cold electric glow that springs to life in the cabin, it is the moment when all the decisions, big and small, well thought out or not, that led you to this precise moment are suddenly seen in a new light. I'm not sure I know why—perhaps the fact that all devices have to be turned off, and one is left with no choice but to look inwards. You are too close to landing to begin a new film, your mind too tired to continue reading, and the passengers around you have no desire to chat: they look away, ashamed to be surprised in the state of vulnerability that comes with waking up, their face disfigured by the lack of sleep. It's perhaps also because the brain, already having too much to do just to remain more or less functional, no longer has the energy necessary to react to the onslaught of questions with all the responses provided by the normal defense mechanisms. These have dropped; they're too heavy to mobilize. You can't kid yourself when you're devastated by insomnia: you no longer have the strength.

I experienced one of these moments as we approached New Delhi. I didn't really know if I was exhausted by the trip or by everything in my life that had preceded it. I saw myself again as a child. A hyperactive kid playing in the streets of Mumbai. With this minuscule existence of a boy born toward the end of the 20th century, I could do so many more things. A leap across three decades, and here I am in this airplane. Anthropologist and specialist of the Andamanese: well, why these tribes and not others? And why this profession for which nothing in my family environment predisposed me (my father worked for the post office, and my mother was an English teacher)? My papers say that I'm a permanent resident of the United States, and that my Indian nationality authorizes me to stay here as long as I like: why did I go so far from my home if it was only to return there? And I have other papers that say I'm married to Eleanor, while nothing will ever reveal the world of repressed, confused feelings that I have for Eva. Why this life and not another? If I took into account all of the causes and effects, the mature decisions, the bad luck, the assumed risks, the opportunities I managed to seize and those I missed, would this aggregate whole suffice to understand what led me to this moment, to the fact that I'm here, my back stiff, beside this matron who has been ignoring me since Dubai and is handing a cookie to the sulking child in the seat next to her?

The captain announces that we've begun our descent toward the capital of India. No, we cannot be reduced to the sum of our choices. There is something else, something that makes our choices and decisions for us but also sets lucky breaks on our path and prepares, far in advance, scaffolding that will come crashing down on our head—all of which justifies the betrayals we do not deserve and the happiness of which we are not worthy and drives us into the arms of certain people while others are carried away on rails forever parallel to our own. I became an anthropologist because, as an adolescent, I happened to see the documentary of Prem Vaidya, *Man in Search of Man*. I could say that the enchantment experienced that day set the course of the rest of my life, that I was captured, determined by this instant conviction that adventure is still possible, and that we are living, our hearts full, in a world that remains to be explored. Experiences like this one offer conventional explanations, the ones you give when you have to justify your profession. Others are satisfied by it, but you, yourself, know full well that they leave something unresolved, a shadow, a mystery. After all, who decided what I would desire? Why did I choose a life of travel and study that for others, preferring calm and money or the comfort of their family above all, would have no appeal whatsoever? A baby is crying a few seats away: the descent of the plane is rapid, the increase in pressure must be affecting it. Can I say that I chose this life? Or is it in fact desire that chose for me without my knowing where it came from? What infinite possibilities we are, and what limited creatures we become.

The plane sets down on the runway with an excessively violent bounce, the pilot badly miscalculating the landing. The passengers wince; some rub the back of their neck. We have to be patient while the *sari*-clad women gather up their belongings after looking under the seats, while their husbands get up to retrieve their unreasonably heavy suitcases from the packed baggage compartments, and while this whole crowd, brought here for various and sundry reasons—thirst for discovery or nostalgia for their home—pours into the airport before coming to rest, finally, somewhere in the city. I stay in my seat, looking through the window at the airport without seeing it, thinking of Markus, that night on Block Island when he had spun his theory on déjà-vu, a theory I had considered whacky, bombastic, even inane—and which, nonetheless, I had never forgotten. Perhaps he was right; perhaps everything is decided in advance, and if it's not by a god whose absence by this time has become self-evident, it just might be by the errors we've been guilty of, by a whole set of laws, very finely drawn and invisible, rigorous and inflexible, more omniscient than all the surveillance services in the world; and even more than remorse, more equitable than the most impartial of judges, it is what we have formerly been that puts in us the original root of desire, the conglomerate of appetites and repulsions that makes us what we are, and while believing ourselves to be free, we're only following the script dictated by the countless incarnations of which we are, without knowing it, both the result and the descendants.

I spent around ten days in New Delhi, just the time I needed to recover from my jet lag and, especially, to ask Dr. Pandit all the questions I had prepared for him. For three whole afternoons, I noted down the jumble of memories of his meetings with the Sentinelese, his opinion of the condition of the Jarawas and Onges, the fears he harbored regarding the new arrivals, Bengalis, Tamils, Sikhs, and Pendjabis, whose growing numbers threatened the first inhabitants of the archipelago. Alas, he feared more than ever their extinction since a road—the Andaman Trunk Road—now cut the Jarawas' reservation in two. "You'll see that for yourself," he told me sadly. While accompanying me to his door—he was always extremely courteous—he left me with these words about the Sentinelese: "You know, we are tremendously lucky to have people like them in our country." I said goodbye to him, taking those gentle words away with me.

It would only have taken five hours to reach the Andamans by plane, but I preferred to go by boat to be able to fully appreciate the prodigious isolation of this archipelago, fulfilling a very long-held desire of mine. This decision was nonetheless the source of numerous vexations. Having arrived in Calcutta, I went to the offices of the Shipping Corporation of India intending to rent an individual cabin but, alas, after waiting in line for two hours, the employee at the window informed me that all that was left were bunks in dormitories for eight people. The crossing was shaping up to be memorable; I began to think it would never happen. The ship that was supposed to leave the next day wasn't ready to cast off for another seventy-two hours, and when the departure time came, we had to wait on the quay another afternoon before the passengers were finally allowed to go on board.

This boat, of Polish origin, hardly inspired confidence, appearing to be a good decade beyond the age when it should have been scrapped. The passageways, oozing humidity, ravaged by rust, were invaded by cockroaches. My dormmates played with dice or chatted until an ungodly hour while sipping, despite the ban on alcohol on board, from plastic bottles filled with a colorless liquid they claimed was water, but which was actually gin. They were nice enough guys, who asked me all sorts of questions about America, but the following night I preferred to sleep in a hammock that the crew let me set up on deck. It was the most gratifying night I've ever spent. I was delighted to escape the stuffy atmosphere of the dormitory, delighted to be outdoors, cozy in my sleeping bag as if it were a cocoon swaying with the eddies of the Bay of Bengal, still calm in January. And as I had bought one of those illicit bottles of "water" from another passenger, I could sip it while admiring the glowing sunset, then the stars that emerged from the darkness one by one, happier in my hammock than a first-class passenger has ever been.

The color of the sea became lighter as the trip progressed. From the navy blue off the coast of Calcutta, it had turned turquoise when our ship docked at the wharf at South Andaman Island. A flotilla of tuk-tuks awaited the passengers, and I got into one that set off for Port Blair. On the way to the hotel, I reflected on the staggering distance that separated me from Eleanor, the continents, the mountain chains, and the ocean between us. In leaving for India, I understood that I had attempted to get closer to her. It was paradoxical, of course, and my reasons were not entirely clear to me. How many things have I done in my life without knowing what was impelling me to do so? But I believe I was hoping to get over the relationship I had dreamed of with Eva and rediscover why I had fallen in love with Eleanor—rediscover my need for her, my missing her, the qualities that attracted me to her, those qualities that shine more brightly in the distance, and that you become insensitive to when they are constantly in front of you. It was only three weeks since I had left, and the sadness at the idea of not seeing her until the following summer was already making my heart heavy.

Since landing at New Delhi, I couldn't stop feeling the absurdity of what I was doing, suspecting the vacuity of this book that I had come here to finish: did the world really need a scholarly work on the religious beliefs of a people on the verge of extinction? But I thought, if you look at it clear-headedly, whatever you do, whatever the goals to which you attach your fortunes, all of them leave the same impression of emptiness, since in the end, if you're honest with yourself, they're all just ways to fill your time before you die. The impression of absurdity when you examine how you're using your life is a little like ugliness when you look at yourself in the mirror: it doesn't take long to emerge. There is, however, an exception: what one does for others. And I thought that my coming to India was perhaps not so useless as I feared, because it would allow me to finish my book, which would allow me to get tenure, which would permit me to take care of Eleanor and the child we would have one day. Yes, I was right to undertake this monumental trip, and my place was here, precisely here, in this vehicle that I feared was going to roll over in the sharp turns, that was brushing dangerously close to pedestrians on the street and aggressively passing cars, speeding by the merchants' stalls with their pyramids of fruit and ugly concrete buildings covered with garish signs announcing the presence of jewelers, clothing stores, kitchen utensils, and electronic devices while the radio blared out a Latino hit in Bengali. In coming here, I was accomplishing an act of love, and that alone requires no justification.

I was planning to spend most of my time here in the Jarawa reservation. Obtaining the authorization to go there had taken colossal efforts. The Indian government doesn't like people messing around in the Andamans: it's a sensitive territory. The Indian navy chased off the famous Jacques Cousteau when he came to the area to make a film, and Claude Lévi-Strauss himself received a refusal from Indira Gandhi when he requested permission to send his doctoral students to meet the Jarawas. The fact that I was born in India made all the difference: had I been a foreigner, my application would've been dismissed out of hand. I nonetheless had to persevere for a year to get the necessary permit. I had had to appeal to high-level bureaucrats in the Ministry of Tribal Affairs to convince them that I was a serious researcher whose work would contribute to knowledge of the Jarawa culture. Dr. Pandit had supported my initiatives with a recommendation letter, and I owed to him, as well as to Dr. Roy's insistence, the opportunity to do real fieldwork. I mainly knew the latter by his articles. He had written his dissertation under the guidance of Dr. Vishvajit Pandya, a giant in my discipline, and published numerous studies in linguistics, studies of breathtaking precision. It was agreed that he would accompany me throughout my research, which made me somewhat apprehensive, for I knew almost nothing about him: other than some brief conversations on the phone, we had had no personal contact.

Paradoxically, I have little affection for academics. I speak the same language they do when necessary, but I don't really seek their company outside of work. As a rule, they come from a social class far above mine, and since, in most cases, they've scarcely risked taking a step outside of it, their narrow-mindedness soon annoys me. I immediately understood that Dr. Roy—"Sonu," as he asked me to call him—was my type of professor: someone who has a life beyond the confines of the university. We met at the front desk of a four-star hotel away from the city center. "The first round is on me," he declared, as he pulled me toward the bar where a stuffy waiter, with a fake British accent, gave him a severely disapproving look. I have to admit that Sonu clashed singularly with the hushed atmosphere of the establishment: he was barefoot in beige sandals, his short, hairy legs revealed by his khaki shorts, as were his large, round, slightly fat biceps by the rolled-up sleeves of his shirt, which was partly open on a broad, hairy chest. I thought that we would eventually leave our stools and go into the hotel restaurant, but the kitchen had closed after Sonu followed my round with a third one—he didn't like to lose at that game.

Undernourished and passably intoxicated, we had discussed

this and that, jumping from one subject to the other without ever touching on our research, except once when I tried to broach this topic, and he snapped back: "Stop right there: this evening, I'm not on duty." On the other hand, we discussed weightlifting at length since Sonu was a devotee of this discipline. He tried to impress me with his personal records, bench presses, hang cleans, back squats, and others, but since I didn't know what those movements were, I simply nodded hypocritically with an appreciative expression. He also spoke to me of his wife—a German woman he had met during his postdoc at MIT—and of their three daughters who lived in Chennai, in a large house by the sea where he invited me immediately to come vacation with Eleanor. We parted ways when the bar closed, a fact that the waiter conveyed to us curtly before the lavish tip that Sonu left him magically transformed his contemptuous manner into an obsequious smile. And in the doorway, just before getting into the tuk-tuk that would take him to his hotel, Sonu told me to get ready: in forty-eight hours, we were leaving for the Jarawas' forest.

8

The Primrose

"The survival of the crew isn't guaranteed." That's the distress
message received in Hong Kong by the owner of the *Primrose*,
a sixteen-thousand-ton cargo ship that was traveling between
Bangladesh and Australia when a typhoon blew it onto the reefs
of Sentinel Island in the night of August 2, 1981. Behind the
portholes of the ship run aground, pinned down by the fierce
winds, drenched by the heavy sea, the terrified sailors watched
the preparations of the black men bustling about on the beach.
Emerging from the depths of the island, from the secret of the
trees tormented by the storm, they streamed in by the dozens,
armed with bows and lances and dragging behind them boats
that they launched into the rough sea. Standing at the rail, the
sailors prepared to drive them back with whatever they had found
to defend themselves—fire axes, extinguishers, rocket launchers,
metal pipes. The boarding, however, never took place. The wind
blew the arrows off-course before they reached the *Primrose*,
and the skiffs of the Sentinelese, launched into twenty-foot
troughs, capsized immediately, throwing their addled occupants
onto the shore. The hostilities suspended, a long stand-off began.
Night and day, the men of the *Primrose* stood guard while the
Sentinelese waited for the moment to send them back to their
own world.

That's when Captain Robert Fore—a former fighter pilot in
Vietnam and the Middle East, now working for a drilling platform
in the Bay of Bengal—comes into the picture. Contacted by
the authorities at Port Blair, he agrees to go to the aid of the
shipwrecked crew. Despite the thirty-knot gusts that are shaking
his S-58T Sikorsky, he succeeds in setting it down on the deck of
the *Primrose* between two cranes scarcely fifty feet apart. Masterful,
he repeats this exploit three times, carrying off the last sailors who,

from the air, scan the forest where the invisible Sentinelese wait to take possession of the deserted ship.

Wrecked on the reefs, the *Primrose* is still there. Over the years, the Sentinelese have armed their arrows with the metal of its carcass that, gleaming like a whale skeleton polished by the elements, stubborn as the ruins that survive the disaster of ancient civilizations, reminds those who dream of exploring the island's depths of the danger of even approaching it.

9

In the Forest

The day before my departure for the reservation, I found a message from Eleanor. She missed me, and, on a large calendar in the kitchen, she was drawing a line through each day until my return. Her responsibilities helped her pass the time, her workload having increased since she had been put in charge of a project trying to address the opioid crisis in Ohio. The Vekner Foundation was attempting to make Naloxone more widely available, a medicine designed to block the effects of overdose. She was also working to facilitate care for addicts by offering them outpatient treatments. Eleanor eventually came to a request that she hoped wouldn't upset me. Part of her work consisted in finding donors. She had thought of my friend Markus, of whom I had often spoken when we were living in New Haven, and whose acquaintance she had made one evening, long ago, at Saint Andrew. His father was a famous philanthropist, involved in various charitable activities: he had written a huge check after Hurricane Katrina and donated enormous amounts to the public education system in Baltimore. Would I be willing to put her in contact with him, or his son, so that she could solicit a contribution from them?

I sat in front of my screen for a long while before answering. Her request put me in an awkward position, and I was tempted to refuse. I had never wanted to ask for anything from the Holmbergs, because asking for their help would've confirmed my social inferiority. To make matters worse, I hadn't been in contact with them for months, and I didn't like the idea of resurfacing in their life when I needed something from them. On the other hand, Eleanor rarely asked for my help, and I didn't want to compromise the improvement of our relationship by refusing to give it. I didn't have much time to make a decision; Sonu and I were leaving the next day, I hadn't finished preparing for the trip, and many weeks would pass before I would have access to the Internet again. Ultimately, it was my desire to be useful to Eleanor—and, indirectly, to those she wished to help—that dictated my decision: I wrote to Markus, and, to my surprise, he replied very courteously to us a few hours later, saying that he would be happy to see her the next time he was in New York. I sent a final message to Markus to thank him, to Eleanor to give her another hug, and Sonu and I left the next day for the Jarawas' reservation.

Daybreak comes early in the Andamans, and we were out by five-thirty. I was waiting for Sonu, bag and baggage in front of the hotel, when he appeared in a taxi. I shoved all my stuff into the trunk, and we drove through Port Blair. There is something evanescent in this city. The cracked walls of the houses disappear beneath layers of mold. The alleys tumble down toward the sea between rows of temples, orphanages, merchants, and haberdashers and come out onto the open sewers of Junglee Ghat. On the surface of the water, the pollution seems alive. Banks of foam break up as they flow by and then vanish when the bubbles burst one after the other. The jetties in shambles that are strewn along the coast have long been ready to collapse. They are assaulted throughout the year by the storms that traverse the Bay of Bengal by the dozen. Some cities are monumental and crush you with their lunatic pretension to last to the end of time. Port Blair is in essence temporary, as if it were apologizing for being there and preparing to pack up and go set up its camp of sheet metal and cinder blocks under more welcoming skies.

Even at this early morning hour, the traffic was dense, the air thick with the smoke of exhaust pipes. Scooters, tuk-tuks, cars, and buses were fighting for their share of the road in the pale glow of a badly besmirched dawn. I thought: these are the last images of our world that I'm taking with me. Soon we'll be living in the forest where all this—the garbage and the slaughterhouses, the blaring horns, the rows of electric poles—will seem to belong to a distant past, almost to another life. Sonu grew impatient with the driver, who was going too slowly for him; like me, my new friend was eager to leave the city far behind.

Many of us were traveling north. Ahead and behind us, buses sped along the Andaman Trunk Road. We had to slow down, move at a snail's pace, stop: a growing line of vehicles was waiting for the authorization to enter the Jarawas' territory. A few years before, the Indian Supreme Court had forbidden access to their reservation. This decision had followed on the heels of a revolting video broadcast on the Internet. The images showed an Indian policeman forcing some Jarawas to dance for a group of tourists; between two photos and three selfies, the onlookers threw them handfuls of food. The scandal had been enormous, provoking vehement appeals to close the human zoo. The decision of the Supreme Court could have put a stop, definitively, to these abuses, but it had been reversed in the end. The administration of the Andamans had obtained this turnabout by promising to ban tourism inside the reservation. Henceforth, signs prohibited the feeding of the Jarawas or filming them; it was permitted to cross their territory but forbidden to stop there. Anyone violating the new rules risked five years in prison—at least, that was the penalty set by the law. To enforce the new rules, worn-out policemen armed with old rifles came on board each vehicle, peering wearily at the visitors clumped together at the windows dreaming of catching a look at the "Stone Age tribe." In sum, nothing had changed: for around ten dollars, it was still possible to buy yourself a tribal safari. The tense atmosphere around the entrance to the reservation, the loudspeakers that recited the rules before the buses were allowed to enter, everything added, paradoxically, to the attraction of the experience for the tourists. The barrier rose, the convoy moved forward: they felt like they were entering Jurassic Park. This whole circus was no less repugnant than it was hypocritical.

The local authorities had been informed of our arrival. We nonetheless had to produce our papers and undergo the suspicious gaze of the chief of police while he called his superiors to be sure that he was taking no personal responsibility in letting us pass. After these formalities, which could have taken three minutes and dragged on for three hours, we received the permission to launch our expedition. The convoys were still waiting to enter the reservation. Their passengers pointed at Sonu and me upon seeing us enter the forbidden forest alone.

I felt a strange happiness come over me as each stride took us a little farther away from our world. I hadn't come here to seek some kind of return to the past, a presumed plunge into I know not what primitive era, what original society. I hadn't come in search of a hypothetical golden age, inspired by nostalgia for a state of nature supposedly superior to the modernity that was fading behind us. I had come to understand a different way of structuring social existence, a divergent organization of the life span allotted to us by our common condition. And I had come because the surface of the tangible world must be breached to discover the invisible universe that is revealed with its laws once you are initiated into it; and because I hoped to deconstruct my own categories of understanding of reality, of what constitutes a good and just life. I believe, in fact, that I've always dreamed of a new beginning, of being but an empty surface, a *tabula rasa* on which would be inscribed, in their irreducible specificity, the values and dreams of the people I was going to study, without ever relating them to an earlier experience to assess them, to judge them. My goal—and I remember thinking this as I followed Sonu, my eyes glued to the huge backpack he carried so spryly—was to someday achieve this ideal encounter: the meeting of a virginal mind and otherness.

The "otherness" emerged from between the branches in the form of Yaday. One would be well advised not to be fooled by his youthful air, his gentle smile, his habit of laughing between two utterances, the somewhat comical appearance he owed to his headdress decorated with moss. He had already killed—and a lot. Killed three poachers just a week before, when they had ventured into the reservation to trap wild pigs. By a twist of fate, they had become the prey. The Jarawas had hunted them down in their typical manner, several of them driving the intruders into an ambush where Yaday had, three times in a row, given the fatal blow. He wouldn't have been able to say how many of these interlopers he had killed in all. Fifteen, twenty? Perhaps more. It no more weighed on his conscience than having smashed the head of a fish on a rock in the river; it just made him feel a kind of annoyance, a general concern for the future. He didn't know when others would come, how many of them next time, and, yes, it did affect his happiness. He truly had the impression that, without them, without the threat of all these outsiders coming who had no business being there, taking what didn't belong to them, he and his people would be at peace, would enjoy a more contented life. But what irritated him above all was the hypocrisy of those people; neither he nor the other members of the tribe were taken in, they weren't fooled, not for a second. He had understood long ago that the outsiders were capable of saying one thing and thinking something else, but it still shocked him and seemed despicable to him, which proved, incidentally, how far it was from his way—from their way—of understanding the relationship between human beings. Chewing tobacco, for example (he told me this weeks after our first meeting): the poachers want to get them to do it, but they know *very well* that it's not good for them! And, nonetheless, they try to convince the Jarawas to get into the habit! And it's the same thing with alcohol: they want to get them to drink while they know *very well once again* that it's bad for them! Yaday was not to be messed with; he eliminated the poachers as if they were common pests, and that was perfectly normal, since they were worse than bad: they were deceitful.

That Sonu and I did not meet the fate of their previous visitors was due to the fact that, contrary to them, we carried no firearms; only a machete hung from my backpack. Yaday is the first to appear, and soon, all around us, other men named Bapa, Apay, Raja, Lula, Tanisha, Tangatay, and Takulu—who, for the moment, had no name since they were still strangers come out of nowhere— revealed themselves one after the other, warily, ready to use their bow at the first suspicious movement. Speaking in their language, Sonu reassured them about us; they listened to him explain that we had come in peace, that we wished them no harm, and that we were their friends, *lalay*. They told us to follow them: the adventure was beginning.

It took time, a lot of time and patience, before they finally accepted us. We were tolerated, and that was already an accomplishment, given that they were a people that had excellent reasons to mistrust outsiders. But being tolerated is still being intruders, and what we wanted was for them to open to us, truly, the doors of their world. Entire weeks went by before it was possible to begin asking them questions. To prove our good intentions, we helped them out in all sorts of ways. Sometimes, when the men were going off to hunt, they asked us to stay behind to take care of the most fragile among them. Sonu and I made sure that the older folks lacked nothing, bringing them honey and boiled pork, listening to them sing softly while the women wove baskets or those rustic headdresses with which they adorned their heads and those of their spouses, moss tiaras that made them look like little rural gods.

Sometimes the mothers asked me to watch the children. I quickly became attached to these mischievous, laughing, intrepid kids, with their inexhaustible energy, always ready to act up in the forest, whose harmonious names rolled off my tongue: Telo,

Teonay, Tawalay, Mitaela, Umamay, Idamowo … With them, I had to restrain many expressions of concern stemming from my upbringing. It wasn't uncommon for a little child to use a sharp knife to eat, and a voice in me cried out: he's going to hurt himself! But no, not at all: baby Pilu handled the blade without anyone becoming alarmed and without ever doing himself the slightest harm. Or the children ventured into the jungle, and I thought they could get lost there, meet a wild animal; I feared everything for them, the ground with its jagged stones, the river where they risked drowning … But Onia—one of the Jarawas mamas, always in good humor and coquettish with her crown of white bark, her red dress, the fine edging of yellow pigment that streaked her skin—watched them leave with her customary laugh and without worrying about them. "The babies need to have fun!" she said before breaking out in a fit of giggles, her neck bent backward, eyes half-closed and turned toward the sky, as if she were inhaling, like a plant in the sun, the joy that defined her.

There was a river in the forest that the kids knew well; it was one of their favorite playgrounds. They headed there in groups, dashing through the jungle. I followed these naked little children, with their plump bottoms and round bellies, accompanied by the older ones, as elegant as deer with their long, slender legs. Some of them had necklaces of fine white pearls around their hips, others a purple ribbon sticking to their skin. Having arrived at the river, the kids climbed along the roots of a kapok tree, climbing as high as possible and, with no hesitation, jumped into a waterhole, jumped with their legs straight out or their knees upwards, jumped with their legs spread, all alone or several at a time, into the flowing water where they disappeared for a moment, emerging a little further away grinning from ear to ear and ready to begin the adventure again. Quickly, they climbed back up the roots and threw themselves again into the cold water that was streaming down their backs, following each other so closely that it was a row of gleaming toddlers hurling themselves into the river, a veritable waterwheel of flesh, rapid and nonstop.

The adults too have their games. One day I accompanied a group of Jarawas to a sumptuous prairie that stretched out between two curtains of jungle. There were eight of them— Bapa, Apay, Raja, Lula, Tanisha, Tangatay, Takulu, and Yaday—precisely the same hunters we had met, Sonu and I, the first day in the forest. They were practicing with their bows, trying to shoot their arrows as far as possible. Included in their group, I admired how they drew back the bow aiming high, their knotty muscles as tense as the string, their gaze as piercing as the projectile that suddenly sprang forward at an incredible speed, traveling such great distances that it was impossible for me to see where it landed, while they, with their superlative eyesight, clearly identified its position when it embedded itself in the grass. They shot, and when the arrow disappeared, their body accompanied it momentarily in its flight, their torso bending forward, one leg remaining straight and planted in the ground, while the other lifted gracefully to serve as a counterweight behind them.

In its leisure activities, the so-called prehistoric tribe proved to be remarkably restrained. Each arrow drew very simple, rather redundant, remarks: "that arrow went far"; "it's way over there!" But there was nothing aggressive in these judgments, nothing, in any case, that resembled the savagery of sports rivalries in America. It was as if each arrow was independent of all the others; each one a full-fledged act in its own right, with no connection to any past event, and no relationship either to any following arrow that would renegotiate its meaning, transform the master stroke into a lesser exploit. Each arrow was like the present moment when you conceive it alone: eternity itself. When they handed me the bow to try my hand, I understood that I had just taken a prodigious step toward them.

Yes, Sonu and I progressively gained their confidence by living among them, like them, eating and sleeping as they did until they felt comfortable enough with us, in the evenings, when we were resting at the camp, to have with us the personal conversations on which we took detailed notes that we then had to protect against the humidity and rain. The Jarawas shared with us their memories of British colonization and of even earlier times, when they first arrived on the island. They had only retained vague notions of this; all they knew was that they had come from somewhere else, perhaps by boat, and that since this infinitely distant period, they had remained here, hunting wild boars and living happily. Their myths were like the flames that, at night around the campsite, projected flickering signs on the dark canvas of the forest: I sought all the hopes and fears, all the aspirations and worries that were embedded there.

When the Jarawas referred to what was outside the reservation, they invariably said, "the other world." They saw it as something appalling. "Your world is bad, it smells bad. The forest gives us what we need, we have no need of you," Yaday explained to me one day. "Here, everything is so beautiful. The flowers are magnificent. In the evening, we're together, we stay near the fire, we talk, we sing songs, there are so many songs." Yaday was serious when he said that; his gaze, usually joyful, grew deeper, weighed on me, and I had the impression that he saw in me not just an interlocutor but a spokesman, someone who would eventually go back to where he came from and would convey his hope, the hope of all of them, to finally be left in peace. Yaday had good reason to be concerned. He saw clearly that major changes were underway, that this road that cut through their territory was the precursor of still more dramatic upheavals, and after it, if the Jarawas weren't careful, more and more outsiders would come until they replaced them, the people who had been living here from time immemorial.

Four months went by on the reservation. Sonu was perfecting his knowledge of the Jarawa language—this bulky bodybuilder was a subtle linguist—while I studied their beliefs. It is important to understand that the Jarawas conceive the universe as a structure of multiple dimensions between which the spirits move. With neither soul nor bones, these spirits fall into two categories. The first includes the natural phenomena like earthquakes, thunder, rainbows, and storms whose occurrences indicate the movement of the spirits throughout the archipelago. The second category is comprised of the dead and is itself divided into two groups. When someone dies, their body undergoes funeral rites that transform it into a benevolent spirit. But if the dead do not receive the appropriate rites, they enter the class of hostile sprits that fight with the Jarawas over their resources. The post-mortem duties thus take on a vital importance for them.

I had already observed this metaphysical struggle between the human and the spirit worlds among the Onges and noted the way in which, far from being in servitude to supernatural forces, the living possessed the power to affect their decisions. Among the Jarawas, I discerned a similar belief in the interdependence of the visible and invisible worlds, the practice of rituals being the means to orient the actions of the spirits that, in turn, influence people. In other words, the Andamanese idea of space is remarkably dynamic.

For them, there is no fixed hierarchy between, let's say, the sky, the earth, and an underworld where hell would be located, no more than there is a Creator and creatures who would be naturally subordinate to it. In their perspective, reciprocal power relations characterize the interactions between human beings and spirits, who constantly renegotiate their relative situations. The visible world and its spiritual counterpart communicate permanently while demonstrating their underlying identity, each of them liable to find themselves in a situation of subjection or authority. I published a book on this subject, *Of Spirits and Men: The Religion of the Andamanese People*—the culmination of a decade of studies and these months of research among the Jarawas.

Difficult in many respects—I lost twenty-two pounds in the forest—this time with the Jarawas nonetheless passed too quickly. We had received the authorization to stay four months with them, and it is precisely when it finally seemed to us that we had found our place among them that we had to leave. In saying our goodbyes—and, several days later, in taking leave of Sonu too, who couldn't wait to get back to his wife and daughters—I felt an immense fatigue. Leaving Eleanor had been a much more difficult test than I had imagined, and I suffered again in leaving the Jarawas, who, from the vague group they were initially for me, had been, little by little, transformed into a collection of irreplaceable individuals, each of them engaging for various reasons. The fact is, you leave a part of yourself in all those you meet, and perhaps traveling, quite far from enriching us as is commonly thought, is in fact this experience of progressive dispossession, shreds of ourselves clinging to the places that have touched our hearts and to the beings who found their way there too. Traveling: a loss of oneself by successive pieces rather than an awestruck initiation into the world's beauty ... We left the reservation all the sadder as the likelihood of ever returning was virtually nonexistent.

Before returning to the United States, I had a dozen days left in Port Blair. I spent them typing on the computer the handwritten notes I had taken in the forest, talking on the phone with Eleanor for hours to relate to her what had happened during the months without contact, and answering an interminable list of emails. When I wasn't working, I was walking the streets mulling over the impression—and all the melancholy and calm that came with it—of having arrived at the end of an era in my life. Something was coming to its definitive end; I could feel it. I had finished my fieldwork, my return home was imminent, and more deeply, I was done with this period in which an abstruse need drove me to flee to the end of the world. I wanted to be back with Eleanor and begin a family. I won't deny that my resolutions were still sometimes shaken by the memory of Eva, but every time it came back to me, I repelled it immediately, repeating to myself the list of all the things that separated us, her and me. I had finally understood that being an adult was precisely that: foregoing possible things. And putting all the energy you waste by dreaming of another life into an effort to enhance your own. Mine would continue with Eleanor and, I hoped, the child we would have one day; all the time spent with the little Jarawas had increased my desire to be a father. But before leaving, I had something left to do. It was my last chance: I didn't think I'd ever have the opportunity to return to the Andamans.

One Sunday morning, I took the bus to the Mahatma Gandhi Marine National Park, a dozen miles west of Port Blair. On the way, I saw everything I had forgotten about while in the forest. There were fitness centers and recreational water parks, luxurious and interchangeable hotels like the ones in Miami or San Diego, and, a little farther on behind a fence, open garbage dumps where piles of filth arose in a vile mixture of broken plastic, maggots, and rot. Parabolic antennas stretched up into the sky from the roofs of concrete buildings with pieces of colored canvas serving as doors, and we passed by sawmills that were patiently gobbling up the forest to spit it back out in the form of beams and pencils. As we approached the coast, the rice paddies gained territory beside, here and there, patches of jungle that were surviving for the moment but would eventually be wiped out in their turn. In five, ten years at the most, this is what we would see everywhere on the archipelago: modernity without aesthetics, urbanization without any central planning, the rich in their gated compounds and all the others in their tumbledown shacks open to the winds. The days of the Jarawas were numbered. Soon their forest would be destroyed, replaced by hotel complexes and amusement parks. Throngs of foreign tourists would jostle to take a selfie with the last member of this thousand-year-old tribe before moving on, happy with these spoils, leaving the ancestor to die at the side of the road.

At the entrance to the Mahatma Gandhi Park, the passengers got off the bus and onto a ferry. There were around twenty of us, a handful of Europeans—I could hear snatches of German and French as I strolled on the deck—and a majority of Indians come from the subcontinent, members of the middle class sufficiently wealthy to vacation on the beaches of the Andamans. The ferry set us down on a desert island where we were free for three hours. Young married couples held hands on the shore, striving to appear perfectly happy before the lens of a photographer seizing this exceptional moment that would find its place, framed, on a piece of teak furniture in a Calcutta suburb; and in a few decades, after their deaths and those of their children, would finish in another open garbage dump. A little farther on, obese gentlemen ventured into the water up to the waist and, stretching out on the surface with a mask, floated around looking for fish that fled at their approach.

I had come here because I had heard that, from this island, when the sky is clear, it's possible to catch sight of *it*. So, I began to walk up the coast to the northwest, leaving the other visitors behind me. When we left Port Blair, the weather report promised a sunny day, but the horizon had darkened since then, somber masses moving across the sky. Sitting on the bank at the westernmost point of the island, entirely alone, I was looking for it through the clouds when, finally, it was revealed, very far off, like a minute mirage. Sentinel Island. My trip was over. Something in me finally let go at this precise moment: I had reached the end of what I had come to do in the Andamans. All I had left to do was go home with the nostalgia of those days spent with Sonu and the Jarawas, while knowing full well that it was good and normal that they were finished, and that I had the whole rest of my life to build.

But before I began the return trip, I spent a long moment observing the forbidden island, whose very view made me feel an immense joy. An immense joy at the idea of never going there. My fascination with it, encouraged by that of Markus and reinforcing his when we spoke of it for hours, tipsy, in the lounges of the secret society, now appeared to me as something childish; it was one of those objects that the words of others lead us insidiously to desire, but which, upon closer examination, reveal no actual link with our true ambitions. I was filled now with an experience that compelled me to sweep away this project that I had once contemplated with Markus: going to Sentinel Island. It would have been—how should I put it?—a sacrilege. I thought again of the Jarawas, threatened by the development projects on their territory.

I thought again of the Onges, melancholic, confined to their Dugong Creek reservation, whereas the entire Little Andaman had once belonged to them. And I hoped that the Sentinelese would be able to stay as far from us as possible—in their interest but in our own as well. They held the torch, you understand, the torch of everything that is enchanting and remains inaccessible, of everything that is spellbinding but escapes you, of everything that lets you glimpse marvels but never comes true. They were like my love for Eva: the frustration of our desire and the guarantee that it is possible to desire again. For all of us, it was essential that they survive, for they preserved, intact and fragile, something of the beauty of the world and something like a promise that one day we would be pardoned.

10

A Moment of Epiphany

The profession of anthropologist is thankless, I should know. Work relentlessly to gain the confidence of a people, and you will perhaps experience, after twenty-five years of efforts, a brief moment of epiphany. Dr. Pandit had his *in extremis*. It was in February 1991, when his career was coming to a close. Instead of repelling him with cries and arrows as usual, the Sentinelese greeted him graciously when he went on one of his visits to them. They came to meet his team pleasantly, smiling, and unarmed. Four Sentinelese were confident enough to come on board his boat to grab a sack of coconuts. Meanwhile, Pandit was handing out others to the Sentinelese who had come to meet him in the lagoon where he was standing in water up to his waist. A photograph immortalized him at this moment: the one I saw, three decades later, in his living room in New Delhi.

His companions slowly move away—move away so far that Pandit is now nearer to the Sentinelese than to the lifeboat. This is the moment. A moment of joy, of devotion to the task at hand, of complete forgetting of the risks, and, especially, of familiarity with these men who expose the sumptuous beauty of their black skin, the vigor of their naked bodies, the light of their radiant smiles. Pandit forgets the time and the danger. But the youngest of the Sentinelese suddenly becomes suspicious, pulls out a knife, and threatens with an angry gesture to cut out his heart. Is he afraid that Pandit intends to stay on the island? The young man reminds him that he is just an intruder among them. The moment has already passed. The boat returns for Pandit, who climbs in, shaken but safe.

That moment was like a day of beautiful weather that pops up in the middle of winter and is soon only the delightful memory of a spring long gone, like those loves that you desire for a long time, and that give you a fleeting pleasure—a kiss, a brief embrace—before being denied, leaving us the keen regret of something that will never be. It was like all the happiness that one feels before cloying has replaced enjoyment: an interval stolen from the implacable logic of time.

A few months after this miraculous visit, Pandit reached retirement age and said goodbye to the Sentinelese. And four years after his epiphany, the contact missions were put to an end once and for all. The Sentinelese had resumed their usual mistrust of outsiders, going so far as to hack one of their dinghies to bits with their adzes. The winter of 1991 will have been a mysterious exception and not the end of the tribe's resistance, without the return to the former order of things being more comprehensible than the brief calm of the Sentinelese. The moment of grace had passed, and the temporal parenthesis had closed, this time for good.

11

December 23rd in Newark

I returned to America at the beginning of the summer, and we left immediately, Eleanor and I, for the house on a lake that a friend was lending us. We filled the car with groceries and books, resolved not to leave the place until the end of the vacation. Our friend had described this property to us as a simple "cabin in the woods," so we thought we would find a rudimentary log cabin like you see in the West. Concealed by the woods on a foothill, it was in reality a huge three-story house whose superimposed terraces looked over a narrow lake of blue-green water. Other houses were scattered throughout the forest, but most of them were vacant, or their occupants, just as protective of their peace and quiet as we were, avoided emerging when they saw us outside. When I think back on this period, I recall a perfect solitude, as if we hadn't seen or met absolutely anyone for ten days; a period so calm that it too, perhaps, is floating somewhere outside time, with Eleanor and me continuing to rediscover each other after a six-month absence, embracing in the living room or swimming in the lake, a period that was like a ship adrift, unfettered, lost forever.

Eleanor and I would go down the steps that led to the dock and dive together into the lake, then swim along the shore. In the evening, we would go back out on the water in the boat, with chilled wine; I would row along the banks where slender trees rose up as straight as columns, guide us to the center of the lake, and let us drift at the mercy of the waves in the waning daylight. Lying on the floor of the boat, our heads touching, we would talk and talk for hours about her plans for the Foundation and about all I had seen over there, in the Andamans. It was on such an evening that we decided to have a baby. I took us back to the house, and in the master bedroom on the top floor, we made unprotected love.

Back in Columbus, I continued the manuscript of my book, *Of Spirits and Men.* My goal was to finish it in a year because my tenure depended on it. The idea of becoming a father was ever-present in my mind, and I was working even harder than before, as if I already had a responsibility toward this unborn child. I was more in love with Eleanor than I had ever been and was no longer drawn to Eva, whom I saw on campus regularly when the semester began. I was still surprised by my complete lack of emotion when I learned that she had become engaged to Edmond during my stay in India. I was happy for her and couldn't have cared less for myself. I had made a choice, the choice of this life with Eleanor, the choice to have a child with her. Sometimes I thought that without Eleanor I would be about as lonely as one can be in life. My parents and my sister had been dead for ten years; my closest friends, like Markus and Victor, were disappearing little by little from my existence; I was living thousands of miles from my birthplace; my only family was Eleanor. She traveled regularly for the Foundation, and our relationship had never been so harmonious. One Sunday at the end of November, when she had just returned from a two-day trip to New York, she said to me, "Let's go for a walk this afternoon."

We took the car to go to a park we liked, a park whose turquoise lakes are astonishingly deep, having flooded former quarries. Eleanor was wearing a chocolate-colored coat. We were walking along the shore when, out of the blue, she retreated a couple of steps to observe my reaction and announced, "There, I'm pregnant." I began to cry, as if I needed to be consoled for what I wanted more than anything, as if it wasn't precisely what I was hoping to hear. But intense joy always leads you to pain, because it is impossible to feel it without thinking of those who will not share it, of what they would have said about it, and how they would have experienced it; and perhaps also because in receiving what you desired so intensely, you discover how deeply you needed it, and you are sad for all the sadness you would have felt if you had been denied this happiness you had so yearned for. If we had a boy, he would be named Oliver; if a girl, we would call her Iris. I would've liked to give the child an Indian name, but Eleanor disagreed, saying that it would create problems at school; as always, I gave in. We began preparing for the holidays, and when Eleanor handed me the decorations for the tree, I told myself, "It's wonderful; next year we'll be a family."

Two days before Christmas, Markus's was broken. Returning from Newark airport, his parents died in a car accident.

12

9.1

9.1 is the size of the 2004 earthquake off the coast of Indonesia. The energy released is one thousand five hundred times that of the Hiroshima bomb, enough to make the planet shift on its axis and the effects felt in Alaska. The resulting tsunami is the most destructive in the history of the world. It measures 115 feet, the height of an eight-story building. Forty countries are struck across the Indian Ocean and as far as East Africa. Located near the epicenter, the Nicobar Islands are devastated. A fifth of their population is wounded, killed, or missing. On the island of Sumatra, the city of Banda Aceh mourns sixty thousand deaths, a quarter of its inhabitants. In all, the tsunami counts two hundred and thirty thousand victims of around sixty different nationalities.

Sentinel Island is not spared. Before the disaster, it had a surface of approximately twenty-eight square miles. A wooded islet, Constance Island, was located around six hundred yards from the southeastern coast. The earthquake tips the tectonic plate beneath the island, lifting it up six feet. Vast stretches of coral reefs are exposed and become dry land, increasing the area of Sentinel Island and uniting it with Constance Island.

On December 28, 2004, the Indian government sends a helicopter to take stock of the damage to Sentinel Island. The pilot observes thirty-two individuals at three different spots on the island without seeing a single corpse; he pulls away when a volley of arrows is shot at his aircraft. After that, the world is astonished: the Sentinelese have survived the catastrophe better than the Indian colonists. Just look at that indomitable courage! The brave natives stand up to the flying machine just like they defied the tsunami! This exceptional resilience is accompanied, nonetheless, by an enormous fragility. In redrawing their territory, the earthquake profoundly affected their way of life. All around the island, in place of the ribbon of sandy shores that once enclosed it, there was now reefs of dead coral that separate the Sentinelese from the sea. Since 2004, it is much more difficult for them to reach their fishing grounds, and their chances of survival are further diminished.

The catastrophe separated us even more from them. Those coral plains come between us when we observe them from the deck of a ship, and they watch us from the edge of their forest. For the Sentinelese, too, the 2004 earthquake is a key event in their history: their entire world has changed.

13

Mourning

Samantha and Joakim were returning from Singapore. I can imagine them getting into a taxi, impatient to get home after a twenty-hour trip. The driver hurries to load their baggage into the trunk and get back behind the wheel; for a moment his face disappears behind the fog his breath causes when it encounters the frigid air. There is snow on the shoulder of the road; the traffic is dense and the outskirts of the most fascinating city in the world are extraordinarily ugly, with all those rows of houses backing up to the freeway and all those signs advertising an umpteenth fast-food restaurant or the next strip club. Samantha and Joakim have made this trip over and over again and know that it will take at least an hour. They lean against each other, ready to doze. Irritated by a car going to slow for him, the driver changes lanes, overtakes, loses control of his vehicle, and crashes into the guardrail. He gets off with a few bruises; the Holmbergs are not wearing their seatbelts and are killed instantly.

Joakim lost his life just as he was savoring a new triumph. In Singapore he had attended the inauguration of his fifth gallery. It was going to increase an already incredible sales figure: during the two days they covered his death, the media all reported the staggering sum of a half-billion dollars in annual profits. In the segments on CNN and MSNBC, and in the articles devoted to him in the *Times*, the *Tribune*, and the *Post*, the focus was on his philanthropy rather than his activities as a gallery owner. Joakim had built hospitals in Haiti and orphanages in Honduras, given colossal sums to Baltimore's public schools, and underwrote the fight against the opioid crisis in the Midwest. The Vekner Foundation was mentioned several times, Eleanor having persuaded Joakim to make a donation after meeting him through Markus. She was shocked by the disappearance of the Holmbergs; I was, too, with a mixture of ill-defined feelings. I thought that if I could choose my death, Joakim's would be to my liking: leave without seeing it coming, with the person I loved …

I send my condolences to Markus. I was hurt when he did not invite me to the funeral: I didn't know Samantha very well, it's true, but I had a sincere affection for Joakim, and I would've liked to say my goodbyes to him. When I shared my disappointment with Eleanor, she replied that Markus must be overcome by grief and receiving so many expressions of sympathy that he didn't know what to do with them. He had forgotten to invite me, okay, but how could I hold that against him in these circumstances? I felt guilty and told her that she was right, as always. She had to go to New York for her work and, among other appointments, meet with Markus to learn if his sister and he intended to continue their father's commitment to the Foundation. She would take advantage of their meeting to give him my best and tell him how sad we were for him and his family. Before she left, I had a bad feeling about it, and I said to her repeatedly, "Are you sure you want to go? Isn't it a little risky?" She laughed, replying that I was being stupid or saying that she was in her first trimester, and there was nothing "risky" about taking an airplane. It's because of what happened afterwards that Markus's theory on déjà-vu became little by little a sort of key to understanding the events of my own life: I had *already seen* the moment when I drove my wife to the airport. I also recognized, when they occurred, those several seconds while Eleanor was walking down the hall after going through security. The shape of things was bathed in a different light, a light that set this moment off in the flow of my consciousness, giving me the troubling sensation of a premonitory lucidity.

The next day I call Eleanor in the afternoon, for no particular reason, just to say hello and make sure that everything is alright. No answer, so I let it drop: she must be in a meeting. I try again around an hour later: still no answer. Then another time and another. I put the phone down and return to my computer. I have a class to prepare; it's no use continuing to call. She'll find my messages when she finds them; there's nothing to worry about. The minutes go by. I can't concentrate, I can't stop thinking about the disturbing impression I had yesterday when I left her at the airport. I see her again leaving with her bag over her shoulder and little suitcase covered with stickers rolling behind her, her black hair flowing down to her shoulders. I pick up my phone again and leave her a voicemail. A half-hour goes by. I hesitate, telling myself I shouldn't bother her while she's at work; then, what the heck, I call the office of the Foundation in New York. Yes, Eleanor was there this morning. Yes, she's already left, around noon. No, she didn't say where she was going. Okay, we'll let you know if she comes back. I set the phone down, another hour passes. Anguished, I give up trying to work; to find some relief I tell myself that I just need to do something to keep busy, anything, clean the house for example. I run the vacuum cleaner, stopping every ten seconds because I think I heard the telephone ringing beneath the humming of the machine. Night falls, it's already six o'clock. The anguish has become intolerable, transfixing me as I sit in the armchair beside the living-room window. I go over all the perfectly possible and banal explanations of Eleanor's silence: she lost her cell phone or forgot her charger or ... But from the beginning, I suspect that *something* has happened—in fact, I *know* what is behind this something: it's our child. Eleanor had an accident, and the baby is dead; I'm more and more sure of it with every minute of silence, every minute while the night thickens outside the window. I think of Markus: the major mishaps in life, we know them in advance, for the mind of a human being contains its entire future from the moment of birth.

Eleanor called at around 11 p.m. Her voice was so weak that I could barely hear it; I had to hold my breath so that it wouldn't blot out her words. She was at the hospital and bashed me immediately with the truth: "I miscarried; the baby is dead." I answered, "I'll be there as soon as possible," but she said, "No" with the peremptory tone she always adopted to put an end to a discussion, "I want to be alone. They have me under observation until tomorrow; I'll be home in two days." I tried to insist, but she repeated, "No!" angrily, "listen to what I'm telling you for once; I don't want to see anyone." I knew that my place was beside her, just as I knew she would not budge. "Okay," I answered, "tell me what happened, how you're feeling." The doctors weren't sure but thought that an infection could've caused *it*. She had lost a lot of blood, but all in all she was doing well, she just needed to rest. She hung up quickly saying, "Goodbye" and nothing else, as if we were taking our leave after an argument, as if, for reasons she alone knew but that would be revealed in due time, I was responsible for this new misfortune. I looked around the room. I was sitting in the same living room as two minutes before, and nonetheless I had entered another universe where the child I had imagined in this very place, one day, lying on its stomach and then taking its first steps on the rug, would never come home to us.

I went to get her at the airport. She was wearing the same clothes as the day she left; everything was identical in appearance. In the crowd of travelers, who could have suspected, seeing us so calm and reserved, the priceless thing we had lost and the torrent of emotions we were managing to control? She remained silent and hostile until we were on the freeway, then began to weep silently, her face against the car window, with a low, continual moan, as she must have done as a little girl when she was the victim of some injustice, and I held her hand as I drove her back to our empty house.

14

Flight MH 370

Ten years after the 2004 tsunami, the Sentinelese are involved in another catastrophe. No one has forgotten the Malaysia Airlines flight that disappeared between Kuala Lumpur and Beijing with two hundred and thirty-nine passengers on board. "Good night, Malaysia 370" was its last communication, on March 8, 2014, at 1:19 a.m. What ensued is a mystery. Did the plane go down in the China Sea or in the Bay of Bengal? Did it land in Kazakhstan? Was it blown up by a bomb? Did the pilot commit suicide, or did a drop in cabin pressure cause him to lose control of the plane? He might have continued his flight above the waves for hours until the lack of fuel plunged it in. The investigators searched throughout the Indian Ocean and in the pilot's past, digging up troubling details that yielded nothing definitive. False passports among the passengers did not prove it was an act of terrorism. And among all the theories that arose at the time, one of them is related to the Sentinelese.

It originates with a note by Roy W. Spencer, an American meteorologist. Reading it today, one is struck by its careful tone. The scientist shares a simple observation: while he was visiting the NASA Worldview site in March 2014, he noticed a plume of smoke coming from Sentinel Island. "I doubt," he writes, "that there is a connection to the missing Flight MH 370, which would be a real shot in the dark. But it is a strange coincidence." The very same day, the theory of a crash on Sentinel Island is dismissed by a certain Jim Thompson, who publishes testimony from the Andamans: the smoke began several days before the vanishing of the Boeing 777; it was certainly coming from a fire lit by the Sentinelese. Spencer thanks the contributor, and that's the end of the story for him. But it's only the beginning for the internet crowd, who transform his conjecture into a plausible explanation. There is a flood of articles online: Flight MH 370 went down on an island of prehistoric hunter-gatherers; imaginations soar at the idea of the cannibal feasts they undoubtedly organized.

Paradoxically, it is the history of a people with no knowledge of the Internet that provides a textbook case of conspiracy theory. A simple hypothesis is advanced in a corner of the worldwide web to call into question some official conclusion. Since no one goes to the trouble of verifying the credibility of the source, the initial supposition becomes a proven fact that takes on gigantic proportions through the embellishments of the prejudices, exaggerations, obsessions, and gratuitous allegations of anonymous contributors throughout the world who respond and encourage each other. This anecdote also demonstrates how, beneath an appearance of something new, the perennial obsessions persist. The castaway of yesteryear becomes the survivor of today; the smashed fuselage replaces the wreck on the reefs; and the phantasm of a Westerner facing savages on an island, this phantasm of returning to the past that always implicitly proves the so-called superiority of the White Man, endowed with his industries and the innate advantages of his race, likewise remains identical.

15

The Labyrinth

Eleanor decided that her name was Iris. In fact, no one knew the gender of the child we had lost, but she was convinced that it was a girl, and that we would have named her that: Iris. The months that followed her miscarriage became a countdown before the "birth"—Eleanor had arbitrarily chosen a Sunday in August to celebrate it, and we were approaching it as one would an inevitable catastrophe, with the inexorable progress of a ship heading straight toward an iceberg when it is too late to change course. I remember this as the past conditional period: we *would have been* at four, three, two months from the birth; we *would have organized* the baby shower; we *would have bought* a stroller ... Sometimes Eleanor spoke of these things in hushed tones, sadly, with tears, and I understood: she was grieving. We were mourning what *should have* happened. But other times, she evoked the alternative world in which Iris wasn't dead, with—how should I put it—a kind of detachment. She could declare, "At this stage, Iris would've been kicking in my stomach" in a completely factual way, with the same tone she would've used to talk about the weather report; the next day, she began to sob, repeating, "We would've already sent the announcements." I tried to console her as best I could, but our relationship worsened dramatically after the so-called "birth" she had obsessed about for months. That's when the nightmare really began.

An idea had taken root in her mind, whose progression I could follow by the suspicion-laden look she gave me, a look that seemed to say, "I can't believe what a monster this guy is," as if she were becoming aware of a monstrous plan of which I was the Machiavellian author and she the innocent victim. It had begun with a cutting remark directed at me out of the blue: "In fact, you never wanted this child." I answered calmly that she was mistaken;

I had even waited for many months for her to make up her mind to begin a family. She made no reply, but a little smirk made it clear that she was unconvinced. A week later she attacked again, this time with a direct accusation: "You didn't take care of me enough when I was pregnant; it's your fault if I lost the baby."

At these words, and before replying, by a strange turn of mind, I again thought of Eva. Eva: my way out and my refuge, Eva now married to another and whom I had let slip by once again, although, by an extraordinary combination of circumstances, the vicissitudes of life that had called her back to Moscow had also brought her back to me. Eleanor was looking at me, waiting for me to respond, with the bestial agitation that grips people when they prepare to tear each other apart, but I lingered a last time, before plunging into this struggle, in the mental company of this other woman who henceforth appeared to me in a new light. I had thought that her return was a sort of test that I had to pass to preserve my marriage and build a family with Eleanor. But what if it had been just the opposite, that I had been offered this final opportunity to be joined with her before resigning myself to seeing my life ruined one more time, one time too many? The death of the child was not just an accident. It was foreseen, written that it would come to pass; it was the result programmed from the very beginning, the one that was awaiting me inevitably if I missed the chance embodied by Eva, the chance I had stubbornly turned down, and which would have freed me from Eleanor for good. Markus had perceived something, something fundamental, in sketching out a still incomplete theory of the inexorable and foreseeable character of key events in one's life, a theory through which I was now reading my own. Have you ever held in your hands a game that consists in guiding a marble through a labyrinth and out the other end? People are like those metal balls: enclosed in their labyrinth, they bump into one obstacle after another before disappearing. But, very rarely, a door opens on the side letting them into another story, a second labyrinth that they zigzag through before arriving where we all end up, but by a different path. I had missed my exit with Eva and was now locked in this maze, locked in with Eleanor.

I knew I had to be patient, knew she had lost a child, and that my role as husband was to support her. But I too had lost this child, and it was never about my sorrow, it was always she who had to be consoled, protected, patched up after this misfortune or that disappointment, and her saddling me with the responsibility of the miscarriage was an additional burden, one load too many for me to bear. I began to yell with a sudden aggressiveness that surprised me and shocked her, revealing to myself the depth of the exasperation she was provoking in me. To yell that she had no right to accuse me, that she was crazy, nasty, and self-centered, that I would not let myself be destroyed by her, she should get that through her head. She was stunned for a moment, like you are when you get hit on the head and stagger before responding to the violence with even more violence, and that is exactly what she did: she spewed out a litany of reproaches, and even more than their cruelty, it was their sickly coherence that shocked me the most, the rigorous manner in which they displayed an internal logic without ever relying on the slightest objective criterion. I was astonished to discover their articulation, the faulty but implacable reasoning that bore witness to the long hours spent brooding over them, weaving in her head this web of specious arguments in order, once again, to force me to admit that I was guilty, a hundred, a thousand times guilty of her setbacks.

I had forced her to become pregnant; she hadn't wanted a child. I exploded, telling her that she had said the opposite the week before—which made no difference to her: for Eleanor, the truth consisted in what served her interests at that moment. What's more, I had abandoned her, neglected her, more concerned with my work, my career, and my book than with her, who had felt sick and sad, which had led her—she was sure of it, she felt it deep down in her heart—to suffer this miscarriage. She was crying, and there was something demented in her eyes, eyes in which I was the enemy, the one she was looking at with a mixture of anger and indignation for all the wrongs he had done her. A couple is sometimes like a cavern where two chained animals tear each other apart. I told her that her concussion had changed her, damaged her, that every year she was becoming a little more abnormal; I couldn't stand her constant depressions and crises anymore, and if she didn't stop it, I was going to leave her. She dared me to do it. The next day I rented an apartment, and two days later I was gone.

I found myself in an outrageously expensive one-bedroom apartment in the center of Columbus. I had taken no furniture from the house, except for the mattress of the guest bedroom and an armchair in black leather that I had placed in the center of the living room where it sat, absurdly alone, in front of the windows from which I observed the roofs and lights of the neighboring buildings while the vague murmur of the city drifted up to me, sometimes intensified by the siren of a police car speeding on its way. I told myself, "We're taking a pause, that's all, a pause in our marriage, that's what we're doing. We're not going to divorce, well, perhaps not, it's just that, for the moment, it's better to stay apart and reflect." But I had to admit that I wasn't reflecting, not at all; I sat for hours on end in my armchair in the middle of the empty room, my mind full of memories, flashes: I saw again our meeting one spring evening, when some friends had introduced us at the Thirsty Scholar, a bar on Second Avenue in New York. I also thought of the death of my parents and my sister and all the ordeals Eleanor and I had been through, convinced that they were what had held us together, like two battered wrecks that eventually lock together and make common cause against their disaster, always tossed about but withstanding the torment, finding some comfort in the struggle but in fact two wrecks all the same, with their empty hearts.

It is in this context that my friend Victor, now a lawyer in New York, sent me a message to see how I was doing. I didn't have the courage to pretend I was doing fine, so I told him, "I'm having problems with my wife; we're probably going to divorce." He immediately invited me to come see him: being in the big city would give me a break. I took the plane one Friday after my last class, my return scheduled for the following Monday morning. Most of what happens in our life is predictable, more or less identical to the following week or the one before. Without really knowing why, I was convinced that this weekend in New York was full of possibilities, that *something* was going to happen, something that would reshuffle the cards of my life, redesign my labyrinth.

16

Soli Deo Gloria

I do not wish to speak ill of John Chau. He's a young man who died far from home. Repeat those words after me while imagining what they mean: he's a young man, who died far from home. Of course, our era makes it easy to judge. On the Internet, mobs of anonymous people tear to shreds anyone who dares to disagree with their beliefs. Conservatives or liberals, it's the same intolerance, the same quickness to demonize others. I do not approve of the reasons that prompted John Chau to go to Sentinel Island; I think they belong to another time, and that living with too many certainties, you end up dying for them. But it would be inconsistent on my part to condemn him. That would suppose that I too am sufficiently convinced of the soundness of my ideas to take pleasure in the misfortune of those who do not share them. So I wish to keep in mind these very simple facts: John Chau was twenty-seven when he died; he left a family that loved him, and, from his perspective, sacrificed himself for the felicity of the Sentinelese.

Of course, his fascination with the forbidden island reminded me immediately of that shared by Markus and I. It also forced me to face this question: how is it possible for an idea, a single idea among the billions that a brain is likely to conceive, to colonize it like a parasite, to go from a peripheral to a central position so that everything is related to that idea and depends on it, like a monstrous spider lurking at the heart of the neuronal connections? The obsession of John Chau—bringing the Gospel to the Sentinelese—took hold of him by stages.

The first stage comes from his childhood: the idea intruded into his mind by way of a dream, an innocent-looking dream born from a book. John is ten when he declares that one day he'll live on a desert island. It's 2002, and he's just finished reading *Robinson Crusoe*. Yes, he continues, when he's grown up, he'll live all alone on an island like the one described by Daniel Defoe, and he'll spend his days harpooning jellyfish, swinging in the trees, and jumping into the sea. His father laughs at this child's dream. But the idea does not go away over time; it adjusts its form to continue more effectively its gradual domination of its host.

The second stage takes place in 2008. John is a junior in high school when he participates in the building of an orphanage in Mexico. This experience persuades him that being a Christian, a real Christian, consists in changing one's life to obey Christ's commandments. And didn't Christ command the following: "Therefore go and make disciples of all nations, baptizing them in the name of the Father and of the Son and of the Holy Spirit, and teaching them to obey everything I've commanded you"? Upon returning to the United States, John wonders which peoples have never heard the Good Word. He does some research on JoshuaProject.net and discovers the existence of a mysterious island in the Bay of Bengal, an island whose inhabitants have had no news of Christ. The "Sentinelese people need to know that the Creator God exists, and that He loves them and paid the price for their sins ... Pray that the Indian Government will allow Christians to earn the trust of the Sentinelese people, and that they will be permitted to live among them ...." At this stage, the idea grows incessantly; day after day it grows stronger through all the efforts it calls forth. It becomes a goal, a project, a life choice. A year after learning of their existence, John announces his decision to bring Christ to the Sentinelese. He is seventeen years old. He is convinced that the island and its people were created for him.

Years go by. Sentinel Island does not appear to be his priority; one might even believe that he is no longer thinking about it at all. He enrolls in Oral Roberts University in Oklahoma, an evangelical institution where his father, brother, and sister had been students before him. What will he do after graduation? He speaks of becoming a doctor. But far more than his studies, it's the outdoor life that excites him. He spends all his free time fishing, hiking, climbing, and kayaking. With his bachelor's degree behind him, he begins to travel: he visits South Africa and Israel, India and Kurdistan. Back in the US, he takes solitary hikes along the Lost Coast in California and in the mountains in Washington. He trains as a "Wilderness Emergency Medical Technician." The life he lays out on Instagram is that of an adventurer, although he calls himself an "explorer." He survives a fire in North Cascades National Park and narrowly avoids an amputation after being bitten by a rattlesnake in California; he goes cougar hunting, rappels down cliffs, feeds on strange berries. He counts among his heroes the naturalist John Muir and the American missionary Jim Elliot, killed in Ecuador by the Huaorani. John belongs to that long American tradition that includes Henry David Thoreau and Christopher McCandless: the tradition of metaphysical vagabonds. More precisely, he is a Christian vagabond: to be a missionary is to combine the thirst for adventure with the passion for Christ. "Soli Deo Gloria," he writes as a caption for his photos on social media: "Glory to God alone." It's a clue, a clue that he is not losing sight of his objective. He says nothing to anyone, but he is thinking of it constantly. All the experience he is accumulating is preparing him for his goal: to reach Sentinel Island.

In 2015 and again the following year, he spends time on the Andamans. He keeps to himself the real reason for these visits. It is forbidden to set foot on Sentinel Island; he'll be expelled if the authorities learn his intentions. His father, for his part, suspects what he is preparing to do. When John returns to America, he tries to get him to change his plans. He tells him repeatedly that he has brainwashed himself, that he's chosen in the works of the preachers he admires all the passages that can justify his so-called "mission." John replies that it is his duty to go to Sentinel Island. The tribe is condemned to eternal damnation if its members never hear the Good Word, and who better than he, who has been preparing himself for it forever, to save them? God himself is calling him to go there. He chose him for this role before his birth; everything confirms his vocation, including the initials of his name and the color of his skin. An American of Chinese origin, in the Andamans he physically resembles a Burmese minority, the Karen, and fits easily into their group. His father can do nothing to shake this conviction. They quarrel at the end of 2016; two years later, John lost his life.

During the months he has left, he fine-tunes his preparation. In Kansas City he joins an evangelical organization whose specialty is making contact with isolated peoples. His training finishes with a full-scale simulation exercise: he hikes for hours through a rural area until he reaches a pseudo-native village where Americans dressed in strange costumes greet him babbling in an incomprehensible language. John distinguishes himself during the exercise; he is, according to his instructors, one of the best participants ever to face this. Then, for nine weeks he takes courses at the Canada Institute of Linguistics on how to learn unknown tongues. The other students remember how he always had his nose in phonetics and phonology texts, unless he was reading work upon work on anthropology. His preparation is physical as well. In Cape Town in the dead of winter, he launches his kayak into the frigid waves to toughen himself up. He watches what he eats, jogs regularly, gets vaccinated against thirteen infectious diseases, and engages in constant strength training sessions. John takes all possible precautions to be in excellent health in order not to bring any illness to the Sentinelese. He doesn't know how much time he'll spend with them: five, ten, twenty years perhaps? For that, he has a plan: he'll draw in the sand or in his waterproof notebook; he'll learn their language in order to translate the Good Word. He'll make his first converts among the most influential members of the tribe, who will then help him persuade their fellow tribesmen. And when he has built his church, he'll send to the Jarawas native missionaries who will bring them the Gospel in their turn. John calmly envisaged spending the rest of his life on the island. He never came back. His body stayed there, under the sands of Sentinel.

Autumn 2018 is the last trip: he returns to Port Blair. Barely arrived, he begins the first phase of his plan. Okay, numerous sources repeat that no one understands the language of the Sentinelese, but he had read a minority theory put forth by certain historians of the island according to which it is possible for the Sentinelese to communicate with other Andamanese peoples due to the partial overlapping of their vocabulary. John will not go to the Sentinelese alone; he'll convince a member of another tribe to serve as an interpreter. He tries his luck first with the Jarawas, visiting their territory illegally. First failure. Then he turns to the Onges. He takes a ten-hour ferry ride to reach their reserve on Little Andaman Island. He attempts for two weeks to persuade them: in vain. He returns to Port Blair alone. An important part of his plan has just collapsed, but he is not deterred. He passes immediately to the next stage. A friend on Grand Andaman serves as an intermediary with a crew of fishermen. They're Karens, members of that Christian minority John has integrated. For twenty-five thousand rupiah—around three hundred and fifty dollars—they agree to take him to the forbidden island. On November 14, 2018, John meets them at nightfall. In the diary that records his last moments, he cries out again: "Soli Deo Gloria."

The crossing begins badly. They have to avoid the coastguard that prevents people from reaching Sentinel Island. Under cover of darkness, the narrow rowboat—discreet, almost invisible—should be able to thread its way through. But there is the Milky Way in the crystal-clear sky that casts light on them and the luminous plankton in the sea that reveals them from below. The halo is so bright that when a fish happens to jump out of the water, it looks like a Siren draped in light, cutting through the night like a shooting star. But God—John is convinced—favors his mission. He and the fishermen accompanying him pass under the nose of the Indian navy, as if the Almighty Himself were wrapping them in a mantle of darkness.

In the Bible, Peter renounces Jesus three times before the cock crows. John's faith is similarly put to the test—at least that's how he interprets the repeated warnings of the Sentinelese. On November 15, he approaches the shore for the first time. He's in his kayak when two Sentinelese armed with bows emerge from the forest screaming. "My name is John," he calls out to them. "I love you and Jesus loves you. Jesus Christ gave me authority to come to you. Here is some fish!" The Sentinelese nock arrows and turn their bows toward him. John is frightened and paddles with all his strength to get out of range. As he rows away, a Sentinelese with a crown of flowers around his head stands on the highest rock on the beach and scolds him loudly in a language he cannot understand. When John tries to reply with hymns and sentences in Xhosa, a South African language, the Sentinelese are silent for a moment, then burst out laughing. He returns to the boat where the fishermen are waiting. It was his first test—or his first admonition. John is disappointed that the Sentinelese didn't accept him immediately; he implores the Lord to grant him His holy protection.

The same day, John decides to return to the island. He stands on the shore, his waterproof bible in his hand, in front of a group of Sentinelese, men, women, and a child. He recites to them the beginning of Genesis: "In the beginning God created the heaven and the earth. And the earth was without form and void; and darkness was upon the face of the deep, and the Spirit of God moved upon the face of the waters. And God said ...." The child shoots an arrow. It pierces the bible that John is holding chest high and stops at Isaiah 65:1–2. John breaks the arrow and rushes into the sea, abandoning his kayak. The Sentinelese do him no harm, letting him swim away to the boat that is waiting for him. They've just given him a second warning, but John again believes he's received a sign. What does the Bible say at the verses that stopped the arrow? "I revealed myself to those who did not ask for me; I was found by those who did not seek me. To a nation that did not call my name, I said, 'Here am I, here am I.' All day long I have held out my hands to an obstinate people, who walk in ways not good, pursuing their own imaginations." This obstinate people that is seeking the Lord without knowing it is the people of Sentinel Island. John is convinced of it. "Lord," he writes in his diary, "is this island Satan's last stronghold where none have heard or even had the chance to hear Your Name?"

Then comes November 16. John hesitates, considers retreating to Port Blair, wonders who will take up his mission if he abandons it, and finally decides to return—a third time—to the island. He is completely aware of the danger and has a premonition that this attempt is one too many. In a farewell letter to his parents, he asks them, if he is killed, to pardon his murderers and make no attempt to recover his body. And he defends himself one last time: no, he is not crazy, and his plan is in no way futile; the eternal life of the Sentinelese is at stake, and he expects to meet them one day, assembled at the throne of God, singing His praises in their language. "I hope this isn't my last note," he writes, "but if it is: to God be the glory—I'm heading back to the hut I've been to. Praying it goes well." John asks the fishermen to let him off on the island and not to return until the next day. Two reasons drive him to make this decision: he thinks he has a better chance of being accepted by the Sentinelese if they see him alone; and in the opposite case, he wants to spare his friends the spectacle of his death. They take him to the island and leave with his diary and farewell letter. And following his instructions, they return on November 17. It is then that they observe, from their boat, movements on the beach. They approach. Enough to see the Sentinelese dragging something on the sand, a body dressed in black trousers, John Chau's body, that they bury in the sand.

Perhaps you remember the debates his death occasioned. For several days people spoke of recuperating the corpse of John Chau. Consulted on this subject, I was strongly opposed. It was on CNN. I had been contacted a few hours before to give my views on his disappearance. My book, *Of Spirits and Men*, was going to be published soon and made me one of the few specialists of the Andamans in the United States. I explained, live, that an operation on their island would put the Sentinelese in danger by exposing them to germs that their immune system is unable to fight. And I rejected the arguments for a possible punishment, since voices were calling for the Port Blair police to go and arrest the murderers of Chau. I reminded people that he had gone to the Sentinelese of his own accord, illegally, and declared that it made no sense to seek the guilty ones in a tribe that does not have the same concept of justice, and who, in this instance, had protected itself against an intruder after giving him several warnings.

That evening I spoke rather harshly of John Chau and, as soon as the interview was over, felt guilty about it and never entirely pardoned myself afterwards. I accused him of irresponsible behavior in putting the Sentinelese at risk uselessly; of having sought to impose his religion on them without having the slightest knowledge of theirs. I even ascribed to him a form of "cultural imperialism." In setting myself up as a defender of the Sentinelese, I was revealing that I too was convinced of the justness of my cause; I had certainties as unshakeable as his while I was reproaching him for having shown arrogance in prescribing for others his conception of the world. This inconsistency became clear to me later when I read the message his parents had posted on Instagram after his death, a message full of dignity in which they asked people to respect their son and pardon him. In the preceding pages, I hope to have shown more compassion.

Here ends my history of the Sentinelese. I began it with their origins, fifty thousand years ago, and followed it up to the death of John Chau in 2018. It is the last important event in the series of contacts between their world and ours—or the last at least before the one that directly involved Markus and me.

17

Manhattan

You find yourself singularly vulnerable when a misfortune appears on the horizon but has not yet occurred. When a parent is in the hospital, and no one can tell you if he will survive; when you fear you're going to lose your job, but your employer hasn't yet made their decision; when you are perhaps going to divorce, but a reconciliation is still possible. It's in those moments that living becomes really dangerous. You no longer follow your normal routines. Especially, you have less to lose than ever before—or that's what you think in any case—so you take risks that you normally never would. It is in this psychological disposition that I arrived in New York: ready for anything and not knowing what to expect, as if what was going to happen was no longer up to me but consisted in a series of situations that would decide my future without my being able to exert the slightest control over them. I'm not sure I'm making this state of mind clear to you. It is a rare experience, and it suspends your normal thought processes so that you think of it later like you remember a bad dream, without knowing what really happened ... I had the feeling that chance and my will power no longer existed, that I was only an empty shell that would let its behavior be dictated by the circumstances, whatever they were, because they would indicate a predetermined plan that it would be inconceivable not to follow. In those moments, everything is a sign, a premonition, destiny; everything is fraught with meanings and enigmas. In those moments, a life can just as well change direction as return to its former course, and the difference was due to almost nothing. That's what you think of again later, imagining, filled with dread and regrets, the future that did not come to pass.

It was a surprising pleasure to see Victor again. He came to get me at the airport in his Miata convertible—"I hardly ever use this bad boy; thanks for giving me the opportunity"—and even if we hadn't seen each other since graduation, it was as if we picked up our friendship exactly where we had left off. Conversation flowed easily between us; I saw that he was being tactful where my wife was concerned. We would get around to talking about it, but later, after two or three drinks no doubt. Meanwhile, he questioned me about everything that had no direct relationship to her, about the Midwest and the university and about that guy: "I've forgotten his name, the one who went to your island to convert those poor Sentinelese. Bravo, by the way, for your interview on CNN: that was a class act." Victor was in great shape, still slim but more muscular than before—"I'm into CrossFit; don't get me started or I'll talk your ear off about it for two hours." His only problem consisted in finding his work too easy; things were going so well that it was becoming routine; sooner or later he would need some new challenges. Perhaps he would try to get himself transferred to an Asian office: "Have you ever been to Hong Kong? I can see myself spending two or three years there." Yes, really in great shape, with the joyfulness of people who have a bank account with a six-figure balance and, an added insolence, are young enough to take advantage of it.

"Do you have any news of Markus?" I finally asked him as he poured me a second Japanese whisky in a crystal glass. We had already spoken of friends we were slowly losing sight of because they were pursuing their respective ambitions thousands of miles away, knowing all the while that at the first contact—which was precisely what was happening between us—our friendship would spring back immediately, as lively as before, abolishing time. Truth be told, I wasn't at all sure I wanted to talk about Markus; I was even pleasantly surprised we had been able to discuss Saint Andrew for a good quarter hour without feeling obliged to pronounce his name, since the kind of authority he exercised over us then now seemed irritating and unjustified to me. But at the same time, he was beginning to blend together in my mind with those years at Yale that, from a distance, and all the more so since my personal life was beginning to unravel, appeared to me in that deceptive halo of nostalgia that conveniently obscures the worries that plagued us then and highlights, as if they were part of a continuum, moments of happiness that were in fact rare and scattered.

Victor's face darkened. "I never could stand that guy," he answered. I remembered that they weren't particularly close when we were in college, Holmberg Junior being very selective in his friendships. Individuals who didn't interest him for whatever reason didn't exist for him; that is, he did more than just ignore them, intentionally show them what little regard he had for them: he simply did not register their presence, his mind being a photograph with holes in it, like when you're determined to forget a former partner after a breakup and cut them out. Victor had belonged to those figures missing from Markus's vision of things, and he still resented this negation of his person. I took a petty pleasure in encouraging someone else to speak ill of the absent party, without being guilty of it myself, to listen to all the reproaches we shared, but that I didn't have the courage to articulate. Victor didn't need much encouragement to say what he thought of Markus; there were, indeed, volumes to say about his infinite pretentiousness. But what proved to me that my feelings toward him were really complex was the concern I felt when Victor peddled the most recent rumors about him: "The guy is going off the rails, if I understood correctly."

"You are, of course, aware of his parents' death," he continued. "I wasn't invited, but it appears that the funeral resembled the Oscars, with all the rich and famous people who attended. In short, weeks went by after the ceremony, and the pressure very quickly became intense: Markus had inherited the galleries, and he had to make all the decisions. In addition, there's the annual exhibition to organize, so everyone was waiting to see what he's made of, the artists and, even more so, his competition. It was the moment to make a name, or rather a first name, for himself. Except that Markus suddenly disappeared."

"What?"

"He left without telling anyone for that island where his parents had a house, not Nantucket but a posh place of the same type ...."

"Block Island?"

"Yes, that's it! He disappears off to his island, and while His Majesty plays at Robinson Crusoe, his sister Alexandra takes over the business and manages to organize the art show."

"Good grief! When did this happen?"

"Last March. You'll say that he's perhaps going through a rough patch, and this is his way of mourning or taking a step back before assuming his new responsibilities, but the problem is that six months later, the guy is still frittering away his days. When he got back to the city, he started haunting night clubs and posting on Instagram with Youtubers and starlets. If you search online, you'll find a mess of "celebrity" articles that track him in all the trendy spots. Meanwhile, it's his sister who's managing the galleries while he does nothing, *nada*, *niente*. He's not even working for the publishing house his father put him in charge of. A pensioner before thirty."

"Frankly, I can't believe it. He was so brilliant, so ambitious ... He'll surely get ahold of himself; he just needs a little time."

"Do you really believe that? You're pretty generous. You know what I think?"

It was a rhetorical question. Victor continued immediately.

"It's the first, the *very first* time in his life that he has to respond to a real challenge. All the rest, everything he had before, was given to him; he never had to work seriously for anything. And when the Little Prince finally has to show what he's made of, his only response is to flee. Pa-the-tic," Victor concluded, separating the syllables with utter contempt. Then he emptied his glass, smacked it down on the table, and asked, "Wanna go out?" in a manner that made it clear that as far as he was concerned the matter was closed, and he didn't want to hear any more about it.

We got back around two in the morning, and at six-thirty, Victor was already up. I heard him lock the door behind himself; he had informed me that he would be back early evening. Indestructible, Victor was going to spend an hour at his famous CrossFit gym before putting in ten hours at the office. A real machine, with a minimal need for sleep: for certain things, people are really not equals. I had the whole day to enjoy New York, and I began by going back to sleep until ten. Wrapped in the linen bathrobe Victor had lent me, I had a cup of coffee while answering my email. Then suddenly, although I hadn't written him since the death of his parents, I sent a message to Markus to let him know I was in Manhattan for two days, and if he was free, I would be pleased to see him. In fact, I wasn't at all sure that I would really enjoy spending time with him; two minutes after closing my computer, I no longer knew why I had contacted him, and somewhere within me I hoped he would be too busy. But when I received his brusque answer that afternoon as I walked up Fifth Avenue, it hit me with the violence of a breakup: he wasn't in New York this weekend and would see me another time. That's all. It felt like I was losing everyone at the same time, my wife and my best friend. The crowd around me reminded me how alone I was.

Back from work, Victor changed immediately to go out again: it was Saturday night, and the city was ours. My professor's clothes looked old-fashioned beside his Italian suit, and when I commented on it, looking pitiful, he led me into his dressing room saying, "That's no problem, you and I have about the same build." I tried on shirts with cuff links and fitted jackets until I found something Victor wouldn't be ashamed to be seen with me in, after which he took me to dine in a Korean restaurant. Then we took an Uber to the Upper West Side. The streets were full of girls with short dresses who could've been models, and since Victor was a regular, the bouncer let us cut in line and go up to the roof where he had reserved a table. Victor must have felt that he had been sufficiently discreet, because he asked me, as soon as our drinks were served, "So, what's the problem with your wife?" I hesitated, stirring the ice cubes in my Old Fashioned, then told him everything, beginning with Eleanor's concussion, and taking him through our quarrels and incompatibilities, up to the miscarriage and our separation.

"You know I'm not qualified to give advice to a couple. I've only had one serious relationship, and it finished so badly that he moved to San Diego to put the whole continent between us. But do you want me to be honest?"

This time it wasn't a rhetorical question. I knew that if I answered yes, it was at my own risk: Victor would not spare me. There was sometimes a ferocious glee in his sincerity, as if he took pleasure in trampling those conventions that, most of the time, raise strict barriers around what we can do and say.

"Go ahead."

"I believe you haven't been in love with her for a long time. You speak of her as if she were a constant burden. That isn't normal. Note: I'm not saying that *you* aren't normal; I'm saying that it isn't normal in a marriage."

"You think I'm wrong to see things as I do?"

"No, that's not what I'm saying. It's neither true nor false, good nor bad: it's just what you are feeling at this point in your relationship. You can't always control everything, you know."

It was a very simple idea and, nonetheless, I felt he had just articulated a fundamental truth for me.

"In fact, you're afraid above all to find yourself alone. You're staying with her because you consider her your family, and family is, by definition, something you can't leave; you always remain attached to its members in some shape or form. Even me, despite everything that's happened, I still worry about my father ... And after the death of your parents and your sister, what could be more normal? You sought comfort and stability wherever you could, and Eleanor, at least at the beginning, brought you precisely that. But a spouse is not a father or a mother, someone with whom the bond remains indestructible no matter what; it's—how should I put it?—always your solitude bound up with theirs, and if the contract that consists in making each other happy is broken, it's better to give each other their liberty back."

I had come to New York to drown my sorrows and forget my problems; Victor was forcing me to face them and make a decision. I was going to answer when I spotted, a few tables away, a face that seemed familiar to me. Victor turned to see where I was looking: "You've got to be fucking kidding me," he blurted out, confirming that he too had recognized Markus. As soon as he saw us staring at him, Markus said something to the two young women sitting at his table and got up to come greet us.

"Good evening, gentlemen. How're you doing?"

Standing beside us at our table, he forced us to twist our heads to look up at him. I got up to shake his hand, immediately regretting my show of deference. To counteract that, I asked, a little too brusquely, "What are you doing here? I thought you weren't in New York this weekend."

"My plans changed at the last minute. Happy to see you, Victor," he said, shaking his hand too.

"Would you like to sit with us for a moment?"

Markus turned toward the table he had left: a young woman with black hair, slender, impeccably made up, wearing a short dress, gave him a fashion magazine smile.

"I imagine I can abandon them for a few minutes."

Markus grabbed a waiter hurrying by, and while he listened to the list of cocktails, I observed him, noting that he had changed. He was still just as handsome as ever, but something in him was different from before, something I could only describe with the word "corruption." His features had softened, and his whole attitude—for example, his manner of listening to the waiter without deigning to look at him—exuded self-satisfaction, whereas he had always seemed nervous and restless before, always in search of something. The calm that emanated from him was not that of an individual who has reached his goals; it was that of a man who has given up pursuing them. When the waiter brought him his drink, and he began to talk to us, that's when the evening changed course, and I began to lose control of the events.

I had decided to come to New York with the premonition that *something* was going to happen, and while Markus—slightly thickened, with sensual wrinkles at the corner of his eyes that made him look older—talked easily, unconcerned with having interrupted our conversation or left his friends at his table, I suddenly became aware that I had *already seen* this scene. I had already seen the black waiter who was passing behind him, the dark blue shirt that Victor was wearing, the jerky movement of the dancers behind him, the very short, gray, glittering dress of a girl who seemed much too young to be here. How can I make you understand what distinguished this instant from all the others? It was as if my mind were a film shot in color, into which the director had inserted an altered, sepia-colored sequence, in slow motion. Ever since the day at the airport in Columbus when I had had a similar experience, just before Eleanor's miscarriage, I had understood what these impressions of déjà-vu really are: warnings.

To my surprise—and even, very quickly, my dismay—Markus began to speak to us of Sentinel Island, like a person who always finds a way to return to a subject they're obsessed with. He began by alluding to my interview on CNN, immediately criticizing what I had said. Okay, John Chau went to the island illegally, but did the Indian government really have the right to restrict access to it? Either the Sentinelese were independent, and India had no business controlling access to their territory, or India owned this island, but by virtue of an illegitimate appropriation that called its sovereignty into question. I answered that the question of rights changed nothing about the duty to protect a vulnerable people, but he didn't listen to my objection, and, as if to justify John Chau's initiative by showing that it was part of a very long history, he began to evoke the preceding contacts between the West and Sentinel Island. Why was he talking to us about that, after all those months of separation? Suddenly, he interrupted his rant and said to us, "Do you want to join us?" That was the breaking point.

Sitting at Markus's table, his two friends were looking at us. I had never seen two women so attractive. In the movies, on the Internet, sure, but inaccessible creatures, belonging to a world with no possible relationship to mine and probably virtual, because, unless the image has been doctored, how can an appearance correspond so precisely to what men desire? I turned toward Victor, who gave me a sharp look. Just as before, in New Haven, I was forced to choose between him and Markus. He awaited my decision, and I knew what I should have answered; I knew I had come to this bar with him, a friend who was concerned about me, who had taken me into his home; I knew that he didn't like Markus, and that he would refuse his invitation. But I also felt that *something* was waiting for me over there, at that table, and that closing the door on this story would leave me with yet another regret. For a brief moment I thought of Eva, of that night when her hand on my forearm had made me draw away; I thought of all those instances when I had done what I was supposed to do rather than what I deeply wanted to do. For once I was going to see what happens, what reward and what punishment there is in following one's desires. I accepted Markus's invitation. He got up immediately, and I could see the annoyance in Victor's look. He said he was tired and was going to go home; I offered to accompany him, but we both knew I had already made my choice. He shook our hands, and I would've liked to see more understanding in his eyes, but I was certain, with an instant pang of guilt, that I had hurt his feelings, and that it would take time to get him—perhaps—to pardon me for preferring Markus to him once again. He disappeared leaving a banknote on the table, and I followed Markus to his table as if I were entering uncharted territory.

The redhead and the brunette were named Jana and Olga. I was so intimidated that I was very nearly disagreeable with them. I felt like an old uncle who was completely out of place here—they were twenty-three or twenty-four years old—and who is acting stupidly reproving. Fortunately, I had Markus on my side; he ordered drinks, and one more glass helped me find it less incredible for them to look at me like that, as if it were perfectly normal for me, an anthropology professor, married, feeling far older than I really was (I was thirty-three that evening), to be sitting at a table with them in a very trendy bar in New York, two friends who were sharing a room in Brooklyn and who—that's how Markus had introduced them to me—"had a *great* future in fashion." They talked at length about designers and photographers I'd never heard of—Markus held forth on them as he used to do on Conrad or Schopenhauer. I began to play a role, that of the intellectual who knows nothing of this world but deigns to show an interest in it. Instead of writing me off as some lame academic (which they would doubtless have done if I had appeared to apologize for my ignorance), Jana and Olga took it upon themselves to educate me—and I pretended to be hard to convince, which caused them to redouble their efforts. By means of one or two exaggerations, Markus succeeded in elevating me in the eyes of the two girls by saying that I was a famous college professor who had lived for months with dangerous tribes and could be seen regularly on CNN. I became as exotic for them as they were for me. Then Markus invited us to have a drink at his place. Jana and Olga looked at each other, smiled, and accepted—I just went along with it. Twenty minutes later, an Uber let us off at our destination.

All four of us were in Markus's living room. Olga and Jana gazed ecstatically at the signed works on each wall. While Markus prepared our cocktails, I stayed motionless in the room, yes, virtually frozen in place, certain that it was my last chance to leave. Markus came in with a tray before I could decide, and I found myself sitting on the couch beside Olga, with Markus on my left and Jana in an armchair. I grabbed my glass and looked around the loft, with its huge picture windows, all the lights of the city, and the dark mass they defined: Central Park. There was a sort of heaviness in the silences between our exchanges, like a weight on my chest that slowed my breathing down. Markus was smiling mysteriously and reviving the discussion each time just before it died out, stretching out this ambiguous moment at will until he said to Jana, "You're so far away; why don't you join us?"

We are taking up all the available space on the couch, so she sits on his lap. She puts her arms around his neck and, with her right hand, gently strokes his hair. Olga and I watch them; she appears amused but at the same time attentive; she finds the spectacle they're putting on fascinating. Markus plunges his face between Jana's breasts and his hands in her smooth red hair. They kiss and, quickly, Jana slides down between his legs; on her knees before him, she opens his trousers, takes out his penis, and puts it in her mouth. Olga turns toward me, and like you jump from a rock into the sea far below, I lean toward her and give her a tender kiss; I'm so afraid of repelling her that I move my hands very slowly, taking great caution, brushing against her breasts rather than touching them. She returns my embrace and opens my shirt, kisses my chest and, sliding in her turn between my legs, takes out my penis and begins to lick it with her little pointed tongue. Markus groans beside me; I see Jana change her rhythm, going very quickly sometimes, then taking his penis out of her mouth and pressing it against her cheek and her eyelids before swallowing it again. Olga turns her large brown eyes toward me and works her mouth up and down my penis. Markus groans louder and, his arm stretched out on the back of the couch, squeezes my shoulder as he goes into a spasm and comes, at the very moment that Jana takes him out of her mouth. A stream of sperm hits her in the face; she licks what is still dripping down his penis and with her finger methodically wipes the semen she has on her cheek and lips into her mouth and swallows it. Olga goes faster and faster, and when she gently squeezes my testicles in her hand, I ejaculate into her mouth with a loud groan. I remain with my head resting on the back of the couch, eyes closed, like a castaway who has just reached a beach and has no idea where he is.

Olga brings me back to life by licking my penis, which soon becomes erect again. I open my eyes: Markus has disappeared with Jana. Olga takes off my shoes, then my socks, my trousers, underwear, and shirt, before leading me by the hand toward a bedroom where she puts a condom on me. She pushes me onto the bed, disrobes in front of me, and does a slow pirouette so that I can admire her body, with a smile like she probably does in front of the camera, and when she is lying beside me, I caress her breasts, hips, and clitoris, penetrating her with one finger then two, and slipping between her legs, it's now my turn to lick her at length while she grips my hair. Finally, she tells me to take her. It's the first time I've been unfaithful to Eleanor; my hands haven't touched another body for years. We can hear cries from the other room; Olga's get louder; for a moment it seems to me that there is a sort of competition between her and her friend; there is perhaps one between Markus and me, too. After the orgasm, I literally collapse. Alcohol and fatigue dig a pit that swallows me up.

Hands on my chest awaken me. I don't know how long I slept; I open my eyes and see Jana. Olga has disappeared. Mechanically, still half asleep, I embrace Jana, take her breasts into my hands, let her take off my condom and put on another one. I'm already inside her when I see Markus's figure in the doorway. He stands there for a long moment, motionless, watching us; then he comes to the bed, and Jana turns her head to kiss him. He takes a bottle out of the nightstand, squeezes some clear lubricant into his hand and, spreading her buttocks, patiently prepares her while she is astride me. Then he takes her by the shoulders and, drawing us onto our side, he sodomizes her very slowly; I can't tell if Jana's groans come from pleasure or pain. Inside her, I can feel his penis a fraction of an inch from mine. In the half-light, he is looking at me over Jana's head and suddenly penetrates her more vigorously, without worrying about hurting her and ignoring her pleas to go more slowly: we reach orgasm together and ejaculate at the same time. The three of us lie on our backs in the large bed, breathing hard, saying nothing. Exhausted, drunk, I fall asleep again. When I wake up, the apartment is empty.

THIRD PART

A belief in a supernatural source of evil is not necessary; men alone are quite capable of every wickedness.

Joseph Conrad, *Under Western Eyes*

I get dressed in overdrive and slam the door shut. Three seconds in front of the elevator, and I'm already out of patience; I look for the exit and run down the stairs. Out of breath, disheveled, I see the doorman, who says, "Good morning, sir." I lower my eyes and hurry by without answering. Outside, I walk so quickly that I'm almost running; I can't wait to get away, to leave something behind me, although I don't know what it is. Early Sunday morning in the swanky districts of New York: hardly anyone in the streets. Women in sports garb, pushing a stroller in one hand and holding a mug in the other, look at me suspiciously as I pass by. Ten minutes at that speed calm me down a bit. I go into a Starbucks, order a black coffee and, leaving with it, walk more slowly while waiting for the burning liquid to become drinkable. Without intending to go there, I find myself in Central Park.

Sitting on a bench, I mechanically watched the jocks go by, one after the other. Hordes of runners were being passed by squads of cyclists, riding fancy, spindly machines that seemed on the point of breaking under their weight. My coffee was lukewarm when I finally brought it to my lips. Christ, what did I do last night? I thought, so that's what you find when you follow your desires: this appalling mixture of pleasure and guilt. I could've stayed with Victor last night; after turning down Markus's invitation, I would've felt a regret tinged with irritation against myself, that's about all. I made the opposite choice, and what did I get out of it? I couldn't deny it, I had experienced a disturbing voluptuousness. Making love to those two young women had given me more pleasure than I had ever had before, but it left me with an immeasurable malaise: I had been unfaithful to Eleanor, which would certainly destroy our marriage if she learned of it. And then there was Markus, what had happened with him. I couldn't even think of that, or rather I couldn't accept what that revealed about him and me. I simply did not have the courage to draw the obvious conclusions, to put into words what had happened. That night put into question the bases of my sexual identity, certainties anchored in me since my adolescence concerning who I was. In the fascination he had inspired in me for years, did I need to recognize a form of sexual attraction, repressed up to now? And in his behavior last night, a reciprocal desire? The violence of the pleasure I had felt did not come from those two women alone, from the emotion provoked by those gorgeous and new bodies possessed by mine; it came also from the participation of Markus. I was stunned by what that night revealed about me.

I wanted to know what time it was, but I had forgotten my watch at Markus's place, which aggravated me no end. My parents had given it to me when I turned twenty—this watch much too expensive for them and on the back of which they had had my first name engraved. Go back there or ask him to send it to me? For the moment, I didn't wish to have any more contact with him. I stopped a passerby: it wasn't nine yet. I had slept less than four hours, and the day that had scarcely begun seemed like an interminable tunnel. I would've liked to be back in Ohio already, not in my desolate apartment but in our home, with Eleanor. I headed for Victor's building; I had to go back to his place to get my things. His expression was icy when he opened the door, but a second later, after looking at me more closely, it turned into concern: "What happened to you? You look awful." I didn't have the courage to lie, so I told him everything, haggard, sitting hunched in his kitchen while he prepared breakfast. When I fell silent, he just said, "Eat," then, when I had swallowed the scrambled eggs and the vegetarian sausages, "Go to bed, you need to sleep." I complied, like a guilty child.

Toward four o'clock, we went out for a walk. I had a headache, and he lent me a pair of sunglasses to make the glare more tolerable. We just returned to Central Park, where we walked for a long moment. The trees were disoriented, ochre and yellow in places, budding in others, caught between the end-of-summer heat and a hint of chill that announced the coming of autumn. While Victor was speaking to me, I thought, I'm extremely lucky to have him for a friend. He didn't hold it against me that I had accepted Markus's invitation the night before: "Hey, I found those two girls pretty sexy too," he said. "You must've had a good time, you little bastard," adding that yes, some part of me was perhaps attracted to Markus, but I didn't have to control my desire; in any case, I wouldn't be able to put it in a cage if it wanted to get out. I was perhaps bisexual or just attracted to certain men, but who cares? He knew I wasn't homophobic, but it was also an opportunity to prove it by accepting that part of myself, as I said I accepted it in others. As for Eleanor, he had already told me the previous day, before I had cheated on her, what he thought of our relationship. For him, the die was cast long ago; I just hadn't yet accepted the fact that it was over, but I would eventually. "You'll see; give yourself some time, and you'll make the right decisions." I listened to him in silence, the mildness of the air and gentleness of his voice taking the edge off of things. When he took me back to the airport the next day, I made him promise to come see me in Columbus: thirty years later, we're still friends. I look at him and see him again on that day when he opened his door to me and forgave me, when he took care of me in a moment of weakness. There are movements of generosity whose consequences last your whole life.

Back in Columbus I didn't contact Eleanor for a long time. I taught my classes, went to meetings, continued my research, and did the administrative work that was required of me, but as if despite myself, or rather as if I were two different people at the same time: the one who did these things mechanically and the other who watched him from a distance thinking what's the use. The preceding summer I had applied for tenure, and I watched indifferently as my file went through the various committees that had to evaluate it. As it passed through each stage, my colleagues congratulated me warmly, and I thanked them with a show of forced enthusiasm. What had seemed to me supremely important a year ago scarcely interested me now. I was living alone; Eleanor and I would never have a child together, and I found little interest in striving for myself alone.

She's the one who took the first step. She wrote me, "Let's have a drink next Saturday," without asking if I was free: I was simply summoned. I let a day or two go by before answering, in part because I wasn't sure I wanted to see her but mostly to show a semblance of independence. I knew what was going to happen if I gave in to her. We were going to meet like two strangers in this bar; we would make love in my apartment and then have discussions and arguments and, in the end, return to our normal situation, our life before—before the loss of our child and that weekend in New York that, a month later, seemed like a monstrous dream of which nothing remained other than a disconcerting mixture of malaise and guilt. Answering this message was tantamount to falling back into Eleanor's web. I finally said yes as if I were bowing before a superior will, as if, in fact, I had never had a choice.

Everything happened as I'd foreseen, except that the violence of the scene surpassed what I had imagined. Eleanor's anger was more intense, her reproaches more bitter: I had abandoned her after her miscarriage; I was a monster. I tolerated her crises by remembering what I had done in New York. Perhaps she was right: I was certainly a bad person. I handed over the keys to my apartment and went back home with a strange feeling of defeat. I agreed to everything, to the appointments with the marriage counselor that cost me a fortune to hear in front of him the same reproaches I endured in private; to all the whims of Eleanor who, to compensate for the love I was incapable of giving her anymore, adopted one, two, three, four cats and soon many more, turning our house into an animal shelter. She spent an untold amount of time on adoption sites, comparing the respective virtues of cats that she subsequently spoke of as if they were children that were going to live with us: "Should we choose Babette or Dylan, he's so cute, he looks like he has a really attractive personality." I finally threw in the towel, answering, "Why don't you just take both of them, if you prefer?" The house was crawling with more or less crippled felines who jumped on us and sank their claws into us without warning, covered our couches with layers of hair, and cost another fortune in visits to the vet and in food that we ordered by twenty-five-pound bags. When I opened the door to the basement where they spent the night, the overexcited creatures scrambled wildly to invade the living room. I put up with that along with the rest, telling myself, there is an abysmal void in Eleanor, she fills it up however she can. Only once, I tried to tell her that, when she was ready, if she wanted to, I would like us to try again to have a child. She began to weep, hugging one of the cats against her on the couch, like a little girl putting a stuffed toy between herself and all the ugliness in the world.

Since I was no longer getting what I needed from this marriage that I was incapable of escaping, I finally registered on a dating site, telling myself that I was just looking. I checked it out at night when she was in the bedroom—Eleanor knocked herself out with antidepressants and usually went to sleep around nine o'clock, while I virtually never nodded off before one in the morning. In discovering one of these sites for the first time, I had the impression of an enormous sexual liberty, as if all those available women were really potential partners. My excitement faded very quickly. The vast majority of the women I contacted didn't bother responding to my messages or moved on to someone else after three distressingly superficial exchanges that I had been naïve enough to consider promising. And since the only women who showed interest in me did not appeal to me at all, I quickly experienced a growing frustration, a humiliation and disgust with myself that considerably worsened the malaise I still felt from the incident in New York. In fact, all my actions were determined by that weekend: the very need to seek other partners was a consequence of what had happened. I hadn't spoken of it to anyone other than Victor, despite the numerous occasions when I was on the point of pouring it all out on the marriage counselor's couch.

With the lucidity that comes years later, I eventually understood what I was seeking at that time. The women with whom I had slept *that night* were uncommonly beautiful—one of them has become a famous actress, and I changed her name to protect her. I wanted to see if, without Markus, without the prestige and consideration his acquaintanceship lent me, I could attract partners who were just as fascinating. The very rare women on these sites who could be compared to them either didn't answer or blocked me at the first contact, which confirmed for me, painfully but unsurprisingly, my lack of attractiveness when Markus's money and aura no longer enhanced my value in the eyes of others. Still more, I was trying to recapture a sexual identity that the night with Markus had shaken; I was hoping that the desire of other women would return to me what he took from me that night.

In the end, I was satisfied, or rather I understood in obtaining what I wanted that this was no path to salvation. I'm not too keen on describing what happened; it was, on the whole, rather distasteful, and all I achieved was more contempt for myself. Within a few weeks, I made love to two other women whom I only found mildly attractive: their foremost asset consisted in not having rejected me. The first was nice enough but a little foolish; she believed to the very end that I was a bachelor, and that I was contemplating an authentic relationship with her. I had to lie to her for days and go through all the conventional steps with her: first date, second date, etc., at a bar, at a restaurant, then, finally, at a hotel downtown where her arms, stomach, and thighs, when they were revealed to me, mostly made me nostalgic for the absolute perfection of Olga and Jana. I disappeared from her life after two or three nights, when my excuse for not inviting her to my apartment—a roommate who was always hanging around—finally began to appear suspicious to her. I lied to her about everything—my name and profession, nothing was true in what I told her about myself—and, behaving like a real bastard up to the end, I blocked her cell number, vanishing into the city after taking my pleasure in her.

The second was a colleague a little older than me who taught in another department. She knew I was married, and that troubled her all the less since she was too. She was consumed by a fierce resentment of her husband, who had been guilty of an offense that she never identified, but that she hinted at in a voice strangled by anger; she used me to take revenge, my phallus being the instrument she employed to settle her accounts with him. One day I met them at a party I wouldn't have gone to had I known they were invited: her husband, a nice guy, all smiles, bore no resemblance to the monster she had described to me. I managed to take his wife aside and speak to her, telling her that we couldn't go on, we had to stop everything. She agreed, shrugging her shoulders, and other than at the university where no words were exchanged between us, we never saw each other again. I left these two adulterous affairs with my disgust with myself increased tenfold and a greater tolerance for Eleanor's depressions, as if all the repugnant and pathetic things I was doing were a way for her to acquire, without even knowing it, longer periods of indulgence.

The month of January arrived and with it the big news: I had been granted tenure. The "party" we organized at our place, after much difficulty making it look presentable with furniture torn to shreds by the cats, was as sad as the rest of my life with Eleanor. I could no longer see any escape from it, just a slow continuation of days spent cohabiting with her, bathing in the tepid waters of her melancholy with nothing, other than the perspective of occasional trips, promising to break this routine. Theoretically, I could have divorced and started my life over alone or with someone else, but I imagined this possibility as if it were just a mind game, a gratuitous and ultimately unfeasible speculation. I was attached to Eleanor by myriad invisible bonds that forbade me to even conceive of life without her.

Eleanor kept hold of me by guilt, the guilt I felt for my undeniable errors and all those she attributed to me besides. She kept me by my deep solitude and the awareness that other than her, there was no one I could count on. She had me by the death of this child for which, by dint of insisting on it, she had convinced me I was responsible; and she kept me also by other secret chains, by the dismal debasement of myself that she cultivated, saying I was incapable of surviving in the real world without her, a dreary intellectual concerned with obscure and vaguely grotesque questions outside of which I understood nothing. At the time, I hadn't comprehended either the workings or even the existence of these perverse means of controlling me; all I knew was that I was miserable without knowing why and unable to do anything about it. The cause of this misfortune—this little woman embedded in my life like a tick in an animal's flesh—was permanently before my eyes and, nonetheless, I couldn't see it.

For want of a dream in common, a desire we would've shared (I had finally accepted the obvious: we would never have a child together), I wanted to strive toward new professional goals. As a reward for receiving tenure, the university had granted me a second sabbatical year. After my last stay on the Andamans, I had resolved to never leave Eleanor for such a long time again. I was now contemplating returning there, mostly because I wanted to get away from her but officially to make a documentary I had begun thinking about.

The rumor was growing: the Indian government was considering opening a railroad line linking Port Blair to Diglipur, a village a hundred and fifty miles north of the capital. According to the Transportation Minister, there were multiple economic and strategic justifications. For years, the government had been trying to turn the Andaman archipelago into a hub of international commerce as well as a major tourist attraction. But in cutting the Jarawa reservation in two, the railroad risked dealing a fatal blow to the tribe who, sooner or later, would be forced to integrate into the rest of the population. Rather than a book, a new scholarly publication that would be dissected by specialists and ignored by everyone else, a film seemed to me a much more effective means of alerting public opinion to the precarious situation of the Jarawas. I decided to return to Port Blair to meet the proponents and opponents of this rail project and, more broadly, to document what I saw as a tipping point in the history of the archipelago, a change in which, from being on the fringe as it had always been, it was preparing to be connected to the rest of the world and sacrificing its native populations.

With this project, much more committed than my previous work, I believe I was also seeking a form of redemption. I could no longer make Eleanor happy; I had been unfaithful on several occasions; I had to find a way to be useful. It also occurred to me that I shouldn't keep selfishly to myself all the love and time I would never have the opportunity to give to a child; I had to put it to work for someone, for something. It seemed all the more necessary that my choice be the Jarawas, since they were declining in a general indifference that, more and more, appeared to conceal some kind of plot: their annihilation was the price to pay for the economic development of the archipelago. For hunter-gatherers, it takes acres of liberty to be happy; modern man only requires a few yards to be miserable in his own way. In Columbus, I thought of the baby Pilu, of Umamay and Idamowo, Onia and Yaday: other than me, who was worried about them?

To carry out my project, a very large budget was indispensable. I needed high-quality equipment to shoot the documentary, not to speak of the funds I would need to get to the Andamans and set up home there for a prolonged period. I applied for a grant from the university but was, unfortunately, turned down. The political dimension of my project may have been the problem, or perhaps I had requested too much money. It's also possible that there was just too much competition that year, and other applications took precedence. In any case, three months before my sabbatical leave, I hadn't found a dollar of the amount I would need. I was contemplating approaching private donors when Alexandra, barging back into my life, offered me a solution to my problems provided that I be party to hers.

She knocked on my office door one October day. I hadn't seen her for years, since graduation in fact. A year before, I had spent that remarkable night with her brother. Since then, I had never contacted him again—I had even decided not to ask him for the watch I had forgotten at his place—but I had continued to keep tabs on him on the Internet, regularly, secretly, without really knowing why. There was no news about him recently. By looking to the past, I dug up old articles that speculated about the role he would play in the family business after the death of his father and more recent ones, in the "gossip" press, that featured his relationship with semi-celebrities. You saw Markus in the arms of a French actress, then in those of a Columbian top model in New York, Los Angeles, or at the Paris Fashion Week. But for several months there was no mention of Markus either in the magazines devoted to the art world or in the tabloid press; he had fallen into anonymity without anyone going to the trouble to wonder why. On the other hand, a search for his sister yielded numerous results. Her last exhibition had been a resounding success; she was on her way to taking the position in the art world that Joakim had occupied before her.

"So, may I come in," she asked curtly, after I had remained motionless for a few seconds, stunned to see her in front of me. I stepped aside and closed the door after her. As I sat down behind my desk, she settled into a chair and cast a contemptuous look on her surroundings. I immediately regretted not having cleaned up. The wastebasket, full of wrapping paper, smelled of cold curry; the shelves were on the verge of collapsing under the weight of the books, dirty clothes cluttered the armchair, and three tea bags lay on a saucer, shriveled up and dry like dead insects. On the walls, the picture frames were slightly askew, those in which I had put my diplomas and those that contained travel photos.

"Interesting décor."

"You're free to leave if it isn't to your taste."

I replied much more aggressively than I had expected, and I was almost as surprised as she was. Before, during that summer we had spent together on Block Island, instead of retorting when she spoke abruptly to me, I just smiled at her stupidly. She didn't remember me being capable of repartee; she was used to more docility from me. A little laugh full of nasty irony escaped her.

"The gentleman has acquired a personality since we last met?"

"Listen, I have no idea what you've come here for. If it's to insult me, you can go back to where you came from on your stilts."

She glanced, despite herself, at her high heels, which must've cost a fortune. A pained expression that soon turned indignant appeared on her beautifully made-up face. I couldn't prevent myself from finding her lovely.

"But since you went to the trouble of coming, you might as well tell me what I can do for you."

"Very well, I'll get right to the point: Markus has disappeared."

"Disappeared? What do you mean?"

"Disappeared. Do I have to draw you a picture? No one knows where he is, and he isn't answering his telephone or voicemails."

"How long has it been?"

"It will be a month this Sunday."

"Wait, didn't he do that already, after the death of your parents? I heard that he had gone to Block Island without letting anyone know."

"Without letting us know, yes, but not without staying in contact. After a few days, he called me to tell me where he was. This time, it's different: he's said nothing to anyone."

"You've reported this to the police?"

"Of course, but they can't do much. There's no crime involved, no kidnapping, and the cops know he's vanished before. All they say is for us to wait for Markus to reappear. For them he's just a statistic: one thousand five hundred people disappear *every day* in this country ...."

"I'm very sorry to hear that, really I am. But without wanting to be disagreeable, I don't understand what this has to do with me. If he were to write to me, I ...."

"I don't think so: I think his disappearance has everything to do with you."

She handed me her telephone. I studied the pictures at length, one after the other, before reacting.

"You don't seriously think he went there?"

"It's a possibility. Markus never does things half-way. If he decided that it's important to him, he'll do everything he can to get there."

"It's madness. Access to the island is strictly controlled; no one has the right to even approach ...."

"Really? I could cite examples to the contrary, and you too, no?"

"But we would've heard of it; something would've trickled out in the press ...."

"Not if he had an accident. Or if someone has a reason to hide what happened to him."

"I still don't see what you expect of me ... You aren't suggesting that ...."

"Yes, I am. No one is better qualified. And as I see it, you have a certain responsibility for this."

"Stop right there. Your brother is a big boy, and I have nothing to do with his decisions. Everyone is responsible for his own actions, right?"

"Okay. But you know very well that you're the one who put this idea in his head. He's been talking about it ever since he met you."

"Perhaps, but why now? Why has he returned to this project after such a long time?"

"You have to understand: Markus was not well at all after the death of our parents. And when I say *not well at all*, it doesn't tell the whole story; the poor boy was a walking disaster. He did nothing all day long, slept with random women. He started hanging out with people who were absolutely not of his world, popping pills that were bad for him. That he didn't want to invest his energy in the galleries, I could understand; it's dad who convinced him to work for him. But he could at least have gotten a grip on himself, found a new goal in life. Last year I went to his apartment and told him that he couldn't go on like that, not with all his potential. We had a long talk, and he brought up the novel he had been thinking about since college but had never dared to speak to our father about. I told him that was maybe what he needed to do: something he desired deeply, now that he no longer had to wonder what dad was going to think. That seemed to make him think. But like I said, with Markus it's all or nothing. He left for Woodstock to be alone in a country house that belonged to our parents and, to the best of my knowledge, stayed there until I sent someone to find out why he was no longer answering my calls. That's where these photos were taken. Now, I would like you to go to his place and see what he's … installed."

"And if he has indeed gone there? You're not really going to ask me to …."

"I told you: who better to find him? And to be honest, I don't see who else I could ask."

"You got to be fucking kidding me! We haven't seen each other for years, and you march in here out of the blue and think I'm going to go to the other side of the planet just to indulge you? Have you lost your mind?"

"No, but I will admit that I have no other way to find out what's happened. I could hire an investigator, but no one has the expertise or the contacts over there that you have. So, are you going to help me or not?"

"And you, what're you going to do for me? I imagine you're used to whistling, and people do whatever you want. Sorry: I owe you nothing, neither you nor your brother, and I'm not going to leave everything simply because you do me the great favor of coming to my office."

"Very well. What do you want?"

I thought a few seconds, then I spoke to her of my documentary project. I believe that if I wasn't persuaded I was acting for a good cause, I never would've dared make this deal with her: I would help her find Markus if she would finance my film. When I had prepared my grant application, I had established a budget that was intended to cover my expenses. Taking a flyer, I added twenty-five thousand dollars to this amount, telling myself that for people like her it was nothing, and given the enormity of what she was asking me to do, I deserved a bonus. She was silent for a moment and— either because she didn't want to waste any more time or because she couldn't resist the pleasure of humiliating me by showing me that this sum, a lot for me, was derisory for her—she wrote out a check on a corner of my desk and handed it to me curtly.

"I'm counting on you going to Woodstock as soon as possible. When will you be free?"

She asked me this question in giving me a set of keys. I had the brief, disagreeable impression that everything was going exactly according to her plan.

"I can be there at the end of the day on Friday."

She got up and, for a moment, studied me before saying:

"You've changed."

"You haven't."

And I closed the door behind her.

I went home a few hours later. Eleanor asked me how my day had gone, and I couldn't bring myself to tell her the truth. I preferred not to say anything about Markus's disappearance until I came back from Woodstock. I had considerable doubts about this whole business and was already contemplating returning Alexandra's check. While I waited to make a final decision, I told Eleanor the lie I had prepared on my way home. I told her that Victor—"You know my Saint Andrew friend, the one who's a lawyer in Manhattan"—had just lost his father and I was going to spend the weekend with him to give him some support. Eleanor encouraged me to go, suspecting nothing. I packed my suitcase and left the house early on Friday morning—officially for the airport, where I would supposedly leave my car until the following Monday—but, in reality, for western New York.

Six hundred miles, more than nine hours of driving. I had plenty of time to think about what Alexandra had told me, what I would do if it was true that Markus had gone there. And I thought of all the promise he had shown when we were younger, of what I had accomplished myself since that day when, in front of the Sterling Library, we had taken opposite paths. Audioslave's hard rock accompanied me through Pennsylvania. "Pearls and swine bereft of me / Long and weary my road has been …." Drenched in darkness, mixing red and ochre, the great Chris Cornell's voice was like the vast sky when evening falls: full of melancholy and yet illuminated by the promise of a renewal after the night. "I was lost in the cities / Alone in the hills / No sorrow or pity / For leaving, I feel." My mind followed the winding of the melody as the car negotiated the bends in the road that bordered the fields and forests. The sun had long disappeared when, at the end of a narrow twisting road, Markus's house appeared in my headlights.

I turned off the ignition and took out my cell phone to use as a flashlight. The residence was set in the woods, and I couldn't have said where the nearest neighbor was, having left the main road a good quarter-hour before. With the keys in my hand, I went up the flight of steps that led to the front door. I entered a huge room with a picture window that looked out onto the night and reflected a wavering, blurry image: mine. Exhausted, I took my suitcase up to one of the bedrooms and fell into a deep sleep.

I awoke very early the next morning in the empty house. The solitude, the cold—snow had begun to fall during the night, and the branches were bending under its weight—conjured up images of the end of the world, as if I had traveled across a hostile countryside before taking refuge here, after the death of the occupants, in this lodging whose door I had forced open, and which would serve as a shelter until hunger or enemies forced me out. Quite rightly, I had assumed that the cupboards would be empty, so, as a precaution, I had brought with me enough food for the weekend. When I had finished breakfast, I began to explore the bedrooms.

I had the impression I was visiting a show home in a development reserved for the wealthy. Everything was luxurious, comfortable, and yet terribly impersonal. The granite of the kitchen was exactly what you would expect in a luxury home; the bathrooms offered all the modern conveniences you could want, but even if the décor was elegant, it was also stereotypical, as if all the decisions concerning the furniture and the style had been made by a professional interior decorator. Among all the bedrooms, I found it impossible to tell which one had been occupied by Markus. The house had been cleaned since his disappearance, and I found nowhere any distinctive features that might have recalled his tastes. It's for that reason that the discovery of the basement was so surprising: the contrast with the upper floors could not have been more striking.

It was one of those spacious furnished basements that serve as rec rooms. I found a billiard table, leather armchairs, and a gigantic flat screen—but stored beneath the stairway to make room for the insane display that had invaded the space, colonized one wall, then another, all the walls in fact, even part of the floor and ceiling. On Alexandra's phone, it had been impossible for me to realize the stupefying quantity of texts and images accumulated by Markus. There were handwritten notes, photocopies, lists, a lot of lists: of place names and surnames, some crossed out, others circled in red in the enthusiasm of a discovery; and then freehand drawings, maps, satellite images, black-and-white, color, and sepia portraits, landscapes, sketches, bibliographies, everything tacked to the walls in an apparent hodgepodge countered by a long red line that established a connection between these heterogeneous documents, or a sort of narrative continuity for the moment still indecipherable. And in the center of the room—an enormous room without the slightest partition to divide it—there was, lit up by the glow coming from the basement windows and by the spotlights set in the lacquered ceiling, a magnificent finely worked desk, on which was sitting alone—and the nakedness of this table contrasted sharply with the monstrous rash of papers on the walls—a laptop computer, closed.

After getting over the first second of astonishment that had brought me to a halt, I approached the documents to inspect them. They were all related to Sentinel Island. Despite the apparent chaos, the general organizational principle was easy to figure out. You had to read the room like a frieze that began on the wall facing the stairs and whose progression was chronological. Slowly, like an Egyptologist discovering hieroglyphics in a temple visited for the first time in centuries, I followed the progression of the texts and images as they recounted the history of the island. On the walls there were excerpts from Ptolemy and Marco Polo and a fragment of a text written by a certain Buzurg ibn Shahriyār al-Rām-Hurmuzi. I recognized photographs I had seen in the course of my research on the Jarawas: portraits of Maurice Vidal Portman and images that exhibited men from the Andaman archipelago, caught in erotically troubling poses.

A series of texts illustrated with diagrams mixed in with the others didn't seem to belong there. I didn't see their relationship to the selection of ethnographic works they were placed beside. They were excerpts of books on the functioning of the brain and, reading the paragraphs Markus had feverishly highlighted, I understood that they were about the causes of déjà-vu. This phenomenon must have been linked, in some way or other, to the book project revealed by this astounding display, though I was unable, at least for the moment, to guess by what bias. I continued my exploration of the room until I came to the central panel; I stopped and stared longer than I had at any other material. How could I stop looking at it? It was entirely devoted to me.

Markus had put up several dozen documents that concerned me. At the center was the portrait from my university's website and, all around it, texts that were related to my works. I immediately recognized an excerpt from my book, *Of Spirits and Men*, in which Markus had underlined in red a long passage devoted to the Sentinelese, as well as photocopies of the majority of my articles, in their entirety, tacked to the wall. There were also photos of Eleanor and me that I had shared several years before on social media, and even some hard-to-find writings, like the copy of an article I'd published in the student newspaper at Columbia when I was doing my bachelor's degree there. Markus had done an in-depth investigation of me—not only of my anthropological research, for which I could easily understand his interest, since it was connected to the Andaman archipelago—but of my personal history as well, the journey that had led me from Mumbai to Columbus and including my time on the east coast of the United States. I felt a violent anger grow in me, an indignation that I had to control so I wouldn't tear down all these fragments of my life that he had collected without my permission. Then I found a newspaper article that described the attack in 2008 in which my parents and sister had been murdered. Rather than allowing myself to be overcome by emotion, I went and sat down at the desk, trying to understand what I could possibly have to do with Markus's novel.

It seemed to me that the answer was there, in front of me, in this computer that asked me for a password when I opened it. I sat for a long time looking at the cursor blinking on the screen. Raising my eyes, I could see right in front of the desk all the documents that involved me. That's when I thought: this is precisely where

I was meant to be. Markus had no doubt anticipated that his disappearance would lead to the discovery of his workplace, where a substantial portion of the texts had a direct connection to me, and that I would visit it sooner or later. Once again, I suddenly had the distinct impression of doing exactly what was expected of me, of finding myself in a place I had been led to by someone who maintained that I was free not to go there. It was like when Alexandra handed me the keys to this house after giving me to understand that I could choose not to take them. If I was playing a predefined role in some story worked out in advance, I might as well accept it right now and contemplate how to close this chapter and move on to the next one. Before making any attempt to access the computer, I mused: when Markus decided to block it, did he select a password that he and I alone would think of?

I began to think about what had created a special bond between us, and the secret society that had brought us together in our youth immediately came to mind. On the off chance, I tried "SaintAndrew": the screen shook it off. Then I thought of the address of the hall we often used to allude to it: "82CollegeStreet." The screen shook again, but this time offering a clue: "Formula." It was a critical moment, because the system was warning me that I had only one chance left to unlock it. This threat did not worry me; I now understood what the password was. The members of Saint Andrew alone know the ritual formula that they write at the end of their exchanges, as a reminder of what unites them and a sign of belonging to the same community. I typed the entire four-word phrase, without spaces, and that was the gateway to Markus's computer.

On the screen there was a folder labeled "Documents," a file named "Sentinel Island," and a second file, "Markus Holmberg." That's all. They were lined up horizontally, and I opened them one after the other. In the folder "Documents," there were other folders: "Portman," "Modern Period," "Chris" … I opened this last one, and a quick glance showed me that it contained the texts and photos that were hung on the wall. It was the same thing with the other folders: I found only the digitized versions of the articles, books, and images Markus had arranged around himself. The "Sentinel Island" file, however, was another story.

I skimmed it first, through all the chapters, eager to come to the end of the story: it hadn't been written. It stopped at a blank page, preceded by the roman numeral "III." I went back to the beginning and started reading again. Here, in essence, is what the first part of the book said. I was clearly the hero or, at least, the source of inspiration. The main character—Aman—came from Kolkata and had lost his family in the same attack that had taken the lives of mine. The tale was told from the perspective of his best friend, a slightly younger man who had met him during their studies at Princeton. This switching of universities was indicative of the modifications Markus had made to the biographical material he had appropriated. All in all, his innovations didn't go very far. Whether from lack of imagination or because he thought that reality yielded an adequate narrative, he had just transposed large stages of our life in describing them as he had perceived them or in making a few superficial changes. There was our vacation on Block Island (changed to Martha's Vineyard), his father's fortune (made in the music industry and not in the modern art market), and also, albeit rarely, Eleanor (rebaptized Ashley). Overall, everything in the first part of the book was about events I knew perfectly, since they were fragments of our youth in New Haven.

What surprised me the most, however, is the way he looked at me, I mean the way he looked at Aman. He expressed, with respect to his friend, an admiration that was comparable to what Markus had always inspired in me. The narrator attributed to him qualities he was convinced he himself was lacking. Aman had the fierceness in battle, the resilience, the courage, the zeal in his work that he had never succeeded in developing in himself. More favored by his circumstances but in a certain way weakened by the ease he had encountered throughout his life, he had never been toughened by overcoming real obstacles. He considered himself insignificant and unstable, hesitant; he perceived his friend as an irresistible force. I didn't recognize myself in this description. The misgivings that the future inspired in me, the unbearable grief, the fear of failing in my undertakings, my oversensitivity, all those flaws that seemed to be inherent to my character appeared nowhere in the more heroic portrait that Markus had created of me. Had he never suspected my numerous weaknesses? Or had he chosen to ignore them in order to make of me an ideal image? Whatever the case may be, the whole novel demonstrated that I had preoccupied him as much and perhaps more than he had ever fascinated me; that he had seen in me virtues that he lacked, just as I had considered myself incomplete without the advantages I felt he enjoyed. When I understood this, it was, how should I put it, like a Copernican reversal of perspectives, as if the axis according to which I had interpreted the world and my place in it had just been brutally inverted.

In the second part of the book, Aman became substantially different from the model I had represented for Markus. The most notable difference consisted in the pathological reoccurrence of the impression of déjà-vu that plagued the character. Aman believed he was constantly reliving the same day; each new action appeared to him like the phantom of a prior act. The narrator did not explicitly formulate this idea, but he at least implied that Aman wished to go to Sentinel Island for the following reason: because he hoped to break there the cycle of infernal repetitions, to enter a new temporality by visiting the island, which he could not have seen before, the island that was by definition *never seen*. This orientation of the narrative struck me, as if Markus had merged our two persons: he had taken my origins, my profession, and many other things, but he had also lent to this *Doppelgänger* certain of his own characteristics, beginning with the distress, or the lapses, of which he had told me years earlier on Block Island and which, it seemed, he had never surmounted.

The second major difference between Markus's story and the model that our lives had provided him consisted in the protagonist's obsession with Sentinel Island. I had never seriously considered going there—except, perhaps, when Markus and I discussed it in the lounges of Saint Andrew—and the Jarawas and Onges had given me enough work that I felt no need to investigate their neighbors on an island whose access was forbidden by the Indian navy. Aman, however, dreamed day and night of the Sentinelese and was convinced he had a clear advantage over all his predecessors: he knew how to communicate with the tribe. In the course of the text, the narrator cites an excerpt from Vishvajit Pandya's *Above the Forest*: "Early ethnographic accounts suggest that each tribal unit on the islands spoke mutually unintelligible languages. However, linguistic records, compiled by the islands' administrators and more recent research, suggest a great degree of overlap in terms used by each group." This hypothesis is then explored later in the story: in the Jarawa reservation, Aman was determined to find a translator who would accompany him to Sentinel Island. He was counting on this "great degree of overlap in terms" to communicate with the inhabitants of the island. The same idea had occurred to John Chau, who had sought, in vain, a travel companion among the Jarawas and the Onges before deciding to undertake his trip alone. Where Chau had failed, Aman was convinced he would find a way to succeed: the second part of the novel ended with his departure for the Andamans. Beyond the numeral "III," the page remained blank.

I closed the file and clicked on the last document, the one named "Markus Holmberg." It was a copy of a plane ticket. Markus had reserved a flight to Port Blair leaving from JFK, and unless his plans had changed, he had been on the ground there since the end of August. I was motionless for a long moment to give my various, contradictory emotions time to settle. The strongest among them was, ultimately, anger. A violent anger at the idea that he had freely plundered my personal life and not bothered to ask my permission to use the experiences I had shared with him in complete confidence. That he had taken this deep wound in my life—the loss of my parents and Kamala—to use as a simple narrative element, a convenient justification of what he had perceived as a manifestation of my determination to win, made me positively furious.

Kamala and my parents weren't abstractions that played an explanatory role in the "psychology of the hero." She was Kamala, my older sister, mocking and so strongly attached to our family that she had never wanted to leave it, probably to compensate for the fact that I had chosen to live in America. He was my father, with his sharp sense of duty, his principles, and his odd little habits that we smiled at among ourselves. And it was my mother and her gentleness and devotion to her students, so strong that she always felt she could do more for them. It was that and so many other things; entire libraries would not have sufficed to contain everything they were, these people Markus had so coldly used. That is the first thing I could not pardon him for; I still can't, in fact. His consciousness of his privilege was so deeply anchored in him that he never questioned his right to take whatever he wanted, including the private life of a friend, and disclose it in a book.

My anger was so intense that I again contemplated going back on my agreement with Alexandra. I could've concealed what I had found on Markus's computer and claimed it was impossible to tell if he had taken a plane to the Andamans; that would've been a way to extricate myself from all this business and move on to other things. He'd just have had to get along without me, this failed novelist, false friend, and phony adventurer ... But it was the anger itself that suggested another plan. I called Alexandra and told her that I had proof that Markus had reached Port Blair, and that I wouldn't go looking for him unless she agreed to increase the amount she'd offered me. A harsh negotiation ensued. I demanded more money, and she wanted me to leave immediately; I answered that I wouldn't leave the US before the end of the semester, and if that didn't suit her, she was free to go find another specialist on the Andamans with a decade of experience, contacts throughout the archipelago, and a knowledge of the local languages. I succeeded in getting her to promise three times my annual salary; for her, it was becoming a disagreeable sum to part with; for me, it was paying off my mortgage early. We agreed that she would transfer half of the payment the day before my departure (which would give her a chance to pay nothing if Markus reappeared in the meantime), the second half to be paid when I had found him. In exchange, I committed to leaving as soon as my classes were over, six weeks later, on December 3.

The following day, on the drive back, I reflected at length about what I would say to Eleanor. Was I going to reveal Markus's disappearance to her, and the money I had just—call it by its name—extorted from Alexandra? Or invent a pretext to justify moving up my departure for the Andamans? There are too many lies between us, I thought, let's try to begin a new chapter. When I got back home, I asked her to sit down, and I began by telling her that I wasn't coming back from Victor's. She remained impassive and bolt upright on the couch, without reacting when a cat crossed her lap and stretched out limply a little beyond. And she showed scarcely any emotion either when I informed her that Markus had disappeared, then told her about my weekend in his country house. Her coldness surprised me; I didn't expect her to have a fit, but she didn't appear particularly irritated that I had hidden the truth from her. What concerned her, on the other hand, was my certainty about the whole story: was I really convinced that Markus had left for the Andamans? And was it really possible that he had gone to Sentinel Island? I showed her the copy I had made of his plane ticket. As for whether he had attempted to reach the forbidden island, I seriously doubted it, for he was not unaware of the difficulty of getting there, nor of the risks he ran if he did. And since his success was much less probable than his failure, his doomed attempt would've been reported in the media; there was no chance that the papers would not feast on the misadventures of an American millionaire who had set foot on "cannibal island." In my opinion, he must have been springing for expensive private cruises to islands similar to Sentinel but deserted, to bring back images and odors, impressions that would be found in the novel he was finally finishing after all these years.

I was reassured to see that instead of focusing on my lie, Eleanor was encouraging me to go to Markus's aid. I even had to remind her that it was impossible to cancel a month and a half of classes when she asked why I didn't leave immediately to look for my friend. The last question, concerning the money, did not leave her indifferent: she suggested several uses for the sum I was going to receive from Alexandra. Discussing our plans and the perspectives this windfall opened up for us was one of the most agreeable conversations we had had in a long time, as if this whole business that I had feared would increase the tensions between us was instead bringing us closer together. During the weeks that preceded my departure, Eleanor helped me get ready for it as best she could. She often asked if I had news and said repeatedly that she was proud of what I was doing for my friend. When the day came, she drove me to the airport—no, she would not feel abandoned in my absence; her mother was coming to visit a few days later (she always chose to come when I wasn't there, a "coincidence" I had given up remarking upon many years before), and they would leave together for Texas at the beginning of Christmas vacation. She embraced me at the terminal entrance, drove off, and I found myself alone again, leaving for the other side of the world.

How many times I've thought of that precise second—the second Eleanor drove away—imagining the consequences, all the woes and joys, all the horror—yes, the horror—but also the redemption I would never have experienced if, as I was tempted to do, but too late, I had motioned to her to stop, to come back to get me and take me back home where my future and hers would've been transformed, this second during which the future of Julia and even the life of our little one was at stake—which, of course, we hadn't the slightest idea about. And nonetheless, something tells me that I was never free to call Eleanor back, that an eternity of errors and good deeds would've weighed on my arm if I had tried to raise it, and that the labyrinth had been in place for a long time already: all I had to do now was reach its end.

A heavy rain was pounding Port Blair when I arrived at the town center from the airport. I moved into my hotel and, the next day, went to see Subbiah, a local guy I had met during my last stay in the archipelago. In anticipation of my return, he had begun to ask questions everywhere about Markus and had made good progress in his investigation. Subbiah had in fact succeeded in identifying the luxury hotel where Markus had spent a week before leaving for the north of the island, for Mayabunder. This name immediately struck me, because I remembered that John Chau had gone to this village next to the Jarawa reservation when he was preparing to visit Sentinel Island. A cousin of Subbiah's lived there and had advised us—without wishing to say anything more—to see a local fisherman named Jyoti. We took the ferry and went straight to his home.

Jyoti stared at me a long while without saying a word. I was a fellow countryman and could answer him in Bengali but, nevertheless, he looked at me with the special distrust reserved for foreigners. That's what I had found the most wearing in the emigrant experience: the fact that in the final analysis you become a stateless person. The Americans had, for the most part, accepted me; they cared little about the reasons that had brought me to the United States, a country that—there was wide agreement, especially among those who had never left it—was superior to the rest of the world. But I'll never be one of them, I could see it clearly in the way they asked me, without meaning any offense, if I "often went back home," which meant that my home would never be in their country. It was the same thing for Jyoti: for him too I was an intruder, and what brought us together—the language, the color of our skin—ultimately proved to be much less important than what deepened the gap between us, namely that I had come from a country where it takes two weeks for the average employee to earn more than he did in a year of toil. In these circumstances, the cultural references you have in common carry little weight; being a foreigner is less a question of your passport than of belonging to a distinct social category—and the wealthy know it better than anyone, living in a cosmopolitan world disconnected from any national affiliation.

Since I couldn't persuade Jyoti to answer me, I simply paid him to tell me what he knew about Markus: a hundred dollars bought me my first lead. He began by recognizing him on a photo I showed him. Then he told me that toward the end of the summer, Markus had asked him to take him within sight of Sentinel Island. He had been clear about it, he just wanted to "see Sentinel Island," go around it, observe it for a moment and take pictures, but he had no intention of setting foot on it, he just wanted a boat to approach the forbidden island, that's all. Jyoti had sent him away and explained to me why. His brother-in-law had helped that other American, the one who had died on Sentinel Island—yes, John Chau—to get into the Jarawa reservation and, after the missionary's disappearance, had had serious difficulties with the local police when they had tried to reconstruct the foreigner's actions. It was too risky, Jyoti didn't need these kinds of problems in his life, so, to get rid of Markus who would not take no for an answer, he had given him the address of the owner of a fleet of boats in Junglighat specialized in the transportation of tourists, a fellow who had a reputation for providing them with whatever they wanted in illegal pleasures, mainly weed and whores. Perhaps an expedition into the forbidden waters around Sentinel Island was one of his services? That is at least what Jyoti had advised Markus to check out for himself. I wondered for a moment if he had told me the whole truth. I observed his hard, mulish expression as he looked me in the eye with a rising aggressiveness and concluded that I wasn't going to get anything else out of him. I thanked him, he nodded, and Subbiah and I returned to the port to inquire about the return crossing.

Subbiah knew the man Jyoti had steered us toward, a certain Zlatair, whose reputation left a lot to be desired. Derogatory stories about him had been circulating since 2004 and the tsunami that had ravaged the Andamans. At that time, Zlatair had influential connections at the Port Blair chamber of commerce and significant capital that he had used to set up an economic development project of a very particular type. With several Phuket hotels in Thailand, a region known for its translucent waters and prostitution rings, he had established an innovative market. In exchange for a percentage of the profits, the hotels gave their clientele the opportunity to take an excursion to the Andamans. The official pretext was "helping a region hit hard by the earthquake" by supporting local businesses, but it was the young women of Port Blair, reduced to extreme poverty, that they offered the tourists upon arrival. Discreet vehicles will bring them "to your room in twenty minutes" was the sales pitch used by Zlatair. Subbiah explained to me that after one or two seasons, Zlatair's business had drawn too much attention: there was the sordid affair of a traveler from Northern Europe who had broken the jaw of one of the girls. Plain-clothes policemen had posed as clients, and his operation had been dismantled. After many clashes with the courts, Zlatair, now over fifty, had started another business, a company that organized day tours to Rutland Island, even if, according to rumors, he hadn't entirely given up his former trade and still proposed, on a smaller scale, the products he offered before. Subbiah contacted Zlatair through a friend, and we met him at Junglighat the day after our return from Mayabunder.

Zlatair's house was the largest in the neighborhood. It had a kitchen, toilets, and a real roof with a frame instead of the sheets of corrugated metal that covered the rest of the houses on the street. This cement building was all that remained of his former fortune and his dreams of creating a vast network of international sex tourism. Zlatair was left bitter and ill-humored, as I clearly saw when he received me in his kitchen, sitting at a table at ten in the morning with a bottle of Johnny Walker and a glass. He wasn't toasting with the three men standing around the room, potbellied, arms crossed, imposing, and ready to intervene. An anthropology professor weighing a hundred and fifty-five pounds was no great threat to them; they seemed relaxed but never took their eyes off me. Subbiah waited for me in the street, so I was alone in front of their boss, who asked me what the fuck I wanted from him. He emptied his glass in one gulp and served himself another that he downed before I had finished speaking to him about Markus and the search I had undertaken.

He didn't waste any time: he had information, and I could have it for a thousand dollars. I was delighted to have come to the right place but, at the same time, I thought it best that he not suspect the extent of the means I had at my disposal by obtaining too quickly what he was demanding, so I pretended it was a lot of money for me. He retorted with an evil smile that "foreigners always say that"—confirming, incidentally, my theory about expatriates all becoming stateless people. Keeping my calm, I answered that nothing guaranteed he would tell me the truth when I had paid him, a fear I begged him to excuse; he shouldn't take my lack of confidence personally but, you know, I confided, suddenly solemn and sad, people have tricked me in the past, and since then I've promised myself to take all necessary precautions to avoid it happening again. He poured himself another glass, acting as if he was wondering why he was wasting his time with this clown, and, after a long bout of bargaining, I managed to bring him down to five hundred dollars and get him to agree to share his information before receiving the money. With the three bodyguards around him, it would've been difficult for me to skip out on him.

Markus had visited Zlatair at the end of September after returning from Mayabunder—I was clearly following in his footsteps. He had proposed to him the same project he had discussed with Jyoti: he wanted to see Sentinel Island, circle it, take a few photos, shoot some video, that's all. Zlatair always tried to gain a clear profile of his clients, and Markus was no exception. He had asked him why the hell he wanted to see Sentinel, what was it with the Yanks and this shitty little island with its fucking cavemen, and wasn't it enough, what happened to the other fanatic, the guy who had wanted to convert them and got his hash settled instead? He couldn't remember Markus's explanations very well, or he hadn't entirely understood them, but the American had spoken of his novel, of how he'd been studying this island for years, reading everything that had been written about it, and he wanted to see it once, only once, that was why he'd come from the other side of the world and, if he left without having set eyes on it, he would have "a feeling of incompleteness."

"A feeling of incompleteness": the phrase had struck Zlatair, and he repeated it several times, still incredulous, irritated, not believing his ears. "How can people bother with such bullshit?" he asked. "That's stuff for rich pricks, stuff for White dudes, foreigners" (he looked me straight in the eyes to let me know that, as far as he was concerned, I was all of the above), and I couldn't disagree with him entirely; you had to be Markus to put yourself in danger not to satisfy a need but an idea, a personal notion of what constitutes success. A need, Zlatair could have understood that; he even had an open mind on the question and responded indiscriminately to any whim, woman or girl, little boy or young man, everything was good as long as you paid. But simply an idea? No, really, that was beyond him, and from his viewpoint, that of a guy who emptied bottles of whiskey at ten in the morning, who had a large golden chain around his neck with the links embedded in his salt-and-pepper chest hair, who had thick rings on his paws, and who earned his living by renting out penises and orifices, it was scarcely possible to see it otherwise.

Ultimately, Zlatair had made Markus pay—he didn't tell me how much, but with the radiant look that appeared briefly on his face, I understood that the memory of the sum was enough to delight him—to put him in contact with some fishermen who would agree to take him where he wanted to go. He had refused to get involved himself; it was too dangerous in his situation, he'd already had enough trouble with the police and preferred not to make any more waves. I reflected that Zlatair had badly misread his client, not suspecting the true extent of his means—in all likelihood, very few dollar millionaires had flocked to his kitchen—and I, who knew Markus well, had no doubt that he wouldn't have hesitated to reward Zlatair richly for the risks he would have taken. I said nothing of this in order not to upset him; something told me that this missed opportunity would've eaten away at Zlatair, and looking at his soft body, perspiring despite the fact that he was motionless, perched on a stool that seemed too narrow for his backside, I thought that Zlatair must've already had a good number of things eating at him and didn't need one more.

A new round of bargaining began. He didn't want to tell me where he had sent Markus until I promised him two hundred dollars more. When I finally caved, he gave me the address of a certain Mainak Sharma who lived in district no. 15 at Dairy Farm—another slum but farther to the west, just next to the temple of Shiva. And thereupon Zlatair dismissed me, raising his hand to get rid of me while ordering his men not to let me out of their sight before I had given them the eight hundred dollars. "Seven hundred, we agreed on seven hundred!" I insisted. "Okay, okay," he responded, with a tired look, repeating his previous gesture of irritation. My audience was over, and the three guys stuck to me like glue until I had handed them the wad of bills.

Subbiah, all the more obliging since I was paying him generously, proposed to accompany me to Dairy Farm. He'd never heard of this Mainak Sharma, but with the information provided by Zlatair, it shouldn't be too difficult to locate him. On the other hand, he advised me to wait a little before showing up at his place; fishermen get up early and return home late, so we would have greater chances of finding him after nightfall. I took advantage of the free time that day to meet a newspaperman from the local daily, *Andaman Times*, one Pranab Samaddar, who agreed to speak to me in front of a camera. At this point, I hadn't yet given up on my documentary and wanted to make the most of the break from the investigation of Markus's disappearance to move this project forward. Pranab was a fired-up young man who appeared immediately to belong to that very rare category of idealists whose ability to make decisions based solely on the search for truth make them both worthy of admiration and particularly vulnerable to reprisals from all those who, more powerful because dishonest, tolerate large and small compromises of their principles to satisfy their interests. He had just published an article concerning the sexual exploitation of the Jarawas. No further back than the previous month, poachers from Tirur, a godforsaken hole in the forest, had persuaded some young girls to go hunting with them and had raped them for days on end. Such crimes took place regularly, too regularly ever since the poachers had gotten into the habit of bartering with the Jarawas, intruding little by little into their social network, becoming more and more integrated into their life, and it had been impossible to punish the guilty ones, even though they had been identified, because the girls had refused to testify against them.

The sexual exploitation of women and children was already revolting in itself, but what Pranab most apprehended—and that wasn't an empty word in his mouth, it was real fear—was the introduction of diseases to their island, the devastation that a virus like AIDS could cause in a tribe already fragile and threatened on all sides. The survival of the Jarawas sincerely preoccupied him, and he had enthusiastically consented to speak with me when I informed him of my intention to make a documentary that would bring their fate to the international community's attention. Such a plague could bring them to the point of extinction, as had been the case of other peoples of the region in the past, such as the Great Andamanese, decimated by syphilis in the previous century. Pranab went so far as to predict a return to violence between the Jarawas and the colonists. It should not be forgotten that the tribe had only laid down its arms at the end of the 1990s, and that it would take them up again if the law and the police proved incapable of protecting them—or, still worse, were in collusion with the wrongdoers. Before taking his leave, he made a comment about the Sentinelese: strange things, he announced with a mysterious air, were happening among them. He had to verify his sources before saying anything further, but I would be able to read an article in which he would take stock of things, very soon, perhaps even in the next issue of the *Andaman Times*. I tried to get more out of him, but he refused, firmly but politely; all he could add at this point was that there was a rumor circulating that concerned the forbidden island, a rumor that, if it turned out to be true, was going to be a real headache for the authorities. I shook his hand warmly, promising to let him know when my documentary was finished. I had just enough time to drop off the camera and the rest of the material at the hotel before I had to leave for Dairy Farm with Subbiah.

Having arrived at the temple of Shiva, we stopped passersby to ask if they knew where Mainak Sharma lived; one of them finally gave us the information. As soon as the door opened, I understood that a domestic incident had just taken place. The woman who appeared precipitously in the doorway had reddened eyes, angry voices could be heard behind her, and the expression on her sad, tired face, upon discovering these two strangers, went in a flash from surprise to fear. She cried out, "Mainak!" and a man in his forties arrived a moment later, replacing his wife at the half-open door. He too seemed astonished and stammered, "Are you from the police?" I shook my head, and he continued immediately: "So what the hell are you doing at my house?" I realized that we only had a second before he would slam the door shut in our faces, so I went right to the point: "I'm looking for an American, Markus Holmberg." His face fell, and he seemed to hesitate, then, in a tone people use when they are forced to admit defeat, when they have to accept the inevitability of something they had long feared, he mumbled, "Come in" with an infinitely tired look, walking away with his head down, back bent, disappearing into the hallway where we followed him.

In the main room there were four children, two men sitting at a table (they too with serious expressions and drawn features), and three women in their forties whose eyes still shone with tears. They watched us come in, dismayed, and Mainak, reacting to the questioning looks directed at him, declared darkly, "They're here for the American," before adding, "It would be best if you all left."

The men asked him if he was sure, and he replied, "I'll take care of this; I'll see you tomorrow at the port." They all headed toward the door, and Mainak's wife took the kids into the other room as we sat down at the table, Subbiah, Mainak, and I.

"My name is Krish, and I'm a friend of Markus Holmberg. He disappeared at the end of the summer; his family is worried about him and asked me to find him. Do you know anything?" Once again, I felt that it was best to be direct. Mainak was silent for a long time, so long that I began to wonder if he would answer at all. He seemed to be weighing exactly what he was going to say, as if he feared incriminating himself by revealing too much. In the end, he made up his mind to ask, "And how do I know you're not from the police?" I thought for a second, then took out my wallet in which I had my American driver's license, an identity card from my university, and a Bank of America Visa card. The sight of these plastic rectangles plunged him into new abysses of uncertainty, and after another long, long silence that Subbiah and I respected as if one word, one gesture could at any moment dissuade him from ever telling the truth, he finally murmured, "They didn't come back."

He continued, his voice very low, as if the reality were too horrible to be named, as if speaking quasi-inaudibly were the way to master it, to avoid it smacking you in the face. "They didn't come back," Mainak repeated a little louder this time, "they had an accident." I let him talk, fearing he'd fall silent again; I breathed slowly, not taking my eyes off him. Subbiah, on my right, didn't move a muscle either, and we listened to him, respecting the pauses, wondering if they would be definitive, then following him through the twists and turns, the digressions, the backtracking, and leaps forward in his discourse. Certain facts, too serious to be approached head-on, you have to attack from one side then the other, revealing each time a nub of truth.

Markus had come to his home in September, recommended by an acquaintance (Mainak refrained from mentioning Zlatair—was he ashamed of this contact in the underworld of the archipelago?), and had explained his plan for an excursion in the vicinity of Sentinel Island. Mainak had a wife and four children. The idea of entering the forbidden waters was all the more frightening as the John Chau incident was still fresh in everyone's mind here; they all knew what had happened to the men who had helped him: they had been convicted of involuntary homicide and violation of the laws protecting the aboriginal tribes. Their lives and those of their families were ruined. The more Markus raised the promised amount, the more Mainak grew firm in his resolution not to have anything to do with such a dangerous, futile, senseless plan. His younger brother Anvita was in the room when Markus tried to convince him. Anvita was twenty-three, and those thousands of dollars up for grabs finally got to him; he waited until Mainak had given Markus a categorical refusal to tell him, "I'll take you there."

Mainak had done his best to talk him out of it, but Anvita had just married and was tired of a life spent in misery, breaking his back every day from dawn to dusk; he wanted better for his wife and the family he wished to begin. He stuck stubbornly to his agreement with Markus, and when Mainak tried to force him to change his mind, they nearly came to blows. Anvita insisted repeatedly that the foreigner didn't want to go *to* Sentinel, just within sight of it; there was a difference, it wasn't so dangerous, and he wanted more, more than all *that*—and by *that* he gestured at the corrugated metal roofs beneath which you roasted in the heat, the shacks that people were crowded into, the water that you had to go fetch at the neighborhood tap, filling bucket after bucket, and the intense suffocating stench of the slum that sticks to your skin and follows you like a bad conscience wherever you go.

I asked Mainak when the accident had taken place, and I had to ask him to repeat his answer, because I thought I had misunderstood when he said, "Three days ago, Anvita and Markus set out three days ago and have given no sign of life since." At first, Markus wanted to leave much sooner, in October, but the monsoon had forced them to be patient. On this question at least, Anvita was reasonable; he had refused to take him before the end of the rainy season, saying, "Alas, the waters around the island are notorious for their violent currents, many ships have wrecked in this area. You've heard of the *Primrose*, haven't you?" It took me a moment to digest this new information, that Markus, having left the US thirteen weeks before, had waited until December to head for Sentinel Island—which meant that when I was looking for him at Mayabunder, he was getting ready to leave Dairy Farm.

Anvita refused stubbornly to have another boat come along as insurance against an accident: "Too expensive, that would cost too much," he repeated, determined to keep for himself the whole amount paid by the foreigner. Markus had hypnotized him with this fortune; he'd always used his money to bend the will of others, to control them by letting them glimpse a sudden opening of new possibilities. Anvita had arranged to meet him at night, and they had headed for Sentinel. Mainak hadn't had any news for three days—not, in any case, from Anvita himself—but he had heard something: it was his friend Vaishna, one of the men we had met at his home, who had shared with him the strange rumor. He had it from a cousin, a non-commissioned officer who had spoken to one of the witnesses of the scene, a scene that embarrassed the authorities because they were unable to explain it and had no interest in digging into what had really happened. At two o'clock in the morning, this very day, a thin white trace had risen, whistling, over Sentinel Island before changing, a thousand feet up, into a languid comet that had lit up the night while falling with a superb laziness back onto the island, followed in its descent by the gaze of a dozen coastguardsmen at the rail of the ships that were patrolling in the area, dumbfounded to see a flare spring from the forbidden territory. It was to this strange event, I was absolutely certain, that the reporter from the *Andaman Times* was referring a few hours before, and the origin of this call for help, launched from the depths of Sentinel Island, was either Anvita or Markus.

Mainak wondered all day if he should let the authorities know about his brother's disappearance, at the risk of creating enormous problems for him with the police if they found him on the island. And each time he got ready to do it, he was held back by the fear that no one would help Anvita and Markus. If they had ended up on Sentinel, they would be left there; in similar cases, the authorities had always preferred not to intervene, so alerting them would probably be to no avail. Mainak had thus stayed home, not knowing what to do. "But the flare gun," I said, "proves that there is at least one survivor. Won't the navy investigate, search for them?" Mainak shrugged his shoulders: "Don't count on it," he answered. "For them, it's much simpler just to pretend they saw nothing."

"And what about us?" I asked.

"What about us?"

"We can't go there?"

"Where? To Sentinel Island?"

"Not necessarily onto the island, but we could at least go around ...."

"You're talking exactly like him ...."

"Are you sure it's true, the story about the flare?"

"Absolutely. Several people confirmed it. At the port, that's all they're talking about."

"So that means they're still alive. And that didn't happen weeks ago, it happened today, just a few hours ago. We have to do something. We could go along the coast, to see if there are any signs of a wreck and, perhaps, only perhaps, bring them back if they are hiding and waiting for help."

"You're ready to go there? Seriously?"

"You said it yourself: the police will not intervene. We are their only chance. Can you imagine for just one second what it must be for them, to be cast away in such a place?"

I fell silent. I appeared to be sure of what I was saying, and I saw that he was beginning to waver, but I didn't know why I was trying to convince him, for what reasons I was ready to take such risks. Markus and Anvita could have died since the shooting of the flare, and what were our real chances of finding them, in the event we even made it to Sentinel? This island was like a dark door I was terrified to open, and it is precisely because I feared what was on the other side that I was determined to go through it. There were other reasons spurring me on, without my being able to establish the exact role they were playing in my decision: my friendship with Markus—and that which went beyond mere friendship, which I didn't want to think about; my responsibility in his fascination with the island; the certainty that I was the only person, with Mainak, who could help them, Markus and his guide; the reward that Alexandra had promised me; and then this penchant for self-destruction that had gripped me since the loss of the baby. In fact, you never really know what determines your behavior; rationality is only the *a posteriori* justification of our desires.

Ultimately, it was surprisingly easy to persuade Mainak. He too had thought of going to the island, without being able to make up his mind, but for a stranger to arrive like that, out of the blue, and tell him that was the right thing to do was a nearly supernatural incitement in this perilous venture, and, very quickly, it was no longer a matter of deciding if we were going to try to help them but of figuring out how to do it. The budget at my disposal smoothed out the difficulties as they arose, and our mutual encouragement reinforced the idea that embarking on this absurd undertaking made sense. Subbiah listened to us, sitting back in his chair, his arms folded across his chest making it clear that he wanted nothing to do with our business and was henceforth only an incredulous witness. We talked at length, Mainak and I, developing a plan that consisted of scouring the coasts of the island in the hope of finding traces of the wreck and resolved to carry it out the very next day; there was no time to lose. I was to meet Mainak at Wandoor, a village on the western coast of Great Andaman, from which we would embark at night.

I returned to my hotel very late. Unable to sleep, I spent long minutes staring at my computer screen, pondering the messages I was going to send to Alexandra and Eleanor. I hid nothing of the truth from the first: I coldly explained the situation and our plan to save Markus, making her no promises other than I would do my best to bring him back alive. I asked her to deposit to my account, upon receiving this message, the second half of the sum she had promised me. If I didn't return from the island, at least Eleanor would be free from want, this money being added to the life insurance that I had taken out, at her request, a few years before. Alexandra's response came almost immediately: it was the beginning of the afternoon in New York. Astonishingly, for her, Alexandra was understanding and grateful. I had clearly succeeded in communicating to her the seriousness of the circumstances, the trouble I had taken to track Markus down, the deplorable situation in which he had put himself, and the danger I was going to face for him. From the outset, she feared that her brother had vanished on the island and thanked me for doing all I could to help him. She added that she was going to transfer the funds immediately, and, indeed, I was able to confirm a few hours later that she had kept her word. "Don't take any useless risks," she finished. Then I had to write to Eleanor.

By this time, my temples were heavy with fatigue, and I wasn't sure what was best for her to know. I simply wrote her that I was leaving for several days, during which time I would have no internet access. If she didn't have any news from me by the following Monday, she should write Alexandra Holmberg, whose email address I included. Markus's sister would explain everything to her. I sat for a few more moments in front of the message; then I added that I loved her before clicking on "Send." When I awoke, I looked at my messages a last time. Eleanor hadn't written me; she was always hopelessly slow in answering emails—which indicated that she was not sufficiently concerned about me to check them regularly. I felt, despite myself, a look of bitterness pass over my face. This silence was a good summary of our story: we had always lived out of sync; even at home, it was as if we were in two different time zones. I turned off the computer, which was my last link to her, and began my preparation.

What should you bring to the most dangerous island in the world? Every object I chose made me feel how ill prepared I was and contributed to a growing sense of absurdity, as if I were an innocent tourist who was going to be parachuted into a war zone. I placed in a waterproof container my identity papers, binoculars, a camera, a flashlight, three liters of water, and two boxes of protein bars. I slipped on a light pair of trousers and a khaki shirt made of synthetic fibers, put a penknife in one pocket and a pair of sunglasses in the other, then donned a cap and inspected my hiking shoes. My reflection in the mirror hardly inspired confidence: as always, I found myself too small and too skinny, my back a bit bent. There was something floating in my gaze, something I vaguely hoped to leave behind me on the island if I were to return. Subbiah was waiting for me at the front desk. I paid my bill, and he drove me to Wandoor, around twenty miles to the west. Neither of us had much to say on the way. I knew the road; it was the one I had taken upon leaving the Jarawa reservation, when I went to that islet from which you could see Sentinel Island. "This time, I'm really going there," I repeated over and over to myself, not believing it.

When we shook hands, Subbiah looked at me exactly as if he were saying goodbye to me forever. I had never experienced that before, this promise of my disappearance in the eyes of someone else: "Let's have a drink together when you get back!" he said, falsely cheerful, before dropping me off at the entrance to the village. I grabbed my things, and some people in the street pointed out the house where I was supposed to wait for Mainak. He arrived at the end of the afternoon, reassuring me that everything was ready, and that we would leave as planned around one in the morning. It still seemed just as incredible to me that this island I had been thinking about for fifteen years, that had always appeared to be at the very edge of the earth, was accessible after scarcely a few hours of navigation, and, still more incredible, that I was about to go there. I kept repeating it to myself, to accustom my brain to an inconceivable situation that resembled one of those bad dreams from which you awake exhausted, feverish, and soaked in sweat.

Mainak left me to do some final preparations after showing me a corner of the dirt floor where I could put my sleeping bag. Beyond the palm-leaf walls, I heard the cries of the neighborhood children; rain hammered on the metal roof then stopped, and, after a long moment, I fell asleep. At the appointed hour, Mainak shook me: "Wake up," he said, "we have to leave now." I gathered my stuff while he waited for me in the doorway. In silence and guided by his flashlight, we followed a path that wound through a stand of coconut trees. After around ten minutes, we arrived at the shore before continuing on to the jetty that was a little farther away. Mainak pointed to a spot in the shadows, instructing me to wait for him there. I listened to the noise of the waves dying on the beach, accompanied by brushing sounds that I couldn't identify. "A good time to put a stop to this," I said to myself, not moving a muscle.

Mainak emerged from the darkness and motioned to me to follow him to the end of the jetty. Billions of bluish points of light in the sky disoriented me. Were these gently twinkling galaxies luminous organisms at the very bottom of the sea, and this enormous swath of darkness below the border of the cosmos? All this celestial beauty buffeted me. I was moved by it, as if it were the heartrending proof of the splendor of a world I was on the verge of losing. Mainak pointed his flashlight out to sea, turning it on and off three times, very quickly. Out of the vague forms far off in the archipelago, a low shadow loomed toward us, preceded by a rumbling that became slowly clearer: it was a wheezy motor propelling a slender, elongated craft. The pilot stopped the motor a short distance from the jetty, and the boat, continuing to glide forward, came close enough for us to climb aboard. When my feet left the rocks on which I had been standing, the fear of never again setting foot on land crossed my mind.

At the stern stood two small figures whose faces were indiscernible in the darkness. They remained mute, but with Mainak's help they handed me a plastic tarp. In the event that a plane from the coastguard flew over us, it was understood that Mainak and I would hide beneath the tarp while our pilots would get out their fishing tackle. With this precaution in place, the motor sputtered back to life, and we slowly moved away from the shore.

Our boat hardly inspired confidence. Hacked by hand out of teak, it was twenty feet long. There was no bridge or seat, just benches that came from the structure of the tree from which the boat had been dug out. It was so narrow that once seated, my hands clasped on my thighs, I could set my elbows on each side. We were going along the archipelago our pilot had arrived from when Mainak again signaled with his flashlight. Another boat, similar to our own, appeared out of the darkness and followed us. "They're with us," Mainak explained. "It's safer to go there with two crews." I felt the heat of the black water when I stuck my hand into it, lulled by the monotonous noise of the motor that exuded a vaguely nauseating odor. Behind us, the wake we made in the waves grew until it died out.

How was our pilot navigating? He had neither sextant nor compass nor GPS, not to mention no radio. Perhaps he was reading in the stars the path we needed to take, or maybe he had known all his life the location of this island that his father had made him promise never to approach? Now and then he changed direction, suddenly accelerating or slowing down to lessen the noise from the motor. "That's what I was afraid of," said Mainak, pointing toward a distant glimmer of light: "It's the coastguard. After the distress signal the other night, they must have increased the patrols around the island." Our pilot continued to play hide and seek with these ships that, oddly, caused me no concern. I was convinced, deep down, that our expedition would not finish like that, with our little boats taken into custody and accompanied back to the port without our setting eyes on Sentinel. My whole life had been preparing for this moment; I knew that we would go to *that place*, that we would go all the way.

Mainak trusted the pilot so completely that he wrapped himself in a blanket and went to sleep on the bottom of the boat. I would have liked to do the same, but sleep was out of the question with all the excitement and impatience, so I just stared into the darkness, which was punctuated now and then by the sparks that sprang from the motor and died in the sea. After several hours of navigation, a glow arose, far off. For a moment I thought it was the lantern of another ship, but it was just the flare of dawn rising over the sea. Clouds scattered high up in the sky began to brighten, then the light gradually spread out, revealing the features of the pilot and his crewmate, two thin bearded men. The first wore a turban, and the other, younger, looked a lot like him. It was perhaps his younger brother or his son. Their worried gazes were directed out to the open sea, avoiding mine. Despite myself, my eyes kept closing; I slipped under the seat and, my head lying in the bow of the boat, fell asleep in my turn.

When I awoke, the land we had left stretched out far behind us in a thin ochre line. And for the first time since our departure it came into view, black and still far off, deploying its gloomy canopy: Sentinel Island. Lightning fell from the crown of somber clouds surrounding it in the storm. It was really as if we were approaching the end of the world, an end of the world guarded by all the horrors of the sea, with the night and the void as its culmination. Something born of old superstitions—when sailors saw Leviathans in the ocean depths, a sidereal fall of the oceans at the edge of the flat Earth, and head-shrinking cannibals on each strange shore—came back to me fleetingly from the dawn of time. I sat and gazed at the forbidden island, my mind a jumble of disparate ideas. That too is Sentinel: a place that escapes language like water slips between the mesh of a net. The man with the turban prepared a line and began to fish. In the boat that was following us, one of the sailors had also taken out his fishing gear. Fishing would be our alibi if the coastguard caught us in the restricted zone: we would tell them that we had come there by accident, borne by the currents. At regular intervals, the sailors pulled out tunas and snappers that they clubbed to death before throwing out their line again.

As our boats drew closer to the island, we passed by intertwined branches that resembled the tentacles of long cephalopods. Sometimes a slender emerald brushed against the hull; it was the leaf of some tropical tree. The details of the island slowly came into view. We could already distinguish the light ribbon of the beach from the tangles of trees. The closer we came, the more the ocean revealed the secret life in its depths. Dolphins rose up around us, and flying fish passed in swarms across our bow. Turtles swam up from the turquoise sea bottom where the coral formed vast labyrinths, greeting us with a black stare, seemingly indignant at our intrusion. But in a striking contrast the island that pitched on the horizon revealed no trace of life other than its vegetal profusion. It seemed to me at times that only the legend of a people could be born in such complete solitude: had the Sentinelese ever existed, and had Markus and I sacrificed all these years to the cult of a shadow?

One knee placed on the seat, my balance constantly threatened by the rocking of the boat, I observed the island bobbing in my binoculars. I could see tree trunks on the shore that looked like men stretched out on the ground, fog that I took for smoke from a bonfire. The lagoon was filled with an armada of dugouts that, on closer examination, turned out to be stumps adrift. A sudden lurch of the boat flung me down onto my seat; the pilot was taking us on a northwesterly course as we began our circumnavigation of Sentinel Island. He took great care to keep his distance from the wall of reefs revealed by the waves breaking over them; two hundred yards away, the beach seemed both near and inaccessible. Sitting behind me, Mainak looked worriedly at the clouds gathering to the east. It was mid-December, and the rainy season should have been over. At Port Blair, the storms came every two days or so, intense but brief. The weather, which we had expected to be clear, was becoming more threatening by the minute. The waves came more and more rapidly. Grabbing the plastic buckets lying around the boat, we bailed out the rising water. The rescue boat that was following us at some distance was like a reflection of the fragility of our own.

The jungle we were moving past, dense and wrapped in mist, resembled a film played over and over on the backdrop of the shore. It gave way to a succession of dunes dotted with sickly bushes. We were approaching a small island a short distance from the coast; the breakers were over ten feet high, forming a constant barrier. On the other side, waves were smashing against an obstacle that I took for a rock. I finally recognized the vertical form, the metal protruding above the water: we had reached the wreckage of the *Primrose*. It resembled the vestige of a very ancient civilization, gnawed away by the sea.

That is when Mainak cried out, "Look! Natives!" Between the *Primrose* and the beach, I saw a dugout canoe. We were a hundred yards away from it, and we could make out the silhouette of the craft and of two men, one at the bow and the other, behind him, working a pole. I was seeing Sentinelese for the first time. Had they caught sight of us? On the other side of the border marked by the reefs, the two men were on a parallel course with ours—having a much easier time, however, as the waters of the lagoon were calm in comparison to the Bay of Bengal. For a minute, probably less, their dugout, the wreckage of the *Primrose*, our boat, and the one that was escorting us were all on the same axis, like four planets in a line. Perhaps, I thought, time is like this conjunction. The periods coexist over time, never meeting nor disappearing; and from the most distant past to the future, all of the intermediate stages subsist.

Mainak cried again, "Look!" As dense as a cataract, swift and fleeing like a tornado, a column of rain, several hundred yards tall, was moving across a sea bristling with gray waves, a tsunami of dark clouds just behind it. "We've got to get out of here right now," Mainak exclaimed, "or we're going to die here." The sailors were yelling in Bengali, pointing at the storm. As we were going around the island by the northwest, heading for its most distant shore beyond which hundreds of miles of ocean separated us from the next coast, Sentinel Island, complicit, had interposed its forests, concealing from us those cloudy masses torn by lightning. In the lagoon, the dugout had disappeared.

The swells pushed us stubbornly toward the reefs. We climbed up the waves and plunged down the other side faster and faster, diving into and carrying off an enormous cargo of water that we had to bail out before the next mountain hit. Our motor struggled in these extreme conditions, fighting a losing battle against the waves and currents. In this situation, it was just as useless to try to flee toward the empty vastness of the Bay of Bengal as to attempt to reach the island. Before us, the column of rain had disappeared, absorbed by the rapidly approaching wall of clouds. The pilots cried out to each other again and, to my great surprise, changed course to head directly into the storm. They had caught sight of a slit between the clouds: black cliffs rose on either side but, in the middle, appeared a narrow gray pass we could perhaps slip into.

A minute later, however, the cliffs closed ranks, quashing any hope of cutting through the storm. Pushed to its maximum, the motor was at best able to maintain our position. Slowly losing ground in this inequal struggle, we were constantly drawn toward the coral barrier. Suddenly Mainak cast the anchor while the sailors took out the tarpaulins to provide some shelter. They ordered me to unfold my own, and before ducking under I glanced furtively at Sentinel Island drowned in the rain, smothered by the inky sky. For a brief moment, silence reigned everywhere. It was as if, magically, the danger had disappeared as we huddled beneath the tarps. The illusion didn't last, however: gusts of wind began to hiss, and the waves broke more and more violently on the reefs. And the rain beat down on the canvas in dense ribbons, flooding my binoculars and my notebook, seeping into my clothes and my kitbag, pounding this island to which we had never been so close and where we risked foundering with no one in the world to come to our rescue.

For what seemed an eternity we huddled under the water-soaked tarp, our limbs tangled like bodies in a common grave, the deluge drumming down on us. The boat rose and fell precipitously on the waves, and I felt the anchor on the sea floor straining to hold us secure, like a helping hand about to let go, its severely tested links on the point of breaking. Shaken, knocked about, we expected the final shock of the hull against the reefs any second. But the storm pursued its path; the rain battering the tarp began to slacken, the waves lifting us to milder heights and sending us down the other side less wildly. Little by little the boat regained its balance, and we came out from under our plastic shroud to bail out the water as best we could. It was high time: the water was mounting dangerously in the boat, threatening to swallow us up. I heard voices, cries, and turned my head: the other boat was also on the point of sinking, its occupants working frantically to get the water out.

The rain continued to fall in tight vertical sheets, adding to the load we were carrying. When the downpour finally relented, Mainak tried to restart the motor, but it balked. The two sailors and I stopped bailing immediately, petrified, staring at him, scarcely daring to breathe and even less to imagine what would happen if our means of locomotion failed us in the middle of the restricted zone. Once, twice, and more, Mainak attempted to crank the motor into life until a muffled sound, something like the cough of a chronic smoker, rewarded his efforts and allowed us to approach the second crew.

A tense exchange ensued between Mainak and Vidur, the other captain. Mainak wanted to continue our circumnavigation of the island and repeated that "this smattering of rain" (I couldn't help admiring the euphemism) in no way changed our mission. We'd gotten through the worst: we weren't going to let a little shower chase us back to port. Vidur repeated over and over again, "It's too risky, it's too risky," in a disjointed harangue that mixed helter-skelter the paltry sum that Mainak had given him, his three kids, his wife, and his handicapped mother. He punctuated his protests with broad, exasperated gestures, motions that grew more emphatic as he grew angrier, pointing to the island, the monstrous island looming before us, the rain still beating down, the ankle-deep water in the boat, the storm that was moving on, perhaps giving way to a hurricane, and then the island again, the ghoulish island whose mass of tangled trees hid something nameless and dreadful. The exchange became heated: Mainak called him a coward, reminding him of the payment he had already accepted and his promise to come to Anvita's aid, repeating that his brother was probably shipwrecked and wounded, waiting for them somewhere on the island. Vidur shot back that the money, the money, he hadn't received enough to justify such risks. He had already taken hold of the motor to return to Wandoor, and I saw Mainak measuring the distance between the two boats, as if he were going to board the other one, when one of our sailors, the youngest one, silent since the beginning of the argument, the only one who had been observing the island while the rest of us were absorbed with the quarrel between the captains, suddenly cried out, horrified, instantly silencing the two men:

"What's that, over there?"

He was pointing at the shore, far away, where the coast curved, so far that what he was designating could just barely be made out, a vague mark, a dark vertical line on the paleness of the beach. Shading our eyes, squinting, we were all frozen in place, concentrating, as the noise of the waves and the rain enveloped us. The surface of the sea, hammered by raindrops, was punctuated by miniscule craters erupting everywhere, and while the others scanned the horizon, their knees bent against the rocking of the boat, I searched for my binoculars. I wiped them as best I could, and when I finally brought them to my eyes, I was jolted backwards so violently that I nearly fell overboard.

Without saying a word—I didn't want to influence him by naming what was perhaps only a figment of my imagination—I handed the binoculars to Mainak. The sailors looked anxiously back and forth from him to me until he let out a horrified shout when, there could no longer be any doubt, he had recognized, planted on the beach like a barbaric scarecrow, a monstrous Christ, the sagging, limp remains of a black-haired man, his chin hanging down on his chest. One after the other, the sailors took the binoculars, their shocked recoils confirming what we feared we had seen.

Mainak gestured to the sailors to weigh anchor. He immediately engaged the motor without so much as a glance at Vidur, who, his resistance evaporating, followed in our wake. Mainak pushed the motor far harder than he should have, the boat smacking into the waves and soaking us with large chunks of sea. We risked capsizing at any moment, but I made no protest against his rashness; I would've liked us to go even faster. In his mind, as in mine, it was as if any reasoning were suspended; there was a blank, an interlude that would last until we had determined if this body, vilely exposed to the wind, to the rain, and to the wild beasts, was that of Markus or of Mainak's brother, unless it was the body of a poacher—I clung to this hope—come to despoil the Sentinelese of their meager resources while the whole wide world was open to his greed.

Mainak held his course, clenching his teeth, staring straight ahead, and when we had arrived near the reefs, facing the figure, he stopped the motor and, grabbing the binoculars, trained them on the body, staring at it at length. When he removed the binoculars, his eyes were brimming with tears: Mainak had recognized his brother. An obscene wave of relief swept over me. I gently retrieved the binoculars from his dangling arms and scanned the beach, looking for another human scarecrow that the Sentinelese might have left to warn intruders. But the shore was empty and the lagoon too, the lagoon where the rain was still falling while other clouds were splitting apart, flooding the bank with light so that Anvita's body was now crowned by a rainbow—ironic and splendid. Mainak collapsed in the boat and sobbed for a minute or two, then, after conceding this momentary weakness, stood back up while the other boat cast anchor beside ours. In a low voice, one of our men informed the other crew: "Yes, it's Anvita; no, there's no mistake." Then Mainak spoke to all of us: "Over there, three hundred yards away, there's an opening in the lagoon; I'm going to get my brother's body. Who's coming with me?"

Everyone lowered their eyes. Were they thinking, like me, of the Sentinelese arrows, of twenty-five years of expeditions that had never overcome their resistance, of the death, in short, that could strike us the moment we set foot on the forbidden island? I volunteered, and they looked at me with gratitude, relief brightening their faces: one person was enough, another volunteer would be too many they quickly stated. We would have to be quick and discreet, efficient and silent: untie the body and get out of there immediately, a two-man job. Mainak flared up: "Shut your traps," he ordered our crew, "and get out of here." They jumped into the other boat while Mainak was turning to Vidur to tell him, looking him straight in the eye, "You don't budge from here until we get back." Vidur nodded and, as soon as the anchor was back in the boat, Mainak cranked up the motor.

"So, I'm going to Sentinel Island." The sentence turned slowly in my head as Mainak steered the boat, at the same insane speed, toward the entrance to the lagoon. The coast flew by with its colossal trees in whose shadows a muted and persistent threat, incomprehensible and patient, awaited us with the confidence of a predator who knows the advantage of its size, its weight, and its force, who knows the swiftness with which it can strike the intruder who ventures there. And while the clouds continued to open up and flood the island's shore and its gleaming lagoon with a blinding light, and that sentence continued to revolve in my head with the neutrality of an objective statement, "So, I'm going to Sentinel Island," what struck me was the calm and even detachment that pervaded me.

Our boat entered the lagoon. The clouds were now far off, and the rain had stopped. We approached the beach slowly, a beach that seemed oddly familiar to me: I suddenly understood, without the shadow of a doubt, that I had already seen it, and that my entire life had conspired to create the conditions for this instant. Nothing could have prevented this moment from happening, and this intense calm was the proof, this troubling familiarity with fleeting impressions—a certain density of the light, momentary reflections on the surface of the water, a pattern created by interlacing branches. Everything gave me the certainty of being in exactly the right place as well as a disconcerting impression of invincibility, as if the fact that we could not *not* come here was the proof that we would take this business to the end, live through it, return from it, and tell about it. I linger on the delicate description of this singular state of mind to bring out the metaphysical dimension of Sentinel. At this point it seems to me that the lesson should indeed be clear: Sentinel is not only a place but an idea, the irrefutable proof that moving forward in time is nothing other than recognizing in fits and starts something whose inevitable character we already know intimately. But I also linger here to explain the decision, apparently absurd and nonetheless perfectly coherent, that I was getting ready to make a few minutes later. Mainak killed the motor, letting the boat glide forward silently until the bow hit the shore and anchored us on Sentinel—a few yards from the tortured body of Anvita.

I lifted my gaze toward him, immediately wishing to erase from my memory—where it has nonetheless remained like a scar—this face whose cheek was pierced by a gaping wound. The naked jaw was visible from the side, and I would have liked also to forget the slit throat from which a flow of black blood had spread across his chest, and to forget the gashes that the arrows had made there. The sand in his hair, the wet T-shirt clinging to his skin, everything proved that the remains had spent a good while buried on the beach before being exhumed and stood up that way, a rotting scarecrow whose sickeningly sweetish odor filled my lungs. The whole scene felt ironic and monstrous, for the tranquil shore where it was playing out, flooded with sunlight, with the driftwood at the edge of the translucent lagoon, could be taken for the incarnation of a certain idea of happiness.

Mainak remained motionless in front of his brother, incapable of turning away. I handed him my pocketknife to free Anvita, whose hands, tied behind his back, bound him to a branch driven deep into the ground. And while he severed the bonds, I scanned the forest, fearing that the Sentinelese would rush forth to prevent us from leaving with this carnal fetish. With infinite care, Mainak eased his brother to the ground, then asked me to bring the plastic tarp, which I unfolded next to the body. I grabbed him by his wrists—I can still feel his spongy flesh in my palms—and Mainak by his ankles as we placed him in the middle of the canvas that we pulled over him like a shroud. We carried him to the boat where, oh so carefully, we slid him under the seats so that he could rest with his back against the sea.

We spent eight, perhaps ten minutes in all tending to Anvita, and if the Sentinelese were hidden somewhere watching us, they had decided to let us leave with our corpse. In any case, nothing betrayed their presence; the lagoon and the beach were empty as far as we could see, and the only human presence on the horizon was that of our comrades on the other side of the reefs. Mainak got into the boat and asked me to push it and get in. I stood there lifeless, mute. In the course of these critical seconds, he perhaps imagined the arrows of the Sentinelese whistling in the sky, heard their steps as the horde ran up the shore, visualized all the dangers we had escaped and which could still materialize as long as I stayed there, my head bowed, indecisive. He asked me what had gotten into me, why I was just standing there. And suddenly I moved away from the boat and began to dig frantically all around the branch to which Anvita's body had been attached a few moments before, with the fear but also in a certain sense the hope of discovering the face of Markus buried in the sand—Markus who, if he wasn't there, was perhaps still alive on the island after his distress flare had rent the night.

"What the hell are you doing, digging like that? Push the boat and get in, we have to get out of here."

"I'm staying."

"What do you mean, you're staying? Are you nuts?"

"I want to be sure. Markus might still be alive; you wouldn't have abandoned your brother, would you? If the Sentinelese had killed him, they would have stood him up on the beach too."

"We don't have the time for me to tell you how stupid that is. Get into the fuckin' boat, and let's go!"

"No!" I cried—and my shout provoked the flight of a swarm of birds in the jungle, giving another proof of our presence to the Sentinelese. "Come back for me in exactly two hours. If I'm not back, leave without me."

"Two hours?"

"Two hours. Give me a chance to find him."

He promised me to be at the exact same place at the agreed time. I pushed the prow to free the boat. It drifted backwards, Mainak started the motor, and a few moments later it had left the lagoon. I was alone, alone on Sentinel Island. I turned to face the forest, glanced at my watch, and crossed through the curtain of trees. What happened afterwards, minute by minute, has remained in my memory with stupefying clarity; or, more precisely, what happened afterwards has never ceased to happen and is still happening: I close my eyes and another version of myself is still there, on the forbidden island; it has never come back.

Each step brought me closer to the heart of the island—and each step took me further from the rendezvous spot. I'm drawn forward toward the depths of Sentinel and at the same time pulled in the opposite direction where help—life—awaits me. In my head there is a void; sensations, yes, but not a single idea. This is not the time for reflection, not the time to wonder if what I'm doing makes sense, if there's the slightest chance that I'll find Markus, or if he would've taken the same risks for me. Nor is it the time to question myself about what I'm trying to prove, if this adventure will make me a man, and if I will succeed in breaking the spell of Eleanor, this malaise she has imposed on me since she came into my life. I must use everything the Jarawas taught me to make it back to the beach in two hours—no, less than two hours already. Living with them I learned to find my bearings in the jungle. To move beyond the great panorama—the chaos of vegetation, the intertwined branches—to the recognition of details. Not to get lost in the multitude—the trees, the vines, the ferns—but rather to pay attention to what is unique: "this kapok tree with the split trunk next to the three palm trees on my left," or "this mangrove five yards from the arborescent euphorbia bushes." Each memorized image is a landmark on the path back—the link in a mental chain that keeps me alive.

My senses are extraordinarily acute. They've never been so sensitive. The crackling beneath my feet sounds like explosions, the noises from the forest strike me in bursts. I'm a surface where everything is absorbed: the bark of the fallen tree I step over remains in my hand; the odor of the decaying vegetation is almost suffocating. It is fear that gives me this expanded consciousness, which seems abnormal, supernatural. I almost feel divine, for everything flows into my brain and is organized there: the sensation of the sweat that runs down my chest, like the moist heat that cloaks my shoulders and the rustling I hear on my right, perhaps a mongoose or a wildcat. I'm conscious of all these facts, independently and at the same time. I stop for a moment and look backwards while crushing with a slap the mosquito that has been tormenting me. On the other side of the branches and tree trunks—rising so high and coming together to form an arch that the sun struggles to pierce by slipping through the rare cracks—I can see fragments of the beach and sea, disconnected. Soon the forest will have shut completely, and the palm trees will be like the bars of a prison.

I come upon a path, a narrow trail that winds through the jungle with, here and there, footprints that are still fresh. I remember Portman and Pandit, who spoke of these lines of communication in the forest linking the villages to the coast and to each other. I hesitate to take this trail. Among the trees I'm less visible—but noisier and slower too. I have an hour and a half left. I hesitate when I hear, so indistinct that it perhaps only exists in my troubled imagination, a sort of clamor, far off. Frozen in place, I strain to hear and, yes, there are echoes of loud voices coming from the coast. I quickly grab a branch that I set across the path; it will mark the exact place where I left the forest. I begin to run as fast as I can, not knowing quite why. I feel such an intense terror that I'm just obeying sudden impulses that dictate my conduct. I have thirty minutes to find any trace of Markus if I want to have enough time to retrace my steps back to the beach. I run and no longer know if I'm fleeing death or rushing toward it, the death I've come here to confront and that is observing me at this very moment, behind the trees, ready to release an arrow that will hit me in the spinal column and slam me headfirst into the ground. At the horizon the light is changing. A space opens up in the forest. I slow down as I approach the clearing. My heart is beating so hard I can't hear the noises of the jungle, my legs trembling so badly they can only carry me forward with a superhuman effort. I prepare to spend less than five minutes in the Sentinelese's village—five minutes I've spent thirty years pondering.

The clearing is a circle about forty yards in diameter. The trees surrounding it are like the walls of a well soaring up toward the sky. When the clouds pass high above, the entire space is plunged into a momentary twilight, and it's as if something enormous and imperious is punishing you for a misdeed by inflicting night on you—then, satisfied by seeing your fearful countenance pay homage to its power, relents and returns the sun to you. On both sides of the trail that leads to this clearing in the forest, skulls of wild boars form sinister little mounds a yard high. In this open area, there is a village. Against the jungle, around twenty wall-less huts are set in a circle, with leaf roofs that tilt gently toward the back. And in front of these rectangular dwellings, fires are burning, surrounded by stakes. A totem watches over each home: sticks driven into the ground decorated with five twigs that recall the fingers of a hand.

I saw him immediately, in the center of the deserted clearing. The child sitting on the ground, his back turned to me, staring down at something—I soon see that it is an ant carrying a leaf—and cooing its appreciation, its encouragement. I move forward, checking that my first impression was correct: yes, the huts are indeed empty and, other than the little child, there are no other Sentinelese in sight. I'm ten steps from him now, and he hasn't heard me. I'm wondering how I can avoid frightening him when out of the forest comes a noise, vague and louder than before, like a stifled rumbling, losing volume as it approaches. The child raises his head toward the source of the clamor and in doing so catches sight of me over his shoulder.

What immediately crosses his face is the broadest smile, the most radiant, most touching, most disarming smile, filled with affection, naivety, and joy. He claps his hands, beaming, this little baby, at most a year and a half old, who only possesses this disarming smile, and who begins to warble melodious sounds, sounds that spin in the air, that tumble out with inflections and tremolos, trills, sounds that mean in the universal language of children, "You came!" and "I'm happy to see you!" He is looking at me with his charming little nose, his eyes sparkling with a joy that is going to turn into a fit of giggles. Clumsy, awkward, his flapping arms betray his excitement, and he reminds me of the Jarawa babies I watched with such pleasure in the reserve, reminds me of a photo of myself when I was around his age and, in fact, of all the toddlers I had met in the course of my life, with their gentleness and native sweetness, their emotions varying like the reflections on the water's surface and, like them, pure.

For the first time I begin to suspect that I was mistaken in taking the Sentinelese for a figure of Difference. It's true that I've always refused to consider them "primitive" or "Stone Age warriors," for these words, borrowed from other peoples' language, seemed to stem from racist prejudice. But I nonetheless viewed them as a certain incarnation of Otherness and a face of Exoticism. Well, this child is me and it's all of us, it's our common humanity, it's the voice that says *mama* and *I love you* in a thousand different languages. It says nothing else; it's the same yearning for happiness and the same desire to escape suffering, the same craving for dignity, and the same need of love. It's all of us, exactly as we are, here and now, not as projections of a bygone age, memories of a proverbial time offering a so-called reflection of our origins, but our present condition in all its surprising fragility and beauty. And I wonder, looking at this child—still keeping my distance to avoid both frightening him and transmitting to him the germs I know I'm carrying—why I was fascinated by his people, why I felt the desire to come here, what dreams attached to this sea of foliage led Markus and me into such solitude while I could have returned this baby's smile in Columbus or New Haven, New York or Mumbai, in all the places I've lived and all those I might yet go, in the reflection in my mirror too, since this little being was me, and he was you as well.

Something is moving to the side: the baby and I turn our heads at the same time. I jump when I see, standing beside one of the huts, a very old woman, her hanging breasts, her hollow stomach, petrified at the sight of this intruder, this invader. I raise my hands instinctively, my palms turned toward her, chest high, but before I have time to utter an expression of peace in Jarawa, in the hope she will understand, she disappears into the jungle with a speed I wouldn't have expected from her skinny thighs and emaciated body and cries out a loud warning to her tribe. I glance at my watch: I had left Mainak an hour and a quarter earlier. It is time, past time, to start back toward the shore before the others respond to her call. And since the Sentinelese, alerted, might burst out at any moment, I give myself one last chance to accomplish my mission, one last chance to get Markus out of the hiding place where he may have survived: I scream his name with all my strength, twice. Then I hold perfectly still and count ten seconds, waiting for the response that never came.

I frantically hurry past all the huts, looking inside for any trace, any object that might reveal Markus's presence, and I'm in luck, for after having found in one dwelling a boar's skull decorated with paintings, in the next one a bow, arrows, harpoons, wooden buckets, and a fishing net, and in a third a curious board covered with inlaid stones and seashells that resembles a chessboard, I discover in the corner of the last one a waterproof jerrican that must weigh at least five kilos. I open it and look inside. There are various objects: a wallet, papers, an empty red and black plastic flare gun, and, at the very bottom, a revolver. I have no time to think: I shove the revolver into the back of my pants, quickly grab the can and, after glancing one last time at the baby—who responds with a final smile—rush out of the clearing. I have less than forty minutes to get back to the beach. I give up any thought of finding Markus; the only thing that counts now is not to end up a prisoner of the island. I have no way of knowing it at this point, but I'm carrying off with me the secret that is going to destroy my life.

Retracing my steps as fast as my legs can carry me, I try to recognize the exact place where I left the jungle. And just as I catch sight of the branch I left as a landmark a cry rings out behind me. I turn around, and there they are, twenty yards away: four Sentinelese, two women and two men armed with a bow and an adz whose blade is attached to the handle by a piece of rope. I slowly set the can on the ground and show them my empty hands. I can feel the weight of the revolver against my back. The men are strong, with bulging muscles, their foreheads wide and round; one has very short hair, the other a ridge of hair that runs down the middle of his skull; their bodies and faces are covered with symbolic ochre markings. Arrows are stuck in their bark belts, and other bands are wrapped around their biceps. Beside them the two women have yellow bands around their heads and armbands of the same color. One of them has a strap holding leaves to her back; the other is carrying a large basket made of bulrushes, shaped like a cone, empty.

We stand looking at each other for a long moment: two worlds contemplating one another, wondering how to bridge the gap. Before they use their bow, I speak to them loudly in Jarawa, trying to persuade them I'm peaceful, saying things like "friend," *lalay*, "Don't shoot!", *kho patho*, "Leave me alone!", *m-ajigijiya*, and "Go away!," *anathča*. And while I'm wondering if they've understood me, the man with the ridge of hair shoots an arrow that flies off into the trees because just as he let it go, one of the women pushed his arm. He turns to her angrily, but she stands her ground and, while they're arguing, I take out the revolver. They immediately fall silent, and the terror in their eyes confirms what I had heard: the Sentinelese know about firearms. This isn't the first time a stranger has waved one at them. When I point the gun at them, they freeze, and when I fire into the air, they flee toward the village. I scoop up the jerrican and head into the forest.

I hurry through the jungle; I've spent far too much time on the island and am going to arrive at the rendezvous too late. I'm going to end up dead on a stake facing the sea. My body is reaching the limit beyond which asphyxia awaits me, paralysis of my members; I stumble and fall on my face. I get back up in an instant, bloodied, a purple trickle moving down my arm; my trousers are torn, and I can see a piece of my right knee, the size of a quarter, hanging down. I have ten minutes left to reach Mainak. I resume running, ignoring the pain; for the moment it barely registers, scarcely an annoyance although the two wounds are deep enough to leave scars that are still visible today. Fragments of the sea suddenly appear through the branches, and I push on, panic-stricken, for the rendezvous time is past—I'm going to find the beach empty and die on this island. And when I finally emerge from the jungle, panting, drenched in sweat, my mouth dry, my sight blurred, I understand instantly: my situation is desperate.

I'm around five hundred yards from the meeting place, marked by the stake to which Anvita was bound. Mainak is in the lagoon but turned in the wrong direction. I'm a half-hour late, and he's heading out toward the open sea. Behind me I can see them running: thirty, forty Sentinelese perhaps, rushing toward me, still far off and small but growing larger by the second. I dash toward Mainak screaming at the top of my lungs, terrified at the idea he is going to leave me behind. He finally hears me and immediately turns the boat around. The Sentinelese are coming closer, I won't have time to wait for Mainak to arrive. I quickly take off my shoes and trousers, tear off my shirt and fling the revolver into the water, followed by the waterproof jerrican that Mainak grabs off the waves. And I dive into the water, swimming frantically, beside myself, to reach the craft. I expect to receive an arrow at any moment; I can already feel the projectile penetrate my flesh, and, by a strange mental quirk, I suddenly remember the summer day spent with Markus, Alexandra, and Joakim when the threat of the Great White had led me toward the depths of the Block Island strait. The noise of the motor is deafening, I hear a cry, I see the bow and hold onto the boat's side until Mainak hauls me on board, where I lie on the bottom, my chest heaving from the violence of the effort. Mainak says nothing, doesn't head for the entrance to the lagoon as I expected but remains standing, looking toward the shore. I pull myself up, and then I see them.

Several dozen Sentinelese form a solid wall. All of them young and strong, they're close enough for us to read on their faces the determination, the courage, the defiance they feel. They stand perfectly still, immersed in silence. They're armed with bows and lances, and I understand that they could have easily struck me when I was swimming to the boat, that they can still shower us with a volley of arrows. Generous, they choose to let us live. Our craft drifts for a moment, parallel to the shore where other Sentinelese, from both sides of the beach and from the depths of the island, continue to pour in. Now there are more than a hundred of them, and the new arrivals join the wall formed by all the others, among them women and old men, infants suckling at their mothers' breasts, and small children hiding behind the adults' legs. It's the presence of these children that changes the meaning of this moment as it stretches out. They look curious, frightened, and some even amused; they point at us, laughing, while others begin to cry. This is not a moment of confrontation, nor of epiphany, but rather—how to put it—an instant of deep equality during which a mutual promise is made. Each is making a silent appeal to what is best in the other. Mainak and I are standing before a united family that is asking, in return for the clemency it is showing us, that we leave, forgetting forever the path to their island and letting our peers know that the Sentinelese have no need of them. The boat continues to drift slowly, floating past the last Sentinelese at the end of the line. Mainak cranks the motor, and we move away as the Sentinelese continue to watch us until we leave the lagoon. When we do, they break up their wall along the water, intoning a song we can hear faintly in the distance.

Mainak and I said nothing before rejoining Vidur and his crew. There, behind the barrier-reefs, they gave me something to drink and some clothes before asking, "So, what happened? Did you find your friend?" I pointed at the waterproof can in the bottom of the boat, answering, "That's all that's left of him." And for many, many years, I kept speculating about the circumstances of his disappearance. Could he have drowned at the approach to the island, when Anvita's boat broke up on the reefs? I imagined his incredulity in looking up at the night, seeing it vanish and then rise back up over the waves, the forbidden island he had dreamed of for years on end, to die without having touched it and without having accomplished any of the things he had hoped to build in his life. Or was his corpse waiting somewhere beneath the shore, perhaps just beside the place where I had looked for him? And I imagined this time his rigid body, his glassy pupils open on the sand, and his disembodied spirit screaming into the void, inaudible, *Here I am, here I am, you can't leave me here!* Unless an argument had taken place between Anvita and Markus, an argument that had degenerated into an accident or crime? And there was a kind of revenge in that particular ending: that Markus would find death at the hands of a man whose misery he had exploited to satisfy his whim to live an adolescent dream that had bound him to this island in which he saw the final stage of the age of discovery, the last theater where he could live a Conradian adventure, whereas it was, more sadly, the home of a fragile people surrounded by billions of greedy, hostile strangers.

I opened the jerrican as the others watched as if it were a treasure chest. I extracted a first-aid kit, a waterproof plastic bag containing a cellphone, Markus's passport, and a wallet containing his driver's license, credit cards, and some large bills that I distributed to the members of the crew. I pulled out various other items: a mosquito spray, a tube of sunscreen, and, in a second plastic sack, red and closed with a cap, a USB flash drive. There was also a flare gun, the one Markus must have used when they wrecked. I closed the can and explained what had happened on the island. They too had a lot to tell. After leaving me, Mainak had gone back to his comrades on the other side of the reefs. And little by little a group of Sentinelese had grown on the beach, larger and larger, making obscene or threatening gestures in their direction. Mainak and the others went back into the lagoon to create a distraction, draw the Sentinelese to the coast while I was looking for Markus deep within the island, and it was because of them that I had found the village deserted. At the rendezvous time, Vidur had guided his boat to the east, drawing the crowd of Sentinelese after him while Mainak went the opposite way to come get me. After waiting for me beyond the time we had agreed on, he was resigning himself to leaving without me when I finally came out of the jungle.

We remained moored away from the shallows while waiting for night to fall. I used the first-aid kit to disinfect the wounds on my arm and knee. Then I began to take a series of photos that I've only shown to a handful of people, photos that will be discovered in my office after my death. Mainak and I agreed on a plan, that we carried out upon our return to Port Blair, to explain the disappearance of Anvita and Markus and to cover the truth like the lid of a tomb. Stretched out in the boat, occupying nearly all the space between us, Anvita's body was like a metaphor for mourning and the outsized place it takes in one's life. We all travel with our dead; we just have to learn to move forward with them.

Little by little the light faded, and I stared at the island still hoping, against all odds, that the figure of my friend would appear on the shore and wave to us. But the only forms on the horizon were those of the Sentinelese who stayed on guard as long as we remained in sight of their coasts. They had brought dugouts that they held ready in case we again crossed the barrier-reef, the border between our two worlds. Four scrawny trees, their bark bleached by time, stood out from the forest canopy and looked like guardian deities of the island: before all the others, they were set ablaze by the twilight. The still waters of the lagoon shimmered with purple, ochre, and violet hues, then night seized everything in its embrace, bearing away Sentinel Island to which, I thought, I was saying my final goodbye.

Far away, scattered lights signaled the shore of Great Andaman, very weak and blurred by the distance. Nearer to us, the headlamps of the coastguard dictated the dodging we would have to do to slip stealthily between them. The crossing would be long, and as soon as it was completely dark, we moved away from Sentinel, from which neither sounds nor glimmers of light could be detected, and which had so completely gone from sight that it could just as well have been swallowed up by the sea. I remember freezing during this return trip; I was trembling, and my teeth were chattering from fatigue and lack of food. I also remember thinking of Markus, apologizing for abandoning him. We tacked in the night, keeping away from the Indian navy; Vidur's boat escorted ours, and, after taking our two crewmen on board, the captain headed for the islands from which, a few hours before—unless it was in another era, almost another life—he had left to follow us to Sentinel. Mainak took us to the jetty we had left the day before; I had the impression of seeing it too after a long absence, as if the feeling of having undergone a profound change on the island, of having lived more in twenty-four hours than in a decade, increased the distance between me and the material world.

Mainak moored the boat; we jumped into the waist-high sea and, taking our belongings, left behind Anvita's body, rocking in the waves. Walking slowly like old men along the coconut tree-lined path that wound through the night, we returned to the village of Wandoor. Barking dogs greeted our return, and we finally slipped—collapsed—into Mainak's house. I expected to fall asleep the moment my paralyzed limbs touched the ground, but anguish, a veritable terror prevented me from sleeping, as if I were only now becoming aware of the enormity of the risks I had taken to find the person for whom I was beginning to mourn: my best friend.

At daybreak, Mainak, who hadn't slept any better than I, made breakfast on a portable stove. We ate in silence, and he left me for two whole hours while he entrusted Anvita's body to his cousin, giving him instructions for the preparation of the funeral ceremony. Then we set out on the road to Port Blair to go to the main police station. We had to wait a long time on plastic chairs, not far from other visitors, Indians especially but a few Westerners as well, surrounded by a swarm of men and women walking all over the place, talking loudly, and answering constant telephone calls. It was Officer Pramod Manjali who received us in an orderly office devoid of personal photographs or anything else that indicated he had a private life, a broad-shouldered fellow in his forties with a close-cropped mustache whom I never saw smile. We gave him the story I had concocted the day before with Mainak, and which we had refined on the way to Port Blair.

Mainak and his brother had taken Markus and me on a fishing trip that went bad. We had been caught in a storm off Boat Island, and Markus had fallen overboard. Anvita had dived in to save him, the two men had drowned, and we had only been able to recuperate Anvita's body, the currents having swept Markus away. The policeman asked if there were other witnesses to the events, and Mainak gave him the name of Vidur, who went to the station the next day to confirm our version of the facts. I showed Markus's papers to Pramod Manjali, filled out a notification of death, left my contact information, and promised not to leave the island before the conclusion of the investigation. Afterwards, Mainak took me to the bank, where I paid him more than the agreed-upon sum in order to cover his brother's burial expenses. Then he dropped me off in front of the hotel, saying, "I hope I never see you again."

Back in my room, I literally collapsed. It was three in the afternoon; night had fallen when I opened my eyes. I plugged in my computer and found a trivial message from Eleanor. She wished me a good weekend and had seen absolutely nothing to worry about in the email I had sent her before my departure. All the better, I thought, in responding in the same tone, without saying a word about Markus's disappearance or Sentinel Island, instinctively avoiding any written reference to what had really happened. Then I called Alexandra. She picked up at the first ring and said simply, very calmly, "So?" Giving her all the details, to prepare her for the disastrous news awaiting her at the end of my story, I told her what had happened on the island. "Markus has left us," I finished. "No one can do anything more for him."

What she answered just stunned me. She asked if I had made a notification of death, with the falsely detached tone you use when you're trying to hide the deep interest you have in some news. Stammering a little, I explained to her that we couldn't, neither I nor the men who had helped me, admit that we had gone onto the island—in any case not without exposing ourselves to extreme difficulties with the Indian police, and that we had therefore decided, to account for the disappearance of both Anvita and Markus, to make up a story about a fishing accident. She wanted to know if there would be an investigation, and when I said yes, she urged me to keep her abreast of the situation. I fell silent, to allow her to ask other questions about the death of her brother and to thank me for risking my life to find him. Instead, she reminded me coldly that the truth would do me no good if it got out; the story of an anthropologist who went illegally to the territory of a protected tribe would destroy my career, and it was in my interest to maintain the false statement I had made to the police and never retract it. After this threat, she hung up.

I remained frozen in my chair, telling myself I always knew these people were despicable. And I only understood a few weeks later the cause of her barely contained jubilation at the announcement of Markus's death, the cause of the satisfaction she exuded in admonishing me to keep quiet after getting from me precisely what she was waiting for, when I received the news amid the appalling chaos my life had become. Alexandra was taking over the leadership of the Holmberg galleries, replacing Markus whose death, based on my testimony and the investigation by the Port Blair police, had been registered by the American authorities. The position she already held *de facto* was now hers officially. She had the talent and perseverance, the business sense and the preparation needed to assume it effectively, all the things missing in her brother whom Joakim, in a patriarchal reflex perhaps, because he was his son and oldest child, had persisted in trying to make his heir while Markus's deepest ambitions took him toward other horizons.

And for several years, Alexandra did indeed excel in her new responsibilities: I saw her smiling—when my resentment drove me to look her up online—in the photos taken during exhibitions in one of her galleries or another. She only lived this dream life for a short decade, however. Before the age of forty, a devastating cancer took her life, a cancer of the pancreas, one of the most pernicious forms, if I can believe the information I recently received on the question, since I too am ill and, according to the doctors, only have six to eight months left to live. Like before, at the end of that day spent with Alexandra, Markus, and Joakim, that day on the boat when I sensed, as it wore on, that it was surrounding me with symbols whose sense, one day, at the end of my life, would be revealed to me, Markus, then Alexandra, preceded me, preceded me into the night after beating me to the sailboat where their father, a faraway figure that stood out in the twilight, beckoned us to join him. It's the announcement of this illness that convinced me to tell my story, now that neither the fear of Saint Andrew nor the threats of Alexandra, nor the interests of my career are there to force me to keep my silence, now that the time has almost come to meet you—you who I loved and lost, and you too whose secrets, finally revealed, provoked my hate and, more rapidly than I would've believed, my forgetting.

After the call to Alexandra, I needed to go out and have a drink—or rather several drinks—and that's what I did. I left my room, forgetting the USB flash drive from the jerrican brought back from the island that I had resolved to explore but hadn't had time to think about in the subsequent twenty-four hours. That evening, I couldn't yet imagine anything of the upcoming problems, and I followed the impulse that drove me to dive into the glitziest and most vulgar clubs and pubs that Port Blair had to offer, as if to prove to myself, by shocking all my senses, that I was back in our world, that I hadn't remained there, on the island, that I was indeed alive. So I wandered in the streets, passing gaggles of Germans and Australians, all of them rowdier than the next, drinking a beer in one of those clubs that don't fill up until around two in the morning and whose dance floor remains forlornly empty until then, with the exception of the florescent beams that sweep across it, creating intangible choreographies. After that I moved on to whisky in a pub; it's remarkable, the ability they have, the Irish, to recreate a parcel of Dublin everywhere in the world; wherever you are, their place always feels familiar. And then I stuck with the whisky, but in another bar, a pathetic little café where I perched on a stool watching a cricket match without seeing it up on the screen on the other side of the counter, while clients went in and out through the beaded curtain attached above the door and Bengali hits played much too loudly, stifling the conversations and even one's thoughts. I don't know what I was attempting to dispel with alcohol, perhaps the terror that had gripped me ever since the objective reasons for it had disappeared, as if I had repressed it for such a long time that it was now returning, with interest. Or the sadness I felt when I thought of Markus, of what he could've become, and of the bizarre end he had met by his own fault, and also the shame at the idea of having been manipulated by Alexandra, whom I began to hate with an unreasonable intensity. Then, there is a void in my memory: I can see the old TV set again and the cricket players, very clearly, the posters of Bollywood actresses and figurines of Ganesh and Shiva, but nothing of the way back to the hotel, which I must've found since I awoke on my bed a few hours later, still fully dressed.

Everything sped up that day. The telephone in the room rang at around ten in the morning, rang for a long while in my dreams, it seemed, before rousing me from my sleep. I answered, my voice slurred, to hear that Pranab Samaddar was waiting for me at the front desk. "Pranab who?" and the voice at the other end replied, "Pranab Samaddar, a journalist from the *Andaman Times*." "Of course," I cried, remembering the idealistic reporter who had become defender of the Jarawas. I washed my face and quickly combed my hair to make myself presentable—in vain, ultimately, because I looked precisely like what I was: a wreck who ran on alcohol, frighteningly sleep deprived—and went to meet Pranab at the desk. This time, he seemed much less pleasant. When he had perceived me as an ally of the Jarawas, he had been charming, offering his help in every possible way. Now he was on assignment for his paper and was asking me questions in a crisp manner, as if he were lying in wait for all the non-verbal signs that, in addition to my spoken words, would reveal to him what was really going on inside my head. He didn't tell me how he had gotten the news—I imagine he must have his contacts in the police—but he knew about Markus's disappearance and wished to hear my version of the events.

I had been caught in the middle of a hangover, and the fear of contradicting my statement of the day before set off all my red warning lights. At the same time, I couldn't turn down this interview without giving him the impression that something suspicious had happened—which he seemed convinced of in any case, as I could see in the insidious questions he asked me. Slowly, perhaps exaggerating my emotion a little but developing my narrative as if I were in a mine field, I repeated in the same terms what I had told Officer Manjali. And when Pranab cried, "How is it that you couldn't recuperate the body of your friend, whereas you were able to pull onboard the pilot's brother?" I described the terrible currents that had swept Markus away and added a dramatic detail about the motor that had taken a while to restart. Pranab didn't seem convinced, but I pretended not to notice it. "Heavy night?" he asked finally as he was getting up from the breakfast table where he had refused to order anything while I had swallowed some scrambled eggs and a good quart of coffee. "Yes," I replied, "I've just lost a friend, you know." And as I didn't need to act to show my sadness, he looked at me sympathetically and shook my hand, saying, "My article will appear tomorrow."

When I went back up to my room, I saw that I had missed five calls. I called the number back, and it was Officer Manjali who answered at the first ring and asked me to come by the station at two o'clock. I understood that it was less a request than an order, and I promised to be there. Too tired to wonder what he had to say to me, I set my alarm clock for a one-hour nap, dropping asleep as if I had pulled out the plug of some electrical appliance. When I arrived at the station, Manjali made me wait a good while, which didn't anger me for I understood that this must be one of the police techniques they use to work on suspects. He finally received me in an office where there was also a stranger whom he introduced me to as Officer Narang, a huge guy who did not respond when I greeted him and whose only role was, clearly, to intimidate me by his massive presence. "We have a few questions for you," said Officer Manjali.

"OK."

"We're trying to reconstruct Markus Holmberg's itinerary on the Andamans. As far as you know, when did he arrive in Port Blair?"

"Toward the end of August."

"What did he come here to do?"

"He told me he was writing a novel about the archipelago; he had been thinking about it ever since he was in college."

"A novel about what exactly?"

"He was always evasive on that point."

"Really? You have no idea?"

"He only mentioned one day that his novel had something to do with the history of the Andamans, from the beginning of the British colonization to the present day."

"And he never said anything about the Sentinelese?"

"The Sentinelese? Yes, he did speak to me about them. He knew of their existence, like everyone here, but what interested him for his novel was rather the history of Indian independence as seen from the Andamans. Anyway, that's what I understood, and I could be mistaken; whenever we began to discuss his book, he would change the subject immediately. It was his first novel, and he refused to show me any passages until he had finished it."

"Interesting. Do you know why I'm speaking to you of the Sentinelese?"

"Not the slightest idea."

"I'm talking about them because a distress signal was sent from their island last Friday. You haven't read the papers?"

"No. After what happened to Markus, my mind was elsewhere."

"That's understandable. But you're sure that your accident didn't take place in the area of Sentinel Island?"

"Absolutely certain. Like I told you yesterday, it happened to the south, during a fishing outing off Boat Island."

"When did you meet your friend?"

"Two days ago, the morning we went out to sea."

"And you, how long have you been in Port Blair?"

"Almost three weeks."

"You mean you waited three weeks before meeting with your friend?"

"That's right. I was very busy; I'm working on a documentary on the Jarawas."

"A documentary on the Jarawas? Tell us more."

"As you know, I'm an anthropologist. I wrote my doctoral dissertation on the religious beliefs of the Jarawas and Onges, and I returned to do a report on the changes affecting the Andamans."

"What changes?"

"You know: the Andaman Trunk Road and the new railroad line that risks cutting the reservation in two ...."

"And you don't approve of these changes?"

"It's not a question of me approving or not. I'm here to document them and measure their impact on the Jarawa reservation, that's all."

"And the Sentinelese?"

"What about the Sentinelese?"

"Do you have any ideas about them?"

"In all honesty, I'm not a specialist. Access to their island is forbidden, and no one knows much about them."

"And you, an anthropologist, you were never tempted to go pay them a little visit? Just out of curiosity?"

"To tell them what? No one knows their language. And I had too much work to do with the Jarawas to get involved with another tribe."

"Still, it's strange, isn't it?"

"What's strange?"

"Your meeting your friend after he's been here for four months and you for three weeks—and that same day one of you doesn't return to the port."

"It's an accident that will torment me for the rest of my life. I'd known Markus since college. It's an enormous loss for me."

"And what if I told you I have a theory?"

"I would say that a good theory is based on facts."

"Facts, I have more than I need. You're not interested in my theory?"

"Sure, of course I am. I'm listening."

"Imagine two college buddies. One of them is an anthropologist, the other a millionaire. Both of them get it into their heads to visit Sentinel Island. Don't ask me why, I've never understood the obsession some people have with this island, but there are stranger things happening in the world. The millionaire arrives ahead of time to prepare things, the anthropologist gets on a plane a little later, to cover their tracks. Then they go to the island with the help of some local accomplices and, there, something awful happens that forces them to send up a distress flare. In the end, one of the local guys gets killed, as well as the richer of the two friends, while the other, the anthropologist, manages to get away and has to make up an accident story that doesn't hold water. What do you think of my story?"

"And you, what do you think of it?"

"What do you mean?"

"Does it hold up for you? Because, from my point of view, it is based on a series of conjectures but not on any known facts. May I be honest with you?"

"That's all I'm asking."

"Markus Holmberg was my best friend. I joined him in the circumstances I've described to you, and what happened is precisely what I've told you: we met for a boat trip, there was a storm, an accident, and, in the end, two deaths. The reality is already hard enough for you to spare me, in addition, these baseless accusations."

"So you know nothing."

"About what?"

"About the distress signal."

"No, I've already told you, I've just learned about it from you."

"You're going to find me repetitive, but you must admit, all the same, that it's a strange coincidence. Everyone is wondering how a primitive tribe began to send distress signals like that, with no warning, and it's precisely at the very moment you come in here to inform us of an accident that made two victims."

"Yes, it's strange, yes, it's a coincidence, but, frankly, I'm not so stupid as to approach Sentinel Island."

"OK. One last question all the same."

"As you wish …."

"Do you know which hotel your friend was staying in? Because it's been impossible to find any trace of him beyond the month of September."

"I'm sorry, I have no idea."

"And other than the identity papers you brought us yesterday, he left nothing else? No trace, for example, of this famous novel he came here to write?"

"No, I know nothing about that. I gave you everything he had with him on the boat."

"Very well. Now it's my turn to be honest with you. It's going to take time to wrap this matter up. In the meantime, we ask you not to leave the city and to have no contact with reporters."

"I'm sorry, but I've already spoken to someone. This morning, just before you called."

"Who was that?"

"Pranab Samaddar. He works for the *Andaman Times*."

"Believe me, I know very well who he is. I've already had to deal with him. And what did he want from you?"

"He had questions about the accident."

"And what did you tell him?"

"The same thing I told you: the truth."

"OK. You couldn't have known. I hadn't yet asked you to steer clear of reporters. But let this be your last interview. The Andamans really do not need this kind of publicity. We want to avoid the media influencing the course of the investigation as much as possible."

Officer Manjali must've been deeply upset in the following days. Announced by the *Andaman Times*, the news of Markus's disappearance was picked up by the media all over the world within twenty-four hours. I stayed cloistered in my hotel room and had requested that the front desk stop putting calls through to me—reporters were trying to get to me from morning to night. On my computer, I could read articles in *The Times of India*, *The South China Morning Post*, *The New York Times*, the *Guardian*, *El País*, and *Le Monde* that, with tiny variations, repeated the small amount of information available on Markus's death. Something in this event had caught the collective attention. Drowning was in itself a banal accident, but what fascinated people, I believe, was the proximity of Markus's death with that of his parents. There was in this story the markings of an American tragedy, of a family curse that was targeting the elites of this world. The young heir, handsome and fantastically wealthy, lost his life soon after his parents in a far-off country. It was an illustration of the fragility of life and a welcome reminder that death, egalitarian in nature, strikes the powerful and the humble indifferently and holds in reserve absurd endings for everyone, including those whose birth showered them with advantages. Yes, there was a sort of plebian enthusiasm in these articles that complacently evoked Markus's fortune, the prominent people he had frequented in the world of art and politics, the identity of his various girlfriends, articles that pretended to deplore his premature disappearance while one could read the poorly disguised *Schadenfreude* between the lines, the satisfaction that comes with revenge. He was dead. His superiority was no longer of any use to him; people could pretend to have compassion for him.

Alexandra was interviewed in most of these articles. Photos showed her in a black dress, wearing sunglasses, grieving for this exceptional brother who was leaving her all alone after the death of her parents. My name was regularly cited, the comments that Pranab Samaddar had gotten out of me reappearing in article after article. I think that ultimately the decision to close the investigation, made by Officer Manjali a week after our second session, resulted in large part from all this media hype. His questions had shown that he seriously doubted my story and, by a process of deduction, had gotten far closer to the truth than I would've liked. But he had no way of confirming my presence on the island with Markus, and as long as my witnesses continued to support my version of the facts—a version they couldn't contradict without incriminating themselves—it was impossible for him to prove his theory.

Paradoxically, the very suspicion that it was possible that he was right must've dissuaded him from going any further. If Markus had indeed died on Sentinel as he was convinced he had, the authorities of Port Blair could anticipate a series of enormous complications. They would have to explain both the inability of the coastguard to enforce the safety zone around the island and the death of an American citizen on it. They would also have to confront those who would demand that his body be repatriated, as well as those who would strongly oppose an intrusion presenting a risk to the health of the Sentinelese. It was wiser to stick to my story, to avoid creating a mountain of additional difficulties for everyone that would do nothing to change the fact that Markus had disappeared. Officer Manjali called to inform me that the investigation was closed, that he couldn't prove it, but he was certain that he was right about me. Consequently, he personally invited me to leave the archipelago as quickly as possible and never set foot on it again. I answered that I'd like nothing better.

And I was not lying, for since my return to the hotel, after the conversation with him at the police station, I experienced an anger—no, a rage—that prevented me from sleeping, caused me to go around in circles in the room, and drove me systematically to reject the calls from Alexandra and Eleanor, the calls from Sonu and Victor that popped up one after the other on my cell phone, a rage that made me give up my documentary project on the Jarawas and decide to return to the United States immediately.

And while I awaited authorization to do so, I continued to look at my discovery on Markus's USB flash drive, the key I had hurried to open upon returning from the police station, where I suspected there was a copy of his novel. I wasn't wrong, for during his stay on Great Andaman, Markus had indeed begun the third part that remained to be written when he was still at Woodstock. And beside the book, in another folder, I discovered something, a proof, like a time bomb that he had left there—on purpose perhaps, or so I asked myself a thousand times—and that shattered my life.

I've never forgotten that trip back to the US. Twenty hours with no sleep. Twenty hours with hell in my head, this hell that opened up the second I had found the photograph on the flash drive, twenty hours mulling over what I was going to say, imagining what had happened, the lies and evasions, the equivocations and accusations that would meet my questions, twenty hours during which I tried to read, to work, or watch films, but my mind returned stubbornly to this image, to all it meant for me, for us, if nothing could refute what I clearly understood. Sometimes I thought that my last trip to the Andamans was behind me; I thought that my documentary would never be made, and that I would have to rethink my professional life. But these problems only preoccupied me in fits and starts, seeming miniscule in relation to the one question that obsessed me. Twenty hours went by like that, feeling my energy fade little by little, worn down by all the discomfort and all the little abuses that airlines and the security systems impose on you—narrow seats, no room for your legs, interminable waits standing around before going through passport control, then seated again before the next flight, all these tests of your nerves that mistreat your body and were all the more painful for me in that I couldn't count on rest and sleep upon my arrival but a terrible struggle, putting to death what we had been.

Perhaps I went about it badly. Perhaps, instead of just turning up after weeks of silence and without alerting her to my return, I should've taken a hotel room, gathered my thoughts, and mused about the best way to formulate my questions. But I had repressed them for too long; for days I had refrained from calling her because it would've been too simple, for her, to unplug the video, claiming there was a technical problem, or to hang up after calling me crazy. I wanted to see her face as the truth came out, and for it to be impossible for her to flee and continue to lie.

Upon arriving in Columbus, I took a taxi home. It was six p.m. when it dropped me off, and it was already completely dark outside. Scattered lights at the windows indicated that Eleanor was at home. I stood there for a long time, motionless, telling myself, "Nothing has to change: it depends on me." The night was freezing and the road empty. The lanterns on the façade of the house made the snow covering the lawn sparkle, snow still fresh, whose crystals hadn't been broken or sullied. And then I thought that it was too late, that nothing could put that devil back in his box, and that we would take this story to the end, whatever the cost. I opened the front door.

She appeared at the top of the stairs. The emotions succeeded very quickly on her face: fear at first (who was this intruder?), surprise upon recognizing me, a beginning of joy, feigned or real, and then a calculating, cold look. She must've understood, instinctively, that something abnormal was about to happen, perhaps even guessed the nature of the exchange to follow and decided, like a formidable adversary, that she would stand up to me, that she would admit nothing, that she would be victorious in the combat that was coming. Eleanor walked slowly down the stairs and said, "You look awful. What's the matter?"—the first words she had spoken to me in two months. In an authoritative voice, that sounded false because it was completely at odds with our normal relationship, I answered, "Sit down." She put on an ironic, nasty smile, as if to let me know that my macho act didn't impress her, and that she would soon put me in my place.

We were in the half-light, she sitting on an ottoman, I on the couch. Only the light from the hall was glowing behind her, so I got up to turn on a lamp. Suddenly, it was as if we were at the theater, as if spotlights had lit up the stage where the dialogue on which the rest of our life depended was about to begin. She said nothing, and everything confirmed my doubts. Shouldn't she have been surprised by my sudden arrival, reproached me my long silence, plied me with questions about what had happened to us, Markus and me? She was looking at me too calmly for it not to be affected, always with that smile that slowly stoked an anger I had more and more difficulty controlling. I took out my computer and, staring at her so that I wouldn't miss anything that crossed her face, I showed her the photograph on Markus's key. A photo of her, radiant, taken on the High Line in New York.

At first, she said nothing. Then she exclaimed, "Yes, it's a photo of me, so what?" She was annoyed, aggravated, like a mother irritated by constant questions from her child. I had to try again; I don't remember what I answered. And from question to question, from evasions to exhortations, all night long the list of partial confessions went on, each time preceding something worse.

I was the one who had put her in contact with Markus.

For the Vekner Foundation, yes, for her philanthropic project.

They had met in New York.

Then seen each other again.

They had kissed on the High Line.

Yes, the day of the photograph.

Then kissed at his place.

They had made love there.

How many times, I don't know, does anyone remember how many times?

It had lasted a long time.

For weeks.

For months.

She had become pregnant.

Not by me.

By him.

The baby she was awaiting was his.

She had returned to New York to tell him.

He hadn't wanted to keep the child.

She hadn't had a miscarriage; she had had an abortion.

She is the one who killed the child.

Not mine. The other guy's.

It was my fault.

Everything was my fault.

My fault for working so hard.

My fault for leaving her for months for my expeditions.

And for what?

For whom?

My career?

My book?

Savages who didn't speak a word of English?

My fault—everything she had done.

Eleanor fell silent, the infernal fandango began. It went on for several weeks, weeks of hate and recriminations, weeks of horrors and reproaches, sleepless nights where we didn't really know when they finished and when they began. We emerged from our nightmares when the garden was still bathed in darkness and the day that was breaking was just like those that preceded it and those that would follow: this constantly renewed litany of our mutual loathing. We endlessly bled from the wounds we caused the other as from the ones inflicted on us. Blame bounced between us like a birdie between rackets: "It's your fault, no, yours, you're responsible for my faults," and sometimes I was gripped by remorse, I felt guilty for everything she had done while she observed me with a nasty victorious look on her face because I was absolving her of her mistakes, which suddenly became light, so light, nonexistent. Then I changed my mind like you free yourself from someone's grip on you, and the fandango, subdued for a moment, began again, the fandango that was playing in our house that had become a cage whose key we had tossed away. Eleanor was the victim, and I was the torturer, I became the prey and she the hunter, the madness grew between us like a fever, her madness, mine, mine added to hers and hers to mine, it went on and on, back and forth, remnants of a very old affection gleaming sometimes in our night but soon eclipsed by new cries and angry shouting: it was the infernal fandango starting back up.

I went to a gun shop and asked to see a semi-automatic pistol. "A classic," the clerk answered, "a Beretta M9. Kosovo, Somalia, Afghanistan: this little toy has proved itself. On special offer to you for only four hundred and ninety-nine dollars (plus tax)." I filled out the form and waited for a half-hour while my criminal record was checked out. The authorization came over the Internet, and ten minutes later I was in my car with the weapon and the ammunition. I sat there motionless behind the wheel for a long time, a very long time, the motor running, suspended between two destinations. I finally drove off to the east, at around five in the afternoon; the traffic was heavy and the daylight fading. I parked the car next to the boathouse, went down the slope, and walked along the river without meeting anyone until the lights from the houses vanished, until the rustling from the forest alone broke the silence. The snow crunched beneath my feet; the pristine path hadn't been trampled. I came to a bench installed before an opening in the curtain of trees. I sat down and looked at the water caught in the ice, long enough for night to fall completely. Sometimes the snapping of a branch betrayed the presence of a deer; its shadow fled into the woods, and everything became still again. I took out the Beretta. Then I inserted the bullets into the clip and the clip into the gun, as the salesman had shown me. And I set the pistol in my lap, like a sleeping child. I released the safety and pressed the weapon to my temple; it was, how should I put it, like a morbid game: I don't really want to do that, well, not really, it's just to see how it feels, unless ... Ice cold, the metal burned my skin ... Does anyone know why they pull the trigger, why they don't? I had, I believe, the premonition that I still had some happiness awaiting me in my life. I stood up and threw the weapon into the flowing water.

Epilogue

It is to be remarked that a good many people are *born curiously* unfitted for the fate waiting them on this earth.

Joseph Conrad, *Chance*

Sentinel Island is empty today.

Under the Andaman skies, the people of forever have disappeared. The Jarawas died out first. The construction of a railroad through their territory sped up the inevitable process of their extinction. Hotel complexes rose where the little Jarawas used to play. It will soon be twenty years since the last representative of the Onges died of distress and alcoholism in the Dugong Creek reservation, the final survivor of his people, speaker of a language now forgotten by everyone, in a hurry to join his own kind in the night. And then, finally, it was the turn of the Sentinelese. All it took for that was a Birman poacher, infected with the flu virus, to sneak in among them. He was the one, the patient zero of an epidemic that swept away the Sentinelese in a few weeks. For a while, promoters tried to take advantage of the opportunity to develop luxury tourism on this virgin island, but the Indian government decided to protect Sentinel Island by transforming it into a national park. Two companies are authorized to organize tours there, but with a specific proviso. They are obliged to introduce visitors to the history of the Andamanese people, Sentinel Island having become an open-air memorial.

Eight years ago, I asked Julia if she would agree to accompany me. She pushed a lock of her long blond hair behind her ear and directed her turquoise gaze straight at me, with the seriousness that had charmed me from our first encounter. We met two months after my separation from Eleanor, when the divorce papers hadn't been signed yet. At the time, my friends advised me not to go too fast, feeling it premature to begin a new relationship before I had put an official end to the preceding one. They were right in principle, but once they had spent some time with Julia, they quickly changed their tune, mentioning her composure and seriousness, her classical beauty, her kindness, and her thoughtful, affectionate character, as if I hadn't noticed all of that before them. Victor, who told me repeatedly over the phone not to get carried away with this woman, is, of all my friends, the one whose turnabout was the most spectacular. Two days after arriving at our home for a visit, he took me aside to tell me, as if he feared I was dumb enough to squander my chance, "You've found a rare gem, my friend. Whatever you do, don't let her fly away!" mixing his metaphors along the way. I've never forgotten the wink he gave me when, the day of our marriage, he handed me the box containing the wedding ring.

I had told my story to Julia. The whole story. So I didn't need to explain to her the importance of this return to Sentinel Island for me. She agreed to go with me, and we left with our daughter, Tara, who had just gained admission to the University of Chicago. The atmosphere was heavy on the boat taking us to Sentinel. It was a launch moving at astonishing speed; it took scarcely a few hours to cover the distance separating the island from Wandoor, which had become a wealthy city since the day when, in another life it seemed, I had left it with Mainak to make our statement at the Port Blair police station. At the tourist office, the employees had made it clear to us that it was a cultural visit, not just another day at the beach with a snorkel mask. The repeated warnings about "the historical importance of this exceptional site" left little doubt as to the targeted clientele: educated, wealthy people eager for cultural enlightenment during a vacation in the sun. They also demonstrated the underlying guilt that permeated this troubling staging, as if the Indian government were striving to evince posthumous concern for these peoples they had failed to protect. The launch cut through the sea on a beautiful day; loudspeakers were playing recordings of Jarawa songs that, despite their joyous melody, left me as heavy-hearted as if they were dirges, since these voices were coming to us from beyond the grave. I was moved, far more than I had expected, to find myself here with my wife and daughter. It was as if two periods of my life that were absolutely not fated to meet suddenly collided. Sentinel Island, all things considered, was also an emblem of my youth.

Our boat came into the lagoon. The guide turned on her microphone to greet our group of twenty people, all Westerners except for me. Her name was Noor, and she had a violet flower behind her ear, a white T-shirt with spaghetti straps, and a violet skirt. Noor was under twenty-five but had clear authority owing to her vast knowledge and the seriousness of her mission; these people, after all, only continued to live through her voice. While a sailor jumped onto the wharf to dock our ship, she explained to us that it was, along with the museum we would see later, the only modern structure permitted on Sentinel Island. The commission in charge of the island, composed of civic leaders from Port Blair and government officials, had set as its goal not to alter it from its natural state. "It is unfortunate that, when they were still living, the Sentinelese were not the recipients of so many precautions," Noor stated with a frankness that surprised me. She had distributed earpieces that allowed us to follow her talk without having to raise her voice. "We are walking," she observed, "on a territory that the Sentinelese defended for fifty thousand years. That should inspire deep respect in all of us and lead us to ask: what should we have done, while there was still time, to prevent this island from being reduced to a place of meditation?" Even the two children in our group, rowdy and noisy when we were on the boat, settled down now, impressed by the solemnity of our guide.

We had been warned before our departure: a mile-long hike was on the program. Walking slowly, Noor related the history of the Sentinelese. She was precise in her explanations and, like an excellent teacher, summarized the most important information while being ready to develop an idea, cite her sources, or explore a related subject according to the interests of her audience. A couple of German tourists, botany enthusiasts, questioned her on the vegetation of the island; the children wanted to know if there were crocodiles and poisonous snakes; and a French visitor engaged her on the subject of Portman to show her that he wasn't just anyone and had read more about him than she. More and more incisive, Noor didn't let herself be intimidated. Finally, we arrived at the village.

It was much larger than the one in which, all those years ago, I had come looking for Markus. The clearing was twice as big, and around fifty huts with sloping roofs had been preserved in their original state. The researchers had discovered three other villages on the island. They had speculated that each of them gave shelter to a separate community within the Sentinelese family, and that unions were arranged systematically between the members of the different groups. Since the village we were visiting was the largest, it had been dubbed "the capital," while the three others bore the names of artifacts exhumed there: "the chess board village," "the ax village," and "the great dinghy village." Other products made by the Sentinelese awaited us in the museum we would visit after the lunch break. Outside the "capital," a picnic area had been set up where we ate the food we had brought, under Noor's careful supervision to make sure that the wrappings and even the crumbs ended up in the bags provided for that purpose. A quarter mile from the picnic area, a long one-story building housed the National Museum of the Andamanese People. Noor pointed out the most beautiful pieces for our admiration, explaining what they revealed about the Sentinelese culture. We lingered before the bone necklaces that horrified and fascinated the children. Our guide took advantage of this to describe the funeral rites of the archipelago's people and their custom of exposing bodies between the roots of huge kapok trees. "That brings us to the great mystery of the island," Noor said, leading us into the next room. "I'm going to introduce you to Mister Krish." Tara and Julia stopped in their tracks and turned to look at me, astonished. I indicated my complete bafflement, and we joined the other visitors. Blocking our view of its content, they were standing around a display case lit up in the darkness.

Noor was saying that the skeleton of "Mister Krish" had been discovered outside the "chess board village." In a state of advanced decomposition, the bones had provided little information but enough to create an enigma. The specialists had succeeded in determining that it was a male individual, around thirty years old at the time of his death. Even more surprising, he was five foot nine inches, taller than the average Andamanese man. And this individual was Caucasian, as the DNA from the bones proved. "So why do you call him Mister Krish? That doesn't sound very Caucasian," the Frenchman asked. "Because the skeleton was found with this watch, on the back of which the name 'Krish' is still legible. Surprising, isn't it? No one has ever understood what this man was doing there." Concocting theories among themselves, the members of our group followed Noor as she led them toward an exhibit devoted to the British colonization. Julia, Tara, and I stayed behind and approached the display case.

It contained the photograph of a skeleton in a cradle of roots, whose bones were almost indistinguishable among the vegetation that had grown all around them. Inside the case there was also a skull set on a cushion, its empty eye-sockets staring out at us, and, beside it, on a little stand, a watch without a bracelet, covered in rust, a watch I recognized immediately since it was mine, the one my parents had given me when I turned twenty, and that I had forgotten one morning in an apartment in Manhattan.

I had found Markus, and for all eternity he would bear my name.

Acknowledgments

During my research on Sentinel Island and the Andaman archipelago, I learned a great deal in reading the following texts, whose authors I wish to thank: Triloknath N. Pandit, *The Sentinelese* (Calcutta: Seagull Books, 1990); Vishvajit Pandya, *Above the Forest: A Study of Andamanese Ethnoanemology, Cosmology, and The Power of Ritual* (Delhi: Oxford University Press, 1993); Madhusree Mukerjee, *The Land of Naked People: Encounters with Stone Age Islanders* (New York: Houghton Mifflin, 2003); Satadru Sen, "Savage Bodies, Civilized Pleasures: M. V. Portman and the Andamanese" (*American Ethnologist*, May 2009); Vishvajit Pandya, "Through Lens and Text: Constructions of a 'Stone Age' Tribe in the Andaman Islands" (*History Workshop Journal*, Spring 2009); Vishvajit Pandya, *In the Forest: Visual and Material Worlds of Andamanese History (1858–2006)* (Lanham: University Press of America, 2009); Pankaj Sekhsaria and Vishvajit Pandya (eds), *The Jarawa Tribal Reserve Dossier: Cultural & Biological Diversities in the Andaman Islands* (Paris: UNESCO, 2010); Pramod Kumar, *Descriptive and Typological Study of Jarawa* (doctoral thesis, Jawaharlal Nehru University, New Delhi, 2012); Gethin Chamberlain, "Andaman Islands Tribe Threatened by Lure of Mass Tourism" (*The Observer*, January 2012); "Human Safaris May Be Banned, but Still Tourists Flock to Andaman Islands" (*The Observer*, September 2012); Adam Goodheart, "The Last Island of the Savages" (*The American Scholar*, March 2016); Ellen Barry, "A Season of Regret for an Aging Tribal Expert in India" (*The New York Times*, May 2017); and Fehmida Zakeer, "Meet the First Woman to Contact One of the World's Most Isolated Tribes" (*National Geographic*, December 2018).

The quotation from Dr. Peter Underhill in the chapter "Mysteries" comes from the article of Nicholas Wade, "An Ancient Link to Africa Lives on in Bay of Bengal" (*The New York Times*,

December 2002). The comments attributed to Dr. Triloknath N. Pandit during his discussions with Krish are borrowed from interviews he granted to various media. The version of events by Robert Fore in the chapter "The *Primrose*" was reconstituted with the help of a letter sent to the journalist Jack Mottram. To write the chapter "Soli Deo Gloria," I consulted, among other sources, "John Chau's Death on North Sentinel Island Roils the Missionary World" by Eliza Griswold (*The New Yorker*, December 2018); "The Sentinelese of North Sentinel Island: A Reappraisal of Tribal Scenario in an Andaman Island in the Context of Killing of an American Preacher" by Mundayat Sasikumar (*Journal of the Anthropological Survey of India*, June 2019); "The Last Days of John Allen Chau" by Alex Perry (*Outside*, July 2019); "The American Missionary and the Uncontacted Tribe" by Doug Block Clark (*GQ*, August 2019); and "Dead Missionaries, Wild Sentinelese: An Anthropological Review of a Global Media Event" by Michael Schönhuth (*Anthropology Today*, August 2019). The chapter "In the Forest" owes much to the splendid documentary of Alexandre Dereims, *Nous sommes l'humanité* ("We Are Humanity," 2017), that includes testimony from members of the Jarawa tribe. In the chapters "Portman 1/3" and "Portman 2/3," the speech of Maurice Vidal Portman to the Royal Geographical Society of London is adapted from his work in two volumes, *A History of Our Relations with the Andamanese, Compiled from Histories and Travels, and From the Records of the Government of India* (Calcutta: Office of the Superintendent of Government Print, 1899).

I would like also to thank Martin Munro for welcoming this novel into the "World Writing in French: New Archipelagoes" collection; Anne-Solange Noble and Ludovic Escande of Éditions Gallimard for their enthusiasm for this project; my friend Pierre Huguet, whose comments helped me to improve the first version of the text; Sarah-Grace Heller, Dana Renga, and The Ohio State University's College of Arts and Sciences, for supporting the completion and translation of this book; and Vishvajit Pandya for answering my questions about the beliefs of the Jarawa people. Special thanks are due to my friend, Alan J. Singerman, for translating this novel with passion and care: only rarely in life do you get to work with somebody with whom you have so much in common.

Thank you, finally, to my friends and relatives who accompanied the writing of this novel: Janice Aski, Jean-Valère Baldacchino,

Acknowledgments

Antoine Bello, Arnaud Bertrand, Bruno Cabanes, Michaël Ferrier, Pierre Frantz, Brigitte Hoffmann, Maxime Maillard, Ananda and Vita Roy, Lucille Toth, Jennifer Willging, the MacEwan Family, and, above all, my much better half, Sarah.